FOR THE LOVE OF A MARINE

SHARON KIMBRA WALSH

For the Love of a Marine
ISBN # 978-1-78430-785-1
©Copyright Sharon Kimbra Walsh 2015
Cover Art by Posh Gosh ©Copyright September 2015
Interior text design by Claire Siemaszkiewicz
Totally Bound Publishing

Published in 2015 by Totally Bound Publishing, Newland House, The Point, Weaver Road, Lincoln, LN6 3QN, United Kingdom.

FOR THE LOVE
OF A MARINE

Dedication

To my husband, who portrayed the patience of a saint
with my nocturnal wanderings
and key bashing in the early hours of the morning,
and to my work colleagues, who gave me excellent
feedback and criticisms —
without you all this book would never have left my
laptop. Thank you.

Author's Note

May we stand together in honor and memory of our
fallen heroes.
Never forgotten.

Chapter One

A blood-soaked combat boot, reclining on its side, lay tossed carelessly in a corner of the operating theater among torn and shredded webbing. Bandages and gauze soaked with crimson coiled in clumps on the floor, mixed in with remnants of charred and torn camouflage uniform. Personal effects, pitiful, tragic reminders of those who had been medevacked to the combat trauma hospital — CTH — lay scattered on a metal trolley, waiting to be identified and returned to those who had survived — or returned home with those who hadn't.

Although the CTH was temperature controlled throughout, within Theater One it was hot and humid, the air thick with the coppery smell of blood and an all pervading stench of feces and urine. Dark blood had trickled then dripped from each operating table to pool in splatters on a dark green, rubberized floor, with smudged crimson footprints leading to and from the accumulating puddles where surgical teams and medical technicians had unknowingly trodden through them. Stainless steel instruments clinked mutedly against each other while in the background was the continuous whirr of an air conditioner, the periodic hissing of recycled air flowing in and out of the theater and the soft repetitive clunk from a clock on the wall.

CTH personnel clad in full-face plastic visors used to prevent blood spatter, white mesh face masks underneath, smears of blood adorning green surgical gowns or scrubs and gloves, crowded around the two occupied operating tables. Despite the blood-soaked surroundings and an atmosphere filled with palpable tension, there was no evidence of panic and no anxious overtones overriding smooth, professional voices as the two surgical teams bent all their efforts to saving the lives of the two unconscious young soldiers. Intense expressions of concentration were etched on many faces and requests for assistance and instruments were uttered in quiet, clear monotones. Both the blood and gore was ignored as though it did not exist.

Anyone looking into the busy room would have wondered at the almost emotionless and dispassionate air of the people working there, as though each one possessed an invisible mental shield that prevented them from becoming emotionally involved with their patients, something that each had subconsciously cultivated over the months of their deployment to protect themselves from the daily scenes of carnage and death, harsh realities of a combat zone. The shield was a necessity, a psychological barrier subconsciously erected to prevent burnout and breakdowns caused by unrelenting exposure to the cruel and unavoidable pressures of working in a combat hospital.

Corporal Katie Walker, twenty-six years of age, was a senior combat trauma medic—CTM—attached to the CTH. She was in her seventh year with the British Royal Army Medical Corp—RAMC—and on her first deployment to Afghanistan, assigned to Surgical Team One alongside another CTM. She had been in-country since March 2014 and had completed four months of a six-month tour.

During the early weeks of her deployment, Katie had experienced her own personal battles with trauma and stress. There had been many times when she had wondered if she would ever find the strength to complete her tour. Nightmares of explosions and maimed bodies had awakened her from sleep night after night, and on one occasion after a particularly lengthy duty, she had taken flight in tears to hide in the female locker room, saddened by the sight of so many brutally wounded and mentally shattered men and women being brought into the CTH. There had been other occasions when she had been on the brink of making a formal request for redeployment back to the United Kingdom, despite the adverse ramifications to her career that this might have brought about. The unpleasant experiences that she had been exposed to had caused her to reconsider how the human species treated one another.

As the long months had passed, however, like everyone deployed to Afghanistan, she had learned how to emotionally protect herself, had unknowingly developed the self-same protective shield as her colleagues — an ability to distance herself from adverse emotions and feelings. It wasn't that she was emotionally cold or numb to the brutal daily truths of the combat world she inhabited. She was a human being with a great deal of compassion and sympathy for those she treated and tried to save, but her detachment was for her own protection, an emotionless armor that helped to harden her mind against the overwhelming pressures that she had to face.

That particular day had been an emotional one for them all. Three British soldiers out on foot patrol in a remote area of the Afghanistan desert had been injured in an improvised explosive device — IED — incident. One of the soldiers had stepped on a hidden mine lying undetected by a mine detector. The explosives, covered by a pile of razor-sharp stones and rocks, blending in with the surrounding terrain, had detonated, the resultant blast throwing shrapnel-like debris through the air, catching the soldier who had trodden on the mine and two others at ground zero. All three had sustained severe injuries and a combat trauma team — CTT — flown out by a Chinook combat trauma flight — CTF — had stabilized the casualties in the field before extracting and medevacking them back to the CTH at Camp Churchill, located in the British sector of Base Independence.

Three trauma teams, waiting outside the CTH, had immediately assessed the casualties then, while surgeons from three surgical teams scrubbed for the surgeries, the gravely injured soldiers had been swiftly taken to the trauma rooms, where the trauma teams standing by had immediately brought heavy bleeding under control, given full body assessments and checked vital signs then, following X-rays, all three were connected up to IV solutions and blood products to replace blood loss and stave off the onset of shock. A decision was made to prep the casualties for immediate surgery and rush them through to the operating theaters.

Three operating tables within Theaters One and Two were now in use. Each surgical team carrying out the surgeries consisted of surgeons who were specialists in their various fields, anesthetists, two surgical nurses and two CTMs. All the medical personnel excelled at what they did, each selected for deployment to the Afghanistan war theater specifically for their specialist skills and for their ability to be able to work under intense levels of pressure.

The surgeries that had been going on for most of the day were almost over, the casualties having come through their ordeals safely. If they remained stable and there were no complications over the next forty-eight hours, they would continue their recovery and rehabilitation back in the UK.

The tension in Theater One slowly began to dissipate and each surgical team began to relax. Conversation around the operating tables lightened in tone and there were a few subdued chuckles as someone made an obscure joke about a subject totally unrelated to the present situation.

Katie checked the IV line attached to her own patient again, tracing the fragile tubing leading from the triple branched cannula in the back of the young soldier's hand up toward a collection of bags containing blood, plasma and saline fluid, ensuring that the life-sustaining products dripping downward were doing so at the correct speed and as freely as they should. She then placed two steady but sensitive fingertips on the casualty's carotid artery and, with a sense of satisfaction, felt the strong throb of a pulse, confirming that the young British soldier continued to remain stable.

Nodding to the attending anesthetist that all remained well, Katie paused, taking a brief moment to gaze down at her patient. A hasty pre-op wash had removed much of the blood and dirt from the young man's face and body, and now that she had a few minutes' respite, she noticed with a deep sense of sadness that he was much younger than she had at first thought, probably in his early twenties, with shorn, dark hair. Stubble covered his chin and jaw line as though he had not shaved in some time, and his skin was pale, almost translucent, making him look as vulnerable as a child, a telltale sign of the trauma that had assaulted his body. He had obviously been out in the field for some time, as he appeared not to have washed in days and a strong smell exuded from his still body. Body odors from soldiers brought in from the field were a normal occurrence for the medical staff. The fetid smells barely stirred or offended their senses.

The young soldier's injury from the IED explosion that day had resulted in the complete destruction of his lower left leg. Even though the golden hour for medevacking him back from the field to the CTH then assessment followed by surgery, was not breached, the leg had been too damaged and had been amputated just above the knee.

So young. The sad thought often intruded into Katie's weary mind of late. *What will he do now?* His Army career had been abruptly and cruelly terminated, the lifestyle to which he had been accustomed had changed irrevocably. He could go on to lead a relatively normal life — most amputees did, and adapted and coped well. With counseling and rehabilitation, the young man would resume his life, but the harsh reality was that it had changed forever. There would be no going back to reclaim what he had once had and moving forward would be the ultimate test for him.

A sudden movement caught Katie's attention, disturbing her thoughts about the patient. Leading surgeon Major Josh Macintyre of Surgical Team One had stepped back from the operating table. Stripping off his bloody surgical gloves, he raised his plastic visor and pulled down his face mask. Rubbing his eyes tiredly, he once again inspected the heavily bandaged stump of the soldier's amputated limb before commenting wearily in a broad but lilting Scottish accent, "Well, that's it, ladies and gentleman. That's all we can do for the poor wee laddie. As long as infection does'na set in and he remains stable, he'll do. Thank you all for your assistance."

Major Macintyre turned away from the operating table, his body posture stooping now as though all the adrenaline and energy that he had drawn on to save his patient's life had drained away. He walked toward the door of the theater, feet shuffling in their protective bootees, and left, Katie knowing full well that he would make his way unerringly down the long corridor to the R&R — rest and recuperation-room — at its far end.

Lance Corporal Henry Barrow, Katie's CTM colleague on Surgical Team One, left the theater unbidden, unknowingly leaving a trail of bloody footprints behind him. He returned moments later pushing a gurney that he aligned lengthwise against the operating table. The five remaining members of the surgical team positioned themselves to each side of the patient and, with Katie carefully handling the IV stand, lifted the young soldier gently onto the gurney.

With the lance corporal pushing and Katie wheeling the IV stand and keeping an observant eye on her patient for any downward turn in his condition, they left the theater, turned left down the long corridor and, moving at a steady pace, guided the gurney with its precious passenger some meters until they arrived at the critical care unit — CCU — beyond the wards on the right. Lance Corporal Barrow and Katie wheeled the patient into the brightly lit CCU where four trauma nurses awaited their arrival. Working in well-honed synchronization, the two CTMs transferred the still-sleeping soldier to a pristine white hospital bed, ensuring that the sheets and blanket were tucked securely about his motionless body.

Two trauma nurses immediately took over from Katie and Henry, deftly arranging the IV bags, checking the IV line for kinks and air bubbles and placing a finger heart rate monitor onto one of the young man's fingers before turning on the heart rate and electrocardiogram monitor. It immediately began to beep quietly in rhythm with the patient's heart rate and a normal, if slightly rapid tracing in green began to show on the LED screen. Katie moved to the end of the bed while one of the trauma nurses unclipped the patient's blank chart and returned to his side to check his vital signs. Methodically, the nurse took the patient's pulse, noted it on the chart, then took his temperature and listened to his heart and lungs. Katie heaved a deep sigh of relief as the nurse hung the clipboard back on the end of the bed without comment, and glanced at her colleague.

Henry pulled his face mask down around his neck, sighed, rubbed his eyes and smiled at her wearily. "Are you all right?" he asked.

Katie rotated her neck tiredly, stretching the stiffness out of her shoulders and spine. "I'm okay, I suppose," she answered, her voice muffled by her own face mask. With irritation, she pulled it down so she could speak more clearly. "Although I wonder sometimes if I'll ever get used to all this, day in, day out. It makes me so bloody mad and sad at the same time. All these people are so young. They don't deserve injuries like these. What a waste of young lives." She suddenly felt exhausted and depressed and it showed in the flat tone of her voice.

"I hear you," Henry responded sympathetically. "It's a hard call and no, nobody deserves to end up injured or dead, I agree with you on that one, but—and this is going to sound pretty harsh—it's what we all signed up for." He stopped speaking, studying her face closely. "Are you sure you're all right? You're looking pretty pale."

"I'm just tired," Katie explained, lightly brushing off his concern, then she chuckled quietly. "Perks of the job, I suppose." She was not about to admit to her work colleague that she was beginning to feel ill. She felt lightheaded and nauseated, and while she was positive that the symptoms were simply the effects of the long hours she had spent in the hot and humid operating theater, her self-diagnosis did nothing to help her to feel any better.

At that moment the second patient from Theater One, accompanied by the two CTMs from Surgical Team Two, was wheeled into the CCU. Transferred to a bed next to the first, the remaining two trauma nurses commenced their post-op observations and procedures, identical to those carried out on Katie's still-sleeping patient. Katie and Henry, nodding to their CTH counterparts, left the CCU to go back to Theater One.

Outside in the corridor, the temperature was far cooler than it had been in the theater and the CCU. While Lance Corporal Barrow went on into the now-empty theater, Katie paused, taking a deep breath of the fresher air. Leaning against the cool wall, she raised a hand to wipe away clammy perspiration from her forehead. She would never get used to the heat, no matter how long she stayed in Afghanistan. Her earlier nausea becoming worse, she tried to distract her thoughts from her unsteady stomach by studying her surroundings.

The CTH was one of the few solid builds on Camp Churchill. A large, single story, sand-colored structure, it sprawled over an area of two thousand square meters, its rigid, straight lines at odds with the khaki canvas tents, sand-colored office containers and dun-colored, hard-packed sand and dusty earth that comprised the rest of Base Independence. It had started life as a MASH-style field hospital but as the base had expanded and become more developed and permanent, so had the Role Three Combat Trauma Hospital, a medical facility in miniature with state-of-the-art equipment, giving it the ability to be able to cope with the most complex of cases, something that was paramount in a war theater.

Its interior décor was spartan in its gleaming whiteness with spotless walls and dark green, rubberized flooring that ran throughout each room and the long central corridor bisecting the length of the building. A large, red-lettered sign — easily observed by all who entered — was placed just inside the double entrance doors, prohibiting the carrying of weapons beyond a certain point. Camp Standing Orders stipulated that everyone entering the building, including all medical personnel, had to leave their personal weapons in a small room simply called the weapons room, just inside the double doors, and collect them when leaving.

Leading off from the corridor were two operating theaters, each containing two operating tables. This gave the CTH the ability to perform four surgical procedures at the same time. In addition, there were two trauma rooms, each with a portable X-ray machine, capable of keeping four casualties stable until taken to surgery. The main rooms consisted of an MRI room, a twelve-man critical care unit, two twenty-man wards, the R&R room, shower and locker room facilities and a number of other rooms, all making up the labyrinth that was the CTH.

A lifeline to the sick and injured, the CTH was a safe haven for those who needed to know that in the midst of war there were people who cared—that there was a place of peace and protection where wounds were treated and damaged limbs and psyches healed. It was where the medical teams and staff worked beyond the call of duty to offer survivors compassion, care and an unfailing hope of survival, together with dedication and commitment. All the skill and competence in the world, could not save some, but the majority of the casualties who passed through the CTH's doors survived and went home to their families. This ultimately gave all the medical staff a sense of victory and achievement over those whose sole intent was to maim and kill.

Katie jerked herself from her reverie. There was more work that needed to be done before she could rest, so straightening up from her weary slouch against the wall she went to the door of the theater. She paused there, her weariness intensifying, dismayed at the mess that greeted her. The room—the scene of the two earlier surgical procedures—now lay silent and empty but there was blood everywhere—droplets sprayed on walls, smeared liberally across countertops, the operating tables, and staining instruments and instrument trays. A curdled miasma of smells inside the room, combined with the heat and humidity, were such that Katie felt as though she was about to suffocate. Perspiration immediately broke out on her forehead and her stomach churned rebelliously with a surge of the earlier nausea. Attempting to ignore her escalating discomfort, she swallowed and moved into the theater to commence the task of restoring it to its prior cleanliness.

After use of the theaters and trauma rooms, each needed to be thoroughly cleaned and sterilized. An infection control policy was in force and all surfaces — including walls, floors and anywhere that had come into contact with a casualty's bodily fluids — needed washing with an anti-bacterial, water-based solution. Instruments had to be autoclaved for optimum sterilization and all equipment used, cleansed thoroughly in boiling water. Every swab and retractor had to be accounted for, instrument trays replenished and drug cabinets re-inventoried, depleted drugs replaced. Each room was always restored to its pristine condition smoothly and quickly, those personnel that carried out the tasks aware that there was always the chance of further casualties arriving at the CTH.

Katie joined Lance Corporal Barrow, and while she worked, she listened to the muted voices of medical personnel drifting to her from the direction of the R&R room where everybody had congregated for a much needed coffee or cold drink and where, she knew having been party to the discussions herself, they would be going over the surgical procedures of the day and discussing the status of the patients. She longed to join them but the bloody mess in the theater needed tending to.

Although they were both tired, Katie and Henry were adept at doing this particular task, and they cleaned the theater quickly and thoroughly, collecting all the bloodstained bandages, pieces of uniform and swabs together before sealing the bundles in bags to prevent further contamination and throwing them into a waste receptacle in preparation for incineration. At one point Katie discovered a set of dog tags lying in lonely isolation on the floor in a small pool of blood. Picking them up, she allowed them to dangle from her gloved fingers for a second then ran them under hot water and set them aside to place with the other personal effects.

The CMTs from Surgical Team Two eventually joined them to assist with the clean-up. All four went about their work in silence, exhausted but with a quiet sense of efficiency. When they had finished cleaning Theater One, the four moved on to Theater Two then to each of the trauma rooms. It was when they had nearly completed their tasks in Trauma Room Two that Katie's nausea abruptly returned with a vengeance. Breaking out in a cold, clammy sweat, she paused in her task of wiping down an examination table and swayed dizzily.

Glancing down at her gloved hands in an attempt to distract her thoughts from how ill she was feeling, she noticed a liberal coating of dried blood on them, and geometric swathes of quickly drying red down the front of her scrub smock. She gagged slightly and put a hand to her mouth, remembering at the last minute about her stained gloves and jerking her hand away from her face. She knew instinctively that at some point in the very near future she was going to be very ill, and to avoid the embarrassing scene that this might create, she needed to get outside the CTH in the hope that some fresh air might help her feel better. Her face pale and covered in perspiration, Katie turned to Henry. "I need to go outside for a few minutes," she announced, her voice shaking slightly.

"Okay, no problem," Lance Corporal Barrow replied, glancing at her. Seeing how suddenly pale and unwell she looked, his expression became one of concern. "Katie, you look terrible. Are you feeling all right?"

"No, not really," she answered abruptly. "I'm feeling a bit sick. I'll be back in a couple of minutes."

Sensing that it might only be a matter of time before the unthinkable happened and that she was not going to be able to make it to the female toilets before it did, Katie about-turned and left the theater. Turning immediately right, she headed quickly for the wide double doors at the front of the building. As she neared the entrance, her stomach began to churn, prompting her to run, certain that she was not going to be able to make it outside before she vomited. There was no time for her to collect her weapon, and with one hand leaving a bloody handprint on the white paintwork, she thrust open one of the doors and hurried outside.

It was a late mid-June evening, one of the hottest months of an Afghanistan summer, and even though Katie stood beneath a jury-rigged canvas canopy, erected to shield patients from the glaring sunlight when ambulances arrived to unload them, the temperature was searingly hot, the air dry. Now the heat, dust and stench of aviation fuel, together with exhaust and oil from vehicles, pervaded the air and Katie began to feel even more unwell.

Fine dust, nicknamed moon dust because of its silvery color, added to the discomfort of those living on the base. It coated the air, getting into mouths, eyes and noses, and was a constant reminder that Base Independence was located in the middle of a desert. The dust was only one of the never-ending problems of this environment. Base personnel made regular efforts to try to prevent it from invading buildings, engines and even clothing, but it was an impossible task.

Stopping abruptly outside the main doors, Katie took a deep breath and tried without success to calm her roiling stomach. Standing in the shade, she began to shiver, perspiration quickly cooling on her skin. She swallowed, head pounding, unsteady on her feet, and reached out a trembling hand, groping blindly for something she could hang onto, finding the solid doorframe, and grasping on tightly so that she could support herself. She bowed her head and closed her eyes, gritting her teeth and willing herself not to be sick.

She focused on her breathing, opened her eyes and glanced around, trying to occupy her mind with more mundane things, but even these preventative actions failed to make her feel any better and suddenly she became aware that her struggles were failing dismally and she was going to be ill. Spinning to the left, she hurried around the side of the building in an attempt to remove herself from the view of anyone who might come out of the doors. She immediately vomited and continued to do so until her abdominal muscles contracted in rebellious protest then, moaning softly, retched dryly until her stomach eventually decided that it would allow her temporary respite. She straightened, tears of reaction trickling down her face, sweat-damp hair clinging to her forehead where it showed from beneath her floral surgical cap. She coughed slightly, clearing her throat, feeling weak and tired, stomach sore, as though it had been squeezed through a wringer and spat out. All she wanted to do at that moment was take a shower, change into clean scrubs and have a much needed rest.

"Are you okay, ma'am?" a deep, husky American voice suddenly asked from behind her.

Chapter Two

Ma'am! Who's ma'am? The question popped wildly into Katie's exhausted mind as she jumped violently. She had believed herself to be alone and now she uttered a small unladylike squawk of surprise and spun round. The harsh sunlight blinded her, her vision blurring so that at first she could not make out who it was that had spoken to her. Blinking her eyes quickly, she finally made out the figure of a tall, broad-shouldered man clad in Army combat fatigues — ACFs — standing immediately behind her. Not expecting him to be standing so close, Katie took an involuntary step backward. Her boot sole slipped on the tiles laid haphazardly on the sandy ground and she promptly over-balanced, pin wheeling her arms to prevent herself from toppling over. A hand instantly shot out and grasped her arm, pulling her back to a safer footing.

Gasping, embarrassed and irritated with herself, Katie shook off the rescuing hand and glanced up at the soldier in front of her. She was tall for a woman at five feet ten inches, but the top of her head barely came up to his chin. Against her will and totally alien to her character, she couldn't prevent her eyes from traveling first down then up his body, taking in the dusty combat boots, desert camouflage combat trousers and khaki T-shirt that molded itself to a flat stomach, broad, well-muscled chest and tanned, powerful arms. An M4 carbine hung by its carrying strap, over one shoulder. Her eyes eventually settled on his face, and despite feeling wrong-footed and having just spent the last ten minutes being violently ill in front of this stranger, she noticed his eyes. They were a deep, almost cobalt blue fringed with extraordinarily long, dark eyelashes. There was a sharp, evaluating expression in them, as though he ran across women vomiting outside buildings every day and took it in his stride. His deeply tanned face had a firm, square chin, and beneath a military camouflaged cap, Katie could see cropped, dark blond hair.

Katie was startled at the sudden surge of attraction she felt for the unknown man and it unnerved her. There was something about him that had started her pulse racing erratically and if she had been feeling a little better and the situation had been less humiliating, she would have been amused at her reaction. To make matters worse, she finally realized that she had been staring at his face for far too long and that the man was returning her stare just as intently, as though taking in every detail of her features. Katie found the directness of his gaze a little unsettling, and she cleared her throat nervously. Attempting to speak, she found herself struggling to form an adequate response to the soldier's question, which she had almost forgotten. She wanted to let forth with a cutting response, to put this man down and divert the unnerving intenseness of his gaze, but found that she was completely tongue-tied.

Anger and humiliation that a complete stranger had observed her being ill began to surge inside her and she wished that a hole would open up at her feet and she could crawl into it and disappear. To top it all off, he was a Yank to boot, and probably had all the arrogant character traits of one. Katie's irrational annoyance at what she perceived to be a breach of her privacy increased twofold. A decent person would not have stood watching her be physically sick without announcing their presence. As she reached this conclusion, she straightened, raised her chin defiantly and snapped, "I'm fine, thank you..." She abruptly realized that she did not know the man's rank and again, another wave of embarrassment washed over her and her cheeks flushed a bright red.

"US Marine Staff Sergeant Joe Anderson," the man volunteered, appearing to ignore her rudeness. "I'm glad you're feeling better."

There was nothing in his tone except concern and sympathy, certainly no evidence that Katie could hear of contempt or ridicule, and a friendly smile played about his lips. Katie's ire rose another notch because the staff sergeant's voice was a deep, husky drawl and rolled over her like balm, easing her embarrassment and irritation and doing strange things to her nerve endings. She felt confused and this irritated her further. The unexpected attraction she felt for this man was unwelcome, unwanted and out of character. She was decidedly uneasy at the feelings he was triggering inside her and she had the urge to dismiss him rudely and run back inside the CTH like a frightened child.

Watching the display of emotions flitting across the woman's face — something that he had been studying intently and with a great deal of interest since he had startled her — Joe Anderson was uneasy at the strong surge of feelings she was arousing in him, and his observation of Katie was just as avid as hers of him had been. He had immediately noticed her tall, slim figure and, as he considered himself a normal hot-blooded man, had noticed that she had curves in all the right places, even beneath her shapeless scrubs. Her hair was short and curly and a color that he could only describe as burnished copper. Her skin was lightly tanned although at that moment her face was pale. A liberal smattering of freckles across her small, pert nose and highly defined cheekbones stood out in stark relief, which he found undeniably cute. A tilt to her chin led him to believe that she might also possess a stubborn streak and probably a temper to go with it. The most stunning feature of all, however, was her eyes. A clear emerald green, fringed with long, dark, curling lashes, Joe could picture how they might flash and spark when she got upset or angry. He wondered how old she was and guessed her age to be in her early twenties. He felt sudden disappointment. He was thirty-six, probably a grizzled old man in her eyes, far too old for her — if he had any intention of getting to know her — which, he was attempting to convince himself, he had no intention of doing at all.

Joe found himself feeling as uncomfortable as a schoolboy with these new and uncharacteristic thoughts. Attempting to dismiss them, he noticed a smear of blood on one of the woman's cheeks, the bloody gloves and the dark red stains on the front of her top, and realized why she had been vomiting. He felt sympathy rise inside him. "Bad day, huh?" he asked casually.

Acutely conscious of the staff sergeant still staring at her, and responding to that stare, Katie nodded. Trying to regain some shreds of her lost dignity, she attempted to distract herself by pulling off her gloves and shoving them into the deep pocket of her scrub smock. She noticed vaguely that her hands were white and wrinkled and remembered that she had forgotten to put medicated talcum powder on them before pulling on the clinging nitrile.

"I've had better days, Staff Sergeant," she finally answered politely. "I apologize that you had to see my..." She stopped speaking again because Joe Anderson was shaking his head.

"No need to apologize, Corporal. I've seen grown men throw up over a lot less. Believe me."

Katie nodded, grateful for the casual dismissal of her apology. She sensed that he was attempting to make the situation less humiliating for her and again she felt calmed by his calm voice. Straightening, she smiled slightly. "Well, thank you for that, Staff Sergeant, but I do need to get back to work. Can I help you with something?"

Staff Sergeant Anderson nodded. "Yeah, I do believe you can," he answered casually. "One of my marines—a Private Hanson—was admitted to you this morning with injuries from an IED incident. I've come to see how he's doing."

Relieved that their conversation seemed to be back on a more general footing, Katie said politely, "Of course, Staff Sergeant. Please follow me and I'll take you to him." She went to step around him as he was blocking her path and without another word, he stood aside then fell into step behind her.

Katie and the staff sergeant entered the air-conditioned coolness of the CTH and she waited while he offloaded his weapon in the weapons room before they continued walking down the corridor, Katie trying to think frantically of some polite conversation she could make but unable to kick-start her brain into formulating a sentence that might sound even remotely intelligent. She found herself feeling distinctly shy — which had never been an inherent part of her character — and tongue-tied again.

She led the staff sergeant past the first ward and eventually arrived at the second. On entering, she took him to the second bed, where the young US marine private was sleeping. Involved in an explosion while out on patrol a few days previously, the young soldier had had to have his left leg amputated from just below the knee. The bones in the limb had been completely shattered, and to save his life, removal of the limb had been the only solution. Again, he was just one of many who had arrived in-country full-bodied and would be returning minus a part of himself.

One other bed was occupied by a young British soldier who had been involved in a separate IED incident from that of the marine private. The rest of the ward was empty and silent, the beds neatly made, each with a green blanket tucked around white sheets and green curtains hanging beside each. The other three casualties from the IED incident that morning still remained in the CCU under observation.

An air conditioner hummed in the background, together with the soft beeping of a heart monitor machine. It was cool inside the ward and Katie felt some of her equilibrium return. The unsettled feeling in her stomach was beginning to fade, although her humiliation at making an exhibition of herself outside was not. Stopping at the foot of the hospital bed, she gestured to the staff sergeant to proceed and he approached.

Moving to the patient's side, his combat boots squeaking on the rubber floor, the staff sergeant looked down at the young face of his man. His eyes glanced from the ashen complexion, down the white and green bed covers to where it was clearly evident that a limb was absent. "You had to amputate?" he asked quietly, a tone of sadness in his voice, verbally confirming what he could see.

Hesitating slightly, Katie moved to the man's side. "Yes," she answered softly, although the young marine was still asleep. "I'm sorry, Staff Sergeant, his leg was just too badly damaged to save. Everyone out in the field, the CTT and ourselves here at the CTH, did everything we could. The only thing that could save his life was amputation. He's stable now and is doing fine. He'll remain here for a while then, as long as he continues to remain stable and doesn't develop an infection, he'll go back to the US. With rehabilitation and some counseling, he could go on to lead a relatively normal life. He's young and strong and he'll get plenty of support and assistance. I know it's no consolation right now, but he's lucky to be alive."

The staff sergeant remained unmoving for long minutes, still staring down at the marine, then nodded. "I understand," he acknowledged at last. "You've done a good job with him."

He turned around to look at her and Katie, stirred at the emotion on his face, felt a surge of sympathy for him. They all tended to forget that the men in charge of the men and women who were injured or killed felt a great deal of responsibility, loss and guilt. It was almost as tough on their leaders as it was on the patients. "He'll be fine," she reiterated, wishing that the expression of sadness would leave the staff sergeant's face. "We'll look after him, Staff Sergeant. I can promise you that."

The staff sergeant nodded again in acceptance. A small silence rose between them until, at last, he cleared his throat nervously. "Well, I guess I'd better get going. I'm glad you're feeling okay, and thank you again." With this last parting remark, he strode away from her and left the ward.

Katie remained standing beside the bed, staring after him then at the vacant doorway after he had disappeared, decidedly confused about what had just occurred between herself and the staff sergeant. Now that he had gone, she felt slightly lost and alone. "Oh my God, woman," she scoffed at herself. "Where are you coming from? You barely know the man. Get a grip."

She felt stupid and naïve and wondered if her reaction to him as a man had been obvious to him. She was unable to pinpoint exactly what it was about the staff sergeant that had set her pulses racing and an undeniable surge of attraction flowing through her. She had always been independent. Her parents had been killed in a car accident some three years previously and, with no siblings, she had been left on her own. The Army had been her life. She had vowed right from basic training that she would focus on her career, steering clear of any relationships, and the complex problems that always seemed to go hand in hand with them, until she was completely ready. Now, after only a few short hours, Katie suspected that this US marine staff sergeant had unknowingly succeeded in blowing all her hard-won promises and emotional reservations out of the water.

Mentally shaking herself and uttering an exasperated noise, Katie busied herself checking the young private again for any adverse changes in his condition, noted his vital signs on his chart then left the ward, going out into the corridor. She could hear voices coming from the R&R room and started the long walk toward it, desperate for a strong cup of coffee and a chance to collapse into one of the old armchairs there.

* * * *

After collecting his weapon and slinging the strap over his shoulder, Joe Anderson strode out of the CTH, across the gravel and sand forecourt, and turned out onto the road. Keeping up his brisk pace and heading toward Camp Roosevelt—where the United States Marine Corp—USMC—was based—and an arranged exercise run with his squad, he couldn't turn his thoughts away from the young CTM whom he had just met at the hospital. He could not dismiss the image of her face from his mind. He remembered her expressive green eyes, her quiet voice and the stubborn tilt of her chin when she had snapped at him. He found himself smiling at his thoughts, and with a startled awareness and a good deal of uneasiness, realized that he was attracted to the woman, more so than he had been to any other. Instantly quelling his wayward emotions, determined not to think about her any further, he forced his attention to his squad and the next two days' training that he had arranged for them and that he knew was likely to emphasize his reputation as 'the old man'—or harsher language at his expense, if his men were anything to go by.

* * * *

Back at the CTH, as Katie approached the R&R room and the noise coming from it grew steadily louder, Sergeant Ron Webster, the senior non-commissioned officer in charge of the CTH, approached her from his office. "You look healthy," he commented bluntly, eyeing her with a certain amount of concern.

"Why thank you so much for the compliment, Sergeant, but I'm fine, thank you," Katie answered her tone heavy with sarcasm.

"I'm really glad to hear you say that, Corporal," Sergeant Webster responded dryly. "But you'll have to excuse me if I don't believe you. Just do us all a favor. Go and take a break before you keel over. The night teams will be here shortly then we can all get the hell out of here."

"Yes, Sergeant," Katie replied, "but can I say with all due respect that if you'd been paying attention, you'd have seen that I was already heading for the R&R room before you waylaid me." With this parting remark and a falsely sweet smile to go with it, she continued on to the area where the medical staff gravitated to when the CTH was quiet. With the exception of the trauma nurses who were attending to the three new patients, the US marine and Private Berwick, everyone was present with all armchairs occupied and everybody drinking what was frequently and eloquently classed as the worst coffee in the British Army.

Katie wrinkled her nose at the stale smell that permeated the air. The R&R room was in the last stages of acute untidiness and generally allowed to remain that way. Face masks littered the chairs and floor, the chairs did not match in color or design and their cushions sagged, sadly misused and abused by hundreds of backsides. Magazines, piled and strewn on the surface of the battered coffee table, mixed with empty plastic coffee cups and coffee stain rings. In prime position on the counter, beside a microwave, kettle and portable fridge full of bottled water, was a large coffee percolator with its jug half-full of tarry, black-looking coffee.

As Katie entered the room, everyone glanced up and some of the conversation ceased.

"You all right, Katie?" Leading surgeon Captain Andrew Myers of Surgical Team Two asked.

"Yes, I'm fine. Thank you, sir," Katie replied truthfully, turning as Henry Barrow handed her a plastic cup of stewed coffee.

"Ugh, I don't have a clue how we can have drunk this stuff for so long," she commented to him. "I hate to think what it's doing to our insides." Wrinkling her nose, she thanked him and sat down in the sagging chair that he had just vacated. Sinking gratefully back against its crinkled leather and sighing, she took a sip of the coffee. Disgusting though it was, it certainly hit the spot. As there were no other vacant seats, Henry sat on the arm of her chair with his own cup and everybody turned back to their conversations.

Katie remained silent, deep in thought, not participating in the various discussions circulating throughout the room. She was fully aware that each of the medical staff dealt with the traumas passing through the CTH in their own way. She personally dealt with each issue by attempting to relax for a few minutes following each incident, thinking of what had gone on during the day, analyzing her thoughts then storing them away in the furthest reaches of her mind, refusing to allow them to affect her in any way.

Others dealt with events each in their own individual way—by being loud and jovial, discussing the surgeries in depth, arguing in good humor or just sitting and taking part only when prompted. The trauma teams, surgical teams, CTTs and support staff were highly skilled people, and most of them had been dealing with traumas and emergencies for many years, so the tragedies and events that occurred in the CTH were not unknown to them. None of them, however, could fail to be moved or saddened by the wanton destruction of so many men and women.

After she finished her coffee, wincing at the last tepid dregs in the bottom of the plastic cup, Katie rose, threw the container into a waste receptacle and turned to Lance Corporal Barrow. "I need a shower. That's where I'll be if I'm needed," she said and he nodded.

Feeling even more tired than usual, Katie left the R&R room and went to the end of the corridor, letting herself into the female locker room. She unlaced her boots and kicked them off then undid the ties at the back of her smock shrugged out of it, followed by her baggy scrub trousers. She bundled everything together and thrust it into a large waste bin situated in the room. Returning to her locker, she retrieved her toilet bag and a large bath towel, which she wrapped around herself, then opened another door and went through into the female shower room.

A short while later, Katie uttered a sigh of delight as she stood beneath steaming hot water, face lifted to the sharp, pounding needles, reveling in the feeling the spray caused against her skin. She felt the tension slowly seep from her body and stiff muscles in her shoulders and her neck begin to relax. God, she was so tired. She needed to go back to her tent, collapse onto her camp bed and sleep, but she was still on duty and couldn't leave until Sergeant Webster had dismissed her.

Unbidden, a clear, detailed image of Staff Sergeant Anderson's face popped into her mind and Katie unwittingly shivered, nerve ends quivering. There was something about that man, something dangerously sexy, some element of his presence or character that she had never come across in a man before. Perhaps it was his eyes, which had sent shivers up and down her spine, or the calm strength that appealed to her as a woman. Whatever it was, whatever charisma he had, the memory of him was doing things to her that she had never experienced before and it was making her feel extremely uncomfortable.

Katie lurched from a daze, realizing that she had been standing in the shower with her eyes closed. "Damn!" she exclaimed loudly, her voice echoing around the shower room, "Leave it alone, Katie girl. That man is most definitely not for you and you, my girl, are most definitely not interested in him." As if calling her out on her denial, a small voice piped up in her subconscious and amusedly quipped, *Liar!*

Feeling flustered, Katie soaped herself vigorously, determined to push thoughts of Staff Sergeant Joe Anderson to the back of her mind and mentally labeling them 'dangerous'. Concentrating on what she was doing, she scrubbed her skin to ensure that there was no blood left anywhere, washed her hair thoroughly then turned off the shower. She felt a little better — more alert — and the fatigue had relinquished its hold on her slightly.

With the towel wrapped around her body once more, she went back to her locker and retrieved her multi terrain patterned combats — MTPCs — boots and khaki T-shirt. She sprayed on deodorant, dressed then sat down on the bench to lace her boots. She checked that her dog tags were still around her neck, put on her webbing belt, put a torch into a deep pocket of her trousers and finally put on her military cap, fastening her combat helmet by its chinstrap to her belt. Recently, due to the increase in hostilities on the base, there had been an update to the camp Standing Orders relating to the code of dress, so all personnel now needed to carry their personal weapon and helmet with them at all times. As cumbersome and inconvenient as it was to have to carry a helmet and light support weapon — LSW — orders were orders and were there to be obeyed.

Ready at last, Katie left the showers, intent on making her way back to the R&R room, where Sergeant Webster met her at the door just as she was about to enter.

"The next teams are in," he announced, looking her up and down. "You look a lot better than you did, almost human again. You can stand down now. Go and get some chow and sleep. I'll see you for notes tomorrow morning."

"Thank you, Sergeant. See you tomorrow," Katie rejoined with relief, grateful that she was finally free to go off duty.

On her way down the corridor toward the doors, she popped her head into the CCU to briefly check on the soldiers operated on just a short while previously. All three were still asleep and being attended to by the trauma nurses. The three women and one man raised their hands in farewell to Katie who smiled, whispered, "Goodnight," and walked on. She looked in on the US marine and the British soldier but they too were still asleep. Henry Barrow was checking the young Army soldier's pulse and he nodded his goodbye.

Katie hurried toward the double doors, hoping that before she reached them and let herself out of the building, she would not be stopped by Sergeant

Webster with an order that she stay on. She hastily retrieved her weapon, slung it over her shoulder, thrust one of the doors open and stepped outside, immediately feeling as though she had been released from prison.

It was now 2000 hours but still warm, the air oppressive with heat and dust. Dusk was beginning to fade toward night but Camp Churchill was still busy with personnel either going on or coming off duty, others heading at a brisk stride toward the mess to eat, and vehicles trundling slowly up and down the main road, trailing dust clouds behind them. The sun, a flaming red ball, was low on the horizon, and the first glittering star had appeared like a bright diamond in the deep blue sky.

Katie took a step onto the gravel and sand that formed the large turning area for emergency vehicles and for the second time that day almost jumped out of her skin when a familiar voice behind her asked, "How're you doing, Corporal Walker?"

Chapter Three

Katie spun round sharply and, in doing so, her boots slipped on the sharp stones, somehow became entangled, and she sat down on the hard ground with a heavy thump. Her teeth clicked together, almost catching her tongue between them, and her backside protested at the forceful contact and the countless sharp edges digging into her tender rump. "Oh shit!" she exclaimed beneath her breath, biting her lip in a futile attempt to block any further obscenities.

Reclining against the wall as though he had all the time in the world, arms folded and booted ankles crossed, Joe Anderson chuckled.

Katie, legs bent at the knees with her elbows resting on them, head lowered, murmuring further obscenities at the innocuous ground, jerked her head up, eyes flashing, immediately on the defensive.

"Oh, you think this is funny?" she snapped. "I could have broken my bloody neck. Do you often make a habit of scaring the pants off of unwary females, Staff Sergeant?" Feeling her cheeks hot with mortification as a result of her ungainly fall, she was angry.

Still staring at her with more than a little interest, Joe tried unsuccessfully to wipe the smile off his face. "Nope," he eventually answered casually, "but I do have to say that you look kinda fetching sitting there in the dirt." He straightened up, adjusted the M4 slung over his shoulder and walked slowly toward her, the grin widening on his face.

"So not funny," Katie exclaimed, humiliated at ending up on the ground at his feet, extremely irritated that his presence was causing a resurgence of the feelings of attraction that she had experienced earlier that day and furious at his apparent casual disregard for her predicament.

Joe stopped at her feet, and putting his fists on his hips, stared down at her. After a moment, he bent forward and held out his hand in a gesture of assistance. "Give me your hand," he ordered.

Katie ignored the offer of help, having every intention of getting to her feet under her own steam. However, with her recent luck of embarrassing incidents, she had a nightmarish vision of ending up on her backside again if she attempted it. Relenting reluctantly, she reached up and slid her hand into his proffered one. As their hands touched, her next explosive thought was that his hand felt strong, rough and warm, and a tremor ran up her arm as her palm made contact with his.

With one swift movement, Joe's grip tightened and he pulled her gently to her feet. As Katie regained her footing, she overbalanced slightly, staggered forward and discovered that he was standing far too close for comfort. Quickly, she glanced up at him to find that he was still staring at her with a warm expression on his face. A suffocating feeling of panic rose in her throat and she stepped back abruptly. He promptly released her hand as if her touch had scalded him.

Trying to regain her scattered composure, Katie averted her face from his stare, struggled briefly with the strap of her rifle, which was attempting to strangle her, straightened the military cap on her head, and bent down to pat vigorously at her combat trousers in an effort to get rid of the dust. Her cheeks felt fiery and her heart was racing furiously. *What the bloody hell is wrong with me?*

When there was no further dust to get rid of, she found that she had no option but to straighten up and face him. "What are you doing here, Staff Sergeant?" she asked at last, aware that the tone of her voice was a little less than friendly but unable to do anything about it.

"I was waiting for you," Joe replied simply. "I thought you might like to go to the mess for some chow."

Taken off guard at the invitation, Katie was a little stunned. Her first thought was to immediately refuse and she hesitated, the reasons for turning this man's invitation down turning over in her mind. She did not want to get involved with this staff sergeant. She had always managed to get by on her own and did not want that to change. She was fully aware that her recent thoughts and feelings were out of character for her but any denial of the inexplicable attraction she was beginning to feel for this marine was beginning to make her feel as though she was fooling herself. She hated feeling so vulnerable.

"Hell, I'm sorry for asking, I sure didn't mean to make you feel awkward," the staff sergeant said apologetically. "Look, just forget I did, okay?"

Katie continued to hesitate, feeling uncertain and confused. *What harm will it do?* That small, rebellious voice piped up again in her mind. *It isn't like we're going to go out on a date. That would be impossible at Camp Churchill with the thousands of people living and working here and the lack of privacy and social entertainment.* Feeling reckless and never able to explain to herself later why she did it, she suddenly made up her mind. "I'd like that. Thank you," she answered politely and winced at how formal and British she sounded. It was definitely a day for feeling embarrassed.

Joe Anderson grinned. "Okay, that's great. Let's go then."

In silence, they continued walking to the road and turned onto it. It had now become quite dark and both of them automatically switched on their torches. No street lights existed along any of the roads, so trekking around the base at night was hazardous. All personnel carried torches as part of their personal equipment so white beams continuously flickered like large white fireflies. The main islands of light came from the distant airfield, motor pool, the sprawling mess and the Navy, Army, and Air Force Institute—NAAFI. Other lights from distant accommodation tents were dim and muted by their canvas canopies.

Katie, trying to think of something intelligent to say, noticed that Joe's torch had a red lens thereby emitting a red beam so, for want of better a conversation, she glanced at him and asked, "Why do you carry a red torch?"

Joe gestured with it. "This thing?" he answered, "Well, when we're out on patrol, it's not a good idea to use white flashlights when we're on the move as it gives our position away. Red light is easy on the eyes, doesn't interfere with our night vision and is dark enough to prevent the enemy from locating us."

"I see," Katie answered. "I thought everybody wore night vision goggles out in the desert so you wouldn't need torches."

Joe glanced sideways at her. "We do," he responded. "But we can't wear them all the time. When we make our ORP—sorry, objective rally point—we have to utilize other light and the red flashlights come in handy."

Conversation lapsed between them for a while, although it wasn't an uncomfortable one. Katie was enamored of the idea that this man had made an effort to wait for her. It did, however, make her feel a little gauche and out of her comfort zone, and she was unable to work out how she felt about the whole situation.

"How long had you been waiting?" Katie asked, again trying to strike up an intelligent conversation. She felt shy and was finding it hard to think of something to say.

"Only half an hour or so," Joe answered. "I was coming from a briefing and was passing. It was a spur of the moment thing."

"Really?" Katie asked, an amused tone entering her voice. "Do you often ask strange women to the mess on the spur of the moment, Staff Sergeant, or is that part of your duties?"

The faint gurgle of laughter caused Joe to glance sideways at her, and even though his face was partially hidden in flickering shadow, Katie could see that he was grinning, white, even teeth gleaming faintly in the darkness. "Nope," he answered, "I don't make a habit of it. I only ask strange young women who throw themselves at my feet." He moved the beam of his torch up just to the right of her face in an effort not to blind her, so that he could see her expression.

Katie found herself smiling as well. "I should hope not, Staff Sergeant," she teased and her cheeks flushed a little.

"Please, less of the Staff Sergeant," he said. "I told you, it's Joe."

"Okay, Joe it is, and I'm Katie," Katie responded a little shyly, feeling her face flushing again when she realized that, much against her will, the boundaries she had set herself where men were concerned were thinning and stretching, because of this man. In her mind, she had already been calling him by his first name whenever she thought about him and couldn't have stopped the forward progression of getting to know this US marine even if she had wanted to.

Joe nodded. "How long have you been in-country?" he asked.

"Four months," Katie answered. "What about you?"

"Same," he replied. "It's my third deployment."

"You're a glutton for punishment," Katie exclaimed. "Why anyone would want to come out here for a third tour is beyond me."

Making small talk, they continued walking along the dusty road until they eventually reached the mess. Joe opened the door of the sprawling building, allowing Katie to precede him, and after the door slowly closed behind them, they went on into the main room, removing their military caps as they entered. The mess was nearly empty. Tired soldiers, many looking as though they had just arrived back from patrol or were just going on or coming off duty, sat slumped at tables sipping coffee or eating supper. There was a barely audible hum of conversation.

Joe and Katie immediately found an empty table away from other personnel, leaned their weapons against chairs and going to the hot food counter, collected a tray each and proceeded to choose their food. After they had both selected drinks, Joe led them back to their table, where they seated themselves and began to eat.

"So," Joe Anderson began, setting down his fork, opening his can of Coke and taking a large swallow. "Rough day, huh?"

Katie nodded. "Just a bit," she answered. "Not as bad as it can get but bad enough. We had a young British Army private come in from an IED incident a couple of days ago, your man from an IED and three more IED casualties this morning. The Taliban seem to be stepping up their IED campaign. That's the cruelest way to be injured, I think." She paused, looking down at her plate then back at Joe. His gaze was on her face, his eyes staring intently into hers. "You know," she continued, a little sadness in her voice, "we deal with varying degrees of trauma, from minor to complex, day in and day out, but you never get used to it. You try to maintain a distance—a detachment from situations—but suddenly just one bad day can trigger an overload then everything can hit you both physically and mentally all at once. And there's no warning that it's coming." She smiled wryly. "The result is the rather embarrassing and humiliating display you stumbled upon."

Joe nodded as if he understood what she was trying to say. He held her gaze for what seemed like a long time before managing to respond to Katie's statement.

"I've been in some tough situations myself, where some of the men in my charge have been injured," he explained, attempting to make normal small talk and seeming aware that he was failing dismally. "No matter that it's the bad guys who plant those IEDs or fire those weapons, there's nothing you can do to change the situation. It's tough dealing with the guilt and the feeling that you personally could have prevented the incident from happening. I've been in the US Marine Corp for sixteen years and it still roughs me up when any of my men get injured or killed."

So, a career marine. Tough guy. He has to be about thirty-five or thirty-six then. "This is probably going to sound ridiculous," Katie went on. "I've been on leave a couple of times and, as sick as it sounds, I couldn't wait to get back here. I couldn't function on civvy street. Couldn't get my head around normal. If I can use my skills to help the people serving out here, then that's my goal and I will have achieved something. But the sadness doesn't ever stop, or the wondering about what will happen to those that get sent back home with loss of limbs or disfiguring injuries."

Joe sat back in his seat, fiddling with his fork. "My own job is tough enough, but I have only admiration and respect for the things you medical people do," he said, the sincerity in his tone obvious and the look in his blue eyes confirming his statement, causing a tinge of pink to bloom in Katie's cheeks.

"So, what do you do, Joe, apart from being in the US Marines, I mean?" she asked, quickly changing the subject in an attempt to divert his unnerving gaze from her face. She ignored her meal for a moment, leaning an elbow on the table and resting her chin in her hand. She felt something tickling her forehead, and completely unaware of what she was doing, pursed her lips and blew whatever it was out of the way.

"Me?" he asked hastily. "Okay, well, as you already know, I'm a US marine. I'm part of the One MEF." At Katie's frown, he grinned, "Sorry, One Marine Expeditionary Force, and I have a squad of sixteen men, or four teams of four, a really great bunch of guys. I'm lucky that each one of them is a skilled professional soldier, reliable and would back anybody up in any situation. We carry out patrols, anything from a recon for a distance of a few clicks for a couple of days, to a search and rescue, or attack patrol for four or five days. The attack patrols are the most dangerous, not just because of the enemy, but the MREs are lousy and just as likely to kill you as the bad guys." Joe's tone had held pride and affection on speaking about his men and Katie warmed even further to the man.

She laughed at the remark regarding the field rations. It was a well-known fact in the Armed Forces, that if you dwelt on what the contents of MREs were, you would never eat them.

"Sounds dangerous," she said, her face becoming serious. "Not the MREs, but your MOS."

Joe grinned. "I can't deny that it is," he continued. "But if you keep your head, plan well in advance, trust in your men and your instincts, you can get through anything in one piece."

"What made you join up?"

"My dad was Special Forces," Joe answered. "It always followed that I would join up. I was never good at anything much else. Bit of a rebel in my younger days, I'm afraid. I didn't want to be Special Forces or anything similar so I chose the Marines and it's been a good career. What about your family?"

"My parents are dead," Katie explained. "They were killed in a car crash about three years ago and I don't have any siblings."

"I'm sorry to hear that," Joe responded gently.

Katie straightened up and glanced around the mess. It was even emptier than before. She moved her gaze toward the hot food counter and noticed that somebody was staring at her from behind the hot plates keeping the food warm. Screwing up her eyes, she realized with a stab of annoyance who it was.

Corporal David Hudson was a British Army cook and since the beginning of Katie's deployment to Base Independence had been showing her increasingly unwanted attention. He would not take no for an answer, frequently and insistently asking her out for coffee or a walk or issuing some other such invitation. She had attempted to head him off by explaining as gently as she could that she was not interested, but the young corpora could not seem to grasp that his advances were being rejected. Even though he was British, charming and polite, there was something about those traits that seemed like a veneer, covering up something else, and he made her skin crawl. He just did not want to give up with his persistence, and even though she had given him no encouragement, only refusals, he obviously thought that she should be with him and that they should have a relationship. Now he was staring over at her and Joe Anderson and she did not like the expression she could barely make out on his face.

Katie shifted uncomfortably in her chair and turned her face away. Joe sensed her discomfort. "What's up?" he asked.

"Just someone being a nuisance," Katie answered, brushing the problem aside. She glanced at her watch and groaned. "It's late," she announced. "I need to get back to my tent before they send out a search party. I have to get my kit ready for tomorrow."

A fleeting look of regret darted over Joe's face, but he pushed his chair back and stood up. "I'll walk you back to your tent," he announced. The statement was made in such a way as to brook no argument, but Katie surprised herself by realizing that she had no intention of denying herself the opportunity to be with him anyway.

Retrieving their weapons and stacking their dirty dishes on the plate racks, Katie and Joe left the mess and, watching carefully for oncoming vehicle headlights, crossed the road. It was now very dark. Dust clouds, kicked up by their boots, passing trucks and other military vehicles, shimmered in the sparse flashes of headlights and torch beams. Rich smells of sunbaked earth, aviation fuel and exhaust fumes hung heavily on the warm air. Generator noise thudded in the background, accompanied occasionally by aircraft and helicopter engines as they took off and landed at the airfield.

As they walked, at one point, Katie glanced up at the sky and felt awed by the vast expanse of blackness studded with billions of diamond-bright pinpoints of light. The moon was huge and hung like a massive cream bowling ball, bathed in its own luminosity. "In a harsh, barren sort of way, it really is beautiful," she murmured, "although I think many people would argue that point."

"You should see the desert at night," Joe stated. "It's very bleak with no trees and hardly any vegetation. Dust and sand find their way into places I never dreamed they could get into, and in the winter months, the temperature can drop by as much as twenty degrees. It's a desolate place, inhospitable and cruel, but, on a clear night like this, it's stunning."

"It must be dangerous out there," Katie said, and glanced up at him, her gaze focusing on his face and the way his brow creased when he was thinking. If given the opportunity, she could have stared at his face all night, but suddenly reining in her thoughts, she hastily turned her face away to focus on the direction in which they were walking.

"We deal with it. One way or another, you have to," Joe answered. "If you can't deal with what the Marine Corps throws at you then you shouldn't be in it."

All too quickly, they reached Katie's tent, which she shared with twelve other women. Situated some distance from the main road, it was one of many long lines of regimentally aligned poly-tunnels covered in sand-colored and khaki canvas. Each tent had its own generator and electric lighting with two temporary shower tents and one portable toilet installed out the back of each. The women slept in sleeping bags on low camp beds and purloined, stole or borrowed anything else that they needed, generally from unknown and undisclosed sources.

Katie turned to Joe. "My home away from home," she said, smiling at him wryly.

Joe turned to study the long polythene tent with its canvas canopy and subdued lighting shining out through its opening. "Oh very nice," he said teasingly. "I sleep in the same. Not exactly the Hilton, but when you have to sleep on the ground in the desert more often than not, you learn to appreciate sleeping on a camp bed at times."

They stood staring at each other in silence, Katie not wanting to say goodnight him.

"I'd better be off," Joe announced at last. "It's been real good getting to know you, Katie."

Katie nodded, smiling, "I've enjoyed it too, Joe. Thank you."

Sketching a salute, Joe backed up a few steps then about-turned and strode off. Katie stood watching him disappear into the blackness, feeling disappointed that he had not mentioned anything about seeing her again.

Lowering her head, she toed the hard, dusty ground with her boot. She would have liked to have spent longer with him, getting to know him better. Perhaps it was for the best after all, although she was regretful that he was no longer with her. Sighing, she went into her tent, eliciting a chorus of greetings as she entered.

Chapter Four

Katie's alarm clock, confined by a thick thermal sock and buried beneath her pillow, sounded at 0600 hours the next morning and she instantly came awake, groaning softly as she noticed that the tent was already warm and humid, even at that early hour of the morning. The soft sounds of breathing from the other women, subdued thud of the many generators that were an integral part of Camp Churchill, the distant sounds of military vehicles traveling up and down the camp road together with the dull roar of the engines of a Harrier jump jet as it took off were the normal sounds of the base going about its daily business.

That morning, unusually for her, Katie lay for a few minutes on her camp bed, lazily studying her surroundings. It was all too clear that women occupied the less than ideal accommodation. Some of the camp beds had brightly colored blankets thrown over them, fluffy slippers or flip-flops lay haphazardly kicked off or stuffed neatly under the low camp beds, and damp underwear and other items of feminine apparel hung from every available strut and wire that was capable of holding an item of clothing. Each canvas locker top was festooned with photographs, makeup, toiletries or magazines. There were even soft toys lying on blankets or on the floor, incongruous when set next to various lethal weapons standing against lockers or propped against the sides of the tent. The air smelled of deodorant and sunscreen overlying the odor of damp and additional smells of the camp that filtered in through the tied back flaps at the tent entrance.

Katie was Corporal in charge of the tent. Most of the tent occupants had arrived at Camp Churchill at about the same time as herself, but she had been nominated senior NCO and it fell to her to keep the women in order, the tent as tidy and as clean as possible and to deal with any problems that arose. Not one to lay down the law or order anyone around, by sticking to that policy, she had become a well-liked NCO, having earned the women's trust and having an innate ability to get on well with them. Granted, there were rules and regulations that had to be followed, but she chose to lead by example and not by sitting on her backside and allowing everyone to do it all themselves.

Some of the women worked night shifts, graveyard shifts or were lucky enough to work nine-to-five days so not all of them were present in the tent at any one time. They were a mixed bunch of trades from the British Army, either of corporal or lance corporal rank. They all got on well, helped each other out in times of trouble or if things became too much, there was always an ear to listen or a shoulder there to cry against.

One example of her participation in the lighthearted humor that was prevalent in the tent was that on her arrival, after settling in, one of the women had painted a sign that she had hung on the outside of the tent. It offered a stern warning to trespassers — namely men —

'Tent D Sorority—Enter at Your Peril'. A teddy bear in camouflage and armed with a plastic gun had been stationed outside the tent under the sign.

Having noticed the untidiness of the tent and smelled the odor of damp, Katie knew that it was time she called an admin evening—an evening of washing and cleaning the tent, shower tents and toilet. These nights allowed for some timeout and relaxation together, and also kept the living environment fresh and clean, a complicated and difficult task to achieve in the furnace hot climate with its thick and wayward dust and sand. Katie surmised that the duty wouldn't go down well with some of the women, but all were perfectly aware of the hazards of allowing their living quarters to become unclean. In the climate that they were subjected to on a daily basis, hygiene was of paramount importance, and they all accepted the need for the occasional arses and elbows, the military slang term for the effort put into cleaning, regardless of how much they would gripe and moan.

Another alarm clock sounded with a subdued ringing and Katie's tent companions began to stir. Katie quickly sat up on her bed, unzipped her sleeping bag and swung her legs over the side so she could stand up. She found her bright pink fluffy elephant slippers, thrust her feet into them and grabbed her towel and toilet bag. It was time to bolt for the shower tents before a queue formed. She had to be at the mess for breakfast and report for sick parade and patient notes at the CTH at 0700 hours. Tardiness was one of Sergeant Webster's pet hates, one that would escalate into a crime in the making if she didn't arrive on time.

Katie hurried down the long tent, slippered feet shuffling on the rubber floor, through a makeshift sitting room at the rear and out through the opening to the clearing at the back of the tent where the shower tents and portable toilet were located. She was relieved to find that the showers were not yet in use, although she knew that this wasn't going to remain the case for long as she could hear voices beginning to sound inside the tent. She quickly used the portable toilet, holding her breath at the chemical smell that was a permanent fixture, before negotiating the grid of anti-slip tiles and wiring festooning the ground like multicolored snakes in front of the showers and fastening a notice proclaiming that one of the showers was in use by a female. The idea had come about due to a wandering male, on the prowl for a vacant shower, being discovered about to enter a shower tent occupied by a woman, causing all manner of hysteria and amusement. Lifting the makeshift shower curtain and mosquito net strung across the opening, Katie stepped over the sandbags in situ and went inside.

The inside of the shower tent was its usual dim dankness and the moldy, humid smell of damp tarpaulin and canvas purveyed the air. Thoroughly accustomed to their aromas, Katie dropped her toilet bag in the corner, hung her towel on the looped nylon rope dangling solely for that purpose from the ceiling, quickly divested herself of her nightwear and turned on the shower. She squealed audibly as freezing cold water poured from the showerhead and tumbled over her. Its icy splash raised goosebumps all over her body. She danced about on tiptoe, ducking and diving the spray until eventually it heated to a tolerable temperature and she was able to wash her hair and body.

Having showered quickly, and after toweling herself dry, Katie sprayed herself liberally with deodorant, clothed herself in clean underwear, put her nightwear back on, collected her toilet bag and went outside into the hot, bright sunlight. Short queues of women had already formed at both shower tents and she stopped to speak to those she knew before hastening back into the hot, airless tent.

The interior of the accommodation now resembled a harem of half-naked women. They wandered around in underwear or nightwear as they all hastily tried to find clothing and equipment, borrowed each other's toiletries and shouted good-natured quips across the tent. Katie called greetings to everyone and sleepy sounding voices and good-natured grumbles regarding the early hour of the day responded, a usual morning ritual for the women. Someone had turned on a radio, and although static distorted the reception and therefore was not conducive to good listening, it brought a small sense of normalcy to another morning in a combat zone.

Katie negotiated her way around the milling women and made her way back to her own bed space, placing her toilet bag and towel in the locker. "Morning, Wanda," she greeted a tall, gangly, dark-haired girl who had just risen from the camp bed next to hers.

"Morning, girlfriend," the woman responded and stretched and yawned languidly.

Wanda Webster and Katie had arrived at Base Independence together, formed a friendship almost immediately, and had remained close friends ever since. Wanda was a cheeky, outspoken woman of twenty-seven, a corporal whose trade was equipment supplier at Camp Churchill. It never ceased to amaze Katie that her friend's ribald comments and abrupt manner of speaking never got her hauled up on a charge. However, Wanda kept everyone in the tent sane with her sense of humor—off the cuff though it was—and everyone's spirits up, particularly when things got a little tense during an alert.

"You look half dead," Katie retorted teasingly. "Late night?"

"Nope," Wanda answered, "but thanks for reminding me that I feel half-dead. Now, it's me for the shower, otherwise I'll have to wait until my tour ends to have one."

Katie laughed and turned back to smoothing out her sleeping bag. She left it unzipped and spread out on her bed to allow it to air so it wouldn't become damp with the humidity that tended to linger in the tent throughout the day. After tidying her bed space, she finally dressed herself in a fresh pair of combat trousers, khaki T-shirt and laced herself into her brown military combat boots. Quickly smearing sunscreen onto her arms and face, she finally put on her sunglasses and military cap. She then sat down on her camp bed to wait patiently for Wanda to return from her shower and complete her own dressing.

Finally, Wanda returned to her bed, and at Katie's prompting, obliged her by mustering more speed until she finally announced that she was ready.

Keeping half an eye on the time, Katie waited until almost everyone was ready to leave the tent to go to breakfast before she clapped her hands together. "Hey, ladies, can I have your attention please?" Conversation immediately ceased and everyone turned to face her.

Katie smiled at the tanned faces around her. "It has fallen to me to break the news to you all that tonight we're going to have some fun together. We're going to have an admin evening."

Loud, good-natured groans and some swearing greeted the announcement.

Katie laughed at the various expressions, ranging from acceptance to irritation, on the women's faces. "I'm sorry to have to spoil your plans, ladies, but our living quarters are really in need of a little bit of a clean and a tidy, and I think the shower tents could do with some venting. We'll all meet back here at 1900 hours, and those ladies who have made other arrangements, we should be finished by 2000 hours so there is no need to cancel your plans."

"Thanks a lot, Katie," a lance corporal called out. "I had a hot date for tonight as well. You do know how to curtail a girl's social life." The remark, made in good humor, caused a few chuckles.

Katie dismissed the women and they began to leave the tent in groups of twos and threes, Wanda and Katie being the last to leave after they had claimed their individual weapons.

Outside the tent, Katie glanced around. It was very hot, even though it was early morning. The sky was a pale, hazy blue, the sun a searing white orb, beating down on bare and helmeted heads alike. The ground and tents shimmered in a rippling heat haze. The smell of aviation fuel was thick in the air, enhanced by the heat, mingling with the smell of dry earth, oil and plastic that was quickly heating up in the rising temperature. Dust hung in clouds and burned the throat and lungs. The noise of the base was loud and continuous with the roar and scream of aircraft engines, the chopping noise of rotor blades, shouting and the incessant messages crackling out of the tannoy system, affectionately or not called Giant Voice.

"Damn!" Katie exclaimed, wiping a hand across a forehead that was already damp with perspiration. "This heat really sucks. It's like moving through hot treacle."

"Whatever floats your boat," Wanda moaned in amusement tinged with apathy. "Me? I'm think I'm going to be a gross pile of sludge before I even get to work."

"Okay, here we go," Katie said, laughing and nudging her friend's arm. "Let's brave it."

The two women left their tent, turned left, and moving as economically as possible in the searing heat, passed along the rows of tents. Music issued from open tent flaps alongside female laughter and conversation. Camp Churchill was alive and bustling as it always was, twenty-four hours a day, seven days a week.

The tent accommodation eventually ended and the women turned onto the main road and walked on a little farther, neither attempting to speak, as the hot, dry air seemed to stifle the vocal cords. At last, the huge mess came into sight and both women uttered audible sighs of relief.

Service personnel, both male and female, filed in and out of the building like ants and Wanda and Katie joined the throng before entering the mess. Surreptitiously, Katie glanced slowly around her. Was she perhaps looking for a tall, blond-haired US marine? *No, I most certainly am not*, was the vehement denial that popped into her mind. Then why did she feel a pang of disappointment when she saw that he was nowhere to in sight?

The room was noisy with the hum of conversation, the loud chink of crockery and utensils and the thud of combat boots on the rubber floor. Both American and British service personnel crowded the room, creating a sea of camouflage with equipment and weapons littering the floor. The air conditioning was blissful and Katie stood under a ceiling unit that poured forth almost freezing cold air before following Wanda toward the hot food counter.

The two women collected breakfasts and bottles of orange juice and made their way to two empty seats at a table already occupied by two other women. They all nodded to each other and Katie and Wanda sat down to quickly eat their meals.

"Do you have busy day today?" Wanda asked through a mouthful of cereal.

"Probably," Katie answered, glancing at her watch to keep an eye on the time. "We have four casualties at the moment, all IED incidents — horrible bloody things. They'll probably be able to go home soon if they remain stable enough, although one is suffering some slight complications and isn't quite ready yet."

"Bummer," Wanda responded sympathetically. "I don't know how you do it, kiddo. I know I couldn't."

"Yes, you could if you had the training and you had no choice," Katie responded thoughtfully. "I've lost count of the times that I've asked myself why in the hell I do it then we get a casualty in who's badly injured, who may have lost one or two limbs, and we deal with it and they survive. Then my question is answered."

"I take my hat off to you, girl," Wanda exclaimed. "That's all I can say."

"All the patients are doing okay… Or they were when I left last night," Katie continued. "Hopefully there'll be no more today."

She had no intention of divulging to her friend who she had been with or where she had gone the night before. As lovely as Wanda was, she couldn't keep a confidence to save her life.

"Unfortunately, I have to get my sorry arse to work. Duty calls…" Katie began, starting to get to her feet.

She stopped speaking, whatever movement to leave she was about to make suddenly arrested. A familiar figure had just entered the mess with three other men and was approaching the hot food counter. It was Joe Anderson. He and his companions were laughing and she watched with a great deal of interest as he turned to one of the men and laughed again. Katie's heart jerked violently in her chest and her stomach flipped at the same time. He was definitely a very attractive man, his well-muscled body, enhanced by the combats he was wearing, his movements methodical but graceful for such a tall man. His smile was to die for-Katie was perfectly prepared to admit to that. Unable to stop staring, she watched as the tall marine and his companions collected their food and found a vacant table where they all seated themselves. He sat facing her, although he still hadn't seen her, so she was able to watch him closely.

Katie could hear Wanda speaking to her but didn't respond. As if Joe felt her eyes on him, he suddenly raised his gaze from his plate and glanced around the mess. Eventually, his eyes found hers and their gazes locked. He immediately smiled in her direction and she found herself responding in kind, delighted that he had acknowledged her.

As though no other person existed in the room, Joe and Katie kept their eyes on each other, food and companions forgotten, noise fading into the background. How long it would have gone on for, Katie would never know because a woman approached Joe's table with a tray and sat down next to him. Katie's spirits immediately plummeted to the pit of her stomach and she suddenly felt a sharp, irrational pang of jealousy.

The woman was tall and blonde with hair entwined in a bun and a delicate, aristocratic-looking face. She greeted the men seated at the table as though she knew them then, turning to Joe, she began to talk with him, placing a hand on his arm in a familiar manner.

Katie threw her dirty plate and empty bottle onto her tray and almost ran to the plate racks.

Wanda hurried after her friend, laden with her own tray. "Katie," she called after her, "what the hell?"

"I need to get to work," Katie threw back over her shoulder. "I'm late." She almost flung the tray onto an empty rack and headed for the doors, wanting to get out of the mess as quickly as possible.

Wanda followed her outside and, finding her friend standing stock-still and breathing heavily, she put a staying hand on Katie's arm.

"What's wrong?" she asked. "You legged it out of there like all the hounds of hell were after you."

Katie turned to face her. Forcing a smile, she answered, "Nothing's wrong, Wanda. I told you. I'm running late. I'll see you later." She touched the woman's hand then was gone, hurriedly walking in the direction of the CTH. She did not look back.

Katie, her mind alive with questions regarding the woman who had sat down in the mess with Joe, continued in the direction of the CTH. Common sense chided her that the woman could be a member of Joe's squad and therefore would know him well. There was no law to say that another woman could not sit beside him and talk to him. She tried to convince herself that the proprietary hand on his arm meant nothing. Joe Anderson was not her exclusive property. They had only spoken a few times. Granted, there was a strong attraction on her part and the fact that he had made a conscious effort to meet her after her duties ended seemed to indicate that he was interested in her, but the jealousy she was feeling was something she had never experienced before and it made her angry. She was relieved when she finally reached the CTH and could start her day, safe in the hope that all irritating thoughts concerning the staff sergeant, could then be consigned to the back of her mind and there would be no time to think about him.

After changing from her combats to her scrubs, Katie reported to the briefing room to hear notes about the patients still present in the CTH. The three soldiers injured in the most recent IED blast all continued to remain stable, making satisfying progress. However, they still remained under observation in the CCU and would continue to remain there for a further twenty-four hours and thereafter moved to a ward. Private Berwick was also awake and responsive, although he had asked for an increase in painkillers during the night, and the young US marine was also progressing well. There had been no further casualties during the night, no reports of firefights going on outside the wire, and therefore shift patterns would remain normal with two trauma teams and CTTs on standby and the equivalent number of trauma teams and CTTs stood down.

Sick parade occurred from 0700 to 0900 hours each morning with various personnel arriving with a variety of minor injuries or illnesses such as strains, rashes and, in one case, mild heat exhaustion. Katie performed blood tests if they were required with onward transmission to the laboratory for processing, checked blood pressures, temperatures and distributed medication prescribed by the doctors. There were enough patients to keep her busy and her mind fully occupied, enabling her to push wayward thoughts about a certain man from her mind.

Sick parade over, her duties for that morning—with the exception of a break at 1030 hours—was to replenish the instruments in the trauma rooms, replace white sheets on the examination tables then check over the equipment and instruments in the theaters. She also had to check the drug cabinets and restock specific drugs, if needed.

Lunchtime came and went slowly, with Katie ordering food from the mess and having it delivered to the CTH. After all the duty staff had eaten, Katie joined in a game of poker, the game set out on one of the theater operating tables. As the game progressed and became rowdier, Katie found herself relaxing slightly. She became completely embroiled in the good-humored arguments resulting from blatant cheating in the game until at 1700 hours a young female soldier hobbled into the CTH assisted by a fellow soldier.

While out on a training run, the patient had fallen and twisted her knee. After having the injury examined by one of the doctors, the diagnosis was a minor strain but, to prevent further injury, it needed to be strapped up for support and the woman advised to rest for forty-eight hours. Katie reassured the young soldier that the joint and ligaments would heal and issued painkillers and a sick chit to provide to her section leader. Once treated, the woman left again, assisted by her fellow soldier, and the CTH fell quiet.

At 1800 hours, Sergeant Webster approached Katie and advised her that she could go off duty. Thanking him and wishing him goodnight, Katie went off to the locker room to take a brief shower, change out of her scrubs into her T-shirt and combats, then collected her weapon and left the building. Once outside she stopped, breathing in the hot air.

She glanced around, and when she realized she was looking for a certain US marine who might have been waiting for her, she abruptly stopped herself. Once her duty had finished, her mind had instantly filled with images of the woman who had had her hand on Joe's arm in the mess, and the thoughts irritated her with their persistence. She did not want to see Staff Sergeant Anderson again.

Determined to dismiss all thoughts of Joe Anderson from her head, attempting to achieve some sort of control over herself, she headed for the mess with the intention of getting some hot food inside her then returning to her tent for the admin evening. Nearing the building, she heard Wanda's voice calling her name, waited for her friend to join her, and the two women continued on to the mess together, entering its air-conditioned interior with relief.

Once seated, Katie set about her food with gusto, at one point asking, "How was your day?"

"The usual Numbnuts," Wanda answered, taking a long gulp from her can of Coke, "requesting equipment with no authorization chits or serial numbers — same old, same old. By the way, what the hell was wrong with you this morning?"

"Nothing was wrong," Katie answered, hating to lie to her friend. "I was late for work. I told you." She couldn't help averting her gaze from Wanda's, who was a little too clever to be deceived. "And anyway —" Her sentence was abruptly cut short as from a distance there came the distinct booming sound of a loud explosion. The building and floor shook, and cutlery, cups and plates rattled slightly on the tables.

Chapter Five

Conversation in the mess ceased abruptly, as though cut off by a switch. Everyone froze, holding their breath, hoping and praying that it was not what they dreaded. Giant Voice suddenly boomed then crackled with feedback and a calm, clear, unhurried voice spoke the shocking words that all base personnel dreaded and hoped that they would never hear.

"Attention, attention! This is a red alert. There has been an unidentified explosion on the northeast side of the base. If you do not need to be about the base, remain in your accommodation. All CTTs, trauma teams and medical personnel on standby are to report to the CTH. All infantry on standby are to report to their muster points. That is all."

As the voice ceased and Giant Voice boomed again with more feedback, a deep intermittent siren sounded followed by another and another, all over the base. Adrenaline and tension rocketing up a level, everybody in the mess was suddenly on the move, combat boots thudding heavily on the floor. Helmets slammed hastily on, chairs overturned and tables skidded across the rubber floor as personnel leaped to their feet, grabbed equipment and headed for the doors. Cutlery scattered on the floor, drinks spilled from plastic cups and plates full of food went flying.

"Fuck!" Wanda spat out the expletive and grabbed her helmet from her webbing belt. Silently, Katie followed her example, unclipping her helmet and slapping it on, haphazardly thrusting her military cap into a pocket of her trousers. Leaving the straps of her helmet dangling, she grabbed for her weapon and ran across the room, Wanda following close on her heels.

Slamming out of the doors and still running, Katie quickly slapped her friend on her arm. "Stay safe, girl," she called, and was off jogging down the road toward the CTH.

As she ran, she glanced in the direction of the reported explosion and saw a huge column of black smoke, roiling and curling upward from the distant perimeter wall. Because there was no wind, it hung in the air, a solid, unmoving mass. *So, it's not a drill or a hoax then.* Katie picked up speed, her right arm pinning her weapon to her body, her other arm pumping at her side, dust spiraling up around her from her pounding boots.

The noise was deafening. Sirens wailed. Giant Voice blared every now and again with new instructions and orders, and camp personnel ran or walked hurriedly in all directions. A unit of armed soldiers jogged past her on the opposite side of the road, the unit leader bellowing, "Double time, come on, move it, ladies. Move your goddamned arses."

Just as she was becoming out of breath, Katie arrived at the CTH. The entrance doors had been chocked open and inside medical personnel were milling around, preparing the theaters and trauma rooms for possible incoming casualties.

Panting slightly, her face glistening with sweat, Katie jogged down the corridor, dancing around hurrying nurses and CTH staff, and entered the briefing room, which was already full of people.

"Okay, listen up," Sergeant Webster began without preamble, raising his voice. "There has been a large explosion. It appears that insurgents created a diversion outside the perimeter wall, and while the guards were distracted, they blew a hole in the thing using two vehicles full of heavy explosives. Sadly, there was a squad of soldiers training in the area at the time and one of the guard towers has gone. There will almost certainly be casualties. I want two CTTs down there and CTMs Walker and Wilson. A four-tonner will be here in five to take you all to the incident. You all know what to do. Stabilize the wounded on the scene then get them back here. Understood? Let's get to it!"

Katie darted out of the briefing room and ran to the locker room. Reaching her personal locker, she slammed open the door and quickly put on her combat shirt, body armor and limb protectors. She attached the pouch with her personal role radio — PRR — to the front of her body armor then fitted the lightweight radio headset on over her head, putting on her combat helmet over that and tightening the chinstrap. She finally lifted out her heavy medical bergen and struggled to put her arms through the webbing straps. As a last check, she made sure that her scissors were in their appropriate place on the front of her body armor and that there were fresh field tourniquets and hemostatic dressings in one of many pouches clipped to her webbing belt. Finally ready, she left the locker room, quickly grabbed an emergency medical carrier —

EMC – which contained more complex medical equipment that might be needed to attend to any possible casualties, and jogged down the corridor, retrieving her weapon and going on out into the warm evening air. As she did so, their transportation, pulled up onto the hard-packed sand and gravel forecourt of the CTH, turning three hundred sixty degrees to face back the way it had come.

The two CTTs and CTMs moved around to the back of the vehicle. Someone released the locks of the tailgate and it crashed down, allowing everyone to hoist themselves into the canvas-lined interior. Once everyone was on board the driver of the truck raised the door, slammed it shut and locked it. After a moment, the truck pulled away with a hiss of air brakes.

Katie seated herself on one of the uncomfortable wooden benches that lined the sides, elbows resting on her knees, helmeted head turned sideways so that she could look out of the opening in the canvas at the back. No one spoke each person alone with their thoughts, turned inward on themselves, perhaps contemplating what was about to come, what they would find and how many injured there would be. Katie's thoughts were of Joe.

When Sergeant Webster had mentioned at the briefing that a squad of soldiers had been training in the area at the time of the explosion, Katie's heart had sunk. She had hoped, selfishly, that it hadn't been Joe's squad in the vicinity at the time of the blast, and that in turn made her wonder where he was. *If he was there at the incident, would she get to see him?* The situation was serious with what could possibly be many injured, a breach of security and a sudden escalation of hostilities with heightened tension and fear on the base, but she couldn't help but feel a sense of hope that she might have a chance to talk to him again. Feeling guilty at her thoughts, knowing that they were inappropriate and this was not the time or the place to have them, Katie focused her mind on the present.

Five minutes later, the truck drew up at the motor pool and once the tailgate was lowered, Katie and the other medical personnel jumped down.

As she landed on the hard ground, Katie glanced around, quickly assessing her surroundings. She saw that military police had cordoned off the site of the explosion. Soldiers armed with weapons were standing guard at strategic points around the area while others were carrying out a sweep through and around the motor pool, accompanied by a K-9 unit and their dogs. The animals patrolled the area with their handlers, sniffing beneath parked vehicles and inside and outside buildings in a bid to discover any evidence that insurgents had managed to infiltrate the base. Four Army ambulances had drawn as close to the site of the explosion as possible. They could go no farther because of the narrow approach to where the blast had occurred, so any casualties would need to be treated for their injuries on site then stretchered to the ambulances.

Katie could hear distant shouted commands and screams of pain. Clouds of turbid black smoke, drifting low to the ground, billowed into the area, causing people to cough and their eyes to burn and sting.

Katie's training took over and she began to jog in the direction of the sounds and the source of the black smoke. When she arrived at the scene and saw the destruction and the amount of casualties there were, she raised a hand to her mouth in stunned silence, her mind shocked into emptiness. During her years as a CTM she had been involved in many traumatic incidents and had seen some horrific injuries. It always disturbed her to see the amount of devastation that resulted from an explosion, and the chaos it left behind.

She noticed that part of the reinforced concrete perimeter wall was completely demolished. Caught in the blast, a guard tower had been blown to pieces, wood and metal lying in a pulverized heap. Huge chunks of concrete from the wall lay shattered on the ground, coated with small pieces of the barbed wire that had topped it, blasted into tiny razor-like fragments that would have shot through the air like shrapnel during the explosion. Two vehicles burned furiously outside the wall, with two Army fire trucks in position, spraying foam on the conflagration, surrounded by a protective cordon of armored military vehicles. As Sergeant Webster had already stated, it appeared as though—unseen by the guards in the tower—the vehicles had been aimed at the wall, and loaded with explosives driven at speed to hit it, the resultant impact detonating the explosives on board. Soldiers and medical personnel milled around the site, tending to the many bodies lying on the hard, dusty ground.

Katie could not comprehend how the insurgents could have gotten so close to the base. She knew that besides the high concrete wall with its added protection of barbed wire, guard towers every one hundred meters and both human and canine patrols twenty-four hours a day, there were also sensors, both infrared and thermal imaging cameras, motion detectors and a specially designed radar that could detect human or aircraft movements from twenty miles away. Collectively this dazzling array of surveillance equipment, known as STARS—surveillance, target acquisition and reconnaissance system—should have alerted the base to the impending incursion, but something had obviously failed.

Aware of an immediate need to treat each casualty depending on the severity of their injuries and get them back to the CTH within an hour, Katie noticed an injured soldier lying on the ground to her right attended to by a US Army corpsman. Striding over, she put down the EMC, shrugged out of her medical bergen and dropped to her knees beside him. "What have we got here, Lance Corporal?" she asked quietly, as the attending US corpsman turned to her.

Katie was shocked to see that the young soldier's face was pale and there were tearstains on his cheeks. She also noticed that his hands were trembling. "Lance Corporal?" she questioned gently. "Do we have a problem?"

"I shouldn't be here," was the startling response. "I shouldn't be alive. I should be dead on the ground with my buddies. I should've..." The corpsman's shaking voice trailed off into a stifled sob.

Katie instantly knew that it had been this soldier's squad who had been in the area of the bomb blast and that he was one of the survivors. Even though the young soldier was a medic, the US equivalent of her own role, he was still human so was neither immune to grief nor protected from the consequences of his combat role. Many medical personnel, either in the field hospitals or out in the field, suffered mental trauma if members of their squad were devastatingly injured or killed. Anybody, from the lower ranks to the higher echelon could, on occasion, develop survivor syndrome, a feeling of intolerable guilt at having survived when others died. Nobody was immune in a war theater.

Turning to the shivering soldier, Katie bent her head close to his and spoke quietly. "Lance Corporal," she began clearly and firmly, "your friend is badly injured and we need to deal with him quickly so that we can get him to an ambulance and back to the CTH. If you feel that you can't deal with this, then please find me someone who can. What you are feeling is perfectly natural. It's nothing to be ashamed of, but we need to move on. Your buddies need our help. Now, if you can, I need information on this man."

Katie waited patiently for a response, conscious of time moving on, the golden hour for successfully treating this particular injured soldier ticking down.

The corpsman eventually took a deep, shuddering breath, brushed a hand across his face and spoke in a stronger, steadier tone, "Abdominal wound," he explained. "Left penetrating. I suspect the cause is some kind of shrapnel. He's tachycardic, sweating. Pulse is thready. I've assessed the wound, packed it with hemostatic dressings and given him some morphine. He was conscious at first but now he's out of it and needs to be transfused." The corpsman swallowed. Hands covered in blood from dealing with the wound, voice still trembling slightly, he sat back on his heels.

"Thank you. You've done well, Lance Corporal," Katie praised gently. "I'll take a look then we'll set up an IV line with saline to prevent a chance of shock. It will stabilize him until we can get him back to the CTH."

Katie gently lifted the large gauze packing on the wounded soldier's stomach. An object, perhaps a piece of concrete, fragment of barbed wire or sliver of wood had penetrated the lower left side of the abdomen, tearing through skin, muscle and destroying subcutaneous fat. The wound was large, open and oozing blood, but the corpsman had packed it with hemostatic dressings, reducing the heavy flow, and the blood was now clotting satisfactorily. Katie turned to the EMC and opened the lid. Pulling on nitrile gloves, she took out a length of tubing, a bag of saline solution and a large bore cannula needle.

"We need to find a vein, Lance Corporal. Can you find one for me? If not in his arm, then we'll take one in the wrist."

The corpsman pushed the sleeve of the soldier's combat jacket as far up as it would go and tapped the crook of the motionless arm. It was getting difficult to see in the quickly fading light, but eventually the lance corporal turned to Katie. "I have one, Corporal," he stated.

"Okay, good. Let's do this."

Katie quickly and skillfully fastened a tourniquet above the area where she was intending to insert the cannula, tightened it roughly then palpated the vein. Once she was satisfied, she pushed the needle through the fragile skin, twisted on the tubing then attached the plastic bag of fluid. Taping the needle in place, she finally checked the casualty's vital signs then quickly raised her head and glanced around.

At that precise moment, two portable lights, brought to the site, lit up, their intense white beams flooding the scene and lighting it up in all its macabre horror.

Relieved that she could see more clearly, Katie raised a hand and gestured at a US soldier who was striding past them. "Excuse me, soldier, could you come and help us, please?" she called.

The soldier glanced in her direction, about-turned and came striding toward her. "Ma'am?" he queried and offered a half salute.

"Can you stand by this wounded man and hold this IV above his head for me? I have to move on and so does this corpsman," Katie explained. "There will be someone along shortly with a stretcher to take him to an ambulance."

"Certainly, ma'am," the soldier answered, shouldering his weapon and taking the IV bag, raising it so that the fluid inside it continued to flow freely down into the wounded soldier's arm.

"Thank you," Katie said, offering the man a small smile.

She got up and glanced about the area again. Seeing nobody available, she called out, "I need a stretcher here," and within minutes, two soldiers arrived beside her with the requested equipment. They gently picked up the injured soldier, laid him on the stretcher, then the soldier who was holding the IV aloft moved off with them back to the waiting ambulances.

Katie closed the EMC and picked it up. "Thank you, Lance Corporal," she said. "I'm finished here and need to move on to the next casualty. You can go about your duties—and thank you."

Not waiting for an answer, Katie hurried to the next casualty. The injured soldier was moaning quietly and obviously in a great deal of pain. Tears ran down his ashen, bloodstained face, and his breathing was rapid with panic.

Katie dropped to the ground and rested a soothing hand on the soldier's forehead. "It's all right," she reassured him gently. "Stay with me. You're safe now, and you're going to be fine."

Quickly assessing the torn, mangled arm, she decided that she needed assistance, and turned to see if there was any available. Seeing the young corpsman who had helped her with the first casualty was still standing where she had left him, she called to him, "Lance Corporal. Can you give me a hand here?"

An expression of relief flitting across his young, tired face, as though he was thankful that someone knew what they were doing and had given him an order to do something, the young soldier came back to join her.

"We need to stop this bleeding and stabilize him," Katie explained.

Working quickly, Katie and the corpsman succeeded in arresting the heavy bleeding, packed the terrible wound in the soldier's arm and shoulder as best they could, set up an IV and administered a morphine injection. The soldier began to shiver as the night had grown chilly and Katie quickly wrapped him in a combat casualty blanket to keep him warm. By the time they had completed the treatment, the soldier had lapsed into unconsciousness. Noting that his pulse was becoming weak and irregular, Katie yelled for a stretcher and the soldier was rushed to a waiting ambulance.

As the casualties were treated and stabilized, there were frequent shouts for stretchers overriding the moans of the conscious casualties. Soldiers assisted with IV bags containing saline solutions and blood products or helped to carry the stretchers transporting the injured back to the ambulances.

Katie and the corpsman moved from one casualty to another, treating where they could and assisting the CTTs and other medics where necessary. As much as Katie could work out, there were a total of ten injured with two dead.

After what seemed like hours, all the casualties had been assessed, stabilized and transported back to the CTH, and the medical personnel began to leave the site, heading back with their charges.

Katie was the last to leave, the corpsman who had worked with her tirelessly having already left, dragging dusty booted feet with head and shoulders stooped as though there was a heavy weight balanced on his back. She stood exhausted amidst the wreckage, gazing around, numb and emotionless, at the bloodstained ground, discarded bandages, empty IV bags and ripped open packets of bandages and gauze, smelling the stench of explosives and blood and burning rubber. The white portable lights lit up the bloodstains in all their starkness, throwing into prominence the burned and charred areas of ground and the destruction of the concrete wall. The sight stirred a sick, sad feeling in Katie. She wanted to scream at the utter waste and vent her anger at the people who had done this.

Sighing, she picked up her bergen and thrust her arms through the straps then grasped the handle of the EMC, which now seemed to have doubled in weight. She followed the last of the medical personnel back to where the four-tonner waited to pick up her and her colleagues to take them back to the CTH.

Wearily approaching the rear of the vehicle, she was about to climb aboard when someone called, "Corporal Walker," in a familiar American voice.

Katie immediately stopped in her tracks and spun around. A tall soldier was standing at the perimeter of the motor pool and she felt a reckless sense of excitement when she saw that it was Joe. She hesitated briefly, knowing that it was important that she get back to the CTH as they would almost certainly need her presence urgently, but the sight of Joe waiting for her and the almost desperate need to speak to him was too much to resist. Handing up the EMC to her colleagues already inside the truck, she went around to the driver.

"I have to speak to someone for a few minutes," she said.

"Well, get a move on, Corporal. They want you back at the CTH ASAP," the driver stated, giving her an impatient sidelong glance.

Katie nodded, turned and strode toward Joe. As she approached him, she saw that he too was wearing full combat equipment including helmet, body armor, limb protectors, webbing yoke with a multitude of utility and ammunition pouches, and he carried a large, black weapon in his arms. He stood perfectly still as she approached him, tension evident in his body. There was no welcoming smile on his face as she drew closer, and she realized that this man was very different to the calm and compassionate one with whom she had spoken with the previous day. Coming to a stop, Katie said softly, "Hello, Joe."

Now that she was face-to-face with him, she could see that it wasn't just his posture that was different, or the way he was carrying himself, but the look on his face. His blue eyes were the color of flint, with a cold and distant look in them. His jaw was set rigidly, as though he was gritting his teeth. He was staring at her with that unfathomable gaze and she wondered what he was thinking.

He managed a small smile. "Katie," he finally answered and nodded his head in greeting. He looked away from her and asked shortly, "How many?"

Katie glanced down at her hands. "Twelve," she answered softly. "Ten injured and two dead. Oh my God, Joe, they weren't your men, were they?"

Joe glanced down at the ground then, raising his head, he pushed his helmet back slightly from his forehead. "No," he answered curtly, "but we went along there in a training run about ten minutes before the other squad. If we'd been any later, it could have been us."

God, so close.

"American?" Joe asked.

Katie nodded, "Yes, I'm so sorry, Joe."

"Fuck!" Joe exclaimed, "Motherfuckers!" He spat the words out viciously, and by the thinning of his mouth, Katie could tell that he was furious.

"Joe, I'm sorry. I have to go. I'm needed back at the CTH," she said, wishing so much that she could stay with him, but as had been happening to them over the past few days, their respective duties called to separate them. Continually dragged apart, she suddenly felt heartsick and tired. All she wanted to do at that moment was take Joe's hand and lead him to a quiet place, away from the carnage and blood and the noise and smells of the base, where they could both lick their wounds and comfort each other.

However, all she could do was wait for his response and wish desperately that she could wipe away the anger that was darkening his features. At that moment, the driver of the four-tonner shouted out to her impatiently.

At last, Joe nodded again. "Yeah, I have to get back to my squad. Take care, Katie." He gave her a casual salute, turned on his heel and marched back in among the vehicles of the motor pool.

Katie watched him go, wanting to call him back and talk with him a bit more. Instead, she turned on her heel and walked back to the truck.

By the time they arrived back, the CTH was in organized chaos. Both operating theaters were in use with four more casualties stabilized in a trauma room and two more waiting for assessment. The two dead were already in the mortuary. It was noisy, busy and crowded, with medical personnel monitoring, assessing and assisting where necessary.

Katie quickly changed from her combats into scrubs and gloves and tied on her surgical cap. Taking her cue from the other CTMs, she proceeded to the theaters to assist with the surgeries.

Each surgery proceeded with a professional smoothness, as though each team member had a telepathic connection to another. Surgeons held their hands out blindly and even before a request was verbalized, instruments were slapped into their palms. Trauma nurses and CTMs clamped blood vessels and retracted internal organs within split seconds of an order. There was no panic or pressure, although tension was at its peak.

Katie assisted where needed, taking patients' vital signs, checking IV bags, and changing them skillfully when they became empty. Exhausted as she was, she kept going, maintaining her composure, even though she was screaming inside at the unfairness of it all.

At last, with all the surgeries completed, surgeons removed their protective goggles and stretched the stiffness out of their necks and backs. Medical personnel lifted sleeping casualties gently from the operating tables, laid them on gurneys then wheeled them swiftly to the CCU. CTMs went with their charges to hand them over to the trauma nurses, who were to watch and carry out the crucial twenty-minute post-op observations. The CTMs began the arduous task of cleaning the theaters and trauma rooms and readying and replacing equipment. The surgeons and anesthetists disappeared to the R&R room to fortify themselves with strong cups of coffee.

Like an automaton, Katie cleaned, scrubbed and sterilized. Finally, at 2300 hours, her duties were finished. Exhausted, she stretched luxuriously and offered Henry Barrow a tired, smile. "I'm for some coffee," she announced.

"I hear that," Lance Corporal Barrow answered.

At that moment, Sergeant Webster appeared at the door to the theater. "Briefing in my office," he ordered and disappeared from sight.

"Ah, no rest for the wicked," Lance Corporal Barrow exclaimed, sighing. He and Katie left the spotless theater, and with other medical staff, made their way down the corridor to the sergeant's office. The room was already full when they arrived and Katie and Henry Barrow squeezed their way in.

A huge map of Base Independence, with the Role Three CTH situated in the center, dominated the back wall. Surrounded by concentric squares known as range squares, each one showed, at a glance, the distance a CTF could cover in a set time to reach a casualty. The first boundary was ten minutes away — five minutes out and five back again. Every minute mattered in the event that a CTT went out to a casualty in the field. On a call coming in for casualty extraction, a range was taken from the map and the nearest appropriate aircraft deployed.

"Okay," Sergeant Webster said without preamble, "the base remains on red alert. There are patrols outside the perimeter and inside the base searching for hostiles who might have infiltrated the base itself, and for any IEDs if they have. It's confirmed that two trucks loaded with explosives driven by four Taliban injured and killed our men. The good news is that the bastards blew 'emselves up in the process. We have ten extra patients tonight. Six are on the critical list and are in the CCU. Four others are relatively stable, and we have five who have been with us for a couple of days. Two are dead and are in the mortuary. All patients in the CCU are receiving twenty-minute observations, saline, blood products, and antibiotics via IVs. The roster for tonight is CTT One, Trauma Team One and CTMs Walker and Sheridon on duty. CTT Two, Trauma Team Two and CTMs Harris and Taylor on standby. CTTs Three and Four, Trauma Teams Three and Four and CTMs Windberg and Stanley on stand-down. The rest of you can get lost. That's all, folks."

There were a few tired chuckles at the last remark, then people began to leave the office to change from their scrubs, collect their equipment and leave. The teams assigned to remain trooped down to the R&R room.

Once there, Katie found herself a plastic cup and poured herself some scalding hot coffee. She felt completely exhausted and desperately in need of a strong caffeine boost to keep her senses alert, so she left out the milk and stirred in two spoonfuls of sugar. She perched herself on the arm of one of the chairs, made herself comfortable and sipped at the drink, wincing at its heat and strong, bitter taste. She listened with half an ear to the conversation going on around her, but finally her mind drifted to the motor pool and to the explosion. Patrols would be guarding the area and helicopters would be searching the surrounding terrain for the insurgents. That finally raised the inevitable questions about Joe. Was he out there on a patrol in the dark desert with his squad, isolated and in danger?

She pictured the meeting between them at the motor pool and could remember the way he had looked, so distant and cold, but she could not stop thinking about him. Up until a week ago, she had never had the slightest inclination to have a relationship with a man. She was a normal, hot-blooded woman like any other, but preferred to be on her own, did not want the problems of a relationship or the heartbreak that getting involved with someone created. Staff Sergeant Joe Anderson was different. That evening he had looked dangerous and that look had strengthened the attraction she felt for him.

"Katie! Corporal Walker!" An insistent voice spoke to her, interrupting her reverie.

Katie started violently, spilling some of the hot coffee onto her leg. Jumping to her feet, she turned around to find Sergeant Webster standing behind her, hands on his hips. "Asleep, Corporal?" he asked, a smile twitching his mouth.

"No, Sergeant, just miles away," Katie replied, embarrassment evident in the tone of her voice.

"I'm glad to hear it," Sergeant Webster continued. "I need you to get some food up here. It's going to be a long night."

"Yes, Sergeant." Katie left the R&R room, went to the sergeant's office and used the radio to contact the mess to order the food as the sergeant had requested. She then went back to join the others to finish her coffee. Some of the teams had dispersed to other parts of the CTH to catch some sleep while a few had set up a poker game on one of the trauma room tables. Others catnapped in the R&R room, and the atmosphere settled and finally became quiet, broken only by loud cheers and conversation coming from the location of the poker game.

The night was a long one. After everyone had eaten supper, Katie periodically relieved one or another of the trauma nurses in the CCU so that they could have a break, taking over the monitoring of all the patients' vital signs, making sure that the IVs were working properly and that heart monitors were doing what they were supposed to be doing. She spent a few minutes each hour checking the drug cabinets and replacing drugs. Finally, the clock on the wall of Theater One ticked its way to 0700 hours and the teams on the day shift started to arrive. Everyone congregated in Sergeant Webster's office for patient notes with the status and conditions of the patients discussed at length then finally, at last, Katie was free to go off duty. As was her usual routine, she divested herself of her scrubs and wandered wearily to the showers. A brief hot shower did nothing to relieve her tiredness. The only solution to that was a long sleep. Once dressed in her combats, she put on her webbing and helmet and was on her way toward the entrance to the CTH when Sergeant Webster apprehended her before she could leave. "Everything all right?" he asked, eyeing her tired face.

The sergeant oft times acted like a proverbial mother hen around her, and at any other time this might have caused her some amusement, but this morning she was too tired and too concerned about Joe to muster even half a smile. "I'm fine, Sergeant," she answered.

"Well, you've got a stand-down for twenty-four hours," he announced, surprising her. It was rare to receive twenty-four hours off and even rarer when the CTH was so busy.

"Thank you, Sergeant," Katie responded, smiling at him gratefully, not about to argue, and after collecting her weapon, she left the medical facility to return to her tent and to the comfort of her bed and sleep.

Outside the CTH the early morning was warm and sultry, as if there was going to be a storm. As usual, the air was tainted with dust, which got into her eyes and mouth and down inside her clothing. Due to the high security level caused by the explosion of the previous day, Camp Churchill was busier than usual. Personnel now had to wear combat helmets at all times when outside sections and buildings, and many soldiers marching around the camp were wearing full combat clothing. Katie could hear aircraft taking off and landing with more frequency than usual and the fumes of aviation fuel curdling the air were stronger. Helicopter blades hammered at the morning and there was faint shouting in the distance.

As Katie walked tiredly toward the road, she was convinced that a familiar American voice would hail her from behind, and when that didn't happen, she felt a surge of concern and regret. She even turned to glance over her shoulder once or twice, but there was nobody around. She made her way back to her tent, negotiating squads of soldiers jogging along the roadside and other personnel hastening along to their sections. Everyone moved with a purpose and had a job to do during the alert, and there was no loitering along the roadside.

Katie arrived at Tent D, and on entering, dropped her webbing and helmet onto the floor beside her bed. The tent was empty, hot and silent. Almost asleep on her feet, she stripped off her combats, folded them up, quickly put on her nightwear and flung herself onto her bed. She was so tired that she could barely keep her eyes open. Despite the fact that the last thought on her mind was of Joe and hoping that he was all right, before a few minutes had passed, Katie was sound asleep, one small fist thrust under her chin, the way she had slept since childhood.

Chapter Six

It was 1600 hours when Katie eventually woke up. On opening her eyes, she felt disorientated and fuzzy-headed. Gazing up at the ceiling of the tent, she yawned, her mouth dry as though she had swallowed a mouthful of dust. Sitting up, she glanced around. The tent was still and quiet, the air so humid that perspiration broke out on her forehead. Grimacing, she unraveled herself from her sleeping bag, stood up and stretched, feeling her shorts and T-shirt clinging to her back and stomach with moisture. Reaching for her toilet bag and towel, she quickly headed for the showers.

Katie enjoyed a long, hot shower, courtesy of the other absent women, soaking her head and body under the spray in the hope that it would wake her up, standing with her eyes closed in an attempt to banish the stiffness and tension from her body. Finally feeling a little more human, she toweled herself dry and went back into the tent.

Once she had dressed herself in her usual combats, T-shirt and boots, she sat on the edge of her camp bed trying to decide what to do with her time off. If she was honest with herself, she wished that she was back at the CTH doing something to occupy her time. She felt on edge and restless, something that she always experienced when she knew that there was work to do and she was absent from it. She knew that it was perfectly natural to feel that way. It was always difficult to wind down from an adrenaline-fueled high that was a by-product of an incident. The mind and body could not just switch off at will. This was always a problem for those who endeavored to burn the candle at both ends, and who lived on adrenaline and faced pressures day in and day out.

Katie eventually decided that the mess was the place to be. She needed food to renew her energy, needed to be around other people, and the noise and bustle of the mess was just right. Putting on her helmet and picking up her weapon, she left the tent, making her way out to the road and turned in the direction of the mess.

On reaching the building, she went inside and found it relatively empty and quiet. Finding an empty table, she left her helmet on a chair and her rifle propped against a table leg and went to the food counter. Picking up a tray, she moved along the selection of food. She was hungry and she intended to do full justice to a hot meal. As she mused on her choices, a voice spoke from behind the hot food counter.

"Hi, Katie."

Glancing up, Katie forced a smile onto her face, "Hello, David." By using a formal tone, she hoped that the irritating corporal would back off and leave her alone.

However, Corporal Hudson persisted in his attempt to engage her in conversation. "You look tired," he said.

Katie felt instant irritation and bit her lip, blocking a retort. The cook was always trying to insert a personal note into their conversations, treating her as though he had a right to make personal comments about her, how she looked and how she felt. "I'm tired," Katie replied coolly. "We all had a bad day yesterday and I was up all night on duty."

Corporal Hudson nodded. "Must have been pretty bad for you," he responded, a sympathetic tone in his voice.

Attempting to choose her food and distract the cook's obvious need to talk to her, Katie placed some hot food on her plate and moved on to the fridge to get a cold drink. She chose an orange juice and was just about to move away back to her table when Corporal Hudson spoke to her again. "Katie, I was wondering if you'd like to come to the NAAFI with me tomorrow night for a coffee?"

Katie sighed inwardly. *What a jerk! Will he never give up?* She turned back to face him. "I'm sorry, David, but no. I'm very tired and I'm on duty tomorrow morning. We have lots of patients and we're all working flat out. With what's been going on, most of us are on standby. We could be called back to work at any time. So, thank you, but no."

With a small conciliatory smile, she turned away, and without looking where she was going, promptly crashed into someone standing directly behind her. Her tray wobbled in her hands and the orange drink nearly upended itself onto the floor.

"Oh, I'm so sorry," she apologized with embarrassment. "I wasn't watching where I was going." She glanced up to see who stood in her way and her breath caught in her throat. "Joe," she exclaimed and couldn't prevent a smile from appearing on her face. *He's safe.*

"Hey," Joe Anderson greeted her, a grin spreading across his face, "I was hoping I'd see you here."

Katie's heart did a little dance and her stomach flipped. She saw how tired and wrung out he looked. Dark stubble lined his chin, smudges of dust and dirt stained his skin and there was a dull, weary look in his blue eyes. He carried his combat helmet in one hand and still had on his full body armor with his M4 slung over one shoulder.

"Was that guy bothering you?" he asked, turning to stare intently at Corporal Hudson, who returned the look with a cold regard of his own.

Katie looked back at the cook, whose eyes shifted from the staff sergeant to her. His face twisted with what looked like jealousy, and feeling a little uneasy, Katie averted her gaze. "No," she answered, her tone light and moved away from the counter.

Directing a final steely look at the young cook, Joe stated, "I'll join you. Just let me get some chow. Why don't you go find us a table?"

Katie hastened back to the table she already had and sat down. She watched Joe as he chose his own food and drink then joined her. He hooked a chair away from the table with a boot, put down his tray then propped his weapon against the table and sat down. Katie watched as he rubbed a hand over his face, as though trying to brush away the exhaustion that was evident in the posture of his body.

"Ahh shit!" he exclaimed and sighed.

"You looked shattered, Joe," Katie said softly. "Have you only just come in?"

"Yeah," Joe answered, "we spent most of yesterday, last night and today recceing areas around the base trying to find those Taliban bastards."

"Did you?" Katie asked. "Find them, I mean?"

"Nope. They were long gone. But at least four of the fuckers incinerated themselves in the explosion. No great loss."

Katie winced at the hard note of anger in his voice, but she could understand why he felt that way. There was always a fierce anger on the base when something happened such as an aircraft being shot down, a patrol getting involved in a firefight or personnel killed in an explosion, but it hurt her to hear this man speak so coldly and callously. She wanted to stretch out her hand and hold Joe's, letting him know that he wasn't alone in his anger. Instead, she picked up her fork and began to eat.

"How are the guys getting along in the CTH?" Joe suddenly asked, beginning to eat his own food.

"They're doing all right," Katie answered. "Some are still in critical condition but the others are stable. I was on duty until 0700 hours, so the sergeant gave me a twenty-four hour."

"I have to go back out on patrol again tonight," Joe volunteered casually, "at 2200 hours. We're going to patrol farther out. See if we can't find something to shoot at."

Katie glanced up abruptly from her meal. "You're going out again?" She couldn't prevent consternation from entering her voice, and she belatedly attempted to hide it.

"You have any plans for tonight?" Joe asked, noting the worried look on her face and changing the subject.

"No," Katie replied, her tone equally casual. "I'm on standby in case we have any further casualties. I hope there aren't. It's physically and emotionally draining."

"I get that," Joe answered. "All of you do a great job." He paused. "Look, I hate to do this, but I have to go and attend a debriefing, get my equipment ready for tonight. Walk you back to your tent?"

Bitterly disappointed, Katie nodded. Their meetings were always so brief, and tonight felt worse because of the heightened security on the base and the fact that he was going out on patrol and would be in danger. She felt swift panic rise up in her throat. *What if something happens to him? What if he's shot, injured in a bomb blast, and has to be medevacked to the CTH?* She would know instantly, and have to watch his suffering while maintaining complete detachment from his treatment and care.

As if he sensed her fears, Joe leaned forward and reached a hand across the table, turning it palm up. Katie stared at it. If she placed her hand in his, her destiny as well as his, was sealed. Their relationship would have taken a big stride forward. What came next would be part of their future. She glanced at his face, both frightened and exhilarated at the same time. This man did have feelings for her, and it filled her with happiness. But, they were trapped here with no time for closeness or for being together as a normal couple. More to the point — and harder to think of — was the fact that she would be constantly worrying about him, waiting until she saw him again so that she knew that he was still alive. She wondered if it would be best for them both if this was to stop now, before either was hurt? She studied his face as though she could see inside his mind, saw the warmth and understanding in his eyes, as if he knew why she was hesitating. The look both warmed her and sent a frisson of undeniable sexual tension between them.

Katie raised her hand, hesitated, and placed it in his. He closed his fingers around hers and squeezed. They were both fully aware that the touch had bonded them irrevocably together.

"I'll be fine," he said huskily, his eyes never leaving her face. They were full of emotion. "I'm too old and ugly for anything to happen to me. But you take care of yourself. You hear me?" He squeezed her hand so hard that she winced.

"I will," she whispered in reply. She had a sudden irresistible urge to kiss him, but the mess was certainly not the place to do that, and also doing it in full view of everyone would have very embarrassing repercussions, including giving Camp Churchill something to gossip about for weeks.

Instead, she managed a smile meant purely for him, studying his every feature and finally releasing his hand.

"Come on, we'd better go," Joe said.

They took their trays laden with empty plates to the dirty dishes rack then went back to the table to pick up their helmets and weapons.

Joe led the way outside and together they made their way to the rows of tented accommodation. Outside Katie's tent, they stopped and faced each other.

"Well…" Joe stopped. He suddenly placed the palm of his hand gently against the side of her face, stroking the soft skin of her cheek with his thumb. Without hesitation, Katie placed her own hand on top of his and, turning his palm slightly, kissed the rough, warm skin there.

Joe smiled. "I'll see you in the NAAFI tomorrow night," he stated. "Will you be there?"

Katie nodded silently, not trusting herself to speak

Joe withdrew his hand from the side of her face. "I'll see you then." Striding off hurriedly in the direction of the road, he disappeared.

"Please come back safe," Katie whispered to his departing back, hoping he would look back and feeling disappointed when he didn't. Experiencing a sense of loss, she went into her tent to find Wanda sitting on her bed as though waiting for her to come in.

"You dark horse, you," she crowed. "Who's the guy?"

"None of your business," Katie retorted. "If I tell you, the whole camp will know about it by tomorrow."

"That's a bit unfair," Wanda said, twisting her face into a scowl of mock offense. "How could you think such a thing of me?"

"Yeah right," Katie said sarcastically, smiling at her friend. "Like that's the truth."

"Okay. Well, if that's the way you want it to be, I shall stay silent on the subject."

Katie laughed, "That'll be the day. You'll burst."

For the rest of the evening, Katie tidied her bed space, cleaned her boots and hand washed her dirty combat fatigues, hanging them to dry on a makeshift clothesline out back of the tent. She attempted to sit down in the lounge to watch TV, but was too restless and uneasy. Finally, she lay down on her camp bed and tried to read a magazine. However, the only thing she could focus on was Joe—wondering where he was, what he was doing. At last, impatient with herself, she closed her eyes and attempted to sleep, but the noise from the other women in the tent was too much and so she sat up.

At 2200 hours, exasperated at the fact that she couldn't settle, Katie decided that she would get ready for bed. She was just undoing the fastenings of her combat trousers when suddenly her pager went off. She wasted a few precious seconds frantically hunting for it and eventually found it deep in the pocket of her combats. Glancing at the small LED screen, she saw that a message was scrolling across it, repeating itself over and over again—*Report to the CTH immediately.*

"Oh crap!" Katie exclaimed. Moving quickly, she grabbed her webbing, put it on, and slammed her helmet on her head. "I've been called in," she explained to Wanda. "I guess I'll see you later."

"Take care, girl," Wanda responded.

Retrieving her weapon, Katie left the tent to retrace her steps back to the CTH. She knew that she had been called back because of something potentially serious. *More casualties?* Katie gritted her teeth. *Had someone, or even Joe, been hurt on his patrol?* Common sense tried to dictate that it could be anyone. Joe's squad wasn't the only one out beyond the wire that night but even so, panic gripped her. Images assaulted her mind—of Joe badly injured, bleeding and hurt, of having to call on that unique detachment that medical personnel used as a cloak to protect themselves from emotional involvement with their patients. She wouldn't be able to do it. She just wasn't strong enough.

As though trying to escape from her thoughts, Katie began to jog along the road, threading her way around other personnel going about their duties. She reached the CTH and entered to find Sergeant Webster waiting for her arrival at the entrance to his office. Slowing her breathing, Katie strode to meet him, a look of enquiry on her face. "Sergeant?" she queried nervously, coming to a halt in front of him.

"I'm sending you out with a CTT," the sergeant explained abruptly.

Katie was shocked and taken aback. "What? Sergeant? I'm only CTM trained. I've never gone out in the field to treat casualties, let alone accompanied a CTT on an extraction."

"Katie, you are one of the most skilled CTMs we have here and the other CTTs are already deployed. There are a number of firefights going on outside the wire. Many of the patrols have made contact with hostiles and there have been some casualties. We would normally send two CTTs but we just don't have the manpower. You'll be accompanying leading trauma surgeon Major Webster and trauma nurses Fraser, Turner and Martin." His voice was firmer when he continued. "Go and get on your full combat kit. An APC will be picking you up in five minutes. Get moving, Corporal."

Obeying the order without further argument, Katie jogged down the corridor to the locker room. Aware that she only had a few minutes before the APC arrived, she slammed open her locker and proceeded to quickly don her full combats, body armor, limb protectors and PRR. She checked her bootlaces to make sure that they were tightly laced, for there would be no time to fasten them later if they became loose, then undid the leather thong holding her dog tags, took off one tag and shoved it down under the tongue of her right boot. If she happened to be killed and her body was difficult to identify, someone would find the dog tag in her boot with her ID number on it. Finally, she replaced the thong with the remaining dog tag back about her neck, fastened the straps of her combat helmet, pulled on combat gloves and slid the white armband with its red cross up her left arm before finally shrugging into her medical bergen.

Once she was ready, she felt sudden panic. She could vividly picture the approaching helicopter flight out into the black, cold desert, the coming firefight and having to land in the middle of it, and most frightening of all, having to deal with casualties under fire. For a moment, she rested the front of her helmet against her locker and took some deep breaths, trying to stop the faint trembling in her hands and legs. This was her job, what she was paid to do and she needed to get on with it. This was not the time or the place to succumb to a fit of nerves. She would be no good to anybody if she did not get a grip on herself. Sergeant Webster would not be sending her out if he had any doubts that she could do the job.

Taking a final deep breath, she left the locker room and jogged down the corridor to the front doors. As she passed the theaters and trauma rooms, she noticed medical staff readying them, preparing for casualties. Katie strong-armed one of the front doors open and went outside. The CTT was already waiting and they all turned as she came out.

"Corporal Walker." Major Webster nodded, acknowledging her presence.

Katie saluted. "Sir."

The other members of the team nodded their greetings. Everyone looked pale beneath their helmets and all were tense and restless, eager to be off, shuffling their feet, signs that individual stress was mounting. A sudden rumbling of a large engine announced the arrival of a Bulldog armored personnel carrier — APC — as it pulled up beside them. Immediately Katie and the CTT climbed into the massive vehicle, the door slammed shut, sealing them inside the musty, cloying interior, which smelled heavily of oil and they were off within seconds, heading for the airfield.

Katie sat down inside and rested her rifle across her knees. She was so scared that the fear felt like a lump in the pit of her stomach. Glancing sideways at her companions, she took note of their tense expressions and the pallor of their skin and knew that she wasn't the only one who was nervous.

The APC paused at a checkpoint on the perimeter of the airfield. A soldier glanced in through the window at them all then they waved them on to trundle across to a helicopter apron where the CTF CH-47 Chinook was waiting, its double rotor blades turning slowly, a door gunner armed with an M136 minigun sitting patiently at the large open side door.

The CTT and Katie jumped down from the APC, and without wasting any time, jogged across the dusty concrete apron to the rear of the helicopter where, in single file, they strode up the lowered ramp into the Chinook's interior. As soon as they were aboard, the ramp hydraulically lifted, sealing them inside.

Chapter Seven

Katie spent a few minutes looking around the inside of the helicopter, as much to distract herself from her fear as out of curiosity. She had never been on board a CTF helicopter before and was impressed by its size and the amount of medical equipment there was hanging on the walls, fastened to the floor and crammed into every available corner and space. There were small seats at various points around the interior and Katie found one and perched herself on it.

She heard the rotor blades begin to speed up, chopping at the air with a harsh whickering sound, then the two thousand horsepower double engines suddenly screamed. The thirty-meter helicopter shifted slightly, as if reluctant to move, then the nose tipped upward slightly, and almost gracefully, the Chinook lifted from the ground. The noise of the engines became almost deafening and the upward pitch increased so that Katie had to grab hold of the edge of her seat to prevent herself from falling off. After flying with its nose canted upward for a few minutes, the helicopter started a bank to the left and Katie found herself nearly toppling from her seat in the opposite direction. Eventually the helicopter leveled out and picked up speed.

A cold wind howled and whistled in through the open side door, swirling around the interior of the helicopter, and with the roar of the engines and chopping noise of the rotor blades, it was impossible for anyone to speak without having to shout.

Major Webster approached Katie and gestured to the rifle lying across her knees. "Know how to use one of those, Corporal?" he shouted, a little skepticism evident in his voice.

Katie looked down at the long, black, oily-looking weapon and nodded. "Yes, sir," she yelled back. "I believe I can handle it."

The major nodded at her and went back to his seat.

Katie placed the rifle with its butt on the floor between her knees, clamped it between them, and after struggling to retrieve it, proceeded to insert a magazine into the weapon. She saw that her hands were trembling slightly and she immediately dropped the rifle. It landed on the metal plating of the floor with a sharp crack, bounced and skidded across the decking. Katie took a deep breath, held it, released it slowly and tried to still the shaking of her hands. Major Webster studied the incident with some annoyance on his face and, feeling her cheeks flush slightly, Katie bent down and retrieved her weapon, quickly making sure the magazine had been securely locked into position before placing the rifle, barrel pointed upward now that it was loaded, toward the ceiling.

Major Webster made his way to the cockpit of the Chinook and briefly spoke with the pilot. As he returned, he held up five fingers, a signal to the team that there were five minutes to their destination. At this, the CTT and Katie stood up, laid their weapons to one side and began to ready equipment, placing the stretchers on the floor behind the door gunner then laying combat casualty blankets, IV bags with tubing, blood products and anything else that would be needed to treat possible casualties on top of them. The stretchers with their loads would be readily available when needed.

Barely audible over the noise, the pilot suddenly shouted at them over his shoulder in a calm and matter-of-fact tone, "We've reached our destination, folks. Apologies, we need to circle for a few minutes. The guys on the ground are taking fire down there and they need to secure our landing zone."

Katie took a deep, shuddering breath and closed her eyes, trying to calm her breathing and forget about the terror that was gnawing away at her insides. She would be almost useless if she couldn't get her nerves under control. She found herself repeating the same words under her breath, over and over again, "I will be all right. I will be all right."

Slamming a hand on top of her combat helmet to ensure that it was firmly on her head, she heard a change in the pitch of the helicopter engines and a slight slowing of the rotor blades. The helicopter started to sink toward the ground, the rear end dipping down slightly first. She jerked, startled, when she suddenly heard sharp metallic pinging and clanging on the outer hull of the Chinook. She glanced questioningly at one of the trauma nurses seated opposite her.

"Bullets," the trauma nurse explained in response to Katie's questioning expression. "We're taking fire." The trauma nurse's own expression appeared unperturbed but her voice, although pitched in tones bordering on shouting because of the roar of the engines, was shaking slightly.

Oh Jesus! Bullets! Bullets kill and destroy lives and I'm sitting in the middle of them. Stop! She screamed the word in her brain, panic threatening to overwhelm her. She had to get a grip on herself, had to regain control of her fears.

The Chinook continued its descent, the tail end of the helicopter tilting down even farther, as though the rear landing gear strained for the ground. There came a thud as it touched down then a second one as the front landing gear followed suit.

The pilot shouted over his shoulder again. "Okay. No dilly-dallying please, ladies and gents. We need to get the hell out of here as soon as possible. One more thing, they can't bring the casualties to you, they're being pinned down out there. You'll have to go to them."

Making sure that her bergen was securely on her back, Katie picked up her EMC, slung it awkwardly over her shoulder, checked to make sure that the safety of her rifle was on, held the butt of it against her right shoulder with the barrel pointing down a little to the right of her right boot and joined the other members of the CTT, who were crouched to the right of the open side door.

As the Chinook settled onto the ground and the noise from the rotors diminished, Katie could hear the sound of gunfire from out in the darkness, the sharp crack of single shots, voices shouting and the crackle of static from radios. It was so surreal that she began to feel as though she was in some kind of nightmare.

The major, positioned in front of the CTT and Katie at the door, held up a gloved hand in a signal to wait, and before long two soldiers appeared from out of the darkness, moving at a crouched run. They stopped outside the door of the Chinook, one facing directly to his front while the one on the right of the door raised a hand and beckoned them forward.

One by one, the CTT jumped out into the darkness. Katie was last in line and she hesitated briefly, looking down at the ground. It looked pitch-black beneath the helicopter and she suddenly had an image of herself jumping into an abyss and vanishing forever. Realizing the team were waiting for her, she jumped and landed heavily but safely on the hard-packed dust and sandy earth.

Katie had just regained her balance when a fusillade of gunfire came from the dark and a voice yelled, "On the ground."

A mixture of training and survival instinct caused the CTT to immediately fling themselves down into prone positions. Katie threw herself onto her stomach, releasing her grip on the EMC and instinctively bringing her rifle up into a firing position, pushing the rifle butt firmly into her shoulder and aiming out into the blackness, gloved finger along the safety catch, preparing to release it if necessary.

She was unable to see more than a few meters in front of her. It was almost pitch-black with the exception of a few red torchlights moving erratically about a hundred meters directly in front of her, tracer fire and the blood red whirling flashes of the landing lights on the Chinook behind her. The crack of gunfire was loud and somewhere in the dark was the harsh rattle of a machine gun.

Rolling onto her side, Katie groped for one of her pouches, ripped open the Velcro fastening and drew out her night vision goggles. Still keeping her position low to the ground, she fastened the goggles to the front of her helmet then lowered them over her eyes.

Instantly, everything went green, and she could now see men moving about in the distance.

One of the soldiers turned to face them. "My apologies, folks," he announced almost politely in an American drawl, "but we gotta crawl to avoid gunfire. Follow my lead and keep low." Without hesitation, using elbows and knees, he began to belly crawl along the ground in the direction of the distant figures.

Katie, going last as tail-end Charlie, on hearing the American accent and feeling a cold feeling in the pit of her stomach, obediently followed the CTT member immediately in front of her, uncomfortably encumbered by the EMC and her weapon. Dust puffed up from the ground and every time she inhaled, it traveled up her nose and entered her mouth, causing her to cough repeatedly. Irritably, she shoved the carrier up onto her back, dug her toes into the ground and pushed herself along, gritting her teeth so that they acted as filters for the dust.

The sound of gunfire was all around her and she nearly screamed when a bullet puffed up a small fountain of dust and earth a mere two meters away from her. Breathing harshly and rapidly, sweat trickling down from beneath her helmet, Katie crawled along faster, elbows and knees scraping against the hard ground, her skin stinging with pain through the material of her combats. She was sure that they would be grazed and bruised tomorrow — if she survived, that was. Adrenaline pumped through her body and her heart raced and pounded in her ears. She was more terrified then she had ever been before in her life.

As they neared the red torchlights, Katie could make out a line of soldiers crouched and strung out in front of a low rock wall. Every now and again, she could see tracer fire coming toward them, and the soldiers would raise themselves up slightly and fire back out into the desert, their own gunfire flashing red against the black landscape. Radios crackled and there was the ratcheting sound of a machine gun in the background, stopping and starting sporadically.

To Katie in her terror, sounds seemed to fade away, much like what happened in a nightmare, because all she could really hear was the harsh sound of her breathing and the deep sounding, slowed down whup-whup of the rotor blades of the Chinook behind her.

After what seemed like an eternity, the CTT and Katie belly-crawled the last few meters to reach the soldiers. Major Webster immediately rose to a crouch and spoke to a soldier who had approached to greet them.

"Glad to have you here, sir," the soldier announced in a harsh whisper. "Our casualties are over there." He pointed a red torch beam in the direction of two soldiers, lying on the ground, attended to by the squad's corpsman.

The CTT and Katie ran in a stoop to the injured soldiers. Without wasting any time, Katie and a trauma nurse went to one casualty, and the major with the rest of the team went to the other.

Her training taking over, Katie pushed her night vision goggles up onto the top of her helmet, laid her rifle down on the ground and took off her combat gloves. After putting on a pair of nitrile gloves, she carried out a fully body assessment, running her hands from the top of the casualty's head, down each side of his body then each leg, intent on finding any hidden injuries or bleeding, before discovering an area of the soldier's uniform about the shoulder, soaked in blood. Ripping open the body armor and raising the T-shirt, she discovered a gunshot wound in the upper arm. It was a clean through and through bullet hole and Katie only needed to place a thick pad on the entry and exit holes and secure each with tape before preparing an IV, inserting a cannula into the back of the patient's hand and connecting the IV tubing to it. The trauma nurse took the patient's vital signs and assisted Katie by passing her the medical equipment that she needed. The soldier began to moan and Katie stroked his forehead. "Hey, soldier, you're going to be okay. Just keeping moaning at me. I don't mind, moaning or swearing. Your choice." Leaning her face down to his, she spoke directly into his ear, "We'll get you sorted out, loaded into the helo and back to camp where you'll be safe. You'll be okay, pal. I promise you."

The soldier opened pain-filled eyes at her voice and attempted to smile. "An angel," he murmured hoarsely. "I must have died already." His face glistened with sweat and he grimaced with pain.

"Sorry to disappoint you, soldier, but you're still alive and we aim to keep you that way," Katie answered, giving him one of her best smiles. "And I'm no angel, just an ordinary grunt."

Katie turned to the trauma nurse. "He has a wound in the arm," she explained quietly. "It's not serious. I've packed it and given him some morphine. He'll be out of it in a few minutes. We need to get him on a stretcher and get him into the helo. If you keep an eye on him, I'll go and see if some of these soldiers can fetch the stretchers and get him loaded on board."

The trauma nurse nodded her agreement and Katie crawled toward a small group of soldiers close by. Reaching one particular soldier who was closest to her, she saw that he was, in fact, a US marine. "I'm sorry. I know you're dealing with a lot at the moment but could we possibly have two of your men collect some stretchers from the helo," she asked, "and load the casualties on board?"

"No problem, ma'am," the marine with the rank of sergeant promptly replied, and he turned to two men crouching nearby. "You men, get your asses over to the helo and fetch some stretchers. Bring them back here, collect the injured then load them into the bird."

"You got it, Sarge," one of the men replied, and he and his companion ran to the Chinook. They were back in minutes, clutching stretchers. They gently lifted Katie's patient onto one then the two soldiers, together with the trauma nurse, ran with him back to the helicopter. The trauma nurse climbed into the Chinook, and with the assistance of the door gunner, lifted the stretcher inside. The soldiers were back within seconds, preparing to transfer the second patient.

Katie began to crawl back to her colleagues to collect her EMC and weapon when, without warning, somebody from behind grabbed the back of her medical bergen, jerking her backward so hard that she collapsed awkwardly onto her back. It was so unexpected that for a moment she was shocked and stunned then, kicking the ground furiously, she struggled to turn and get to her knees. Once facing her assailant, she froze and stared, shocked, at Joe Anderson's face and the look of fury on it.

"What the fuck are you doing here?" he shot at her in a loud whisper. He aimed a red torch beam at her face, the beam almost blinding her and fracturing her newly acquired night vision into splinters.

Katie struck out blindly and managed to bat his hand down so that the torch beam fell away from her face. She was stung with anger. *Who the hell does he think he is?* "What the fuck do you think I'm doing here?" she spat back, chin lifting defiantly. "Fucking doing my job, that's what."

A marine, crouching nearby, overhearing the verbal exchange, turned and glanced from his staff sergeant to the female corporal with avid interest showing on his shadowed features.

Joe glared at Katie. He snapped, "Well, get back on the helo. Your team is ready to leave, and that's an order." Without another word, he turned away, dismissing her.

As he passed the man who was expressing a keen interest in their altercation, he ordered sharply, "Focus on what you're supposed to be fucking doing, Marine!"

The soldier jerked. "Yes, Staff Sergeant," was his brief reply, and he hastily turned and faced out into the dark desert.

"Yes, Staff Sergeant, certainly, Staff Sergeant," Katie called furiously after Joe's retreating back. Hurt by his attitude, not comprehending why he had reacted the way he had, Katie crawled back to the other members of the CTT who were hastily collecting medical equipment where it was scattered on the ground.

"Come on, Corporal. We need to get out of here," the major ordered abruptly.

"Yes, sir," Katie responded, her voice shaking slightly both with delayed shock at the confrontation that had taken place with Joe and the onset of nerves at having to retrace her steps back to board the helicopter. She quickly picked up her weapon and EMC and rose to a crouch, waiting for their escorts back to the Chinook. Led at a jog by the two marines who had first met them when they landed, Katie noticed with relief that the gunfire appeared to have abated. She could hear shouting from behind her and boots thudding on the hard ground, but her mind remained focused on the furious expression she had seen on Joe's face and the hard, uncompromising tone of his voice.

She was about to hoist herself through the side door into the Chinook when there was a single gunshot and one of the marines who had been escorting them suddenly screamed and collapsed to the ground.

"No!" Katie yelled, shocked at the scenario unfolding before her. Instantly she darted away from the Chinook, running toward the still figure and skidding to her knees on the ground beside him. At her sudden movement, a volley of gunfire came in her direction from beyond the low rock wall. Bullets ricocheted off the ground around her, raising miniature whirlwinds of dust and little chunks of soil, twanging against the side of the Chinook. The marines behind her at the wall returned fire furiously in response, and the enemy gunfire coming from the blackness fell silent.

The injured marine screamed and writhed, teeth gleaming white in a blackened, grimy face. "All right, Marine, take it easy," Katie shouted, steadying her voice. "We'll get you sorted out. You'll be all right."

She flung the EMC upright and wrenched it open. Working at top speed, Katie checked the marine to assess what wounds he had received. She ripped open his body armor and combat jacket, eventually finding a gunshot wound in his shoulder. There was a small entrance wound with a much larger exit wound and it was bleeding extensively, possibly having nicked the brachial artery. She tore his T-shirt down the front to get access to the wound and was joined by a trauma nurse, and after reporting to her what she had found, they worked together to stop the bleeding, packing the wound, administering painkillers and setting up the usual IV for shock and blood loss.

Gunfire started up sporadically around them and the machine gun recommenced its firing. Katie could hear the pilot screaming at them and she thought she heard the rotor blades of the helicopter begin to pick up speed and the engines grow louder.

A group of marines suddenly appeared beside them, crouching to avoid the bullets. Katie scrabbled backward out of the way as the wounded marine was hoisted into the air and transported unceremoniously at a flat-out run to the helicopter, where the waiting hands of the crew and the CTT were there to take him.

Katie groped for the EMC and her rifle and prepared to beat a hasty retreat to the Chinook when suddenly she found herself jerked into the air. She yelled out and kicked backward, making contact with a shin, but her would-be rescuer ignored what must have been sudden pain and ran with her to the helicopter. Hurriedly placed on her feet, spun round and grasped by the front of her body armor, she was again lifted from her feet and thrown unceremoniously onto the hard metal floor of the helicopter. "Fuck!" Katie exclaimed as her backside hit the hard plating. Pain traveled up her spine and she winced. She was getting thoroughly sick and tired of ending up on her backside. It was going to be black and blue by the time she was finished.

Joe's face suddenly appeared a bare few inches from her own. Enunciating each word slowly and clearly through clenched teeth, his eyes gleaming black in a pale face, he shouted, "Now! Fucking stay there and don't fucking move, goddamnit!" For a few seconds his eyes locked with hers and she was stunned to see in them all the feelings that he had held hidden from her and which she had been longing to see. Speechless with terror, her body trembling all over, all she could do was nod silently.

Joe backed away, still staring at her, then turned, and in a crouching run, returned to his men. Katie watched him go until he merged into the darkness and she could no longer see him then she scrabbled backward on her backside, using hands and boots until she was safely out of the way of the door. The engines wound up to a scream and the nose of the Chinook tilted up and they rose off the ground, hovered for a few seconds, leveled out and flew off at speed.

Chapter Eight

Katie wanted to cry out in protest at leaving Joe behind. She sat on the floor of the Chinook, gasping for air, head between her knees before she suddenly realized where she was. Eventually staggering to her feet, she moved to where the same trauma nurse who had assisted her on the ground attended to the third wounded marine.

During the journey back, Katie knelt by her still-conscious charge. She spoke gently to him, pitching her voice just loud enough for him to hear, trying to keep his fears at bay, reassuring him and holding his hand when he reached up a trembling one of his own. On the surface, she managed to remain calm and detached but involved with the wounded man, but inside she was screaming with reaction from what she had just experienced on the ground.

Finally, the Chinook began its descent toward the airfield at Base Independence and eventually landed with barely a jar on the apron. Waiting medics ran up the lowered ramp and into the Chinook, lifting the wounded marines on their stretchers back down onto firm ground and to waiting ambulances. They were driven to the CTH, where trauma teams were waiting outside the doors for them, and where they were taken directly to the trauma rooms for assessment while surgeons scrubbed for the inevitable surgeries.

Katie and the CTT climbed tiredly into a Bulldog APC. They were driven immediately to the CTH. During the short journey back, Katie sat in silence. She found herself gripping her weapon so tightly that her knuckles ached. If she relaxed slightly, she began to tremble. Reaction had begun to set in and she found that she was breathing fast, at risk of hyperventilating. Closing her eyes briefly, she willed herself to breathe deeply and slowly, and eventually her pulse rate slowed and the trembling ceased. She could still remember the expression on Joe's face as he had flung her into the helicopter, and for the first time was sure that he had developed the same feelings for her as she had for him. It did nothing to reassure her because she was safe for the moment, and he was still out there in the firefight and there was nothing she could do to prevent him from being hurt.

Outside the CTH, Katie paused. Undoing the straps of her helmet, she took it off, running a hand through sweat-soaked hair. She gazed back out to the airfield and beyond, her thoughts and feelings in turmoil. She wanted desperately to be back out in the desert with Joe, as though by being with him and doing her job she could keep him safe. Her burgeoning feelings for him were raw and powerful, and for a brief moment, she felt a surge of worry for his safety. Eventually realizing that she was needed inside the CTH, she was about to go inside to check on the new casualties when the doors swung open and Sergeant Webster came out to join her.

"Well, Katie, everything okay?" he asked, studying her closely.

"I'm fine, thank you, Sergeant," she answered. "Now."

"It's always rough the first time out," Sergeant Webster continued. "But you made it. Major Webster gave some good feedback about you. Well done."

"Yes, thank you, Sergeant," Katie replied, feeling emotionless and empty. "How many casualties were there tonight?"

"We have another six, including the three you picked up tonight, and we are bulging at the seams. Four gunshot wounds, one shrapnel and one amputee. The amputee is still in theater as we speak. The others are stable. Okay, you're done for the night. Go back and get some sleep. I'll see you tomorrow at 0700 hours."

"What about our new casualties?" Katie asked. "Shouldn't I stay to give you a hand with them?"

"Go. That's an order," Sergeant Webster reiterated and turned to go back into the CTH, leaving Katie alone.

"Thank you, Sergeant," she called after him, and turning, began to walk slowly down the road toward her tent, her emotions held severely in check, afraid that if she let thoughts of the events of the night intrude into her mind, she would break down. She trekked slowly back to her accommodation and went inside. Sighing heavily, she took off her helmet and placed it on the floor beside her bed then proceeded to quietly take off her body armor and combats, throwing them down to join the slightly rocking helmet. Suddenly exhausted, more so than she had ever been since she had begun her deployment, she sat down on the edge of her camp bed, wincing at the creak it made. The tent remained silent except for the soft breathing and slight snores from the other women.

Standing up to put on her nightwear, Katie jumped as a torch came on from the direction of Wanda's bed. "You okay, babe?" came a whispered question, tinged with concern.

Katie sat down on the edge of her bed again, running a hand tiredly through her short hair. She hesitated before answering. "It's been an awful night," she eventually replied, equally quietly.

"Want to talk about it?" Wanda asked. The torchlight jiggled and there was the rustle of a sleeping bag.

"No. Go back to sleep, Wanda," Katie replied slowly.

The torch beam came closer and Wanda sat herself down beside her. "What's up?" she asked.

Katie sighed. "It's all wrong," she began. "Everything. We've had so many casualties lately, twenty I think at the last count, and two dead. Tonight they sent me out with a CTT. There was a firefight and I was caught in the middle of it. I was terrified, Wanda. I've never been under fire before. And then there's—" She stopped suddenly, reluctant to proceed any further with the conversation.

"Let me guess." Wanda finished for her. "Then there's the man."

Katie glanced sideways at her friend, just making out the woman's pale face by the torchlight. "How do you know?" she asked. "Oh, wait, I forgot, nothing can get past you, right?"

"I'm not entirely blind, you know," Wanda answered. "I could tell lately by your mood and the way you've been acting that there was something up, man-wise. Plus, you keep looking around the mess whenever we go there. Who is he?"

"Before I say anything, you have to promise me that this will go no further than you and me," Katie stated firmly. "I mean it, Wanda."

Wanda huffed with exasperation. "Okay, okay. Now spill."

"His name is Joe Anderson," Katie finally admitted. "A staff sergeant in the US Marines. About six feet tall, dark blue eyes, dark blond hair, quite attractive—actually very attractive. We met by chance at the CTH. He'd come in to see one of his men who'd been injured in an IED incident while out on patrol. We'd had a pretty traumatic time in the theaters that morning and I got sick, went outside and ended up throwing up. He found me—not very romantic, I must admit—and asked if I was okay. Anyway, we've met up in the mess a couple of times, he's walked me back here a couple of times, and tonight when I went out with the CTT, it was his patrol that was involved in the firefight. He was pretty irate when he saw that I was there. Actually, he was furious. Nothing has happened between us, not even a kiss but…"

"But," Wanda echoed, "you've both fallen for each other, and from the way you're talking, you've really got the hots for him." Her final words were emphatic and all-knowing.

"Wanda!" Katie exclaimed. "That's a vulgar way of putting it. The truth is I'm exhausted and totally confused and scared. I promised myself that I would never get involved in a relationship while I was in the Army, but every time I meet this guy, it's like all the promises I've made to myself fly out the window and I get angry for feeling like it. From his reaction tonight, I'm sure he feels the same way, but as I said, nothing has happened yet. Does that make any sense at all?"

"It certainly does," Wanda replied. "The best laid plans of mice and men and all that."

"What am I supposed to do?" Katie asked, a slight note of desperation in her voice.

"Well, love, I think you may have a problem." Wanda paused. "A staff sergeant, huh? He must be a lot older than you."

"I think he's about thirty-five or thirty-six, something like that. He's hardly old enough to be my dad." Katie felt defensive on Joe's behalf.

"Hey, don't get touchy." Wanda raised a hand in protest. "I'm only here to listen and help."

Katie hung her head. "Sorry," she murmured. "The problem is that getting involved with someone out here is too complicated. There's too much risk for the both of us. I've never really cared about men. I wanted to have a good Army career, move up the ranks, blah blah. You know the recruitment spiel, and now, everything has turned upside down. It's all been so quick. I can't think straight. I know it's been quick but now, all I do is worry about him getting hurt when he's out on patrol. It's screwing up my concentration and I can't afford that to happen in my job."

"My dear, what you need to do is get him out of your system—unrequited love and all that. The place, the time and the excitement of a relationship in a war setting is always far more passionate, but short-lived. What you need to do is get him alone, drag him into some nice dark place and have wild, passionate sex. Jump his bones. That should do it," Wanda suggested matter-of-factly.

Katie laughed quietly. "Wanda, that solution is so typical of you. You always go straight to the crux of the matter in as tactful a way as possible." She paused, her laughter fading into silence. "I don't think he would go for it. He's been a perfect gentleman so far."

Wanda chuffed. "Katie, he's a Yank. He'll go for it. Trust me."

"Oh, I don't know, Wanda. I'm not like that. I can't just go to bed with a man unless there's something there other than...just sex."

"Oh my, listen to you talking about sex," Wanda teased, then, unusually for her, her tone became serious. "I can't tell you what to do, my love, but methinks you're heading for trouble. This is a dangerous place, and as you said, if it's affecting your work, with the type of work you do, it's going to cause all manner of crap to hit the fan. And he's more at risk than you are." Wanda paused then yawned. "Just remember, at the end of your tour and his, you'll both be going your separate ways, not an auspicious future for a relationship."

Feeling suddenly unhappy at Wanda's blunt words, Katie nodded. "You're right," she agreed, her voice sounding sad.

Wanda placed a comforting hand on Katie's shoulder. "You do have it bad," she said again. "I can't say I envy you, but when all is said and done, it's your business, so I wish you luck. Now, I'm for bed. Try to get some sleep, sweetie. You look done in."

With that parting remark, Wanda rose from her friend's bed and went back to her own. Katie sat alone in the dark for a few more minutes, wishing that Joe was with her, hoping that he was safe and that she would get to see him again. As much as Wanda's words had been full of logic and common sense, she was not sure she could dismiss Joe as something casual, and that there was no future in their relationship.

Eventually, Katie slid into her sleeping bag and lay down. Closing her eyes, she saw an image of Joe as he had been tonight out in the desert. She could picture his blue eyes so clearly, in parts so cold and hard, warring with emotions that he had not yet disclosed to her, and she shivered, with warmth and delight at the hidden feelings between them, yet to be brought into the open. Wanda's words played in her head and she experienced a momentary pang of doubt about what she was doing.

It was so hard to sleep. Her head and eyes ached and she was exhausted. The events of the night, including the terror she had experienced, had drained her. Plus she was anxious about her strengthening feelings for Joe. *Can you fall for someone in so short a time? Can the fact that we're both here in a war zone be the trigger for such passionate, intense feelings? Are the brass and Wanda right? Do these sorts of relationships fizzle out because there are no deep foundations for them?* She tossed and turned, the thoughts turning over and over in her head. She could find no answers and eventually, irritated with trying to figure things out, fatigue finally overcame her and she slept.

Chapter Nine

As it did every day, Katie's alarm clock rang at its usual time, waking her promptly. She lay in her sleeping bag for a few seconds, her mind blissfully blank, feeling the soreness in her elbows and knees where they had been in contact with the hard ground the night before. She was still tired, but knew that she had to get up and shower before the others.

Gathering her resolve, she extracted herself from her sleeping bag and stood up. She stretched, easing the stiffness in her joints, collected her toilet kit and towel and made her way through the soundly sleeping women to the showers. Outside, she paused. Today, the air was cooler than it had been over the previous few days and it felt good against her bare skin.

She felt a little low and washed out. Thoughts of the events from the previous night were once more present in her mind, with fleeting images interfering with her usual sense of calm detachment. The image of Joe was paramount in her thoughts, uppermost the question of whether he was safe or not.

Hearing the tent coming to life behind her, she went into one of the showers and turned on the water. That morning it was and she stood under the spray for some time, trying to relax and gather her composure, struggling to retrieve the sense of detachment that seemed to have shredded itself to pieces by the events of the last few days. She finally came to the conclusion that it had deserted her. She felt that elements of her life were speeding out of control and she was fast losing her grasp on the direction it was heading. Finally finishing her shower, she dried herself, dressed and went back to her bed space.

Wanda was awake and offered a greeting. "How are you feeling?" she asked, glancing at her.

"I could feel better," Katie replied, attempting a small smile but failing miserably.

"You'll be fine, girl," Wanda reassured gently. "There's nothing in this world that can't be sorted out."

Katie nodded and went about straightening her sleeping bag and sorting out her uniform for the day.

Wanda wandered off to the showers, and when she returned, Katie was dressed and sitting on the edge of her bed.

"Food?" Katie asked.

As she dressed in her own uniform, Wanda nodded. Before many minutes had passed, the two women left the tent and were making their way toward the mess for breakfast. As they approached the building, Katie found herself looking around for Joe. She didn't see him walking toward the building and once they were inside, she couldn't see him seated at any of the tables. She refused to acknowledge the strong disappointment she felt or the anxious butterflies in her stomach that she felt at his absence. She purposefully engaged Wanda in small talk and spoke about their night out in the NAAFI that evening. However, always, at the back of her mind, was the image of the man with whom she thought she was falling in love, against all the principles and lifelong promises she had made to herself.

* * * *

On a distant part of the camp, on the concrete no-man's-land between the perimeter wall and the barrier of concertina wire that protected the base, Joe Anderson ran as though his life depended on it. Other joggers ran past him in the opposite direction, or he swerved around them if they were heading in his, but he failed to acknowledge the morning greetings — in fact, barely noticed the other people around him. His iPod headphones plugged into his ears, he barely heard the music blaring out its heavy beat. Sweat soaked his khaki T-shirt, trickled down his face and glistened on his tanned, well-muscled arms and legs, but he was oblivious to it. He was pushing himself, even though he was tired from the patrol of the previous night.

He had arrived back from his patrol at midnight, having been extracted by helicopter, and had managed to catch four hours of restless, broken sleep then, wide awake before his alarm clock was due to go off and assailed by unsettling thoughts of Katie, he had gotten up from his camp bed. He was due to go on a patrol the next night and he had paperwork and the Warning Order — WARNO — to prepare and send out to all concerned, so, hoping that the paperwork would occupy his mind and keep treacherous thoughts of a green-eyed CTM at bay, he unearthed his laptop and spent two hours focusing on his work.

Once he was finished, he found himself sitting aimlessly, not wanting to go to the mess in case he saw Katie, needing to get out and find something to do where he could sort out his feelings and thoughts about her before they became his undoing. He had eventually decided to go for a run, convincing himself that the air and space would help him to think.

Now, he jogged along, his breathing easy and relaxed but his mind far from feeling at ease. *Katie.* How had she gotten under his skin so quickly? He could picture her stunning smile, her clear green eyes and the stubborn tilt of her chin when she became upset. He could even hear the clipped British tones of her voice. He finally had to admit to himself that he had fallen for her, had feelings that he had no business developing. In his usual analytical way, he listed the pros and cons of pursuing a relationship with the young woman. She was at least ten or eleven years younger than he. At the end of their tours they would each go their separate ways — he back to the US, she back to the UK. Long-distance relationships never worked — or so went the scuttlebutt. Another bad point to add to the list was that their relationship had started in a war zone, something that — although not banned by the brass — was frowned upon. One-night stands, if you could find somewhere away from other people, were the norm. Trying to maintain a long-term relationship was virtually impossible. The time and place were all wrong and a relationship would be intense and short-lived. His thoughts about her were destroying his concentration and his control while out in the field with his squad, and he couldn't allow that to happen.

On the other side of the coin, she was lovely, feisty, stubborn and brave, something he had seen for himself when she had appeared from the medevac Chinook. He had been completely stunned when he had seen her talking to one of his men, had watched in horror as she had ducked and swerved from bullets, had completely lost it when he had seen an errant bullet strike the ground close to her then, when she had run from the Chinook to the marine who had been shot, he'd acted like a madman. He could still recall with photographic clarity the look on her face when he had picked her up and thrown her into the interior of the Chinook.

As Joe's feet pounded the concrete, he groaned inwardly as he remembered that she had winced as she had landed on the metal plating, and the way she had looked at him with terror in her wide green eyes.

"Crap." He hissed through gritted teeth. She had been just as frightened of him as she had been by the firefight going on around them.

He went on to remember how her eyes had lit up when she had almost cannoned into him in the mess and how he had felt when he had seen her talking to the cook behind the hot food counter. He had heard every word of the conversation between Katie and the young corporal and remembered the feeling of jealousy — completely alien to his character — that had welled up inside him.

Joe checked his wristwatch and saw that it was time he turned back. He needed to shower and dress then he had to attend a briefing with his squad leader regarding the patrol the next night. He U-turned and began to jog back along the perimeter, his stride slower now, thoughts of Katie pushed to the back of his mind. He had his MOS to do, would need to focus. He would get the briefing over and done with then relax until the patrol tomorrow night. He would avoid going any place where Katie might be. He needed to clear his head, get his thoughts together, and seeing or being near her wasn't the way to do it. Feeling a little easier in his mind, Joe jogged slowly back to the US camp and his tent.

After showering, he spent the hours before his briefing checking and rechecking his WARNO and the five paragraph order that he had prepared to let his squad know who was going on patrol, what their positions in the patrol would be and other similar information. It warned them so that they could get ready, and contained intelligence information such as enemy and friendly forces that would be in the area, supporting units—if any, what the patrol was about and what its intention was. It also advised members of the squad what their role in the patrol would be so that they could obtain information or equipment required. The navigator, for example, would obtain maps, special equipment, organize transportation, radio frequencies and call signs, and plot a route based on the area of the patrol. Eventually satisfied with the WARNO, at 1100 hours, Joe made his way to the USMC headquarters and reported to the office of his squad leader.

* * * *

Katie's day was busy. During the morning, there was the sick parade to deal with, with its usual personnel suffering from the heat and minor injuries. Eight of the casualties involved in the bomb blast at the perimeter wall were going home and Katie had to fill in the requisite forms and make sure that all the patients' notes were up to date for handover to the American medical contingents, or whichever country the patients were traveling home to. She kept herself busy helping the nurses with the remaining patients and carrying out her normal everyday duties.

There were no new casualties that day, which was a relief because they had already called on the standby nurses to come in and assist with those patients that they already had in the CTH. Katie was relieved when 1800 hours came and she was stood down for the rest of the night. She opted to go to the mess for something to eat, and on her way there attempted to convince herself that she wouldn't see Joe and probably wouldn't see him at the NAAFI that night either, even though he had said that he would be there. After all, he was a staff sergeant and they had their own post exchange — PX — to go to on Camp Roosevelt, so why would he come to the British one?

Joe did not appear in the mess, and, feeling a little despondent, after eating her meal Katie made her way back to her tent, determined to enjoy herself at the NAAFI that night.

Chapter Ten

The NAAFI was one of the larger solid builds on Camp Churchill. Gone were the long, interconnecting snake-like tents, erected in the early days of the camp. In its place was a prefabricated construction clad in the same khaki and sand-colored paint as the rest of the solid builds on the camp, complete with loud vibrating generator producing both light and electricity.

The NAAFI represented a place where both senior and non-commissioned ranks could meet in the evenings. It was a place that served to act as a safety valve, where tension and adrenaline resulting from the knife-edge existence that all personnel on the base were subjected to on a daily basis, could be released. It was a place where there was much laughter, and where friendships and relationships could start and also end.

Bingo nights took place at one end of the entertainment scale, and at the other end there had been occasions when well-known celebrities had visited and entertained the troops. On some nights, music played and people would expend their energy by dancing. The dance nights were not part of the camp's scheduled events but the top brass turned a blind eye to the impromptu discos. Alcohol was banned on the camp, so they knew that what took place was just a releasing of high spirits. It was a place where both the UK and US Armed Forces gravitated to when they had free time, which wasn't often, so when a NAAFI hop — as it was nicknamed — occurred, it was a night to look forward to.

As Katie and Wanda, both dressed identically in combat trousers, white T-shirts and combat boots with military caps perched rakishly on their heads, approached the building, light and a constant roar of voices and laughter spilled out from chocked open doors and windows. Service personnel, both men and women, lingered outside, smoking and drinking from cans of juice or water bottles, laughing and joking, their conversations mingling with the noises of the camp. The dusty, hot and humid night air neither inhibited their high-octane spirits nor prevented them from relaxing and enjoying their free time.

Katie and Wanda were eager to enter the building and become part of the noisy throng inside. On reaching the crowd outside the doors, both women paused, raising hands in greeting and calling out to those they were acquainted with. There were good-natured catcalls from some of the men, something that Katie and Wanda had come to tolerate, knowing that these voices were good-humored and harmless. Eventually freeing themselves from the quickly expanding crowd, Katie pushed her way to the doors with Wanda following. The brightly lit interior was blinding and Katie had to blink her eyes to get used to the light difference.

An attempt had been made to decorate the interior of the building, but the décor and furniture were purely functional, the drab colors of the paintwork laying claim to the fact that everything was purely temporary. The large room was crowded with a sea of camouflage uniforms, dusty boots and white and khaki T-shirts. All tables and chairs were full, standing room only at the counter.

Katie immediately glanced around the room. Prior to her arrival, she had been determined that she wasn't going to look for Joe or think about him. Unfortunately, she discovered that her willpower where he was concerned was non-existent. *Is he here? Will he be here?* Surreptitiously, her glance locked on to every male that looked tall—either seated or standing—with dark blond hair. She could not see him in the room and the feeling of disappointment was intense.

Katie became aware that Wanda had sidled up to her. "What's up, girl?" the woman shouted to Katie, attempting to make herself heard above the noise. "Is your staff sergeant not here?"

Katie felt the heat rise in her cheeks. "He's not my staff sergeant," she replied hotly. "I barely know him."

"That's a crock of shit if ever I've heard one," Wanda replied slyly. "You watch your arse, girl."

Katie laughed at the other woman's warning. "Yeah, I've had the briefing and all that."

They ventured farther into the room and Katie heard her name shouted, barely audible above the tumultuous din. "There's my lot," she shouted to Wanda and together the two women thrust their way through the crowd toward the counter.

"Evening, Sergeant," Katie greeted Sergeant Webster, who appeared to be propping up the counter.

"Less of the Sergeant, please, Katie," Ron Webster said cheerfully. "Not only does it make me feel old, but it's an insult to downtime."

Both Katie and Wanda laughed and went on to speak to other work colleagues. They each got a frosted can of Coke, and Katie was grateful for the ice-cold beverage. It was hot in the room and getting hotter, and if possible, the noise had risen exponentially with the temperature.

"No music tonight?" Wanda asked regretfully.

"The noise level hasn't risen high enough yet," Corporal Alison Horner, a Trauma Nurse, replied. "Trust me. It will get going soon enough."

As if on cue, at least half of the ceiling lights went off. The crowd cheered, the cheers interspersed with catcalls and ribald remarks. Some enterprising person had rigged an iPod to a pair of obscenely huge speakers and within minutes, music blared from them. Instantly, the NAAFI came alive. The song, one from the Vietnam era, galvanized the more energetic amongst the crowd into action. As if by magic, a large space appeared in the center of the room as personnel moved chairs and tables out of the way, shoving them to line the walls. The space quickly filled with dancers, rapping and stomping. It didn't matter if you couldn't dance or what your dancing technique was like. Dancing was a release, a safety valve.

Wanda grabbed Katie's arm. "Come on, babe. Let's dance."

Katie hastily put down her Coke can and followed Wanda onto the makeshift dance floor, which was now full of singing and whooping men and women, stamping their feet and pumping the air with clenched fists. While dancing, Katie, mindful of her promise to herself, deliberately faced away from the door so she wouldn't be able to see anyone that entered the building.

When the first song ended, Katie and Wanda waited for the next track to start. When it did, Katie began to dance again with a deliberate, sexy gracefulness that began to draw the eyes of a few males seated around the floor. A small space appeared around the two women, and perfectly aware of the attention they were both receiving, Katie and Wanda began to dance as though they were harem dancers. The men around the floor wolf whistled and cheered in appreciation and applauded the exhibition. Katie glanced at her friend and they both laughed exuberantly.

Staff Sergeant Joe Anderson, entering the building, instantly saw Katie, and took in every detail of her appearance in a flash. The attraction he felt for her was even stronger now that he was seeing her again in the flesh. His gaze completely captured by Katie as she danced, he was barely aware of one of his men thrusting a can of Coke into his hand. He was intensely aware of her hair gleaming under the harsh lights, the way the brilliant white T-shirt fitted her upper torso like a glove and showed off her tanned skin to perfection. The way her combat trousers hugged her bottom before widening to cover her long legs caused his stomach to turn over. He continued to watch her as she laughed, throwing her head back, the smile lighting up her face and causing her green eyes to sparkle. He was well aware of the sensation that she and her friend was causing, was acutely aware that the eyes of many of the men in the NAAFI were watching them.

Joe had been determined that he would not attend the NAAFI that evening but, as the day had gone on, he had crumbled. After making up his mind that he would avoid seeing Katie if he could, since the briefing with his squad leader he had tried to keep himself busy, but the tempting thought of attending the NAAFI hop that night and that she might be there had kept intruding into his thoughts and in the end, in exasperation, he had hastily showered and joined some of his men in making their way to the NAAFI — and there she was. It appeared, however, that he would be queuing up for her attention along with every other male in the room. He was neither naïve nor unaccustomed to women's attention, but his undeniably strong attraction to this woman, which had materialized in so short a time, was becoming impossible to deny. She was definitely too young for him, but he was positive that on the few occasions that they had met, she had been as equally attracted to him as he was to her.

The song finished, and laughing together, Katie and Wanda went back to the counter to finish their drinks.

"Hi, Katie."

Katie turned to a new member of the group and forced a smile of greeting onto her face. Corporal David Hudson was standing directly behind her, a smile on his face, a blush highlighting his features. Try as she might, Katie couldn't muster the slightest bit of enthusiasm at seeing him. She wanted him out of her hair. He was becoming an irritation. She felt sorry for him but that was all.

"Hello, David." She finally returned his greeting with as much friendliness in her tone as she could muster.

"You're looking good tonight, Katie," David commented, eyeing her up and down. "Really nice."

Katie could barely suppress a shudder. She felt violated by the admiring look he had given her, eyeing her up and down as though she were a piece of meat for sale. For some reason, the man made her feel uneasy, and she believed that sooner rather than later she would have to use some harsh words to get him to back off. She figured that his ego was so huge that he could not accept that a woman was not interested in him. At present, she had to continue to be polite to him if for no other reason than to avoid an out-and-out confrontation.

"Listen, Katie, there's a film being shown here tomorrow night. Do you want to come with me?"

Katie sighed inwardly and turned her face away. "Thank you, David, but the answer is still no," she replied firmly. "We've been through this before. We can be friends but I'm not going out with you." Turning back to face him in an attempt to soften the blow, Katie was a little taken aback by the look on the corporal's face.

"Not good enough for you, huh?" he asked coldly and with hostility in his tone.

Katie tried to find words to reply to the remark. "That's not it at all, and you well know it. You just can't—or won't—get the message that I don't want to go out with you. Now, back off, David. Please, just back off. No means no in my language."

Corporal Hudson was silent for a moment then he put a hand on her bare arm. "I'm sorry, Katie, believe me. I just… I really like you."

"Well, that's fine, David," Katie answered as gently as possible, shaking his hand from her arm. "I'm really flattered, but I don't want to go out with you." There was a note of finality in her voice.

Wishing that Corporal Hudson would slide out of sight, Katie took a long, cool mouthful of her Coke. Wanda tapped her on the arm to get her attention.

"What a jerk," she exclaimed.

"Yes, he's getting to be a problem," Katie stated. "He just won't give up."

Wanda lowered her head close to Katie's ear. "Have you seen your staff sergeant yet?" she asked.

Katie shook her head. "No," she answered and slowly began to sip her Coke. Sighing, she turned to glance over her shoulder and her heart leaped into her throat as she saw him standing by the door. A sudden surge of excitement made her nerves sizzle and tingles run up and down her spine.

Joe was watching her, standing completely at ease with one hand in the pocket of his combat trousers, the other holding a can of Coke. His dark blond hair was tousled and there was a faint tinge of stubble along his jaw line. He looked tired and drawn.

Katie's and Joe's gazes locked together. Katie felt heat rise to her face and her knees suddenly began to feel weak. Her breath caught in her throat and for a moment she thought she would choke. The impact of the man's presence was so powerful that she could not understand, with some amusement, why she hadn't crumpled to the floor and turned into quivering jelly.

Both Katie and Joe stayed immobile for what seemed like minutes but was probably only seconds, then Joe's eyes moved down to her boots, traveled slowly up her legs and torso and eventually arrived to rest on her face. Then he smiled at her.

Katie's breath shuddered. Thoughts tumbled in her mind and a shiver ran through her body. The feelings this man was stirring in her were, beyond a doubt, speeding out of control, and the way he had just run his eyes up her body had sent heat flooding through her veins. She knew that she was in a very heady and intoxicating situation. All women had attended briefings before being deployed to the Afghanistan theater. Although not specifically ordered against becoming entangled in relationships in-country, it was outlined to them that romances in a war theater were short-lived, passionate and usually resulted in heartbreak. She had scoffed at the idea that it would happen to her, and now this US marine staff sergeant was sending her safety mechanisms flying, her pulses racing and scattering her common sense.

Katie turned away. "Girl," she murmured to herself, "get a grip. You cannot go there."

At that moment, a slow 1950s song began to play, causing a riot of catcalls and booing. Those couples who were married or engaged — or who had become involved in a relationship — were delighted that they now had an excuse to get up and hold each other without fear of being made the butt of ribald jokes.

Katie lowered her head, glanced at her wristwatch and decided to call it a night. She wanted to go back to her tent to sort out her thoughts, try to put some of her feelings in perspective in the matter of Joe Anderson. Just as she was preparing to put down her empty Coke can and leave, someone tapped her on the shoulder.

"David!" Inexplicably angry, Katie spun round to berate the young corporal one final time and stopped. Facing her was Joe Anderson.

"Dance?" he asked quietly.

At his question, Katie, like a fool, instantly became dumbstruck. Her head was swimming with disjointed thoughts and feelings, completely at odds with her usual logical and calm nature. Finally, she nodded her agreement and followed the tall figure out onto the temporary dance floor.

They stood staring at each other while a few other couples moved slowly around them, not seeing them or hearing the noise about them, then Joe put one arm around her waist and pulled her gently toward him, his other hand clasping one of hers.

Katie felt his warm hand on her back, his touch burning through the material of her T-shirt to her skin. The side of her cheek rested against his jaw and neck and she could smell the odor of sand and dust on his combat fatigues and feel the tense muscles in his arms as he held her. His legs pressed against hers, and as they swayed back and forth, her pelvis rubbed gently against his, touching then connecting again as they swayed.

She felt a burning warmth where their bodies touched and the sensual thought that if this man asked her to go to bed with him, she would, popped into her mind, causing heat to rise to her face. She glanced up at him and found that he was staring down at her with a small smile on his face.

"Hi," he mouthed.

Smiling softly in return, Katie mouthed back, "Hi yourself."

At her response, Joe's smile widened and his gaze roamed her face.

As she recognized the warmth in his stare, Katie's smile widened, filled with all that she felt for him. Joe blinked and responded by pressing his hand more firmly against her back, pulling her in more tightly against him. Katie in turn wanted her body to be against every inch of his and she pressed closer until they were barely moving.

She could hear some of the soldiers who were obviously with Joe calling out, "Go, Staff Sergeant," and, "Get in there, Staff Sergeant," and it amused her. However, it was becoming obvious that they were under scrutiny by a few people in the NAAFI and that their blatant attraction to each other would inevitably become the subject of some gossip.

The song ended and Katie did not want to let go. *Will he walk away now? Is this it?* She suddenly realized that he was speaking to her. She focused on his mouth and strained to hear what he was saying.

"Do you want to leave so we can walk and talk?" he was asking.

Katie nodded and together they walked toward the doors leading outside. Loud catcalls and shouts followed them as they wended their way through the crowd, and by the time Katie and Joe exited the building, Katie's cheeks were scarlet with mortification. Her pace quickened as they reached outside and in a few paces, she was almost running. It was only when she heard Joe laughing behind her that she stopped her almost headlong flight and turned to face him.

"What?" she queried. "Why are you laughing?"

Joe immediately tried to straighten his face. "Well, that will certainly give people something to gossip about for the next few weeks."

Katie was about to make a smart retort when suddenly she burst out laughing. "It certainly will," she answered. "And my friend Wanda will be at the front of the queue. It'll give her endless satisfaction and something to wind me up about for months."

They continued walking along the dusty road, mindful of the vehicles speeding past and the many people hastening to and from their duties.

"Where would you like to go?" Joe asked her.

"You choose," Katie answered. "Anywhere is fine with me." She glanced up at him, watching his profile. He was staring ahead as though deep in thought, his face expressionless, and she quickly understood that this man did nothing without thinking things through thoroughly before making a decision.

He remained silent as they walked, and Katie felt uncomfortable at the lack of conversation. As if he sensed her thoughts, Joe glanced at her and smiled again. "Don't look so worried," he said. "I don't bite. In fact, I'm known to be the perfect gentleman."

"Since when," Katie retorted teasingly, "have the US Marines recruited gentlemen?"

"Ah, our reputation precedes us," Joe returned. "A sad fact." He paused. "You know, I had it all worked out, what I was going to say to you if I saw you tonight, but it's all gone to hell and back."

Katie laughed. "Ditto," she replied.

"I know somewhere we can go," he suddenly said. "My men set it up to use when they have downtime and they want to get away from each other. It's nothing special—the usual sand and dust—but it's quiet. Do you wanna go there?"

"That's fine," she said, heart sinking a little. So, he was going to be like all the rest, trying to get into a woman's knickers. Well, he was going to be disappointed. She was not going to put out like some of the other women on camp. As though he had sensed her thoughts, he reached out a hand.

"Hey." He placed a finger under her chin and tilted her face so that she was looking up into his. "It's a place to sit and talk," he said. "Nothing more." His eyes were so gentle that Katie knew instantly that he was speaking the truth. She nodded and cleared her throat. She went to move on but he stayed her movement again.

"I have to say something first," he began, "about last night, out on patrol. I need to apologize for the way I acted. It's just that you appeared from nowhere and scared the crap out of me. I wasn't expecting to see you out there in a firefight, and the thought of one of those bullets...? Well, I'm sorry."

Katie smiled. "It's my job, Joe," she explained gently. "I have to follow orders the same way as you do. I have to go where they send me."

"Yeah, I know," Joe responded, "but..." He stopped talking.

They continued walking along a short distance then Joe grasped her arm again, guiding her away from the road across hard-packed, dusty ground to where high stacks of wooden pallets were arrayed in rows. On passing the first row, Joe turned left then left again, and continued walking straight until they eventually reached the last row of pallets.

They stepped into a clearing where some thoughtful person had used a number of the wooden pallets to create a square windbreak with a gap left to enter its interior. Inside the windbreak were oil drums tipped onto their sides to act as seats. Beyond the clearing, Katie could see the lights from the rows and rows of tented accommodations.

Joe led her through the gap in the upright pallets and into the square space created by them. It was semi-dark and quiet, surrounded as they were by the tall stacks of wood, and the area did offer some form of seclusion for those that needed and wanted it.

"Take a seat," Joe said, and gestured to one of the oil drums. "Not exactly a coffee bar, but it serves its purpose when someone needs a little peace and quiet."

Katie started to move toward one of the oil drums, conscious that Joe was standing, watching her. At that moment, from the direction of the tents, came some music, drifting out onto the night air. The song was a slow one and poignant in its lyrics and tune.

Katie paused, listening and swaying slowly to the music, enjoying the humid air against her bare skin. She glanced up at Joe as he came to stand in front of her and they stared at each other for long seconds, both buried in dim light and shadow. The music seemed to swell around them and other background noises seemed to fade away into silence.

Joe suddenly reached out and took her hand in his. He paused as if unsure of what he wanted to do next, then pulled her gently toward him. Katie went willingly and stood so close to him that she could feel the rough material of his fatigues. His eyes were black in the darkness.

Katie held her breath, waiting for him to speak or to kiss her. He did neither of those things. Instead, one arm went around her waist, the other clasped her hand, and he started to sway to the music swelling out into the night. Katie followed him and they moved together, both sets of booted feet stirring up the dust on the ground.

Katie could feel his hand burning through her T-shirt where it rested against her back. His other hand, holding hers, was rough and firm. She closed her eyes, drinking in the feel of his body against hers. She could feel his warm breath against her cheek and moved closer to him, seeking to feel more of his body against hers. She felt the muscles of his arm holding her flex and grow tighter and the hand against her back made contact more firmly, pulling her even more tightly against him. She nuzzled her head under his jaw line and found that her mouth and nose were bare centimeters from the skin of his neck. She could smell the pure warm odor of a man and the sensations that this aroused were almost overwhelming.

As the music swelled around them, Katie raised her head and found that he had tilted his head down and his mouth was bare inches from her own. "Do you know you're driving me crazy?" he murmured.

The world seemed to stop for a moment then moved on, and she nodded. "I feel the same way," she replied, her voice husky.

Then his mouth came down on hers and Katie responded instantly and without reservation. His mouth was firm, yet warm and gentle at first, but as the kiss progressed, his grip on her back tightened and his kiss became deeper and harder. Katie responded, and matched his ardor equally, and their hot breath mingled and their breathing quickened.

A small part of Katie's mind squeaked a warning but the reckless part of her thought insanely that if he wanted to make love to her, she would do anything he wanted her to do.

She suddenly withdrew her hand from his and put it up behind his neck, her fingers entwining in his hair. Joe put his free arm around her waist and pulled her closer to him, so hard that he staggered backward.

They were both unaware of the song drifting into silence until Joe drew back, leaving Katie feeling strangely bereft. Joe's breathing was rapid and there was a rueful smile on his face. He still held her tightly against him. "Well, this has caused a clusterfuck if ever there was one," he announced his voice husky and choked with emotion.

Adrift in her own sensual feelings, the words suddenly penetrated Katie's mind and she burst out laughing. "A clusterfuck?" she echoed.

"Charlie Foxtrot, colloquial not-so-military slang for a big problem," Joe replied, grinning.

The smile slowly vanished from Katie's flushed face. "Am I a problem, Joe?" she asked slowly.

Joe kissed the top of her head. "No, Katie, you're not, but I think the brass is not going to like one of their marine staff sergeants dating a UK corporal medic. And that guy who was pestering you is not going to like it either."

"David? Oh you saw that, did you?" Katie said. "He's not going to be a problem. I told him that I wasn't interested and I think he got the message. As for the brass? Well, what they don't know won't hurt them."

Joe's answer to her reassurance was to lower his head and kiss her again. He kissed her until she was breathless, until her face flushed, her eyes gleaming. At last, he raised his head and smiled regretfully.

"I think I need to take you back to your tent. I have a patrol tomorrow night so I can't see you. It's only a twenty-four hour, a short one, so I'll be back on Thursday night."

Katie's heart sank. Another patrol, and for twenty-four hours. Only one day by Joe's standards but a lifetime for her. Now their feelings for each other were out in the open, she experienced a new fear for the safety of this man. She wanted to stay with him, envelop herself in these new feelings, spend the night with him if she had to, but common sense prevailed and she knew that this was impossible, besides breaking regulations.

"Be careful…" she began, but a finger Joe placed on her lips prevented her from finishing the sentence.

"Don't wish me luck or say be careful, please, Katie. That'd be a snake bit." When Katie frowned up at him, he laughed. "Sorry. Slang again. It means unlucky."

Light suddenly dawned on Katie's face and she forced a smile. "Sorry. I get it."

He suddenly put the palm of his hand against her left cheek. "Don't worry. I'll be back. I'll see you Thursday night, here, at 2000 hours. There's something on at our PX if you want to go with me?"

Feeling his warm hand on her skin, Katie turned her head slightly and kissed it. "I'd love to," she responded.

His hand twitching at the touch of her lips, Joe withdrew it from her face. "You're asking for trouble doing that," he said gently. "C'mon. I'll take you back to your tent." Taking her hand, he led her from the wall of pallets in the direction of the accommodations.

They reached the neat rows of drab colored fabric and stopped when they neared Tent D, the entrance facing onto a path worn down by hundreds of feet.

Joe turned to face her and took her hands. "I'll be going then," he said, "but you'll see me in a day. Stay safe, okay?" He looked as though he was going to say something more, but seemed to think better of it.

Katie moved closer to him, seeking to feel his body against hers again. "I'll be thinking of you and waiting," she said softly and kissed him gently on the lips. His hands tightened on hers and he made a move to put his arms around her but she stepped back, smiling gently. "Get out of here, Staff Sergeant Anderson, before you get caught out of bounds and before we get seen." She backed away from him, her eyes drinking in his tall figure.

She heard his soft chuckle. "Yes, ma'am. Goodnight, ma'am. Sweet dreams," was his last, softly whispered remark.

Reaching the opening to her tent, Katie stopped. "You too," she whispered.

Joe returned back the way they had come and Katie watched him go, feeling a sensual craving to have his arms around her again and his mouth on hers. As his camouflaged body disappeared into the black and white of the flickering lights, she felt disappointment that he didn't look back. Sighing, she turned, and ducking slightly, entered the humid confines of the tent, releasing the toggles that allowed the tied back flaps to fall down into place.

The tent was in darkness with everyone asleep. Katie undressed, put on her nightwear and climbed into her sleeping bag. She lay for a few minutes, fingers touching her lips gently where Joe had kissed her, thinking back over the last few hours, remembering the heat of his mouth and his tall muscular body pressed against hers, remembering the intense feelings that his kisses had aroused in her, and she shivered with delight. Her last thought before she drifted off to sleep was that she would be seeing him on Thursday, and she murmured to herself, "Please God, keep him safe."

Chapter Eleven

Awakened at her usual time, Katie allowed herself a few minutes' relaxation in her bed before she had to get up and begin her busy day. Eyes shut, the foremost picture in her mind was Joe. She could, with crystal clarity, picture the previous night — the clearing with the wooden pallet fences, the music playing from someone's distant iPod or radio, and their dance followed by the long kisses. In the confines of her sleeping bag, which was already becoming too hot, she shivered with the remembered feelings that the kisses had stirred in her.

She had never felt like this about anyone before, and the strength of her emotions brought a sense of unease in her stomach. Questions popped into her mind. *Does he feel the same way about me? He did say that I'm driving him crazy, but is he stringing me along? What is going to happen between us?* But, Katie argued with herself, Joe was older — more experienced, a seasoned veteran of past conflicts — and she sensed that he was not a shallow person, would not intentionally hurt her. Once again, she envisioned his rugged face and his deep blue eyes, and again she shivered with remembrance. She knew without a doubt that her feelings for the staff sergeant were serious, very serious, with a depth that frightened her.

"Please," she whispered. "Please, God, keep him safe and bring him back to me."

Not wanting to dwell any further on thoughts of Joe going out on patrol again or their newfound openness regarding their feelings for each other, Katie rose from her bed and went for a showers.

After showering, she arrived back at her bed space and saw Wanda making up her bed and opening up her sleeping bag to air it. "Morning, Wanda," Katie called out as she put her toilet bag in the locker alongside her camp bed.

"Hey," Wanda returned, "and where did you disappear to last night?" Katie's friend glanced at her and raised an eyebrow, winking knowingly.

"None of your business, nosy," Katie responded pertly and began to straighten and open up her own sleeping bag.

"Now don't be mean," Wanda returned in an offended tone. "I know who you left with anyway."

Katie turned swiftly to face her friend, "You do?"

Wanda nodded slowly, "Oh come on, Katie. Half the camp probably knows as well."

Katie sank down onto the edge of her bed, feeling uneasy. "Oh, Lord!" she exclaimed.

"Well, what did you expect?" Wanda continued, exasperated. "You left way too early in the evening, the place was packed and, to top things off, you left with a bloody staff sergeant. To make matters even worse, you couldn't have got a damn bayonet between the two of you when you were dancing."

Katie remained silent for a minute or two then glanced back at the other woman, smiling cheekily. "Well, Joe did say it was going to be a clusterfuck."

"A...a what?" Wanda laughed out loud.

"Apparently, a clusterfuck means a big problem," Katie replied, grinning. She stood up and continued getting ready for work. "Oh well. It will give the camp something to chat over for a few days. That's if they haven't got anything better to do."

She waited for Wanda's response, but instead looked up to find her friend standing beside her. Wanda spoke quietly and seriously. "Listen, Katie. You be careful. You remember what we talked about the other night? Don't get serious about this guy, okay? Have fun. By all means, have lotsa fun, but don't get serious. Now you listen to your momma."

Katie turned to her friend, a smile of appreciation on her face. "I get it, Momma. Your words have been noted. Now, you want to shut up and come to breakfast with me?"

"Most definitely. You definitely need my protection. Let me get dressed and I'll be with you in two."

"Meaning five or ten?" Katie quipped with resignation.

Back from her shower and dressed, Wanda sang out, "Ready, girl?" as though Katie had been the one keeping her waiting. They both sauntered outside into the bright sunlight, putting on sunglasses and their caps. As the women exited the tent, they both stopped dead as the heat of the day hit them like a slap in the face.

"Whew," Katie exclaimed, "this heat sucks. I'll never get used to it." Her cap instantly felt like a constricting band encircling her head.

"Let's get a move on," Wanda complained. "This sun is lethal."

The two women hurried to the mess, desperate to get out of the harsh sunlight and into the air-conditioned interior. Once inside, they removed their caps and sunglasses and stopped, relishing the cool air pouring down from the ceiling. As she had done every day since they had met, Katie glanced around looking for Joe, but couldn't see him. She did, however, notice that behind the food counter stood a number of Army cooks in whites.

"Oh crap!" On recognizing one of the cooks, Katie cursed aloud. Wanda heard the expletive and turned to see what had caused her friend to utter it.

"Bloody Corporal David Hudson!" Katie offered as an explanation. "All I need to start my day off."

"Just ignore the jerk," Wanda reasoned quietly. "You don't owe him a thing."

"He thinks I do," Katie rejoined, equally quietly.

They joined the queue, picking up plastic trays and waiting their turn to choose their food. Katie chose some scrambled eggs on toast, intent on avoiding the food where Corporal Hudson was serving. Unfortunately, he saw her. That morning, however, he did not offer her his usual smile, only left his hot plate and moved toward where she was waiting to collect a glass of fresh orange juice.

"Morning, Katie," he greeted.

"Hello, David," Katie replied in as friendly a manner as possible.

"Who was that you left with last night?" Corporal Hudson asked. Katie was taken aback at his tone, which contained a barely controlled anger and frustration.

Angered, she snapped, "That is none of your business!"

"We'll see about that," David Hudson exclaimed sharply and went back to his position behind the counter.

Katie gazed after him in shock then glanced at Wanda, who was also looking after the retreating back, completely nonplussed with a little anxiety on her face.

"What a jerkwad!" she exclaimed. "What's rattled his cage?"

"I think he's going to be trouble," Katie stated worriedly. "He's completely got the wrong end of the stick."

"Yep," answered Wanda, "but that's his funeral. C'mon. Let's go eat... If we can find a table."

Trying to shake off the uneasiness that the altercation with the cook had caused, Katie led the way, looking around for a free table at which to eat. They eventually found one and sat down. There was little time for conversation between the two friends as they consumed their meals quickly, Katie conscious of time ticking on. Having finished, they piled their plates and cups onto trays, rose from the table and went to the racks to deposit them onto one of the shelves. Once outside in the harsh sunlight again, Katie turned to Wanda.

"Have a good day," she said, slapping her friend on the arm. "See you later."

"Take care, you," Wanda said, about-turned and strode off toward her place of work. Katie moved off in the opposite direction, and wincing at the heat, began to make her way at a brisk stride down the long, dusty road toward the CTH.

The long walk to the CTH was particularly difficult that morning as the heat was scorching and oppressive. The whole sky was tinged with a yellow haze, the sun a blurred murky orb. The hot wind that gusted sporadically, created miniature sand and dust whirlwinds particles that stung Katie's exposed skin. As she marched along, she found it difficult to draw in a breath, as though all oxygen had been leached from the air, and she had to grit her teeth so they acted as filters for the clouds of dust that hovered around her face.

At the halfway mark, a light sweat broke out on Katie's forehead and arms. Sand and dust stuck to her moist skin, managing to get down the front of her T-shirt, and the webbing strap holding her weapon, as light as it was, chafed at a sore patch along the strap of her bra. Attempting to ignore the increasing discomfort, she stepped up her pace and then heard the harsh blare of a vehicle horn behind her.

Glancing back over her shoulder, she saw a camouflaged, open-topped Land Rover pull over to the side of the road and was relieved to see Sergeant Webster gesture for her to get into the vehicle. Katie hurried toward him and obligingly climbed in.

"You're an angel, Sergeant," she quipped. "I'm so glad you came along. I was about ready to melt."

"No problem," Ron Webster replied. "An angel I'm not, but glad to be of service."

Walking along the opposite side of the road toward the mess with some members of his squad, Joe Anderson saw Katie getting into the Land Rover. She didn't return his gaze or wave so he knew that she hadn't seen him. He watched as she tilted her head back and laughed at something the male driver said to her, and Joe continued observing her as she rested one booted foot on the dashboard, steadying herself as the speed of the vehicle increased on the uneven, dry road. Even with the cap on her head and sunglasses shielding her beautiful eyes, he still admired the vitality and exuberance that was evident in her actions and the way her mouth curved into her special, brilliant smile.

Joe had woken up that morning with his head teeming with images of the night before, and he knew that kissing Katie had sent his feelings over the edge. She aroused him sexually like no other woman had done before and it was a new experience for him to feel as horny as the proverbial schoolboy. He had become fully aware of the fact that his concentration on his duties was becoming a lost cause and this was not good for either himself or his men. Try as he might, he could not rid himself of the tantalizing imagery of Katie's green eyes or the feel of her soft mouth under his. He had a vague idea that for the first time in his life, he had fallen in love.

In five minutes, Katie and her companion arrived at the sprawling CTH.

"Here we go," Sergeant Webster exclaimed. They jumped out of the vehicle and went into the air-conditioned comfort of the medical facility.

Katie put her cap into her locker, and with a little time to spare before reporting for duty, she hurried along to Ward One to see Private Berwick, who still remained a patient within the CTH. Entering the ward, Katie went straight to the first bed. Private Berwick was lying with his eyes closed, but on hearing movement he opened them, and his face lit up at the sight of her.

"Morning, Jeff," Katie greeted. "How are you doing today?"

"Morning, Katie. I'm doing okay," the young private replied.

Katie picked up the chart attached to the end of the hospital bed and quickly glanced through it. The young

British soldier remained on two intravenous drips, one that fed a number of antibiotics into his arm and another that held a saline solution to keep his body hydrated. She noted in the chart that his temperature had been elevated since the night before and that he had complained of pain in the stump of his leg.

Setting the metal clipboard holding the chart back in its position, Katie walked to his side, and mindful of his injury, gently sat on the edge of the bed. "How's your pain, Jeff?" she asked.

"Not too bad now that I've been allowed to pop some pills," Jeff answered. "It was a little bad during the night and they say that I have a bit of a fever but things are fine now."

Katie's heart ached for the young man. Two weeks in-country and he was now significantly maimed. Sure, there were artificial aids and prosthetic limbs that he would be offered back in the UK, but his young life would be altered forever and he would need much rehabilitation back home once they had him stabilized enough for him to be flown back to his family. But he was young and strong and the one good thing about his situation was that he would be going home.

"That's good, Jeff. I'm glad things are improving." She stood up. "I have to get on now, but I'll come back and see you later. You take care."

"Katie," Private Berwick began.

Katie turned her attention back to the patient, a questioning look on her face.

A smile flitted across the young private's face. "Scuttlebutt tells me you and a staff sergeant have a thing going," he announced.

Katie blushed instantly and was momentarily horrified that the news had gotten around the camp so quickly. But she should have guessed. Composing herself, she laughed, "Well, that didn't take long to get out, did it? How did you get to find out?"

"Some of the guys from my unit came to see me," Private Berwick answered. "I know the staff sergeant and he's a great guy, Katie, and a lucky man."

"That's sweet of you to say," Katie responded softly. "And thank you." She waited for the young man to acknowledge her statement, and with a last smile at him and another smile directed at Joe's US marine in the next bed, she left the ward. She made her way back to her locker, and after opening it, retrieved a fresh set of green scrubs, floral hair cover, blue bootees and dingy canvas shoes. She took the bundle to the toilet, let herself in, locked the door behind her and changed.

Katie made her way to the briefing room where a large white board was regularly updated with patient's details and their medical statuses. There were already two trauma nurses present, Sergeant Webster, an anesthetist, a surgeon and a CTM. Eight casualties and Private Berwick were the only patients remaining in the CTH. All patients had been released from the CCU and were now in Ward Two, doing well. Katie was pleased to hear that Private Berwick was also doing well — improving slowly physically and appearing mentally to be adapting to the loss of his limb. However, time would tell if his positive mental attitude would continue to improve or if he would suffer a relapse. He would continue on the antibiotics for a further week, dressings changed once a day, painkillers on request and a saline drip to keep him hydrated. He would be going home once he was off the antibiotics.

Sergeant Webster then stood up to continue the briefing. "There is a patrol going out tonight so there may be casualties. Before we all go off duty, I want every item of equipment checked and double-checked.

We have to prepare for a worst-case scenario. Well, that's all folks. Let's get on with the day."

Katie left the briefing room to attend to the patients arriving for sick parade then went in to one of the two empty theaters. At the moment, the CTH was quiet. Stainless steel equipment shone and was in position, ready for use, white walls gleamed in the harsh overhead lights and instruments that would be required in the event of an incident were arrayed in neat regimental rows on spotless trolleys and tables. She went quietly about her usual duties of checking the instrument trays, making sure that the surgeons had swabs and scalpels and inspecting the retractors and amputation tools to make sure that they were clean and in order.

She went along to Theater Two to find a British and US surgeon playing a board game, the board itself set out on the operating table with counters strewn across it. They both looked up as she came in. "Care to join us?" Major Burns asked, raising his head to glance in Katie's direction.

"I don't have a clue what you're playing, sir, so I'll decline and leave you to it," Katie replied, smiling. She quickly went about her duties of checking the equipment and instruments, then left to make her way to the R&R room.

Katie collected a plastic cup, one of many stacked haphazardly on a shelf above the coffee machine, and poured herself a cup of coffee. It smelled strong and bitter but she retrieved some milk from the fridge and diluted it to her taste before finding the most comfortable chair in the room and sitting down. Glancing at her watch then the clunking clock on the wall, she noted that it was already 1000 hours. Fifteen minutes' downtime and she would visit Private

Berwick again, check his observations then check in with Sergeant Webster to see what other duties he had in store for her. As of now, she needed to relax.

Leaning back against the sagging cushions, she closed her eyes. Joe's image popped into her mind and she sighed gently. *What is he doing at this moment? Is he thinking of me as I'm thinking of him? Does he feel the same way about me as I do him?* Those questions would probably never be answered because, time in this case, was not conducive to sorting out a relationship, to letting feelings resolve themselves into something long-term. Katie's feelings for Joe however, were deep and true, regardless of how quickly they had developed.

Katie opened her eyes, blinked and sipped at the hot coffee, cringing at the underlying bitterness. At least it would keep her energized and awake. There was nothing like a good burst of caffeine to put things into perspective.

A few minutes later, Katie finished the last of her coffee, threw the cup into a waste bin and left the R&R room. As she walked quickly along the empty corridor, a strident alarm sounded throughout the CTH. Instantly, adrenaline spilled through her veins, her senses switched to high alert and she ran for the briefing room. She could hear pounding feet behind and in front of her as the medical staff hurried to find out what was about to shatter the false peace of the CTH. On reaching the briefing room, Katie went inside.

"Okay, people. Two injured being medevacked in. Info is that one has a gunshot wound in the arm, the other has a shrapnel wound or wounds in the legs. Let's go."

The quiet, relaxed atmosphere quickly vanished and the teams instantly became alert. Katie quickly donned a clean a clean scrub smock then she and a fellow CTM grabbed a gurney each and wheeled them outside the front doors of the building, ready for the incoming casualties.

Both teams heard the siren of an approaching Army ambulance, and within a few minutes, it had pulled up beneath the canopy in front of the doors of the CTH. The back doors opened forcefully and two US Army corpsmen in full combat clothing appeared at the doors. Both the driver and his passenger also leaped from the front of the vehicle and ran around to the rear. Lifted out of the back of the ambulance on stretchers and placed on the waiting gurneys, the two corpsmen traveling in the back held intravenous IVs in the air. As Katie was one of only two CTMs on duty, she took over the role of CTM to one of the trauma teams who, allocated the gunshot wound, rushed the gurney through to Trauma Room One.

After delivering her patient to the waiting trauma team, Katie, armed with a clipboard to which was attached a form, took down the patient's details by glancing quickly at the soldier's dog tags. The injured man was moaning and awake so she quickly went to his head, bent down, and speaking loudly but gently and clearly asked him for some further personal details. Gasping with pain and distress, the soldier attempted to give Katie the answers she required.

The wounded soldier smelled bad. He had obviously been out in the field for quite some time. His face was grimy with a chin covered in stubble where he hadn't shaved in days and his MTPCs were covered in dust and blood. His upper torso was drenched with the bright red liquid.

Working as a well-organized team, one member lifted the soldier's chin to open his airway to enable a high flow of oxygen to be given via a face mask. His breathing was assessed as being normal albeit rapid and shallow with pain, so the team went on to make an assessment as to his general state. Considerable bleeding had occurred, but as the soldier was young and fit, this did not pose a significant problem. Katie managed to obtain good intravenous access with two large bore IV cannula, a necessity in case of delayed tachycardia and hypotension due to shock and blood loss. The leading trauma surgeon performed a rapid assessment of the young soldier's neurological status and a trauma nurse began to quickly remove the grimed combat clothing so that the entire body of the young man could be examined for exit and entry wounds. Katie fastened a blood pressure cuff around the uninjured left arm and noted that the blood pressure, although a little low, was within normal parameters.

"I have a BP of systolic sixty-five mmHg," she reported calmly and proceeded to monitor other vital signs such as blood gases, CXR and ECG output. Once the uniform was, Katie gently and carefully began to wash away dried blood and dirt from around the wound and from the soldier's torso and face. A second trauma nurse hurried into the room with six units of crossmatched blood and Katie promptly hung the bags from IV stands and connected them to the cannula. A portable X-ray machine was then wheeled into position over the soldier's body and X-rays taken above, below and directly over the wound. The surgeon studied the X-rays and beamed confidently.

"No bullet in situ. It's clean. Let's get him to theater, seal him up, put him on intravenous antibiotics and give him a tetanus shot. He's going to be fine."

Having done her part on the trauma team, Katie stepped back and watched as the young soldier was wheeled quickly from Trauma Room One and into theater where a surgical team waited to commence the surgical procedure.

The trauma team who had stabilized the young soldier meandered out of the trauma room into the next one to observe the ongoing treatment of the second wounded soldier with the shrapnel wounds. Katie surveyed the mess with resignation. *No rest for the wicked* she thought. She sighed and began the task of clearing up. The instruments had to be sterilized again, the floor washed and dried and a clean sheet put down to replace the gruesomely stained one on the table.

An hour later, the room was as clean as it had been before. Surveying it with hands on hips, Katie inspected every counter and inch of floor, restocked the instrument trays and made sure the equipment was back in its rightful place. She then went outside into the corridor, where Sergeant Webster approached her.

"Both of the lads are out of theater and doing okay," he said. "The shrapnel wound wasn't deep. He'll be a bit sore for a few days and will be here for a time, but should recover okay if infection doesn't set in. The other lad will have a sore arm and be on light duties for a week or two until his wound heals, but he's going to be okay as well. Do me a favor, lass. They'll need half-hourly observations for an hour or two. Can you do the first lot then order up some chow from the mess? We'll need to eat here, I think. Let's just hope to high heaven that that's the lot for now."

Katie nodded and Sergeant Webster patted her arm.

Katie went to the ward and smiled at Private Berwick. "Looks like you have some new neighbors," she said as she walked past his bed to the two new occupants who were now in the beds next to him. The US marine was gone, discharged and flown home to the States.

"How are they doing?" Jeff asked, glancing at the two pale-faced soldiers who were still sleeping off the effects of their anesthetic.

"They came through their surgeries well and they're going to be fine," Katie replied. She went to the bed that held the gunshot victim, lifted the metal clipboard with the patient's chart from the end of the bed, fished out a pen from the breast pocket of her scrub smock and proceeded to take the young soldier's vital signs. "Lance Corporal John Evans," she noted. She took the lance corporal's pulse and noted the result down on the chart, then proceeded to check his temperature, listened to his heart and checked pupil reaction with a penlight. All were stable and normal. She then moved on to the next bed and proceeded to do the same for Sergeant Ben Johnson, noticing that his breathing sounded slightly labored. Probably a side effect from the anesthetic, but she noted it in the chart.

Once completed, Katie went back to Jeff Berwick's bed. "All okay," she confirmed to him. "Now, I'm going to be ordering some food from the mess. Do you fancy some lunch?"

"That would be good," the young private answered. "Chicken, if they have it."

"Chicken it is," Katie agreed.

She went to the radio and proceeded to order food to be sent to the CTH.

Chapter Twelve

At the USMC headquarters, Joe made his way to one of the briefing rooms where the members of his squad who were to accompany him on patrol that night, were already seated and waiting for his arrival. Sergeant Louis Eastman, assistant patrol leader, greeted him as he walked in.

"Morning, Staff Sergeant."

"Morning, Sergeant. Everyone here?"

"Yes, Staff Sergeant."

Sergeant Eastman turned to face the talking men, "Okay, Marines, let's have some hush now for the staff sergeant," he shouted.

There was immediate silence except for the rustle of combats and a cough or two.

"Okay," Joe began, "let's get to it. I take it you've all received and read the WARNO advising you about the patrol tonight?"

A chorus of "Yes, Staff Sergeant" rang out at his question.

"Excellent," Joe responded. "Then I trust there'll be no problems understanding what we have to do."

"Won't be any clusterfucks from us, Staff Sergeant," Lance Corporal George Westerman, pointman for the patrol, remarked. "It's them other dickwads that are gonna be the problem."

"While I have your back on that, Westerman," Joe responded dryly, "let's stow that shit for now, shall we?"

"Righto, Staff Sergeant."

"Right. If Westerman will allow us to continue." Joe went on, "our patrol area will be grid reference Golf Nine Alpha Five. It will involve a twenty click patrol, NNW three hundred thirty-five and a half degrees five clicks, West two hundred seventy degrees five clicks, South one hundred eighty degrees five clicks and SSW two hundred two and a half degrees five clicks. Our objective rally point will be at position West two hundred seventy degrees two clicks.

"The patrol is a twenty-four hour one. Intel reports that some Terries have been spotted somewhere in the location of our patrol. There is no info on numbers at present. I need to emphasize that we are purely a recon patrol and have no orders to engage. We just get our asses in, have a look-see then get our butts out. No other friendlies will be in our location so if we run into some shit, we're on our own.

"You already know — or you should by now if you've been paying attention — that the local terrain is mostly flat with some rocky hills, dry river beds and very sparse vegetation. There will be little or no cover, so our primary concern will be staying frosty and keeping eyes on at all times. You should all now have your radio frequencies and call signs and know your specific tasks. We have been designated Echo. Everyone is to report to the motor pool at 2330 hours, with no exceptions, Corporal Lewis. So, get back to your pits, get your equipment ready, test fire your weapons and get fed and rehydrated." Joe eyeballed his patrol tail-end Charlie as he concluded the briefing.

Corporal Ben Lewis attempted to look offended, "That's not fair, Staff Sergeant," he remarked.

"Neither is my ass," Joe exclaimed and everyone chuckled. "Now, I don't need to go on and on. It's a waste of my breath and your time. You're not a bunch of cherries so I don't need to tell you that after the fuck up with the blast the other night, we need to be extra vigilant. There will be no fucking around and no heroics. We need to stay focused on the task in hand. If anybody fucks up due to carelessness, I'll shoot them myself. Do I make myself clear? If we make contact, we do our job and get out of there, and I don't want to have to drag anyone out of there in a body bag just because they got themselves killed."

Joe glanced around at the men seated before him, some scribbling notes, all looking serious now and paying attention.

"Okay, let's close this briefing down. I'll see you tonight. Marines dismissed."

"Oorah, Staff Sergeant," came the brief mantra from the squad as the men rose to their feet and left the briefing room.

Joe spent a further few minutes speaking with Sergeant Eastman, discussing the merits of the patrol that night, possible strategies and what the outcome might be, then they both left to go about their daily duties.

* * * *

The rest of Katie's day was uneventful. No further casualties arrived at the CTH and Katie was free to perform half-hourly observations on the two new patients. Both woke up from their anesthetics. There were no complications, and after pain medication, they rested easy.

At 1700 hours, Katie went to the theaters and trauma rooms and performed a final thorough check of the equipment and instrument trolleys, keen to make sure that everything was in order as Sergeant Webster had requested that morning, in the event that they had more wounded tomorrow. She sincerely hoped that they didn't because she had assumed that the patrol that Sergeant Webster had mentioned that morning was the one that Joe would be taking out beyond the wire.

Finally, at 1830 hours, Sergeant Webster approached Katie and said, "Get going, Katie. Go get some chow and some sleep."

"Thanks, Sergeant," Katie responded with a tired smile. "I'll see you tomorrow." Making her way to her locker, she changed from her soiled scrubs into her MTPCs, put on her cap, and after attaching her helmet to her webbing belt, retrieved her weapon and walked slowly out of the CTH into the heat.

It was still daylight, with the sun shining strongly, and Katie blinked in the harsh light. She began the long walk to the mess, initially with the intention of getting something to eat, but ten minutes later she decided against it. She wasn't hungry and was too tired, so she strode past the mess and headed directly to her tent. When she entered, it was empty except for Wanda, lying on her bed reading a magazine. Her friend glanced up as Katie came in, and sat up.

"Wow, you look knackered," she stated.

"Thank you, friend. I feel it," Katie replied, unfastening her helmet and throwing it to the floor where it bounced and rolled to a stop.

"Bad day?" Wanda asked sympathetically.

"Not really. Just a long one. Two wounded came in but they're going to be fine. They just needed patching up and half-hourly observations, then the sergeant mentioned that there was a patrol going out tonight and we may have wounded tomorrow so I had to check and recheck the theaters and trauma rooms." She yawned widely. "Well, it's me for the shower and then I'm going to turn in early."

Katie collected her towel, toilet bag and nightwear and went out the back to the showers. They were both unoccupied and as this was a quiet time with everyone in the mess, she treated herself to a long, hot shower. Once finished, she felt more human and joined Wanda back in the tent. The temperature had dropped slightly and dim lights were coming on all over the base. Katie pulled on a shapeless Army issue dressing gown and thrust her feet into her fluffy pink slippers. Groaning slightly, she pulled a water bottle from her pack, took a long drink then slumped onto her bed and lay down.

"Are you going out tonight?" she asked her friend.

"Nope," Wanda answered. "Quiet night tonight. You?"

"No," Katie answered drowsily.

"Where's your staff sergeant?" Wanda asked casually.

"Going out on patrol tonight." Katie's eyes flashed open. "I'm seeing him on Thursday night, though."

"Oh." Wanda's response was falsely non-committal. "Tough."

"Yes, it is, very tough," Katie murmured and closed her eyes, determined to get the fresh images of Joe Anderson out of her mind. "I'm for sleep." Turning on her side, she plumped her pillow to make it more comfortable and within minutes was fast asleep. Two hours later however, she woke abruptly as somebody shook her arm gently.

"Katie. Katie." She could hear her name being called but felt heavy with sleep and groaned, shrugging off the irritating hand.

The hand was insistent and in the end she opened weary eyes and glared at the offending person. "This'd better be good," she mumbled with irritation.

"There's someone outside to see you," came the response from the woman bending over her.

For a few seconds, Katie remained half asleep then the woman's statement sank in. Sitting up quickly she asked, "What time is it?"

"2130 hours," came the answer.

She'd slept for all of two hours and felt fuzzy-headed and warm. "Damn. If it's that Corporal Hudson," she stated, mostly to herself, "I'll send him away with my size seven up his rear end."

Katie stood up from her bed, smoothed down her short hair, straightened and retied the sexless dressing gown and went outside the tent. Once outside, she stopped dead in her tracks.

Joe Anderson was standing outside in full combats, body armor, combat helmet and gloves. A huge bergen leaned against his leg and slung over his right shoulder was his M4 carbine. For a split second Katie froze with surprise then smiled. "Joe?" she said delightedly.

"In person," he said and grinned.

Katie walked toward him, heart thundering in her chest, suddenly breathless and sure that it was plastered all over her face how she felt about him. As she approached, he suddenly glanced down at her footwear then proceeded to draw his eyes up her tanned legs to the shapeless dressing gown that had a distinct droop on the right-hand side.

He suddenly laughed aloud. "Very fetching," he said, taking off his combat gloves.

Reaching him, Katie stopped. "Ha ha," she said, pointing to the dressing gown. "Compliments of the British Army. And the slippers were a gift from a friend of mine back in the UK. She thought it would add a little feeling of home while I was here."

"It certainly adds something, although I can't figure out what," Joe teased, then his smile faded. "Come with me."

Taking her hand in one of his, he lifted the enormous bergen with the other and led her down the narrow alleyway between her tent and the adjoining one. Halfway down there was a patch of darkness where the lights didn't quite reach. He let go of his bergen, dropping it to the ground, leaned the rifle against the side of a tent, and with one swift movement, put his arms around her and pulled her close to him.

"I've missed you," he whispered.

Katie put her arms around his neck, knocking his helmet slightly askew, and pressed her body close to his. "Me too, Joe," she said softly. "It's been a nightmare. I thought you'd be gone."

"I had to see you," Joe explained. "I couldn't go on patrol without coming here." Then he was kissing her as deeply and as passionately as he had the night before and again, Katie was lost in the sensations that he aroused in her. He held her body so tightly against his that she could barely breathe, but she didn't care. Their breathing became increasingly more rapid as their kiss became deeper. Eventually, Joe raised his head, looking down at her.

"What are you doing to me, Katie Walker? I can't stop thinking about you."

Katie smiled sensuously. "Well, Staff Sergeant, is there anything that I can do to persuade you not to go out on patrol tonight?" She knew that she was using a sexual connotation and it was evident in her tone, her look and her body language. It was also something that she had never done with any man before, and by the look on Joe's face, he knew what she was doing.

He grinned and put a hand against the side of her face. Kissing her mouth gently, he responded softly and sincerely, "Don't tempt me." With that last remark, he bent his head again and once more his warm mouth came down on hers. Katie ran her fingers through his hair at the base of his skull, placed a warm hand on the back of his neck then trailed her fingers along his jawline, resulting in her palm resting against his face. She could feel the faint roughness of stubble against her skin and taste the hot moistness of his mouth, and she uttered a small moan.

"Please don't go tonight," she whispered, pressing her body against his, and his response was to tighten his arms around her and kiss her even harder and more passionately. Eventually he worked his hands beneath the dressing gown, roaming up and down her back until they grasped her buttocks and pulled her hips closer to him. She could feel his erection through his combat trousers and her thin sleep shorts, knew that he was very aroused, and in turn became more aroused herself.

After a slight struggle, but with determination, Katie eventually managed to get her hands up inside the back of his combat shirt and body armor. She could feel his warm skin and the ripple of his muscles through his T-shirt and she moved the palms of her hands in a massaging motion across his back until impatiently, she pulled his T-shirt up out of the waistband of his trousers and thrust her hands beneath it. The feel of his warm, smooth skin caused her to shiver, and she felt him squirm against her and he made a moaning sound. She trailed her fingernails down his sides and this time it was Joe's turn to shiver.

Their kisses began to turn more heated and Joe thrust his hands up inside her sleep T-shirt and placed them on her stomach. The muscles there quivered and flexed and she gasped at the feel of his warm, rough palms.

He suddenly stopped kissing her and thrust her away from him. He was silent for some seconds then said huskily, "God, Katie, I really don't want to go but I have to."

He stepped back and his arms dropped from around her. He lowered his head, breathing rapidly and harshly, and was strangely silent. The noises of the camp came flowing back into their tiny, silent world.

"What's wrong, Joe?" she asked, voice quavering slightly.

Joe remained silent for a few more seconds then shook his head, the strap of his helmet swinging with the motion. Taking a deep breath he replied, "This is the first time in my life that I don't want to leave someone and go out on patrol. But there's nothing wrong, Katie. Everything is fine, but I have to go." He followed this statement up with a glance at his watch. "Shit!" he hissed. "I'm going to be late."

He glanced back at Katie. "The patrol leaves in about thirty minutes. I've gotta get gone." He quickly bent down, swung his bergen up onto his back, shrugged into the webbing straps and picked up his weapon. He stood still for a minute or two, staring at her as though drinking in her image, then he smiled gently.

"Take care of yourself, okay? I'll be back in a day. I'll meet you at the pallets at 2000 hours on Thursday night, like we said. And we'll talk." Taking a pace forward, he gently kissed her on the forehead, then turned and walked away from her.

Katie watched as he disappeared from sight after a few seconds, and she was left standing alone between the tents in the darkness. Finally, tightening the dressing gown around her, she walked thoughtfully back to her tent. The word patrol kept rebounding inside her head. He would be gone, out there in the dark, hostile desert with insurgents hunting the area, the temperature sometimes dropping to below freezing at night, uncomfortable and lonely. *Will he be safe? Will he come back?* The questions tortured her because she could find no answers that could allay her fears. Feeling dejected and empty without him, Katie reached her tent and went inside to sleep and try to make it through until Joe was back.

Chapter Thirteen

Joe Anderson marched briskly away from Katie toward the main road that would lead him down to the motor pool where he would be meeting his squad. It took all his willpower not to turn and go back to her. He wanted her desperately, but knew that there was no way he was going to make love to her in a dark place on the camp like she was some kind of easy lay. Her little plea asking him not to go had torn at his heart, but he had a duty and she knew that. The request in the heat of the moment was purely involuntary from her, and she knew that it was an empty plea because she was as duty-bound as he was.

Joe deliberately blanked his mind to the warm thoughts of the woman he had just been with, knowing that if he allowed one second of distraction to interfere with the next twenty-four hours either he or some members of his squad could be dead. It took an enormous effort to push his thoughts of Katie from his mind, but by focusing on the planning and logistics and what might be waiting for Echo squad out on the flat, dusty terrain of Helmand Province, he succeeded.

He turned sharply out onto the hard, dusty road and strode along it for some time. It was dark but there was enough glow from lights in the tents, from headlights of vehicles passing him and from various buildings to allow him to see. He also had his flashlight, the rubber handle of which he had slid under two pieces of Velcro attached to his shoulder. Due to its position, the red beam angled down to just in front of his feet and lit up the puffs of dust stirred up by his boots, which swirled and shimmered in the intermittent light.

He felt uneasy that night and couldn't place his finger on why. It was stifling hot with a searing wind gusting forcefully every now and again, and he could feel particles of sand stinging his face. As he gazed up at the sky, he noticed that the night's blackness was tinged with yellow and the moon was wreathed in yellow clouds. He had the feeling that bad weather was on the way, and knowing his luck, it would materialize while he was out on patrol.

Dismissing the weather, Joe began to assess each piece of his equipment individually. His bergen, although weighing some fifty pounds fully loaded, rested easy at his back. Items in and on the pack that might have made a noise, were taped down. If he were to take a jump, nothing would move. His body armor fitted like a glove and was worn and flexible in places to allow him to move freely, and he barely felt the weight. His boots, companions on many desert patrols, fit well and were comfortably worn in all the right places. His helmet with the night vision mounted plate and radio headset in its mesh and canvas sling connected to his Personal Role Radio in its pouch attached to his armor, rested snug on his head. He held his M4 carbine by the middle of its stock, liking the feel of the cold, oily metal against his skin, allowing the thought that it was like holding a good woman. That prompted a picture of Katie to pop into his mind again. "Nope," he berated himself. "Don't go there."

He went back to the mental checklist of his equipment. Ammunition magazines, MREs — enough for twenty-four hours — first-aid kit, bladders of water, mess kit, compass, night vision goggles, poncho, sleeping bag and pad. The list went on and on but eventually he was satisfied that he had everything that he should have. If he didn't, then it was going to be tough shit.

He finally saw the motor pool two hundred meters ahead. Aside from the airfield, the motor pool was the biggest section on the base. Situated adjacent to the fuel dump it consisted of containers for the offices and rows and rows of regimentally aligned Jackal Armored Vehicles, Viking all-terrain vehicles, Foxhound vehicles, Bulldog APCs, together with general run-of-the-mill ambulances and ME35s and 4-tonner trucks.

As his long pace ate up the meters, Joe calculated what the end state of this recon patrol might be. His squad consisted of fifteen good men, all seasoned and experienced veterans, trustworthy, reliable and skilled, able to carry out their tasks without supervision. He was optimistic that they would reach the end of the operation safely.

Joe's thoughts wavered a little as he heard the loud roar of aircraft engines. Glancing up and in the direction of the airfield, he saw a Harrier jump jet lift up from one of the runways, hover for a few brief minutes, turn with the aid of canted down thrusters and take off into the night sky. He watched its red and white blinking landing and warning lights disappear into the blackness and a fresh waft of aviation fuel and exhaust came drifting to him on the quiet night air.

As he reached the motor pool, used as the pre-staging area for the patrol, he heard loud voices and raucous laughter. He could see his men leaning casually against vehicles or seated on the dusty ground, supported by their oversized bergens. They all appeared to be in good spirits, unperturbed at the fact that they would be leaving the relatively safe confines of the base to go out into the pitch-black desert. They were all well aware that any one of them could be shot or blown up that night. But that was what a Marine was all about. All of them were career marines, professional and skilled. A marine would continue to do everything 'by the book', no matter how hostile the situation, even when he was tired or believed contact with the enemy was unlikely. A veteran marine would never waste time trying to figure things out but would operate on instinct and training.

As Joe glanced back over his shoulder to see if it was safe to cross the road, he heard one of the marines, obviously on the lookout for his approach, shout out, "Old man approaching," and Joe grinned to himself.

Immediately all conversation ceased and the squad straightened up from their seemingly apathetic positions or jumped to their feet.

Joe stopped, facing them. Sergeant Louis Eastman detached himself from the group and came to stand by his side.

"Headcount, Sergeant?" Joe asked, turning his attention to his assistant patrol leader.

"All present, Staff Sergeant," Sergeant Eastman answered. "Even Corporal Lewis has made the effort. All weapons tested and checked. All call signs and frequencies double-checked and tested. This lot are fed and watered. It's confirmed that no other friendlies will be out there tonight, just us jerks."

"Outstanding," Joe replied and turned to face front. "Okay, ladies, listen up. There is no abort order so the mission is a go for tonight. Our transport will be along in about ten to take us outside the wire and to our drop-off point. We offload and do our recce as we've always done, quickly, no fucking around, with eyes on for everyone, no exceptions. Is that understood?"

There were grunted replies of "Yes, Staff Sergeant" and "Fucking A, Staff Sergeant."

"Excellent," Joe responded, satisfied.

"Is this going to be another Charlie Foxtrot, umm... clusterfuck?" a deep voice asked from the back of the group. A few chuckles broke out at the remark.

"Can that shit, Stoswoski... But roger that," Joe answered, and this caused further outbursts of humor from the marines.

"Okay, okay," Joe announced, "that's enough. Let's have an equipment check."

The men picked up their bergens, shrugged into webbing, then each jumped into the air just once. Observing from which direction the slight rattles and clinks of equipment came, Joe withdrew a role of masking tape from one of his many Velcroed utility pouches and he and Sergeant Eastman walked among the squad, taping down errant pieces of equipment and uniform to prevent anything from making a noise and giving the patrol away. Having finished this task, Joe and Sergeant Eastman went back to the front of the group.

"We have five minutes. If anyone wants a last-minute smoke, get over to the other side of the road. Otherwise, stand easy."

Four of the squad meandered away from the motor pool to cross the road, and in the darkness, Joe could see the small flare of lighters and matches and the resultant red sparks of lit cigarettes. The rest of the men took last-minute drinks of water and reorganized some pieces of equipment, talking in low voices. Once outside the base and in the desert, conversation would be at a minimum.

Sergeant Eastman spoke quietly to Joe. "You think there will be any surprises?" he asked.

Joe shrugged. "You never know," he answered. "Intel says that the group of hostiles spotted was small so we can handle them if the situation arises. There is one thing making me uneasy though, and that's this weather." He glanced up at the sky. "I think we may be in for something nasty. Have we had a weather report?"

Sergeant Eastman nodded. "Weather report was updated about twenty minutes ago. No sign of any bad weather on the way, although I guess that could change," he answered.

"Okay, but I suggest we request weather updates every thirty minutes, just in case it does," Joe advised. "I just don't like this hot wind, the rise in temperature and the color of that sky. It doesn't look right to me."

The men who had crossed the road to smoke began to wander back to the rest of their squad, and at that point, they all heard the sound of a truck engine from the rear of the motor pool.

"Okay," Joe shouted, "form up and get ready to move out."

The men moved quickly, obeying the order without their usual quibbling and jokes, moving into two lines, ready to board the ME35 when it arrived.

Joe fastened his night vision goggles to the plate at the front of his helmet then shoved them back out of the way of his eyes. He would not use them until he and his men were out in the desert in the dark. He finally pulled on his combat gloves.

"Here it comes," he yelled out just as a truck pulled out from behind a row of vehicles and drove slowly toward them. It pulled up and waited for its passengers, engine rumbling quietly.

"Right. Move it, Marines. Get that tailgate lowered and get on board. Let's load it, ladies," Joe shouted.

Somebody unfastened the tailgate and the men hoisted themselves up into the interior of the vehicle, seating themselves on the plank seating lining the inside once they were inside. Joe and Sergeant Eastman were the last ones to board and as they climbed inside the driver came around to raise the tailgate and lock it into place.

It was dark and oppressive inside the canvas-covered interior, so Joe turned on his flashlight. Everybody sat uncomfortably on the benches, leaning forward slightly as their bergens were so large and cumbersome that they prevented the marines from sitting upright against the sides. All had their weapons lying flat across their knees, barrels pointing toward the opening in the canvas at the back.

The truck's engine rumbled louder, then they were on the move. They would be driven through a security checkpoint then down a two hundred meter concrete and barbed wire-lined road leading to another checkpoint, then outside the wire into the desert.

Except for the rumbling growl of the engine, all was silent inside the truck. Most of the men sat relaxed, heads bent, contemplating whatever thoughts occupied them preceding a patrol—family back home, girls back on the base, what they would be missing while on patrol, mortality. Joe himself glanced back out of the opening in the canvas at the diminishing lights of the airfield.

He always hated this part, deliberately and recklessly leaving what was the only safe protected haven in this part of the desert. The base was a place that had become his home over the last four months. There was something else he was leaving behind. Katie. He gritted his teeth. *What the fuck am I doing?* Starting a relationship with a young woman, out here, on a tour that was only to last another six weeks, going against everything that he believed he should do. Then what? She was British. He was American. They would split up, go their separate ways. It would be gut wrenching, probably for Katie as well if he had received the message from her correctly. This was a balls to the wall situation and one that he could well afford to do without. It was affecting his concentration. She had got under his skin and he couldn't get her out. *But do I want to?* His feelings for her had developed quick and hard, something that was completely out of character for him. This wasn't a wham-bam-thank you-ma'am situation. She was not that type of woman.

Just then, Sergeant Eastman leaned toward him from his position on the bench opposite. The loud noise of the truck's engine almost drowned out his voice but it was loud enough that Joe could hear it perfectly well. "Something on your mind, Joe?" was the question directed at him.

Joe glanced up at his friend then back out at the quickly receding base. He had known Louis Eastman for many years. They had been in many conflicts together and had experienced situations where they had had to protect each other's backs and get out of some sticky incidents. He trusted the other man one hundred percent but was unwilling to talk to him about Katie.

Louis Eastman continued, "Joe, if you can't focus tonight then we're going to be in a whole world of shit. Whatever the problem is, fucking get it off your chest and out of your head."

Joe glanced at the deeply shadowed face of his friend, only inches from his own.

Louis suddenly straightened and sat back on the bench as far as he could. Then he leaned forward again.

"Christ, Joe! Don't tell me it's a girl?"

Joe nodded. "Yep," he answered.

"Oh, you fucking dickwad," Louis exclaimed in a whisper. "You know the rules, pal, and in this type of an asshole of a job, you can't frigging afford to have your head up your ass. Have you slept with her yet?"

Joe shook his head, "Nope. Not yet."

"Well, do yourself a favor. Do the tango in the sheets then get rid of her. If you don't get this fucking sorted out, you'll end up in a body bag. For Christ's sake, buddy…"

Joe inclined his head at his friend's blunt advice. "Yeah, I know, but it's not that easy," he stated.

"Well, make it easy," Sergeant Eastman demanded. "For your own sake, buddy, sort it out. Trust me. These sorts of relationships don't go fucking anywhere. It just causes a load of headache."

Before Joe could answer, the truck started to slow then stopped at the first checkpoint, engine rumbling quietly. There were voices from outside the truck then the gears hissed and grated and they moved off again.

"It ain't that easy, pal," Joe repeated again, glancing down at his gloved hands. "It goes way deeper than that."

Sergeant Eastman regarded his friend intently, sympathy etched into the shadows of his face, lit red by the dim beam of Joe's flashlight.

"It wasn't that broad who was out at the firefight the other night—the medic? I noticed that you were having some kind of argument with her."

Joe hesitated then nodded again. "That's her."

"Well, you've got good fucking taste. I'll say that for you." Louis Eastman paused. "Good luck to you, but do me a favor. Put her on the back burner until we get through this. Huh, buddy?"

"Yeah, roger that," Joe responded.

He tensed as the truck stopped briefly at the second checkpoint, then they were waved on out into the desert. A few more minutes and they would be at their drop-off point.

Joe stood up. "Okay, Marines, let's move it," he ordered quietly. "Move off the road and get into formation as soon as you offload. Night vision goggles on, flank security teams out to five meters. Let's go."

The truck began to slow down again then ground to a halt. The driver, a British corporal, jumped out, lowered the tailgate and Sergeant Eastman jumped down, landing lightly enough not to cause any telltale dust clouds. Joe waited while each of the men leaped out of the truck then he followed, landing easily on the hard ground. He turned to the driver and slapped him on the arm.

"Thanks, buddy."

"Good luck, pal," the corporal said and hurriedly went around to the driver's side of the truck and climbed in. He maneuvered the vehicle until it was facing the way that it had come then drove back to the base.

Chapter Fourteen

Left alone and isolated in the dark, hostile desert, Echo squad immediately moved away from the road and got into its patrol formation, which resembled an arrow with the point man up front, the navigator and cover man three meters behind him, then in two lines, each man three meters distant from the man in front, four pacemen, two element men, Sergeant Eastman carrying a machine gun and tail-end Charlie. There were two two-man security flank teams out to the left and right, five meters distant. To make it easy for the marines to follow each other, two reflectorized pieces of material, known as cat's eyes, were fixed to the back of all combat helmets. This also gave the added reassurance to other patrols, if met, that they were all friendlies and on the same side. Night vision goggles in place, tension and silence had replaced the earlier good humor.

All weapons were now held in the ready position to enable each member of the squad to bring theirs up quickly and accurately. The first line of the patrol held their weapons near their right shoulder with the barrel pointing toward their left foot and the second line held them so that the buttstock was in or near the right armpit with the weapon pointing off to the right of the right foot.

Joe took up position just to the left of the point man, the butt of his M4 resting on his right upper thigh, barrel pointed upward, gloved finger relaxed and resting along the trigger safety guard. He slid his own night vision goggles into place and instantly the blackness dissolved to green. Checking to make sure his radio headset microphone was in place, he glanced out to his left and right to see if the squad's flank security teams were in position, checked back along the formation to make sure that each member of the patrol was paying attention then raising his right hand, gestured to the men to move out. Immediately the patrol moved off, boots thudding softly on the hard, dusty ground, each member of the squad following in the footprints of the man in front.

The surrounding desert was dark and silent. The terrain was bleak and barren with low rock promontories, shallow crevices, *wabis* — dry river beds — and shale banks. The hard ground was cracked in places and the arid dryness had caused the terrain to rear upward in some areas in sharp, jagged formations and crumble downward into deep crevices in others. Vegetation was sparse with nothing but thorny shrubs and bushes eking out a poor existence in the shielded crevices and crannies of rocks. The temperature had risen and the hot gusting wind had strengthened, creating man-high whirlwinds of sand and dust. The stars and moon were hidden and the air smelled of scorched dry earth and the copper dry smell of sand.

Joe remained uneasy and restless. He couldn't put a finger on what the problem was, but he knew that he was becoming far too distracted by the weather and not focusing on the patrol. His radio kept issuing short bursts of hissing static and he hoped that whatever inclement weather was approaching and creating the interference would hold itself at bay until they could finish the patrol in safety.

Unimpeded, the marines continued silently on with the patrol at a steady four kilometers per hour. There was no sign of the enemy, no distant noise of trucks or voices. Nothing stirred, neither animal nor human.

The patrol had been moving for about thirty minutes when Joe's radio suddenly spat out a small burp of static. Joe immediately raised a clenched fist to head level, the signal to freeze, and each member of Echo squad immediately dropped down to one knee, facing outward either to the left or right.

"Kite E6 to Eagle E1," came a murmured radio transmission.

Dropping to one knee, Joe thumbed the button on his PRR. "Eagle E1 to Kite E6, receiving," he murmured, barely moving his lips.

"Eagle E1, movement east ninety degrees, ten meters."

"Eagle E1 to Kite E6, roger that. Proceed," Joe responded calmly. He turned immediately to his point man and raised his hand, palm down, and gestured in a throat cutting motion across his throat from left to right. At this signal, which was the signal for a danger area, Lance Corporal George Westerman repeated the signal to the man behind him who signaled to the cover man and so on down the patrol. The marines immediately raised their weapons to a firing position, pointing them out into the dark desert, safety mechanisms off, ready to fire if any enemy approached from the darkness.

Joe strained his ears to see if he could ascertain what his right flank security team had heard but he could hear nothing. Everything was deathly quiet. Five, then ten minutes passed with no sitrep from the squad's security team. Joe was prepared to give them a further five minutes when suddenly his radio squawked quietly.

"Kite E6 to Eagle E1."

"Eagle E1 to Kite E6, receiving."

"Eagle E1, nothing found. Must have been an animal."

"Roger that, Kite E6."

Joe tapped the back of his helmet twice with his open hand, the signal asking for a head count and immediately received, via his radio, each member's call sign. He then pointed the index finger of one hand at the palm of his other hand and immediately the navigator, Corporal Wayne Fitzimmons, hurried over to him, withdrew a folded map from a pouch on the front of his body armor and dropped to his knee beside Joe.

"Position, Corporal," Joe requested quietly.

"Coming up on five clicks, Staff Sergeant. We turn west to two hundred seventy degrees and hump two clicks to our ORP," Corporal Fitzimmons explained.

Joe looked at the map and nodded in agreement. "Excellent, Fitz," he said quietly. Rising to his feet, he raised his hand and gestured the squad forward. The men rose to their feet and continued a further hundred meters before turning west to venture away from the road, deeper into the desert on the second leg of their patrol.

After one click, Joe brought Echo squad to a halt. Corporal Fitzimmons was now pacing alongside him, making it easier to relay coordinates and distance to the ORP.

An ORP was an easily recognizable land feature and set up in case somebody from a patrol became separated from the group. If that happened, all the lost individual had to do was go back to the ORP and wait. In addition, if the patrol came under fire from artillery or mortars, an order could be given and everyone could break up and make their way back to the ORP.

Joe planned to leave the main body of the squad at a designated place of concealment. He and two marines would continue on to the ORP and carry out a recce of the area before allowing the rest of the squad to proceed. Once posting the ORP, they would set up a secure perimeter and sleep for a few hours before proceeding on with the patrol.

Joe ordered the men to take a rest in the shadowy lee of a shallow crevice, which was protected on three sides by large boulders and rocks. Three members of the squad were stationed in a secure perimeter on the fourth, unprotected side. The marines took drinks from their bladders of water, opened some MREs or lit up cigarettes.

Before proceeding on to the ORP, Joe spoke briefly to Sergeant Eastman. "Better transmit a sitrep to base, Sergeant," he said, "and request a weather update."

Sergeant Eastman nodded and spoke into his radio.

Joe gestured to two marines, Lance Corporal Mike 'Wolf' Winters and Corporal James 'Mattie' Matthews, to join him, then waited for Sergeant Eastman to complete his radio transmission to the base.

"Nothing about the weather that's definite, Joe," Sergeant Eastman eventually reported, "but there's a bit of a crapshoot going on back at base. They do think that there's something nasty brewing weather-wise as well, but the Met Office says there's nothing showing up yet."

"All right, Sergeant," Joe replied, slowly. "We'll carry on as planned. Stay frosty for the bad guys as well as the weather. We don't want to be caught on the hop."

Gesturing to the two marines to accompany him and leaving their bergens with the rest of the squad, Joe jumped down into a narrow *wabi* that ran through the area. Shallow as it was, it would provide some cover from possible spying eyes.

Joe, Lance Corporal Winters and Corporal Matthews began to move slowly in a crouch along the bottom of the *wabi*. Thick sand and dust had accumulated at its bottom, together with small stones and rocks. Their progress was an uncomfortable process. Dust swirled up into their faces, and although their eyes were protected by their night vision goggles, they eventually had to stop and wrap scarves around their noses and mouths to filter out choking particles of sand. The wind had become stronger, turning from short, sharp gusts into an almost constant flow of stinging, sand-laden heat.

The *wabi* went on for a distance of a click until it abruptly ended at the ORP, a flat area bordered on the north side by a low outcrop of rock approximately three meters in height. The rest of the ORP was an arid wasteland of tumbled boulders and small sand dunes.

The three marines froze, listening intently for any noise ahead of them. Joe raised his head to peer over the slightly raised stony lip of the stream bed. For five minutes he strained his hearing, however all he could distinguish were the sounds of the wind howling across the clearing, creating fluting sounds in the hollows of tumbled rock as it went and a constant hissing sound as waves of sand blew across the hard ground.

Joe lifted his night vision goggles, scrunching up his eyes to prevent particles of sand, dust and soil from getting into them, and surveyed the sky. It no longer resembled a normal night sky. A writhing dirty yellow mass of clouds was piling up from the south and curtains of sand and dust swept and billowed across the ORP, reducing visibility to a few meters.

Joe replaced his goggles, raised a hand and gestured the two marines forward. Slowly and carefully, they climbed out of the *wabi*, weapons pointing forward and to the left and right. Joe silently pointed in each direction and the two marines split up, spreading out to a distance of five meters from each other to patrol the area while Joe moved forward. Each man paused every few seconds to listen for any suspicious movement and sound, inspecting the ground as best they could for telltale signs of mines. There was no sign that anyone was present in the area but Joe wasn't happy. This whole patrol was beginning to feel like a clusterfuck, not least because the weather was beginning to take a major turn for the worse.

Joe paused, glancing around him through the swirling screens of sand, thinking. Should he radio back to base asking for a mission abort or continue on with the weather becoming increasingly worse and the foreboding in his gut becoming a constant gnawing?

Eventually, he gestured to the two marines and silently pointed back the way they had come. Once again, using the *wabi* as cover, they made their way back to Echo squad. Once they arrived back, Joe briefed Sergeant Eastman. "The ORP is clear," he announced quietly, raising his night vision goggles and lowering his scarf. "We'll move forward slow and easy. But I have to say, Louis, I ain't happy. None of this feels right but I can't place my finger on what's wrong."

"Copy that," Sergeant Eastman responded. "What do you want to do?"

Joe paused. "I don't have anything to go on except this crappy weather," he explained. "I can't see us getting the okay to abort the mission based on my gut feeling. We should just carry on, see what kicks us in the butt."

Sergeant Eastman nodded. "It's your call," he replied.

"Let's get the men geared up and we'll move out," Joe ordered.

Sergeant Eastman strode off to where the men were sitting among the rocks and gave the order to collect their equipment in preparation for moving out. Joe collected his own bergen and shrugged into the webbing. When his men were ready, he lowered his night vision goggles, raised his hand and gestured them forward. The men spread out instinctively, their slow, stealthy nonchalance belying their constantly moving eyes, their weapons raised to shoulder level, feet slowly and carefully placed on the hard ground, always aware that the enemy could have been there before them and planted mines. The patrol was silent, their progress barely disturbing the dust and small piles of rock littering the sand. The tension in the patrol intensified as they investigated the area for any signs of enemy presence.

On reaching the ORP without incident, Joe immediately ordered a secure perimeter set up, placed some of the squad on watch and let the remaining men take time out against the rocky outcrop where they waited for further orders. All the men had now wrapped their faces in scarves and were shielding their weapons to prevent dust and sand from getting into the barrels. The wind had become strong enough that it was now buffeting them from all directions and sand and earth had begun to infiltrate their clothes and penetrate its way up beneath goggles and through the weave of their scarves, chaffing and grazing the skin of their faces.

Raising his night vision goggles again and taking a drink of water from one of his water bottles, Joe joined Sergeant Eastman in the center of the ORP and surveyed the area. Glancing up at the turbulent sky above the rocky outcrop, he noticed a slight glow that seemed at complete odds with the writhing yellow clouds. He quickly identified what he was seeing. Something similar could be seen in a city or town. Above the rock, the sky appeared lighter, as though there were lights shining upward, creating a glow on the underbellies of the fleeing clouds. Joe tensed. Apart from the lights of Base Independence, which could not be seen from their position, there should be no other lights in the desert. Joe turned to Louis Eastman. "Do you see what I see, Sergeant?" he asked and gestured with his head to the glow in the sky.

Sergeant Eastman looked in the direction where Joe had indicated. "Looks like there might be some lights there," he answered. "What do you think?"

Joe continued to gaze at the sky, debating on whether what he was seeing was a natural phenomenon or something was throwing up light, causing the uncharacteristic glow. "I think we need to take a look," he finally replied. "I'm going to take four men and we'll take a recce. I want you to stay here and move the perimeter away from that rocky outcrop. It's too risky to set up there. Someone could come over the top and land right in the ORP. I'm going to radio base and run the recce past them."

"Okay," Sergeant Eastman agreed and strode away to gather the squad around him to brief them.

Joe thumbed his microphone and gave the call sign and password to speak to his squad leader at the base. After he had spoken at length, he terminated the transmission and walked over to the sergeant. As he reached them, four men detached themselves from the main group and came to stand behind him.

"It's a go for a recce," Joe explained to his assistant patrol leader. "Stay extra frosty, Sergeant. Visibility is getting bad and we don't want something nasty creeping up on us."

Joe turned to the four marines. "Have you all been briefed?" he asked.

"Yes, Staff Sergeant," the marines answered together.

"Excellent," Joe responded. "Okay, let's move out."

Holding his M4 with his finger lying across the safety catch and the butt of the weapon supported by the front of his thigh, he strode out of the ORP, the four marines falling into step behind him. He led his men back the way they had come when entering the ORP, using the rocky outcrop on their left as cover. Joe had no intention of scaling the three-meter climb, as they would be in full view of any enemy on the other side that might be scoping out the terrain on the lookout for them. Instead, he was hoping that the outcrop would decrease in height, eventually allowing them to climb over it.

They proceeded slowly until, after about twenty minutes, the rocky wall did indeed begin to diminish in height, eventually petering out into uneven terrain consisting of tumbled rocks and stones interspersed with sand and dust. Joe signaled left with his hand and they clambered as quietly as they could over boulders and crumbled sandstone until they found themselves on the other side of the rocky outcrop.

Before stepping out into the open terrain beyond, Joe glanced up at the pale glow in the sky then crouched down on one knee to carefully survey the surrounding ground stretching out in front of them. It was uneven, littered with rocky screes and large boulders. The wind was now almost gale force and screens of sand and dust blew in heavy curtains across the open space ahead of them. It howled and whined among the rocks and boulders and it was becoming increasingly difficult to speak in a normal tone of voice. The sand had begun to settle into sand dunes and rippled mounds, infiltrating their uniforms, causing acute irritation of their skin.

Some two hundred meters from their position, there was another rocky promontory jutting up into the night, outlined in a deeper black against the glow in the sky. Joe gestured again to move ahead, and using the cover of the rocks and the boulders, they headed in a stooped crouch toward the second rocky outcrop. Twenty-five meters into the march across the open ground, Joe suddenly held up his hand. The four marines behind stopped immediately and dropped to their knees.

Thinking that he had heard a noise, Joe listened carefully. He waited, hearing only the sound of the wind and the rustling and pattering of shifting dust and minute particles of rock against rock. He was unable to hear anything out of the ordinary, so he gestured for the men to move forward again.

The slow walk across to the second rocky outcrop was tense. It was difficult to see the telltale signs of mines and every second was fraught with the possibility of a boot stepping on one. However the careful walk across the open ground went without incident and on reaching the promontory, Joe and the four marines crouched down in a group while Joe surveyed the escarpment, trying to discover a way they could climb up to the top and survey the terrain on the other side. He finally noticed that part of the rock to the right had crumbled away, leaving a steep but accessible slope to the top.

Turning to his men, Joe lifted two fingers, pointed to two of the marines and gestured them to stand at the foot of the slope that he intended to climb. He then lifted two fingers again, pointed at the two remaining marines, and gestured for them to follow him. Silently, they moved to the slope created by the crumbled rock.

With the two selected marines remaining at the foot of the slope, weapons at shoulder height and aimed out into the desert, viewing overlapping fields of fire across the terrain they had just crossed, Joe and the remaining two marines shouldered their weapons and began to climb.

The rock was loose and powdery in some places, and although they moved carefully and slowly, they could not prevent small rocks and sand tumbling noisily down behind them. Their boots, although ridged, had not made for climbing and they slipped constantly, gloved hands grasping for handholds that came loose under their grip. Each footstep upward involved digging the toe of one boot into the sand, waiting until they were assured of a firm foothold then thrusting upward to dig in the other boot. The wind threatened to push them backward off the slope and every now and again they had to pause, clinging to their precarious positions, waiting for a lull in the wind. After what seemed like hours, they eventually reached the ridge of the escarpment. Joe unshouldered his M4 and slowly raised himself up to peer over the ridge.

Chapter Fifteen

Joe immediately saw the source of the glow in the sky. Through his night vision goggles he observed — at a distance of five hundred meters — a Taliban camp. The source of the light came from the blazing headlights of at least six trucks parked in a circle. A large fire was burning in the center of the circle of vehicles with a group of blanket-covered figures seated around it. Joe counted at least two dozen people. He also noted two rocket propelled grenade — RPG — launchers, and he was sure that each person below carried an individual weapon.

"Blatant bastards," one of the marines commented quietly.

"They are that," Joe murmured. He shifted his position and studied the surrounding terrain. "It's pretty protected here. I bet they didn't think they'd be discovered."

"Fucking dickwads," Corporal Matthews exclaimed. "What are we gonna do about them, Staff Sergeant?"

Joe remained silent, thinking. Then he answered the question. "I think we need to get back to the ORP and get the fuck out of here. There're at least twenty-four of the motherfuckers down there. We don't have the firepower. I need to make a sitrep to base, get their feedback. Let's go."

Joe and the two marines carefully moved back down off the ridge, turned onto their backs and gently but quickly slid down the slope of the escarpment back to lower ground. From there, the five made their way back to the ORP, where Sergeant Eastman immediately joined him.

"We have a problem, Joe," he announced. "Base radioed and advised that there's a frigging great sandstorm coming our way. Not one of the biggest but it's gonna be big enough to keep us pinned down out here for a couple of days. The base have already battened down the hatches there."

"Fuck!" Joe exclaimed. "What a bag of dicks." He quickly went on to describe the Taliban camp to the Sergeant then said, "We need to get the hell out of here, put as much distance as possible between us and the bad guys then hole up, wait for the sandstorm to blow over. Get the men together. I need to brief them then we'll move."

Joe and Sergeant Eastman called the squad together and Joe explained about the Taliban camp and the approaching sandstorm. The men were accepting of the worsening weather. They were well aware that the screening sandstorm could offer some protection to the enemy on the prowl at night. The Taliban were used to living in the desert and dealing with storms that started up suddenly and disappeared just as quickly as they came. Inclement weather did not impede the enemy's night patrols and this would create a disadvantage for Echo squad. On the other hand, the sandstorm would also hide their own movements.

"Okay, now you know as much as I do," Joe continued. "I don't need to tell you that the weather is gonna get much worse. We need to find some place to hole up and wait it out. We're not going to be able to make it back to base in this wind and with the decreasing visibility. You'll want to wear your goggles, shemaghs and your ponchos. Make sure that all your emergency kit is at hand. Try to keep the sand and dust out of your weapons. Any questions?"

He glanced at each of the marines in turn, but they were all shaking their heads. Their expressions were unperturbed, as though they were faced with sandstorms every day.

"Okay, you have five to get your gear sorted out."

The marines spent the next few minutes organizing their individual equipment. Part of their desert clothing was a neck and head shemagh, a scarf that used to cover the head beneath the helmet, face then wrap about the neck. There was space left for the eyes and it would keep out much of the windblown sand and dust. They put on their ponchos, generally used for rainy weather but under which they could carry and shield their weapons, protecting the delicate mechanisms from the harsh particles picked up by the winds.

By the time all this had taken place, the weather had deteriorated considerably. The wind was now battering at them continuously, with curtains of yellow sand sweeping across the ORP and wind buffeting the men's bodies, causing them to turn away from sharp particles of sand that stung raw exposed skin. Breathing in the furnace-like heat burned the nostrils and throat, and with all the combat clothing now worn by the men, they were all sweating freely, and they now had to shout to be heard if they needed to converse with one another.

Having sorted out his own equipment, Joe eventually turned to face the men. "Okay, let's get out of here. Remember, stay alert, stay quiet and watch where you're going and don't stop or stray out of sight of your buddy. We need to get as far away from here as we can before we find some place to lie low. Keep your eyes peeled for the Terries."

Moving out of the ORP, once away from the shelter of the rocks, the full force of the storm hit them. The sandstorm was approaching from the south, and to get back to the base they had to march into the wind that was coming from that direction. All thought of completing the patrol in formation was gone. To spread out would be to risk losing a man in the deteriorating visibility. They bunched together, maintaining a meter's distance between each other, those on the outside surveying the terrain for any movement from somebody tracking them. Visibility was almost non-existent with windblown sand forming and reforming around them, obscuring their surroundings. Breathing was difficult so Joe called a number of brief halts so that his men could rest and take on water.

Their march was slow, hindered as it was by wind and uneven terrain with its boulder-strewn ground, gullies and outcroppings of rock thrusting up in hazardous formations. The men fought against the increasing strength of the hot wind — which was always against them — and eventually it began to take its toll. Now and again a marine would stagger — blown off balance — or stumble over an unseen obstacle hidden by the curtains of blowing sand. Their passage grew slower as the men grew more and more weary.

Joe glanced at his watch. It was 0230 hours, or in Army slang, o-dark-thirty, meaning very early in the morning. If they had been back at the ORP, they would have been working on a watch system whereby half the squad would be asleep while the other half would be on watch, turn and turnabout. Now here they were, trying to plow through a raging sandstorm that, he had a sneaking suspicion, had not reached its peak. When and if it did, they would be in serious trouble if they were caught out in the open. It was about time they discovered some form of shelter and got some shut-eye.

When Joe spoke into his microphone beneath the smothering shemagh to radio Sergeant Eastman, he was disconcerted to discover constant static issuing from his radio. He used his call sign and when Sergeant Eastman answered, the transmission was considerably broken up.

Joe halted the squad and ordered them to take a rest. The men turned their backs to the wind and sand and Joe made his way to Sergeant Eastman's position. Joe knelt down on one knee beside his assistant patrol leader, and turning his head, lowered the shemagh from his mouth.

"We need to get the men into some form of shelter," he shouted, immediately wincing at the hot sting of sand and dust on the exposed skin of his face.

Sergeant Eastman nodded, wiping his mouth with a gloved hand. "I'll keep an eye out for something suitable," he yelled back.

Joe rose to his feet, went to the front of the squad and gestured them onward. He judged that they were a good distance from the Taliban encampment and so could begin to scout out some form of shelter. Visibility was now extremely poor and he would not have been able to see an enemy approaching even if he had wanted to. His priority now was getting his Marines to a location where they could rest, take on water and eat. He had no concrete idea how long the sandstorm would last, just the base's two-day estimate. The big ones could take days to dissipate, the smaller ones just hours. He hoped the base was wrong and that this was one of the latter, otherwise they could be stranded for days and run out of food and water. The storm appeared to be causing interference with the radios, which meant that any transmission to base would probably not be received, so in effect they were on their own.

The soul-destroying march went on before Sergeant Eastman approached Joe from out of the sand-laden gloom and tapped him on the shoulder. "Over there," he said. "I saw a good spot when the sand cleared for a second." He gestured to his left and Joe followed his pointing finger.

For a split second, the curtains of sand parted again and he saw that there was a low wall of rock in a rough L-shape. If they sat against it facing north, it would protect them from the wind and sand that was blowing in from the south.

Joe gestured toward the selected location and the men, showing relief in their sudden turn of speed, headed in the direction he was pointing. On reaching the wall of rock, Joe called the men into a group.

"This is as good as it's gonna get," he began, shouting to be heard. "Now, words of warning. Do *not* wander away. If you need to take a piss, only go a couple of feet away from the next man. If you're someone who gets embarrassed at doing bodily functions in front of others, deal with it. Put your bergens at your feet to create some kind of barrier. Eat some chow, keep rehydrated. Cover yourself with your poncho when you go to sleep, otherwise you'll find sand and dust in places you didn't know you had. I want every alternate man to take first watch. The rest of you get some sleep.

I suggest two hours on and two hours off. I don't know how long this will last. I don't think it's at its worse yet. Hopefully it'll blow itself out by tomorrow. Any questions?"

The men shook their heads wearily.

The rock wall was not exactly the most comfortable of places. There were stones littered everywhere and drifts of sand had built up. Echo squad spent precious minutes clearing along the base of the wall until most of the stones were removed then they all sat down with each Bergen placed at the feet of its owner so that together they formed a barrier. The men ate some rations, grimacing at the cold taste and the effects of sand and dust getting into their mouths. Nobody complained. Some lit cigarettes and used their ponchos to shield themselves from the flying sand. Some of the men turned their ponchos backward so the hoods could cover their faces to completely shield themselves then promptly went to sleep.

Joe took first watch while Sergeant Eastman attempted to get some sleep. He sat listening to the howling wind and watched as the curtains of sand whipped across the terrain in front of him. He knew not to stare at one area for too long. With the strange light and the constant movement, it would strain his eyes and he would become tired too quickly. He wrapped himself in his poncho so that he could just barely see and relaxed back against the hard rock. He glanced along the line of men and saw that they had obeyed his orders to the letter. The men alternated, either observing their fields of fire or sleeping.

Satisfied that for the moment all was as it should be, although he would have liked a more concealed position, Joe returned his gaze to his own field of fire, his eyes constantly moving from left to right and back again. Now his body was at rest, although still alert and ready to respond to any danger that presented itself, his thoughts turned to Katie back at Base Independence. He wondered how she was dealing with the sandstorm and hoped that she was safe. He assumed that the base had battened down and dealing with the storm as it usually did, prohibited movement unless it was unavoidable, all flying suspended for the present and all vehicles moved to sheltered locations.

He pictured Katie's face and felt the warm feeling that arose whenever he thought of her. He missed her more than he would have thought possible and knew that before she returned to the UK, they would have to talk. He now knew that he loved her and did not want to lose her. After all these years of fighting and his commitment to the Marines, he had reached a decision that she was going to be his priority from now on. If he had to persuade her to leave the Army and join him in the States, then that would be his goal. He knew that it would be hard on her. She loved her job, was obviously competent at it, and if she rejected his offer then he would have to accept her decision. His heart sank as he thought of how lost he would be without her if she insisted on staying in the UK when their tours finished. The thought of returning to the US without her was something he could not begin to think about. Dismissing the intolerable thought, Joe tried to force his attention back on his surroundings and the worsening sandstorm.

Chapter Sixteen

Back at Base Independence, Katie jerked awake from a sound sleep at the sound of Giant Voice booming its feedback prior to an announcement. As she sat bolt upright in her camp bed, her first thought was that this was another alert because of another incident. Her heart immediately began an anxious pounding and her mouth went dry. Torches came on from the direction of other camp beds and murmurs of protest and startled questions came from the dark.

Katie groped for her torch beside her and turned it on, directing the beam at her watch. Its luminous dial told her that it was 0200 hours in the morning. She threw back the sleeping bag and sat on the edge of her bed.

Giant Voice boomed again and burped forth static. Katie stood up. "Okay, ladies, let's listen to what it has to say."

The women obeyed and the tent became silent.

"Attention all personnel. A sandstorm is approaching the base," Giant Voice announced. "Please restrict your movements outside unless it is unavoidable. If venturing outside, please wear appropriate eye and head protection. Avoid driving vehicles unless absolutely necessary. Cover all generators with tarpaulins and seal all tents, showers, and toilets. That is all."

"Oh crap!" Wanda exclaimed, joining Katie beside her bed. "Absolutely wonderful. Just what the doctor ordered."

Katie clapped her hands. "Okay, ladies, let's get the shower tents and toilet sealed, the generator covered and our own tent sealed. Let's go."

Knowing that sandstorms moved very fast, and if it had already been sighted, they only had a few minutes in which to get everything prepared, the women moved quickly, racing out to the back and zipping closed the shower tents, checking that all loose objects were stored safely, the toilet locked, the generator covered and sealed with a tarpaulin, and the tent flaps at the back of the tent zipped closed.

Due to the unreliability of sandstorms and the danger they could pose, Katie ordered the women to get dressed and organize their equipment ready in case they had to leave suddenly. She was just putting on her own combats and getting her bergen ready with a clean T-shirt and underwear and a book to read and was finishing an equipment check when her pager beeped. Withdrawing it from her combat trouser pocket, she saw that a message from Sergeant Webster at the CTH was scrolling across the LED screen.

Make your way to the CTH. You can wait out the storm here. Bed and shower facilities available free of charge.

Katie turned to her friend. "I'll be waiting it out at the CTH," she explained. "The Sergeant wants me there before the storm gets any worse."

She finished dealing with her equipment, put on eye protectors solely used for this sort of situation, wound her shemagh around her head, face, and neck, completely covering all areas of exposed skin, and finally put on her helmet. She pulled on her combat gloves and slung her bergen onto her back. Turning to the other women and with her voice muffled, she said, "Okay, ladies. You heard Giant Voice. Stay protected. Don't go wandering around. You could get lost. If you need to report to your sections, do so before the sandstorm gets any worse. As Giant Voice says, wear your goggles at all times outside and keep all exposed areas of skin covered. I have to report to the CTH, so good luck everyone and stay safe."

The women wished her goodbye and Katie went to the entrance to the tent and unzipped the flaps. She ducked outside, and before re-zipping the tent, took down the notice on the outside, picked up the teddy bear and placed them both inside the tent flap.

She instantly became aware that a wind had risen. It gusted strongly, bringing with it sand, dust, and earth that swirled around in stinging clouds. Katie could feel the heat through her shemagh and combats and she felt smothered. Miniature sand dunes had already started to build against the sides of the tents. Canvas flapped with crackling sounds and the wind moaned and wailed down the narrow alleyways between the rows of tents. Katie began to walk toward the road. The wind pushed at her back one minute then from the front the next. She bent her head against its force and plowed her way forward. If the wind, dust, and sand were this bad in a confined place such as the base, what could it be like for Joe on his patrol? She wanted him back here, safe, preferably with her somewhere private, but realistically that wasn't going to be possible and she had to deal with it until she saw him — if the storm dissipated as quickly as it had birthed and he got back to the base safely.

Now she battled her way along the road toward the CTH, her torch fitfully lighting her way, its beam barely piercing the spiraling tornados and billowing clouds of sand and dust. It was stifling inside her shemagh and by the time she arrived at the CTH, sweat had started to trickle down her forehead and the wool was moist and cloying against her nose and mouth.

She thrust her way through the doors and into the cool, almost chilly, interior of the building. Once inside, she quickly removed her helmet, unwound the shemagh, removed her glasses, and ran a hand through her damp hair. The air-conditioning was cold against her flushed skin and she stood where she was for a few minutes, letting the refreshing air play on her face and hair. She could hear voices from the R&R room and headed toward it. On entering, she found it almost full with two trauma teams and two CTTs on duty. Sergeant Webster greeted her. "Grab yourself a coffee, Katie, and join us."

Katie nodded, dumped her bergen in a corner of the room, and poured herself a cup of the bitter coffee. She sat down on a vacant chair and sipped at the hot liquid.

"What's it like out there?" Sergeant Webster asked.

"Not very nice," Katie replied. "The temperature is rising and the wind is getting stronger. If it gets much worse, it's going to be hell."

"Well, let's hope our guys stay safe out in the field," Corporal Wendy Turner, a trauma nurse, responded. "I hate to think what they're going through if they're out on patrol."

Katie nodded, the nurse putting her exact thoughts into words. She couldn't bear to think about Joe, what he might be going through out there in the desert. She hoped that he and his squad had found a safe place to hole up in, out of the storm. She missed him so much and the suppressed panic she was feeling at his absence and the threat of the danger he might be under was increasing as time went on. She finished drinking her coffee and disposed of the plastic container then got to her feet. "Me for sleep," she announced and turned to Sergeant Webster.

Anticipating her question, Sergeant Webster said, "We've transferred all the patients to Ward One. We'll use the beds in Ward Two."

Katie nodded, collected her bergen, and wishing everyone a goodnight, made her way slowly to Ward Two. She selected a hospital bed at the back of the ward and drew the green curtain around it, sealing it off from the rest of the room. Turning on the small bed light, she set her bergen on the floor and sat down on the edge of the bed. She gazed abstractedly at the green shimmering curtain then covered her face with her hands. She was tired and felt agitated. Her fears for Joe and her feelings for him were wearing her down. She knew she had to regain control of the way her life was heading but ultimately that would mean breaking it off with Joe and retreating back to her old lonely lifestyle. This action was something that she could not bear thinking about. It was too late to backtrack. She finally found herself admitting that she loved him. It was inconceivable that she could forget him. There had to be another way she could finish her tour in one piece emotionally. The brass were so right. This type of relationship caused nothing but heartbreak, but Joe was there in her heart to stay.

She bent down to unlace her boots and kicked them off. She would sleep in her uniform. She didn't fancy wandering around in her underwear with all the people present in the CTH, and if there were any emergencies during the rest of the night, she would be readily available.

Katie turned off the light and lay back on the bed. She sighed heavily, wondering why love was so painful and difficult to deal with. She thought of Joe again, and after sending warm loving thoughts winging his way — wherever he was — she set the alarm on her watch, and before much more time had passed, her eyes began to close. She slipped into sleep and for the rest of the night fleeting images crossed her mind of howling winds, gunfire, and soldiers floundering in a dark landscape. She tossed and turned, and when eventually the alarm on her watch went off, Katie awoke feeling as though she had not slept all night.

She immediately heard the wind howling around the building. Something sporadically banged against metal and there was the continuous harsh pinging of particles of sand against the outer walls.

Katie sat up on the bed feeling unrefreshed and stiff. Her eyes and head ached and she felt despondent and tense. The only thought that brought her enthusiasm was that Joe would hopefully be back from patrol that night.

She eventually got up from the bed, and glancing around the ward, she saw that a number of the beds had green curtains pulled around them, obviously occupied by other medical staff. She straightened the covers and pillow of the bed she had used then made her way to the locker room. Once out in the corridor, she could hear the murmur of voices coming from the R&R room. There had obviously been no casualties during the night, otherwise there would be far more hustle and bustle within the CTH. Feeling as though she hadn't had a wink of sleep, Katie showered quickly, put on scrubs, and went to get herself a coffee.

Sergeant Webster and a couple of other members of the medical staff were drinking early morning coffee when she entered. They greeted her good morning and when she sat down then Sergeant Webster gave her a brief rundown on the storm. "Looks like it's reached its peak," he said. "It should be blowing itself out soon and moving out of the region... We hope."

"That's good," Katie responded dully and began to drink the rest of her coffee and without thinking about what she was asking. "Will that mean the patrols out will get back by this evening?" Immediately as she asked the question, she cringed inwardly and bit her lip.

Sergeant Webster studied her intently and hesitated before answering. "Looks that way," he said eventually and continued staring at her with a closed expression.

Katie knew that it was pointless to try to justify why she had asked the question. She had dropped herself in it, and the way Sergeant Webster was studying her, she knew that he knew, either via the grapevine and her question had confirmed the rumors or — as he was not a stupid man — he had put two and two together and come up with the proverbial four.

Instead, she changed the subject hastily, mentally shrugging. Well, if he knew about her and Joe, there was nothing she could do about it. It wasn't against the law. They weren't committing a criminal offense. It was just that the brass frowned on it, but they couldn't ban it.

The day was one of the worst of Katie's life. Sick parade that morning kept her occupied with more than the usual attendees, also seeing those suffering from eye irritations due to the blowing sand and grit, raw, chaffed skin from stinging sand, windburn and heat. After that, she helped the nurses with the remaining patients, tidied up the wards, theaters, and trauma rooms then was at a loose end as to what to do next. She took a look outside the front doors to check on the storm. It was almost dark, with visibility reduced to near zero and sheets of sand blown by howling winds piling sand dunes against the side of the CTH and other buildings nearby. It was hot, the air thick and dry, and Katie found it difficult to draw in any air.

Shutting the door, Katie wandered back to the R&R room. Finding the room empty at that moment, she sat down in one of the chairs. She kept looking at her watch, wondering if Joe was making his way back to the base. Surely, he wouldn't continue his patrol in the storm. He and his squad would become desperately lost, run out of water and food and then they would die out there. This thought was too horrible to contemplate. Sighing heavily, she leaned back in her chair and closed her eyes.

Chapter Seventeen

Joe opened his eyes slowly. At first his vision was blurred, his eyes dry and gritty. His neck and limbs were stiff and sore from half reclining on the hard ground and his mouth was dry. He had slept fitfully for a couple of hours, never really sinking into a deep sleep, part of his mind aware of the banshee-like howl of the wind and part of his mind on full alert for signs of danger. It was stifling hot beneath his shemagh and wrapped as he was in his poncho and wearing armor and his uniform, he found it difficult to breathe.

He noticed that what little there had been of dawn had come and gone. The world was now gray-yellow in color with the wind screaming around the boulders and rocks, making strange fluting, and whistling sounds as it soared in and out of gullies, nooks, and crannies.

Eventually Joe moved, and when he did, small piles of sand trickled from his body. He stretched the kinks out of his shoulders and glanced along the line of men. Nobody else was moving.

All members of Echo squad either lay curled on the ground, completely wrapped in ponchos, or half-sat leaning against the rock behind them. The only sign of life from some was the movement of eyes behind scratched goggles and the occasional twitch of a limb. Looking out into the curtains of sand and dust, Joe contemplated their next move. They couldn't stay where they were. If they did, their water would run out, and more importantly, the heat would start to affect them with serious consequences, especially if the sandstorm became worse. He needed to get his men back to Base Independence. The storm would shield their movements. Nobody — not even those who spent most of their time living in the desert — could hunt them down in this type of weather. The Taliban were not omnipotent. They had human weaknesses when it came to being able to survive in bad weather. He would wake the men and talk to them, seek their views on what they wanted to do.

Joe got to his feet, rising above the protective barrier of the rock wall, and instantly felt the full force of the wind battering at his head and shoulders. He staggered and swayed then proceeded to make his way along the line of men. Gently nudging their boots if they were asleep and receiving acknowledgments from the men who were awake, Joe reached the end of the row and gestured to Sergeant Eastman to join him.

As Sergeant Eastman got up from the ground, Joe attempted to send a radio message to the base, but the static issuing from his radio convinced him that a transmission would not get through while the sandstorm was raging. Defeated, he gestured for the squad to gather around him, where they all crouched down behind the protective shield of the wall.

"All right," Joe began, "I can't get through to the base. There's too much interference from the storm. So, I'm gonna put something to you all. The weather hasn't abated much and I'm sure you're all feeling like shit. It's not comfortable being out here in the heat. I think we need to aim for the base. It might be hours or days before the sandstorm dissipates, and we'd run out of water and food long before that. It won't be an easy march back. I wanted to make you aware of that. We'll be on our own, cut off from base. I need to know what you guys think."

Joe surveyed each of the marines in turn, waiting patiently while his announcement turned over in their minds. He noticed that their faces were haggard and tired-looking. Most of their eyes were red and irritated from the dry, sand-laden air, and stubble adorned their faces with sweat glistening on their skin.

Eventually, one of the marines spoke up. "This thing is completely and totally fucked up, Staff Sergeant," he began. "We stay here and things are gonna get mighty uncomfortable. We move out and things are also gonna get uncomfortable. Better that we move out and try for the base than sit on our balls and fucking turn into dehydrated prunes." He glanced at his fellow marines, who were all nodding in agreement.

Joe nodded, accepting their decision. "Copy that. All right. Now, when we move out of here, we stay close together, maintain shoulder-to-shoulder contact. If any of you get lost, stay where you are until we find you. We'll take it nice and slow. Corporal Fitzimmons will take point. We'll take a rest every fifteen minutes. With the storm, I don't know how long it will take us to get back to base. Okay, take twenty, grab some water and chow then we'll move out. Corporal Fitzimmons?"

"Here, Staff Sergeant." The navigator raised a hand.

"I want you to plot the most direct route back to the base. Forget about the route for the original patrol. We need to get back ASAP," Joe ordered.

The navigator withdrew a map and spent a few minutes plotting a route, doing some math on a blank space on the map, and then voiced his conclusions.

"South-southwest ten clicks," he announced, "but it's open terrain, pretty much desert. The wind and sand are going to be pretty rough out there. We'll have our asses hanging out in the wind and be in full view of anyone tracking us."

"A risk we'll have to take," Joe answered, unhappy at the navigator's statement but accepting that beggars could not be choosers in the situation they found themselves in.

While he had been consulting with his navigator, the marines had all been hastily opening MREs and consuming them. Some had gone to relieve themselves and some were smoking cigarettes. Eventually, all members of the squad were ready to leave. Corporal Fitzimmons took point with Joe and the rest of the marines clustered behind, leaving a meter space between each one so that there was room to raise their weapons if the situation called for it. Joe gestured them forward and they stepped out from behind the rock wall, which took them into the full force of the sandstorm.

Immediately the wind tore at their ponchos, battered their heads and bodies, and buffeted them from all sides. Sand and dust found its way into clothes, up under goggles and inside shemaghs. The hot wind tore their oxygen away from them and they all found it difficult to breathe. Their route obscured by flying sand, they came upon hidden shallow gullies, rocks, and boulders abruptly and without warning and had to circle round, sometimes backtracking as their route came to a dead end.

Although Joe called a rest every fifteen minutes and urged the men to take on water, keeping them hydrated, he could see that they were exhausted. The squad was experienced, had completed long patrols in the past over far worse, hazardous terrain, but because of the gale force wind and the curtains of sand and the heat, their energy and stamina were becoming seriously compromised.

Joe and Sergeant Eastman frequently carried out headcounts and checked verbally with each member of the squad, assessing their health and general state of mind. At one point, one of the marines stumbled down into a gulley and fell flat on his face. Tired as he was and weighed down by his bergen, he struggled to get to his feet. Joe hurried to the fallen marine's side while the rest of the squad took a knee, taking out their water bladders to rinse out their mouths and take long drinks of the now lukewarm water.

Joe grasped the fallen marine's webbing holding his bergen to his back and hauled him upright. "All in one piece, Marine?" he shouted, peering closely into the man's haggard, goggle and shemagh-shielded face.

The marine nodded, "Fine, Staff Sergeant," he yelled back. "I lost my footing."

"Ready to go on?" Joe asked. The marine nodded and Joe clapped him on the shoulder and walked with him until they joined the rest of the squad.

They continued on with their slow march, Corporal Fitzimmons constantly checking the map and compass and relaying their position to whomever of them circled the squad, checking for stragglers and surveying the terrain when the curtains of sand parted. The ground and sky merged into one so there was no horizon and no discernible landmarks. Their pace was almost a crawl. What would normally have taken them a patrol of a few hours was now taking them a great deal longer.

The men walked on, helmeted heads bowed to the wind, shoulders slumped beneath their heavy bergens. They stumbled constantly, some going down on one knee, but through sheer stubbornness and determination, gaining their feet and going on.

At last, Joe brought the squad to a halt. The ground under his boots had changed in composition. Glancing down, he toed the sand with his boot and to his relief saw that beneath a covering of sand and dust was the rough surface of a road. They had made it to the road leading to and from the base.

The last leg of their arduous journey went more smoothly, their march unimpeded by uneven rocky terrain, although it remained slow as the marines were exhausted. It was with an uplift of spirits that they finally saw the intermittent faint lights from the base up ahead.

Joe tried his radio once more and found that some of the static had dispersed and he was able to transmit a message to his squad leader, who in turn radioed through to the security checkpoint to advise them that Echo squad was approaching and ordered transportation to be sent directly to pick them up.

It was with a profound sense of relief that they were finally waved forward with a searchlight and within ten minutes, their truck arrived at the checkpoint. The weary marines climbed inside and collapsed onto the benches. They slumped forward with heads bowed, not even bothering to remove their shemaghs, remaining silent.

Joe closed his eyes and allowed himself to relax slightly. He was so tired that he couldn't think straight. All he wanted to do after debriefing his squad leader was to take a long, hot shower and seek out his bed, where he could get some sleep. In addition, there was one more thing he needed to do, and that was see Katie. He so wanted to see her it was like an ache in his gut. "I'm back, Katie," he murmured beneath his breath. "I'm back."

Chapter Eighteen

Katie looked at her watch for the third time and saw that its luminous hands had finally crept toward 1930 hours. There were still thirty minutes remaining until she was due to meet Joe. Her stomach was full of butterflies, mouth dry, and the palms of her hands damp with perspiration. It had been nearly twenty-four hours since she had seen him. Tonight was the night they were due to meet and she was going to accompany him to the PX on Camp Roosevelt. She felt restless, couldn't settle, and didn't want to think about the fact that he might not make it back or that he might not turn up if he was too exhausted from the patrol.

At last, Wanda flung a magazine at her. "For heaven's sake, woman. Sit still for five minutes and read this. You're driving me nuts," she exclaimed in mock annoyance.

Katie grabbed the magazine and laughed. "Sorry," she answered. "I feel as nervous as hell. I don't even know if he's back yet. What happens if he doesn't get back in time? What happens if he doesn't turn up?"

"Bloody hell!" Wanda retorted. "If he doesn't turn up, you come back here. He'll be there if he can be there."

Katie took a deep breath and tried to calm herself. She would be in his arms in twenty minutes, feeling the warmth of him and feeling his kisses. She suddenly flung the magazine onto her sleeping bag. "I'm going," she said. "By the time I walk over there, it'll be 2000 hours."

"Thank goodness for that. You take care, girl. Take your torch and have a great time. I'll want to hear everything when you get back," Wanda said.

"Yeah, right," Katie retorted. "That'll happen." She put on her military cap—Standing Orders had announced that helmets need no longer be worn—and checked her makeup in a small mirror, finally picking up her torch. Wishing her friend goodnight, Katie left the tent.

The sandstorm had moved on but it had left behind its mark with miniature sand dunes piled up against both tents and buildings, with dust and soil laying on the roofs of the canopied tents. Even now, the detritus left by the sandstorm still needed to be cleared away. The temperature had dropped considerably and the wind had died down to a cooling breeze, which was a dramatic change from the fierce gale and heat earlier. Camp Churchill was back to its busy schedule and the usual noise was greatly in evidence.

Katie made her way to the road. It wasn't dark yet but she switched on her torch and hoped fervently that she could remember in which direction the pallets with its makeshift seating area were. She hoped that there would be no one else taking a few minutes out to have some quiet downtime there.

She wanted to do an incredibly childish thing and run to Joe, whooping. She wanted to leap like a child into his arms and hold him for as long as they were together. She was desperate to see him, to feel his warmth, to see his eyes and his smile and hear his voice. Her heart was pounding so hard that she felt sick. There was always the possibility that he had not returned from his patrol or that he had become lost out in the desert, but she could not let herself think about that.

Katie headed in the direction of the NAAFI. It was a lovely evening, with a crystal clear navy blue sky studded with stars and a huge full moon peeping over the horizon. The temperature was balmy, with much of the humidity having dispersed due to the sandstorm. It wouldn't remain that way for long, as it was a peak summer month for Afghanistan, but at present it was a warm summer night and she was enjoying it.

Katie sighted the rows of pallets and checked her watch. It was 1945 hours, she had fifteen minutes to find the place that she and Joe had visited previously. She turned off the road onto the well-worn path and began to wend her way around the stacks of pallets.

Katie found herself almost running with eagerness. She hoped he would be there but if he wasn't, then she would wait for him.

After a further five minutes, the rows of pallets ended and she came out into the space where the wall of pallets was erected. Discreetly flashing her torch around the clearing, she saw no sign of Joe. Disappointed but hopeful, she continued onward, went through the gap in the pallet enclosure and sat down on one of the overturned oil drums. She kept her torch on, a little unnerved at the darkness surrounding her. It was also very quiet, with the noises of the camp seeming distant with just the faint thudding of the generators and a distant aircraft taking off.

A further five minutes went by and Katie suddenly caught the sound of stealthy booted footfalls on the hard ground. Her heart jumped into her throat and she got to her feet. The footfalls were slow and methodical, and she waited for Joe to announce his arrival, but all remained silent. She flashed her torch in the direction of where she expected him to appear from but there was nobody there. Her expectant smile faded slowly from her face and she suddenly felt nervous.

"Joe," she whispered, not wanting to raise her voice in case it was another couple or some other innocent person wanting some peace and quiet. There was no answer and the footsteps had ceased.

Katie started to flash her torch around her, trying to see who was lurking in the shadows. What occurred next happened in a split second. She heard sudden movement from behind, a cracking sound as though one of the wooden pallets had broken, the heavy thud of boots, and then she was grabbed from behind.

Arms wrapped tightly around her waist and she was pulled back against a tall lean body so hard that the breath exploded from her lungs. For a moment, she couldn't breathe. She expected Joe to announce himself but the person holding her remained silent, except for harsh, rapid breathing. It was then Katie knew that this was not Joe but a stranger.

She began to struggle, attempting with her hands to wrench the encircling arms away from her body, but they tightened like a vise and could not be budged. The person was strong, and although Katie was fit and strong for a woman, the stranger was stronger.

"Let me go!" she cried, her voice holding a combination of rage and fright.

"Can't let you go now I've got you, Katie," a voice murmured in her ear, and Katie froze. The hands clenching her stomach to prevent her release began to travel up her body to her breasts and the fingers began to rub her nipples hard.

"David?" she asked. "What...?" She again frantically tried to tear the hands away from her body, clawing at the skin in an attempt to get them to release her breasts.

"Knew I'd get you eventually," Corporal Hudson murmured in a hoarse whisper and his arms tightened, his muscles clamping just beneath her breasts, crushing them painfully.

"Get your fucking hands off of me," Katie spat angrily, fear loading her softly spoken words with venom. "You haven't got me and never fucking will."

She lifted a booted foot and stabbed backward, kicking the unwary corporal on the shin. His reaction was instant and shocking.

He suddenly lifted her so that her feet left the ground and flung her against the pallet fence. She crashed into it and fell, the wooden pallet falling to the ground beneath her. She landed awkwardly, and before she could scramble to her feet, Corporal Hudson had dropped to his knees and was crawling on top of her.

So much stronger than her, he landed on her legs and forced her upper body to the ground. She fought ferociously, twisting and bucking her body in an attempt to topple him sideways, but even though she used every bit of strength she had, the man did not move, only swaying and heaving with her movements. He kept her upper torso on the ground by placing his hands on her breasts and squeezing them painfully.

"We're going to have some fun, you and I," David Hudson said quietly, just loud enough so she could hear him. "You think you're too good for me, so we'll see who has the upper hand."

Katie was terrified. The polite and friendly voice of the cook had changed. The well-spoken and sincere veneer was completely gone. In its place was a deep and sexually charged guttural growl.

"Get off of me, you bastard!" The words came out of her in a harsh croak because she was out of breath and trying to use her strength to get him off her body. She prayed that somebody out on the road would hear her, but strange noises were an everyday part of the camp and she feared that nobody would come to her aid. She could only hope that Joe would arrive soon. She was terrified. It felt like part of her was standing off to one side, looking down at the events unfolding, while another part of her cowered in the darkness of her mind, where it had fled for protection.

Corporal Hudson suddenly released one of her breasts and clamped a hand over her mouth. With the other, he reached down between them and began to fumble with the waistband of her combat trousers. Katie realized at last, shocked, and stunned, what he was after, and she began to pummel his head, shoulders, and arms with closed fists. The blows landed ineffectually and she no longer had the strength in her upper torso to fight him, the strength having drained from her body like liquid through a sieve. He suddenly slapped her face, knocking her head to one side. The soft skin on her cheek immediately sang out with pain and she opened her mouth to scream but he seemed to know what she was about to do and slapped her again. This time the palm of his hand caught the corner of her mouth, a tooth dug into her bottom lip and she tasted blood.

"Now, now," he said nastily, "don't struggle and you might enjoy it — or not. Whatever."

"Never," she spat, tears that she frantically blinked away filling her eyes. "You fucking bastard."

Inside a corner of her mind a little voice was saying beseechingly, *Joe, please hurry. Please, Joe.*

Corporal Hudson had managed to undo the fastening of her combats at the waist and had pulled the zip down and now, one-handed, he was trying to tug the garment down over her legs. She pushed her backside hard into the ground to prevent the trousers from being pulled down and she could hear the man on top of her curse then growl like a frustrated animal.

Katie knew that either way, he was going to win. She was rapidly running out of energy and adrenaline and he had already hit her twice. What was to stop him from beating her if she didn't give in?

A primal survival instinct, however, kept her fighting him, and it was paying off because he was becoming increasingly angry and finding it more difficult to remove her trousers because of her constant writhing and bucking.

Realizing that she was stronger than he had thought and that it was taking too long to get her as he wanted, Corporal Hudson clearly understood that she wasn't going to capitulate to his arousal easily. Suddenly filled with rage beyond reason, he raised a clenched fist to hit her again, only this time his blow did not land. The arm that was raised was suddenly grabbed from behind, another arm went around his neck, and he was suddenly lifted off Katie and flung across the clearing.

Katie landed on the ground and immediately scrambled backward on hands and feet, her breath rasping in her throat, her heart thudding in her chest so hard that it threatened to choke her. Frantically she did up the zip of her combat trousers and watched as Joe

Anderson stalked toward the corporal, who was attempting to get to his feet.

Joe grabbed the unfortunate man by the front of his combat jacket, hauled him up from the ground, and propelled him backward to a tall stack of pallets where he slammed him with force up against them.

"What the fuck do you think you're doing?" Joe asked with cold fury in his voice. He followed the question up by slamming the man up against the pallets again, as if emphasizing the question.

Corporal Hudson's head thudded back against the wood. He promptly lashed out with his foot and caught Joe on the ankle. Joe barely winced and slammed him harder against the unyielding wood.

"Motherfucker!" he spat. "What the fuck were you doing to her?"

"She's free and easy, isn't she?" Corporal Hudson said, his face twisted with jealousy and anger.

Joe answered the statement by lifting the corporal off his feet and throwing him against the pallets repeatedly. "Wrong answer!" he hissed vehemently. "You stay away from her, you fucking bastard. You. Got. That?" Each single word was punctuated by a slam against the wood. "If you don't, you'll be seeing the world through your asshole. Do you understand me?"

For a few seconds, Corporal Hudson hesitated.

Joe spun the corporal away from the stack of pallets and threw him on the ground. The hapless man landed with a thud and sprawled, legs and arms akimbo, like a fallen rag doll.

"You fucker!" Corporal Hudson spat out. He was no longer the good-looking corporal who had pursued Katie so persistently. His face was bright red with humiliation or fury, his eyes bulging, teeth bared like a dog defending its territory.

Joe bent over and hauled the man to his feet. "I ought to beat the crap outta you," he said, dragging the flailing man close so that their faces were barely inches apart. "But you aren't worth shit. But listen to this. Listen very carefully, you asshole, because I won't repeat myself. You aren't worth telling twice. I see you so much as look at her, I'll kill you. And if I don't get the satisfaction of doing it, someone else will. Get my drift?"

With that, Joe flung the corporal away from him. "Now get out of here before I change my mind, you piece of shit."

Corporal Hudson staggered but kept his feet. He turned toward Katie, but it was so dark, she couldn't see his face.

Joe pointed a steady warning finger at him, "Don't even think about it, dickwad. Stay away from her. Do I make myself clear?"

Joe's final warning sounded so quiet and dangerous that Katie herself cringed at the hate and viciousness that she heard in it.

Corporal Hudson hesitated, then turning on his heel and limping slightly, walked away as quickly as he could.

Joe stood with fisted hands on hips, watching the corporal fade into the darkness then, turning, he hurried to where Katie was still on the ground. He dropped to his knees and she instantly flung herself into his arms, her shoulders shuddering and body trembling.

Joe held her tightly, rocking her gently backward and forward. "It's okay," he said softly. "You're okay. You're safe. I'm here."

Katie clung to him tightly, feeling, smelling him, and loving him.

"Did he hurt you?" Joe asked.

"He smacked me in the mouth a couple of times and tried to... He tried to..." Katie's trembling voice trailed off into silence and she continued to shiver against him.

"Ssssshhhh." He gently smoothed her short hair with one hand and rubbed her back in slow, circular motions until she began to relax slightly. He kissed the top of her head.

"Can you get up?" he asked.

Katie nodded, and winced at strained muscles in her upper torso where she had fought Corporal Hudson so frantically. With Joe's help, she got awkwardly to the feet. Once upright, she staggered against him and he put his arms around her again.

"Let me look at your mouth," Joe said and shone his torchlight to the right of her head so that part of the beam lit up the side of her mouth. Katie tilted her head so he could see more clearly where she had been slapped.

Katie saw a burning fury fill his eyes.

"It doesn't look too bad," he announced softly, clearly attempting to control his anger. "We just need to clean the blood away."

"I have some tissues in one of the pouches on my webbing belt," Katie answered, "and there should also be a bottle of water."

"Let's sit down," Joe ordered, and with his arms still around her, led her over to one of the oil drums and helped her to sit down. Shining his torchlight at her webbing belt and its pouches, he hunted through each one until he found a small pack of tissues and the bottle of water. He soaked a tissue in some water from the bottle then proceeded to gently wipe the blood away from her face. Katie winced and hissed through her teeth.

"It looks worse than it is," Joe reassured, and then leaning forward he gently kissed the wounded corner of her mouth. Drawing back, they stared at each other and Katie's eyes suddenly filled with tears that she'd tried not to shed.

Seeing that she still trembling, Joe took her in his arms again, and this time began to kiss her warmly on the mouth.

Katie unhesitatingly put her arms around his neck and returned the kiss with all her heart. All the longing and separation and their love for each other was in the kiss and for a few long minutes what had just happened with Corporal Hudson and the distant sounds of the camp faded away and it was just the two of them alone in the dark. Then Joe felt a warm wetness against his face and he drew back.

"Hey," he began gently, "it's all right, Katie. He's gone."

Suddenly starting to sob quietly, Katie vigorously shook her head, unable to speak. She cried heartbreakingly for some five minutes and Joe held her tightly, rocking her gently. Eventually she managed to regain her voice and hiccupping like a child, she replied, "It's not him."

Joe suddenly released her, stood up slightly from his position on the oil drum, and sat down on the ground. Grasping Katie's hand, he gently pulled her down beside him then turned her and sat her on his lap, pulling her against him so that her head was resting on his shoulder and his arms were around her.

"Tell me," he urged softly and gently.

Sobs still hitching at her breath, Katie snuggled in against Joe. She remained silent for a while, unsure whether to disclose to him how she had missed him and how scared she had been.

Eventually she sniffed. "I missed you," she said simply. "I missed you so much, Joe." She glanced up at him and saw that he was looking down at her. She could just about see his face, features outlined in the shifting shadows. "I was nearly out of my head with worry when the sandstorm hit," she continued, her voice becoming a little stronger. "I knew you were out there and I was so scared that something might happen to you. God, I'm making an utter pathetic mess of this."

Joe remained silent, continuing to stare at her. Katie felt a twinge of fear. *Have I said too much? Maybe he doesn't want commitment. Perhaps his feelings aren't as strong as mine are.*

Chapter Nineteen

"I'm sorry..." she began.

"I love you," Joe suddenly announced, gently and without warning.

Katie froze. "What?" she exclaimed, eyes wide, unable to believe what she had heard. "Really?"

"Yes really. I love you, Katie," Joe repeated firmly and clearly, smiling slightly at her almost childlike question and the look of stunned surprise on her face. "I think I've loved you since we first met. I know it's crazy, we've only known each other for a just a little while, but that's the way it is. I can't stop thinking about you. You are seriously distracting every good intention I have toward my concentration." He continued to stare at her, waiting for a reaction. He could see that her eyes were still wide, and then suddenly a beautiful but shy smile touched her lips.

Reaching up a hand, Katie traced a finger across his mouth with a feather-light touch. "I love you too, Joe," she finally responded. "I didn't want to fall in love with you, but I have. I love you so much."

Joe's arms tightened around her and he lowered his head. He touched her mouth gently with his, but that wasn't enough for them and he began to kiss her deeply, causing their passion to flare into a white-hot flame. The oil drum that Joe had been leaning against rolled away and he sprawled onto his back, pulling Katie with him. Now he was lying half on top of her and his mouth left hers, his lips burning a hot trail along her neck and down to her collarbone.

Katie moaned softly, entwining her fingers in his hair, loving the feeling of his body against hers and the hot, moist kisses that he left against the skin of her neck. Being with Joe, having him kiss her like this, pushed into the background the sordid scene with the cook. There was no comparison to the almost overwhelming feelings that this man could arouse in her. She gently left a trail of light kisses along his jaw line and down to his neck where she nipped gently at his skin, interspersing the gentle sensual bites with small kisses. Joe groaned softly, his body tensing. His mouth found hers again as his hand found its way beneath her T-shirt and his fingers traced light circles on her stomach, causing the muscles there to quiver before his hand traveled slowly upward. Gently, he cupped her breast through her bra and stroked her nipple with his thumb. Katie moaned again, arching her back and pulling his head down harder so that his mouth was crushed against hers.

Wanting to feel his warm skin against her hands, Katie quickly pulled his T-shirt out of his combat trousers and placed her hands on his stomach. She felt the muscles there contract and Joe's hand tightened almost painfully against her breast.

"God, I want you," he murmured softly against her mouth. "I want you so much."

"I want you too," Katie whispered. Her hands moved around to his back under his T-shirt and she tugged on the waistband of his combats, attempting to move him over on top of her. One of his legs moved between hers and Joe's hand went to her waistband — then he stopped.

For what seemed like long minutes, he lay there and she could feel his heart pounding heavily against the palm of her hand where it rested on his chest. His breath was hot on her mouth and his breathing was rapid and harsh. Then he pushed her away gently and sat up, head and shoulders bowed, legs bent slightly.

"Joe?" Katie lay where she was on the ground, staring up at him in confusion. When he didn't answer, she suddenly sat up and got up to her knees. Humiliated and embarrassed, she began to tuck her T-shirt back into her combat trousers.

"I'm sorry," she began in a trembling voice. "I'm sorry. I thought..." Her voice trailed off into a sad silence.

"Hey" — Joe suddenly turned to face her — "it's not what you're thinking. I want to make love to you like hell, but not here." He put a finger under her chin and lifted her face to his. "This place is for quickies and one-night stands. You're worth far, far more than that. Trust me, Katie. If we were somewhere private..." His words trailed off and he leaned forward and kissed her so deeply and passionately that it took her breath away.

Finally, he released her. "I can get us a place, if you're sure it's what you want," he announced.

Katie nodded. "I do," she responded breathlessly.

"A pal of mine has one of those prefab rooms. He's been deployed to a forward operating base and gave me the key to use the room if ever I wanted to...to sleep in, nothing else."

Katie was nodding her answer even before he had finished the sentence. "When?" she asked, her voice breathless with sexual excitement.

"I'm out on patrol tomorrow night," he said. "What about Saturday night? I'll meet you here at 2000 hours."

Katie nodded then shuffled toward him on her knees. She put her arms around his neck, gently kissed his mouth, and again placed small kisses along his face and down his neck, nipping the skin gently.

"Can you wait that long?" she asked, her breath warm against his skin, her voice soft and sensually teasing.

Joe growled softly and laughed. He grabbed her around the waist and pulled her to him. "You're a tease," he murmured. "And yes, I can wait that long if I have something to look forward to at the end of it."

He suddenly put her firmly from him. "Now," he continued, "are we going to go to the PX or are you trying to keep me here by seducing me?" He got to his feet and held out his hand to her. As she put her hand in his, he pulled her to her feet and straight into his arms. "I love you," he said softly. "I love you so much."

Katie smiled up at him, reveling in the emotions that were showing so clearly on his face. "I love you too," she replied.

Joe gently kissed her mouth then straightened, laughing. "We can't keep doing this. We'll never get anywhere tonight," he said. "Come on, ma'am. Let's get to the PX and start the tongues wagging again. That's if you still want to go after what's happened."

Katie hesitated, remembering her encounter with Corporal Hudson and what would have happened if Joe had not appeared in time, but Joe held her tightly in his arms and the fears dissipated.

"I'm not going to let a little bastard like him spoil things," she answered, her chin lifting stubbornly. "If we don't go then he wins."

"Good girl," Joe said and took her hand. They slowly left the stacks of pallets and walked in the direction of the tents. Every now and again Joe would stop Katie, take her in his arms, and gently kiss her as though he couldn't get enough of her, they would then meander on a little farther, keeping to the shadows so that they wouldn't be seen, before pausing again.

Eventually Katie asked, "What happened on your patrol, Joe?"

Joe's reaction was to squeeze her hand. After some hesitation, he replied, "It was bad. I can't tell you some of the stuff, but there were times when I didn't think we'd make it back. We holed up for a while overnight in the sandstorm, but we couldn't wait it out. We'd have run out of water and rations. The radios wouldn't work—too much interference from the storm, so we were cut off. So, after a discussion with the squad, I made the call to head for the base. It took us hours but I've got a top-notch navigator and he got us straight to the road leading to the base."

Katie stepped in front of him and stopped him in his tracks. She placed her hands on his chest and rubbed her palms gently up and down, caressing the material of his combat jacket. Gazing into his face, she smiled slightly. "I was worried sick," she said softly. "I couldn't bear the thought that something might have happened to you. But now I feel selfish knowing that it was hell for you out there."

Joe raised a hand and stroked the side of her face with his finger. "Hey," he said, "I'm here now and we're together." He pulled her closer and nuzzled the top of her head. "Come on, honey. Let's get going."

They continued to walk until they had passed the tented accommodation. Once they had reached the road leading to Camp Roosevelt, Katie felt Joe release her hand. She glanced questioningly at him.

"I don't want you to be the butt of some asswipe's jokes," he explained and shrugged.

After a walk of some distance, they approached a large, brightly lit building from which issued a subdued roar of conversation. Outside the building, a large crowd of uniformed men and women had gathered, talking loudly and full of high spirits. Approaching them, Katie hesitated, falling back slightly. Joe turned to find out why she had slowed her pace.

"What's wrong?" he asked.

"Are you sure about this, Joe?" Katie asked anxiously. "You know what'll happen, gossip, smutty jokes. And I must look a fright with a swollen lip. People will think it was you."

Joe stroked her arm. "Hey," he said softly. "You look beautiful to me. If you don't want to go in, we won't, but I'm sure the majority of the base knows about us anyway. It's your call."

Katie looked at the noisy building, thoughts turning over in her mind, and then shrugged. "What the heck," she answered.

They proceeded toward the crowd at the PX doors, Katie feeling nervous and shy. As they drew nearer, loud, friendly shouts from the men and women, who were acquainted with Joe greeted his arrival with interested and curious glances directed at Katie. Sensing Katie's unease, Joe nodded briefly at the remarks made to him until they entered the building.

The interior was similar to that of the NAAFI on Camp Churchill in décor and layout, but it was much larger and noisier. Joe placed his hand on Katie's back and guided her toward the counter where drinks and snacks were being served. Again, many at the counter hailed Joe and Katie received various glances of appreciation and interest.

Joe bought two bottles of Coke, and while they waited for their drinks to arrive, he bent his head and whispered loudly in Katie's ear, "You appear to be causing quite a stir."

Katie glanced around her and blushed. She had caught the eye of a young soldier who blatantly winked at her and smiled. Offering a small smile of courtesy, Katie turned back to Joe. "I feel like an exhibit in a museum," she said, frowning.

Joe laughed. "No need," he replied. "They're all a great crowd." He took the two frosted bottles offered to him and handed one to her. He then urged her away from the counter and located a space against a wall where they could stand.

"No dancing?" Katie asked, taking a long sip of her cold drink.

"You ain't seen anything yet," Joe replied. "The music will get twice as loud, and then everyone will be prancing around like a herd of buffalo." He took a long swallow out of his bottle, glancing over Katie's head, his eyes distant and thoughtful. Katie watched his face.

"Penny for them?" she asked, loving him so much.

"Heck, they're not worth that much." He hesitated. "But I guess I do have something on my mind. It might cause a problem for you though. Be a helluva decision for you, honey." He stared at her, his dark blue eyes holding a penetrating but troubled expression.

Katie paused, Coke bottle raised halfway to her mouth. "What problem?" she asked warily.

Joe looked down at his boots then glanced at her face. His eyes were intensely blue and there was a wry smile playing about his lips. "You know something? I've never been stuck for words in my life except when I'm with you. I can never seem to find the words to tell you how I feel or what you mean to me."

Katie opened her mouth to say something in response but Joe raised a finger.

"No," he said. "Please let me finish this otherwise I'll never get it out." He moved closer to her so that he didn't have to shout to make himself heard. "I love you like I've never loved a woman before. From the first moment we met in the CTH, I was poleaxed. I was a career marine kinda guy, never wanted to get seriously involved with a woman because I felt it was dangerous, and then I met this CTM who shot all my principles and common sense to hell and back. On my last patrol, my Sergeant gave me a good talking-to and gave me all sorts of advice. Apparently, I'd been distracted and he noticed. Shows how good I was at hiding my feelings. I thought I was real good at it but that was a crapshoot. Anyway, we've only known each other a short time and in some people's eyes that might be a little too brief for comfort. You and I go our separate ways in a few weeks and I can't have that happen." Joe saw Katie's startling green eyes widen. "I want you to come back to the States with me, Katie," Joe continued. "If you want to, that is. I know it means leaving the Army and your career and I can't ask you to do that. I'm just telling you what I feel. You could even join the US Army, or at least work for them. Katie, I don't want to lose you now that I've found you."

Katie was speechless. Her dream of never leaving this man had come to fruition. More than anything, she had wanted to hear him say the things he had, but in her wildest dreams, she had never expected to hear him say that he wanted her with him always. Her smile widened and her eyes filled with unshed tears.

Finding her voice, she nodded. "I will," she answered huskily. "I'll come with you, Joe. I want to go wherever you go."

Joe grinned from ear to ear. "We'll talk more on Saturday night...if we have time." And he cocked an eyebrow at her.

"Doubt we will," Katie responded with a slow, sexy smile.

At that moment, they were interrupted by a voice yelling over the noise, "Good to see you here, Joe."

Joe glanced over his shoulder and grinned. "Hey, pal, how you doing?"

Sergeant Eastman nodded at Katie then turned to Joe. "Okay, Joe. So you decided to join us rowdy lot for a change instead of going over to the other side."

Joe laughed. "Yeah, you could say that. Louis, I'd like you to meet Katie Walker. Katie, this is Louis Eastman, a good buddy of mine and my assistant patrol leader. He keeps me in check and out of trouble."

Louis Eastman held out a hand to Katie, "Good to meet the woman who's managed to turn Joe's head at last."

Blushing, Katie took the proffered hand. "Pleased to meet you, Sergeant," she responded.

"No, no, no." Louis shook his head. "It's Louis, Katie."

"Okay." Katie nodded.

For the next hour, a flow of people came up to Joe and Louis Eastman, greeting them and stopping for conversation. Katie was introduced time after time and it became obvious that there was much interest and curiosity about her and about who she was. During this time, Louis Eastman studied his staff sergeant and Katie. He observed the way they constantly glanced at each other, the small smiles that often crossed their faces, the expressions in their eyes, and the way that they stood close to each other, bodies touching.

Serious stuff, Louis mused to himself. He was concerned. It seemed that the two people before him were besotted with each other, and that was not a good thing for his staff sergeant. Joe had always been an excellent leader. He thought nothing of putting his life in danger to assist or rescue his men, including Louis himself. He had always done things by the book, was strictly a regulation guy. In all the years that Louis had known Joe, he had never seen him so involved with a woman to the extent that it superseded his commitment to the Marines. He had no intention of lecturing him. It was not his place to and none of his business. But he was going to start watching Joe closely, covering the man's tracks if he became too distracted.

At that moment, the music in the PX went up a number of decibels and the whole place erupted into cheers and whistles.

Katie laughed as quite a few men and women jumped to their feet and began to dance where they stood. Louis Eastman made a decision and held out his hand.

"C'mon, Katie. Let's show 'em how it's done."

Katie hesitated then suddenly laughed and went with the sergeant, moving out into some empty floor space. She began to dance, tossing her head back, eyes sparkling, and a smile wide and brilliant on her face.

Joe watched her and Louis and couldn't keep his own smile from appearing. Joe wanted her so badly. He could take her outside and around the back of the building now, but he had meant what he had said to her earlier that evening. He was not about to have quick sex in a dark corner of the camp. She was worth far more than that. He could wait until Saturday, although it was probably going to be the longest wait of his life.

He leaned against the wall, drinking his Coke, watching the woman he adored mingling with the other dancing men and women, pumping her fist into the air, her whole body language exuding joy and enthusiasm.

Joe watched Katie dance with the sergeant until, between songs, he could hear Eastman laughingly protesting. "You've worn me out. I need a drink before I collapse."

Louis led her away from the dance floor, back to Joe. "I return your lady in one piece," he announced. "I can't say the same for myself. I am retiring gracefully to my pit." He glanced at Katie and smiled warmly. "It's been a pleasure, Katie." And he winked, gave a half salute to Joe, and left them.

Joe had taken off his jacket and Katie touched his arm. "Come and dance with me," she urged.

Joe grinned. "Yeah right," he answered. "I think not. I have two left feet."

Katie grabbed his hand and tugged. "Oh come on. You can't be that bad."

Shrugging, Joe followed Katie out into a space and joined her in the dance. Katie admired the way he moved and she played to each one, staying smoothly up against him and laughing up into his face, putting her hands on his waist, touching him whenever she could.

When at last the music finished, laughing, Joe and Katie went back to their little space against the wall.

Katie ran light fingertips down the muscles of his arm, feeling his warm skin and the way his muscles flinched as she touched him. Then she noticed the beginnings of a tattoo on the upper portion of his left arm, disappearing under his T-shirt.

"What's this?" she asked, touching it and rubbing the palm of her hand over it.

Joe regarded her with hot arousal in his eyes. "You'll see it Saturday night," he replied huskily, lowering his head as though he was going to kiss her.

Katie felt a shiver of delight travel through her body. How she wanted this man. She needed his hands on her body, his mouth on hers, and craved to feel his strong arms holding her.

"Don't look at me like that," he murmured, whispering in her ear. He blew gently against the whorls of her earlobe and Katie moaned slightly. She moved closer to him so that her body was touching his and gently bumped her hip against him.

Looking at him, she asked teasingly, "Why?"

"Because, ma'am, you're turning me on and I would have no second thoughts about making love to you right this minute against this wall."

Katie's breath shuddered and her cheeks flushed. "Am I?" she asked breathlessly, "Then why don't you...take me outside?"

"Katie." Joe closed his eyes briefly, "Don't tempt me, please."

Katie leaned her back against the wall and gently tugged at his T-shirt, pulling him closer. Joe placed the palm of one hand against the wall, propping himself against it. "Lady," he said softly, "we are on full view here."

Katie smiled. "And?" she responded. "What's your point?" She ran a finger along the waistband of his combat trousers.

"My point is this," Joe murmured, and leaning forward, he kissed her slowly and tenderly on the mouth.

When he drew back, Katie smiled sensuously, "We have successfully sealed our fates," she stated. "We'll be the talk of both camps tomorrow."

Joe raised his head. "I love you," he said.

"And I love you," Katie answered, "but I need to go and use the ladies." She gave him a quick kiss on the mouth and turned away to leave the room.

She found the restroom and used the facilities. The room was empty and as she was washing her hands, she glanced at herself in the long mirror. Her face was slightly flushed and her green eyes were bright and shining.

"You look like a woman in love who has been thoroughly kissed," she murmured to herself. She dried her hands and left the restroom to rejoin Joe. Thrusting open the doors into the main PX room, she stepped inside and came to an abrupt stop, shocked at what she saw.

Joe was still where she had left him, although now he wasn't alone. He was with a woman who had her hands on each of his arms. Joe himself had one hand on the woman's waist and his head was lowered as though he was listening to something she was saying. The woman had her mouth close to his ear.

Katie recognized the woman instantly. She was the one who had been seated with Joe in the mess.

Katie couldn't move. The pain on seeing Joe with another woman was beyond something she could tolerate. She couldn't believe that five minutes ago, she had been the one in Joe's arms and he had been telling her that he loved her. She had to get out of the PX now, before he saw that she had seen them together. Panic overwhelmed her and she spun on her heel and hurried toward the doors leading outside.

Chapter Twenty

At the precise moment that Katie was exiting through the doors, Joe happened to glance in her direction. He was shocked to see her hurrying out and realized instantly that she had seen him with Dana. His spirits plummeted as he imagined what it must have looked like and what she must have thought. Without a word, shrugging off the woman's hands, he headed after her, almost running. Entering the lobby, he saw Katie through the second set of doors leading to the outside, hurrying away from the building.

"Fuck!" he exclaimed and ran after her.

Once outside, he quickened his speed. He didn't want to call out to her. It would only draw the attention of the crowd standing outside the building. Instead, he ran after her and easily caught her. He reached out for her shoulder, but before he could stop her headlong flight, she heard him and spun around. Joe was shocked to see that her eyes were wild and angry but her cheeks were wet with tears.

"Leave me alone," she spat, but there was the soft sound of a sob in her voice.

"Katie, listen to me," Joe began. "You misunderstood what you saw."

"Yeah right. Tell that to the birds," Katie hissed vehemently. "I'm not dumb. I know what I saw." With that last remark, she spun around again and continued to hurriedly walk away from him.

Angry now, Joe jogged up to her and grasped her arm, "Will you listen, for fuck's sake?"

Katie wrenched her arm away.

Joe suddenly grabbed her around the waist and lifted her into the air. "Okay, we'll do things my way," he said, turned, and began to walk in the direction of the side of the building. Katie kicked her legs and cursed at him angrily.

As Joe crossed the gravel, a military policeman approached them both. Glancing sideways at the staff sergeant with his recalcitrant armful, the MP cocked an eyebrow and said, "Evening, Staff Sergeant. Need some help?"

With his arms full of struggling woman, Joe shook his head and smiled briefly, "Thank you, Corporal, but I think I can manage."

A smile twitched on the MP's mouth and he nodded. "Have a good evening, Staff Sergeant," and continued on his mission to enter the PX.

Joe carried Katie around the side of the PX and continued walking until they eventually reached a patch of darkness. Slightly out of breath, he placed Katie on her feet and waited in silence for the resultant fallout.

"How dare you," Katie retorted furiously, almost stomping her foot. "Who the hell do you think you are? How dare you...you...?" She was so angry that her words ran out and she could only stutter with fury.

Observing her, Joe thought how beautiful she was when she was angry. He folded his arms and, struggling not to smile at her attempts to find the words to berate him, he asked calmly, "Are you going to listen to me?"

"No!" Katie exclaimed stubbornly. "What's there to listen to?"

Exasperated, Joe unfolded his arms and placed a hand on either side of her, palms flat against the wall.

"Katie. You will listen to me. What you saw was nothing. The woman is an old friend of mine. We dated back in the US but it came to nothing. It was all one-sided on her part. Tonight I told her about you and that we were serious. She had to know and she was wishing me luck. Now, you can take it or not, but I don't lie and you better learn that." Joe stared at her still-furious face intently, waiting for her response. Little by little, he saw the fury recede from her eyes, although there was still an air of suspicion and wariness about her.

"I saw you with her in the mess," Katie explained.

"Yeah, I know you did," Joe replied, realizing with relief that she was calming down. "I ran out after you but you were moving hell for leather down the road toward the CTH."

Katie's mouth twitched with a small smile. "Mmmmm, I was pretty angry. I must admit," she answered.

Joe allowed himself to grin now. "You don't say," he remarked. "I would never have guessed."

"I'm sorry, Joe," she continued. "You must think I'm acting like a child."

"No," Joe answered. "It must have looked pretty suspicious from where you were standing but, Katie, I would never hurt you intentionally or lie to you. Never.

I love you and will always love you. And that's a promise."

Seeing that she still needed some reassurance, Joe took his place beside her against the wall and tugged her T-shirt. "Come here, woman," he said and pulled her in front of him, against his body, opening his legs slightly so that her own legs fitted in between them.

"You're quite a handful," he teased, putting his arms around her waist.

Katie snuggled in against him, pressing her body against his as close as she could. She put her arms around his neck and gently teased his short hair with her fingers. She was delighted at his response when he shivered and squirmed.

"Naughty," he murmured, his arms tightening around her waist.

"But you love it," she whispered, softly and huskily.

"Oh yeah," Joe replied and proceeded to show her how much he loved it by kissing her deeply.

As with their other kisses, their passion for each other flared quickly and for long minutes they immersed themselves in each other until suddenly Joe picked Katie up in his arms. Katie immediately swung her legs up and around his hips and he turned and leaned her against the wall, pressing her there gently so that his pelvis was hard against hers. Katie arched her back, trying to get as close to him as she could.

Joe was fast losing control. The promise he had made to himself about not making love to her in a dark corner of the camp was quickly becoming meaningless. It wasn't until he discovered that he had one hand down between them, undoing the Velcro fastening of her combat trousers that he realized how close they were both coming to losing control. He promptly yanked his hand away and stopped kissing her.

"Jesus Christ!" he exclaimed, shaken at the emotions that were burning between them.

Katie put her head on his shoulder and he could feel her trembling and her heart pounding against his chest. She unhooked her legs from around his hips and he gently lowered her to the ground.

She moved her hips slightly against his and said sensuously, "I can feel you." There was no teasing in her voice, just a tone of regret.

"You're not kidding," he said. "Saturday is a hell of a long way away."

Katie raised her head and looked at him, "But worth the wait," she replied softly.

"God, I love you," Joe suddenly said. "I love you so much."

Katie gently traced the outline of his mouth with a finger. "I want you so much," she said simply, without artifice or seduction evident in her voice.

Joe moaned softly and kissed her again. This time it was gentle and showed all the love that he had for her. Eventually they drew apart and Joe glanced at his watch.

"Hey," he said, "it's getting late. Do you want to go back into the PX?"

Katie shook her head. "No," she answered. "I'd much rather stay out here with you."

"Okay," Joe acknowledged and pulled her against him so that she was able to snuggle into his arms.

Out in a war zone nobody made plans or talked about when they were going back home, as that was to risk something happening, fate taking a kick at someone you loved. It was classed as bad luck. So Joe quietly spoke about some aspects of his life in the Marines until at least he sighed and announced with regret, "Time to go."

Katie made a small moue of reluctance, feeling an upwelling of anxiety about Joe going out on patrol again. "I'll miss you while you're away," she said. "I hate these patrols."

"I know, honey," Joe responded softly, "but four more weeks and we'll be together out of this place."

Katie smiled slightly at him, but he saw that there were unshed tears in her eyes and her lip was trembling.

"Hey," he said. "I'll be okay."

Katie nodded with resignation.

"Come on. It's late. I'll walk you back to your tent."

Joe took her hand and together they walked back along the side of the building to the front. The crowd outside was dispersing with much loud noise, and as they joined the throng, Katie attempted to remove her hand from his to save them both from any further gossip, but Joe refused to release it. "Might as well make the gossip even juicer," he announced, and hand in hand, they walked slowly away from the PX in the direction of Camp Churchill.

Once they reached Katie's tent, Joe took her into his arms. "I'll say goodnight for now," he said in a low voice and kissed her thoroughly, not seeming to care that someone might see them or come walking down the path to find their tent. After a few minutes, he released her. "Go," he said, "before I change my mind."

"Goodnight, Joe," Katie said softly. "Take care."

Joe sketched a half salute and turned to make his way back to his own tent in Camp Roosevelt while Katie went into hers.

Chapter Twenty-One

The next morning when Katie arrived at the CTH she found the building in complete pandemonium. There had been a number of firefights during the night and the theaters and trauma rooms were full of casualties. There were patients lying on gurneys waiting for treatment and medical personnel rushing from patient to patient and from room to room. Katie had never seen the teams under such pressure or felt such tension in the air. She ran to her locker to get changed and immediately went to Theater One to assist in any way she could.

The teams had been on duty since the previous night but there was no standing anyone down. The rooms were gore-soaked but the number of casualties did not allow time for the rooms to be cleaned after each surgery or assessment. Everyone was run ragged and exhaustion was beginning to show in short, sharp commands, and irritation.

By late afternoon, Katie was exhausted. Some of the teams were stood down by then but the CTMs, including Katie, remained on duty, seeing to the patients—as there weren't enough trauma nurses—cleaning rooms, replenishing low stocks of drugs and helping out where they could.

At 1900 hours, Katie eventually slumped down into a chair in the R&R room. The place was crowded with exhausted, unusually silent medical staff, people sitting with closed eyes or sipping cups of coffee. There was none of the usual animated conversation or banter and staff discussing the surgical procedures. People looked numb and distracted, locked into their own worlds of fatigue.

Katie was so tired that she could barely concentrate enough to drink her own brew. She wondered briefly about Joe, felt a swift tingle of remembrance from last night, and then jerked as the alarm sounded again within the CTH.

For a moment, nobody moved. Then there was a soft groan and they all rose to their feet. "Okay," Major McIntyre urged strongly, as though rallying troops. "Let's get going, folks. More incoming."

Katie threw her half-full cup into the waste receptacle and headed for the door of the R&R room. She collided with Sergeant Webster, who was just coming from his office.

"Corporal Walker, you're needed on a CTF flight. Get your equipment," he ordered, and without waiting for her response, he was gone, jogging down the long corridor to the front of the building.

For a moment Katie remained standing where she was, numb with fatigue and shock, and her heart sank. Suddenly her training kicked in and she was on the move to the locker room to get changed and retrieve her combat equipment. Within minutes, she was jogging out to the front of the CTH, where the team who she had been assigned to was waiting for their vehicle to take them out to the CTF Chinook. Within minutes, a Bulldog APC drew up and they climbed aboard to be driven to the checkpoint and out on to the helicopter apron.

Katie and the CTT seated themselves aboard the helicopter and rearranged their weapons more comfortably, waiting for takeoff. As on her previous trip, Katie again felt nervous, only this time she was able to keep the nerves at bay, and if she concentrated hard enough on other thoughts — such as Joe — she could almost believe that there was nothing to be concerned about.

The double engines of the Chinook began to wind up to their usual pre-takeoff screams and the double rotor blades began to spin faster, tearing at the night air. The nose jolted upward, followed by the rear, and the helicopter rose up smoothly from the ground, banked to the left, and flew off in the direction of its assigned coordinates.

Katie sat quietly, knowing what was expected of her. Conversation inside the Chinook was again impossible with the big side door open and the wind howling through it and into the interior. To distract herself from her nerves, her thoughts turned to Joe, as they always seemed to do now, and a small smile came and went as she remembered her time with him at the PX the previous evening and what they had discussed. Her life had changed so completely over the last few days that it was never going to be the same. All they both had to do now was make it to the end of their tours, stay safe for each other and out of harm's way. Loving him was a part of her now and she felt a quiet joy whenever she thought of him. Gone were the anxieties of whether she should be involved with him or not. Time would tell whether their love for each other would last, but for now, she was just happy with the way things were.

Katie was jerked from her reverie at the sudden ominous sound of loud repetitive pinging and metallic clanging against the hull of the helicopter. She glanced surreptitiously at her colleagues to discover that they were all looking at each other with expressions of alarm on their faces. It made her feel distinctly uneasy.

"We're taking heavy fire," the pilot suddenly shouted over his shoulder from the cockpit. "This might prove a bit dicey, folks. We need to do a bit of evasive maneuvering, so it's gonna get bumpy."

As the pilot relayed his message to them, the door gunner began firing out into the black night, the continuous ratcheting noise of his gun deafening in the confines of the cabin.

The pinging and cracks against the thin metal hull of the helicopter continued unabated and the Chinook began to swerve from side to side, vibrating and bouncing. Katie felt fear begin to rise in her as she realized that there must be a huge firefight going on below them. The enemy had obviously sighted the Chinook and it would be a great coup for them if they brought it down. She gripped the edges of her seat and tried to calm herself by taking deep breaths. The crew had no doubt been through this many times and she was confident that they knew what they were doing and had a strategy on how to get out of the situation that they now found themselves in. Her belief that they would come through the brief attack was confirmed over the next few minutes as the noises against the hull diminished. Katie breathed a sigh of relief. They had obviously passed out of range of the gunfire.

Katie released her grip on her seat and flexed her tense and rigid fingers. She blew out air and tried to relax her muscles. There were a few nervous laughs from the CTT and a comment of, "That was a close call."

In the next second, everything turned to terrifying chaos.

"Incoming! RPG!" There was a sudden nerve rending shout from the pilot, followed by an explosion from somewhere to the rear of the helicopter. The Chinook shuddered and immediately veered to the left. Loud, strident alarms sounded from the cockpit and over the strained screaming of the engines, Katie could hear the pilot and co-pilot shouting at each other as they tried to maintain control.

The Chinook began to shake then veer violently from left to right, showering medical equipment down onto Katie and the other medical personnel. Although they were all wearing combat helmets, some of the equipment was hard and heavy and they had to shield themselves as best they could.

As though the helicopter had given up its attempt to stay on a level flight, it began to spin in a slow, erratic circle, the even sound of the rotor blades becoming choppy and intermittent, the noise they were giving out now sounding like a harsh whine.

With an upsurge of sheer terror, Katie heard the co-pilot on the radio, "Mayday, Mayday. Charlie Tango Foxtrot Charlie Hotel-47. We have taken fire and are going down. I say again. Mayday, Mayday. Charlie Tango Foxtrot Charlie Hotel-47. We have taken fire and are going down." His voice was calm and controlled but ice formed in Katie's veins as the words impacted her brain.

The sergeant from the CTT suddenly appeared in front of her. He spoke briskly and firmly but remained calm. "Go and stand by the door, Corporal Walker.

When we land, you are not to hang around. You are to get out of the helo any way you can and move as far away from it as possible without endangering yourself. The rest of the team will follow you. Do you understand?"

"Yes, Sergeant," Katie replied in a voice that shook with terror, finally nodding vigorously in case he had not heard her answer above the noise.

The sergeant gripped her shoulder. "We'll be all right, Corporal. Stay calm and remember your training."

The others were all on their feet, but with the wild gyrating and bouncing of the helicopter, it was difficult for them to remain standing, and they had to grasp any handholds that were available.

The Chinook was now spiraling down at speed, almost completely out of control, the crew still attempting to stabilize the spin. If they could raise the nose, then the rest of the Chinook would follow suit and they might be able to land safely.

Even though it was only a couple of minutes since they had been hit, to Katie it felt like hours had passed. She moved to the door, gripping her rifle so hard that the muscles in her hand ached. As she reached the door, the door gunner turned and nodded his head at her. The expression on his face was calm and reassuring.

The rear of the helicopter suddenly plunged downward and there was a rending, tearing crash as it made contact with the ground. Because it had maintained its speed during its spiraling fall, it began to slide along the ground and, almost in slow motion, topple sideways to the left, the long rotor blades snapping with harsh cracking sounds, pieces of metal flying through the air like knife-edged missiles.

The front of the helicopter impacted the ground like a block of concrete falling from a great height and began to roll sideways, following the direction of the tail. Katie found herself somersaulting toward the open door. She heard herself screaming with terror as she flailed with an outstretched hand, trying to find a handhold to hang onto to prevent her from flying outside to be crushed by the tumbling helicopter. Her other hand still retained a vise-like grip on her weapon.

The noise of the dying helicopter was a screaming, tearing cacophony. The engines continued to howl with a tortured sound, metal ruptured and crumpled, struts and steel plating groaned, strained almost to breaking point, warning alarms blared from the cockpit and somewhere in the cabin, somebody was screaming, a howl of human pain. Then Katie found herself in silence.

She became aware of the chilly night air on her face. She could still hear the dying screeches of the helicopter, but they were diminishing as it and she went in opposite directions. Then she hit the ground hard. The breath tore from her lungs. There was sudden pain in various parts of her body. Her combat helmet came off and her head hit something hard. Everything went black.

Chapter Twenty-Two

Katie opened her eyes. For considerable time her mind remained mercifully blank, then gradually she became aware that she was lying face down on cold, hard ground and her head hurt badly. A flickering golden-red light surrounded her and she had no idea where it was coming from. Her mind had stopped functioning and she couldn't remember anything. Something had happened, something bad. She had been... Then everything came flooding back to her and she whimpered.

The helicopter had been hit by some kind of missile and had crashed. Somehow, she was flung from the Chinook after they had hit, and although she had obviously hit her head and was feeling the impact from the ground, she was alive.

The side of her face stung where it rested on the hard earth and she felt bruised all over. Slowly and carefully, she moved each limb, assessing each for any broken bones. It appeared that nothing was broken, but she was bruised and going to ache like the devil in a few hours.

The only thing she was sure of was that her head was pounding severely and she felt sick to her stomach. The cold ground was leaching the warmth from her body and she was beginning to shiver. Inch by inch, she attempted to sit up. At each tentative movement, her head protested, but she persevered until she was in a kneeling position. Once upright, she immediately vomited and instantly diagnosed herself with a concussion — or worse — a skull fracture. She rested for a while with her eyes closed, biting her lip hard, as though another source of pain would force back the much more severe pain in her head.

Gritting her teeth, Katie shrugged out of her medical bergen. Somehow, it had remained on her back, even with one strap broken. She opened up various pockets, searching for basic first-aid supplies, her torch, and a bottle of sterile water. She found all the items she needed and laid them on the ground around her. The flickering golden light and her torch beam allowed her to see reasonably well and she opened up some gauze, unscrewed the top of a bottle of water, and upended it carefully so that some of the liquid trickled out slowly to wet the gauze. She lifted a hand to her head and by feel alone, she discovered a large, painful lump and gash just above her left temple. Hissing through her teeth, she dabbed at the wound gently. She could feel a trail of stickiness coated with sand and dust down the left side of her face and knew that it was probably blood. By touch alone, she located the approximate area of the wound and the blood trail down her face and attempted to clean it, but it was a futile task.

Once she had finished, she repacked everything into her bergen, then spent a precious few minutes locating her combat helmet, which had rolled a few feet away from her position, and her rifle that, because it was black in color and blended with the night, was harder to locate. Once she had retrieved all her equipment, she sat back down on the ground. She felt sick again and light-headed, and she bowed her head between her knees until the feelings passed. She knew she needed to get to her feet and get to the helicopter. The others might be injured and need her help.

She could hear nothing in the area, not a single voice or movement. There was a crackling from somewhere close by and even more distant, there were sharp repetitive cracking sounds that she recognized as gunfire. Sound traveled long distances in the silent desert and she had no idea how far away the gunfire was but knew that she was possibly in big trouble. There was obviously a firefight going off somewhere, not close by, but close enough that if the hostiles decided to come in her direction, she was on her own and she couldn't hope to defend herself.

The pain in her head had retreated a little. As long as she didn't move quickly, it stayed that way, and she finally felt able to get to her feet, although she discovered that she had to use her weapon as leverage by digging the butt of it into the ground and leaning on it to be able to gain her feet.

Once upright, her head pounded another rebellious protest and she groaned quietly, putting a hand up to her forehead as though to relieve the pain. Determined not to give in to her injury, she turned slowly in a circle, surveying her location. It was then she discovered the source of the light and was horrified.

The helicopter was in flames. It had skidded and rolled some distance away from her, coming to rest in a twisted tangle of metal against an outcropping of rock. The highly flammable fuel had obviously exploded and caught fire and it was now a burning beacon for all the hostiles in the area and farther afield to see. Katie knew that she needed to find the others, if they were still alive. They would then need to find somewhere to hide until rescue came, which it surely would, as the co-pilot had sent a mayday before the crash.

Hobbling on bruised and sore legs, she began to limp her way toward the burning pyre. She had come to within fifty meters of it when, by the leaping light of the flames, she saw a body lying on the ground. Hurriedly, she moved toward it and dropped to her knees.

It was the Sergeant who had ordered her to move to the open door before they crashed. Katie quickly put two fingers against his carotid artery and, holding her breath, waited to feel the steady throb of a pulse. There was none. Whimpering, she frantically ripped open his body armor, his jacket and raised his T-shirt, and proceeded to commence CPR. Her head throbbed and pounded at the repetitive movement, but she continued the life-saving technique for ten minutes with no response from the sergeant. Finally realizing that he was dead, Katie sat back on her heels, gasping. Tears began to trickle down her cheeks and she felt as though she could curl up on the ground and cry herself into oblivion.

She was so tired, so weary of all the death and destruction, and now here was this dead man, someone who had done nothing to deserve dying out in a lonely desert when all he had ever done was try to save lives. A sob escaped her, and she put a hand across her mouth to prevent any more escaping. The sob had sounded so lonely and pathetic that it frightened her.

She could not allow herself the luxury of breaking down just yet. She desperately needed to find out if any of the others were still alive. In pain, she laboriously clambered to her feet and proceeded to circle the burning helicopter, glancing around the area for signs that there were others that might be alive. There were no other bodies and she could see no other survivors.

Having circled the burning Chinook, Katie came to a standstill. She was done. Her senses were numb and she was glad of the feeling. But it felt like there was a ten-ton weight on her shoulders and in the pit of her stomach was a ball of unreleased grief that she would have to attend to eventually. But for now, she had to get a grip, maintain an iron-hard control, and piece together a plan from her scattered thoughts. It was becoming obvious that everyone else aboard the helicopter was inside when it exploded and caught fire. The sergeant had obviously been flung out onto the ground as she herself had been, but she was the only lucky one to have lived.

Now, she was alone, out in the desert, and a sudden fear assailed her. She had to find somewhere safe to hide until rescue arrived. She didn't know how long that would be or in what form it would arrive. She listened carefully to see if she could roughly pinpoint how distant the firefight was. The gunfire had drawn closer and now she could decipher the thudding percussions of heavy weapons.

Katie glanced back at the dead body of the sergeant. She had to move the body and hide it in case any enemy happened to appear to check out the burning helicopter. She shrugged off her bergen, dropping it to the ground, and retraced her steps back to where he lay. Hoping that she had the energy to carry it out, she grasped the man under his arms and slowly and with a great deal of effort, began to drag him along the ground toward a small, uneven outcropping of rock that threw its own shadow deep enough to hide both the body and herself. She would lay him there and she would stay by him. The darkness would hide them both, but the burning helicopter would provide some warmth and light. It would also be where any rescue would arrive because it would be their last known coordinates.

Katie laid the sergeant gently in the shadows then stood still for a minute, waiting for the sick pounding in her head to die down and the sudden dizziness to abate. Once the pain had diminished, she tiredly went back for her bergen. Arriving back by the rock, she sank down onto the hard ground and rested against it. She was shivering now, and a clammy sweat had broken out on her forehead. She wanted to sleep but the medical part of her mind knew that with a head injury, you did not sleep. She could feel fresh blood coating her face and she felt very thirsty and sick. Sliding farther down the rock into a half reclining position, she placed her bergen under her head, propped her helmet up so it partly shielded her head — she couldn't put it on because it hurt too much — turned on her right side and curled up into a ball, clutching her rifle with both hands. She thought of Joe and wished that he was there with her. She wanted to feel his arms around her and to hear him say that everything would be all right. The wanting was so strong that it was like a physical pain. "Be safe, Joe," she murmured. "But please come and get me."

Her thoughts became jumbled, and even though she struggled to keep them open, her eyelids began to flutter closed. Finally, against her better judgment, drowsiness overcame her and she slipped into sleep.

Chapter Twenty-Three

"Ma'am, ma'am. Can you wake up for me, ma'am?"

From somewhere in the depths of a deep, dark sleep, Katie heard a faint, persistent voice calling her name. She tried to ignore it, determined not to open her eyes and answer the call, fighting against drifting up through black layers of sleep to the world of reality.

She then felt gentle tapping on her exposed cheek and finally realized that the person calling her name was not going to go away. Katie groaned and attempted to push away the irritating hand. "Leave me alone," she moaned her words slurred and hoarse.

"'Fraid I can't do that, ma'am," came the voice again. "Come on. Open your eyes."

Katie sighed with exasperation and her eyelids fluttered half open. They felt gritty and dry with dust and her mouth and lips felt devoid of moisture, her tongue swollen. She licked her lips and tried to force her eyes open wider. Her vision remained blurred for a few minutes then it cleared and she was able to see her surroundings. She was no longer alone. There were soldiers walking about the area, obviously searching for either the enemy or the occupants of the burning helicopter. Katie blinked a few times then rolled onto her back. She groaned, her body stiff and cold and sore. She immediately saw that a soldier was leaning over her.

"Who're you?" she mumbled, lifting her head so that she could focus on him more clearly. She instantly scrunched up her eyes as a dagger-like pain shot through her skull.

"Bugger," she exclaimed, "that hurts."

"I'm a medic, ma'am. US Marines," the marine answered. "I need to assess your injuries. Ask you a few questions."

"I know what's wrong with me," Katie responded snappishly, feeling very combative. "I have a concussion with accompanying wound, dizziness, my pulse feels a little fast, and I am probably dehydrated because of vomiting. Does that answer your questions?"

The medic looked a little taken aback. "Very good," he commented. "I take it you're a medic yourself then?"

Refraining from nodding her head because of the pain that might result, Katie swallowed and cleared her throat. "CTM," she replied shortly — and shivered.

"Did you lose consciousness?" the medic asked.

"Yes," Katie answered, "but I don't know for how long."

"Okay," the medic continued. "I'm going to need to clean your wound and put a dressing on it. You're covered in dust and you may get an infection." He opened a medical bergen beside him and began to pull out gauze, cotton wool and a bottle of antibacterial wash. He also pulled out a silver hypothermia blanket and slung it around her shoulders, pulling it together around her.

"This might sting a bit," he announced, soaking some cotton wool in the antibacterial solution. He dabbed gently at the gash on Katie's temple, eliciting a sharp hiss from her as the liquid stung the wound ferociously.

The cleansing went on for a while with Katie gritting her teeth and unshed tears springing into her eyes, but she refused to make a sound. The medic then went on to clean the dried blood from the side of her face.

"Nice graze you've got there," the medic commented. "Do you have any other grazes anywhere? I take it you've not got any broken bones or other major injuries?"

"I'm fine," Katie answered sharply. "Sore and bruised but no, no broken bones."

"That's good," the medic responded. "How's your vision?"

"Fine," Katie answered. "I just have a hell of a headache."

"I'll give you something for that in a minute," the medic offered. "Here. Have a drink. Don't gulp it because it'll come right back up. Small sips."

Katie took the proffered water bottle, unscrewed its cap, and slowly drank a mouthful. She swished the first liquid around her mouth, turned her head to the side, and spat it out.

She grimaced. "Sorry about that," she began, "but my mouth is full of dust."

The medic grinned. "No worries."

Katie slowly drank small sips of the delicious water, almost closing her eyes at the blissful moisture in her mouth. She eventually opened her eyes, "Thanks," she said.

"Let's put a dressing on that wound," the medic said, and proceeded to place a thick layer of gauze on the gash and tape it there with strips of surgical tape. "That should do it."

"Thank you," Katie said again.

"You want to try to sit up?" the medic asked.

"Okay," Katie agreed.

The medic shuffled forward on his knees, grasped both of Katie's hands, and gently pulled her up into a seated position. Katie put a hand to her head and froze, waiting for the pounding to cease knocking at the inside of her skull.

"Hurts, huh?" the medic asked.

"Just a bit," Katie replied, briefly scrunching up her eyes, as though doing so would cause the pain to abate.

The medic searched through his medical bergen again and brought out a bottle of tablets. He shook two out into the palm of his hand and handed them to her. "Here you go. They're painkillers. They're not strong, in case you need something else back at the CTH, but they'll take the edge off the pain."

Katie swallowed the tablets, washing them down with water from the bottle.

"Okay, I need to go and report your condition to the old man. He needs to radio back to the base to order a medevac so I'll need your rank and name. He'll probably want to come and speak to you himself, find out what went on here," the medic explained.

Katie gave him her rank and name then slumped back against the rock for support.

The medic repacked his bergen and stood up. "Rest for a bit," he said and marched off toward the other marines.

Katie closed her eyes and willed the painkillers to start working. Her head felt as though it was going to split. A few minutes later, she heard heavy footfalls approaching but kept her eyes closed. She was far too tired to bother opening them. She heard a noise beside her and was just about to open her eyes to see who it was when a warm hand took her own. She would have recognized that touch anywhere. Her eyes flew open and Joe, looking pale and haggard, was crouched beside her, staring at her with a shocked expression on his face.

Katie tried to smile at him, but instead she found the sight of him too much and to her horror, her eyes began to fill with tears.

"Hey," he greeted gently.

Katie's answer was a small sob. She bit her lip hard to prevent the tears from falling. It wouldn't do to cry out here in the desert in front of Joe's squad. She needed to be tough to get through this.

Joe squeezed her hand. "How're you doing?" he asked.

Katie swallowed. "I've been better," she replied in a small voice. "What are you doing here?"

Noting the look of pain on her face, the long scrape on her cheekbone and the ashen color of her skin, Joe felt her pain and fear like a lead ball in his gut. It hadn't even crossed his mind that she would be involved in the helicopter crash. In a way, he was relieved that he hadn't been aware of it until his medic had given him a report of her condition then her rank and name so that he could report back to the base and order up a medevac. His heart had sunk when he had discovered that the only survivor had been her.

"We were out on patrol," he explained, trying to keep the tone of his voice even, "and closest to the crash site. We had orders to check for survivors and, if we found any, get them back to base. There are firefights going off all over the place tonight, hostiles carrying out hit and runs and ambushes. We can't get a medevac out here to this location so we're going to need to march a few clicks to a safe LZ then a medevac will come and extract you. My medic says that you have a concussion but that you're okay to march a couple of clicks?"

"I'll be fine," Katie said, trying to infuse a little firmness into her voice.

"What happened out here, Katie?" Joe asked.

"We got hit by an RPG," she explained. "I think it took off the tail rotor. I was thrown out when we hit the ground. I was already standing at the door, ready to jump. I was lucky. I don't think the others made it. I found the sergeant's body..." She coughed and cleared her throat. "I dragged him into this dark place in case we were discovered. When I hit the ground, my head must have hit a rock and I blacked out." She was unaware of a tear trickling down her face. "Those poor people," she whispered. "They were only doing their jobs." She sobbed a little and put a shaking hand to her mouth. Another tear trickled down her cheek.

"Katie..." Joe reached up and wiped away the errant tears with a thumb. "Hey, honey, please don't beat yourself up about it."

He gently released Katie's hand and smiled at her. "Okay. We need to get you out of here. I need to go and talk to the men. I'll send someone back to help you."

"No!" Katie spoke with vehement embarrassment. "I'll be fine. I don't need any help. You've all got things to do."

"Hey, do me a favor," Joe returned. "Don't go all stubborn on me. You've had a crack on the head, and you as a medic should know what happens with head injuries. Just stay here and do as you're told. Understand me?"

Katie glared at him then finally nodded. "You win," she agreed. "But only because I'm too damn tired to argue with you."

"That's my girl," Joe responded gently. He rose to his feet and turned away, thumbing a button on his PRR.

"Eagle E1 to Hawk E5 and Harrier E11, report to me."

One marine broke away from the perimeter boundary and began to jog toward Joe while another marine appeared from behind the burning Chinook. They came to a halt on reaching him.

"We need to haul ass," he said. "You two are to assist Corporal Walker. Do not leave her side. If she gets sick, just call Doc. We'll form up around you and move out that way."

"Yes, Staff Sergeant," the two men replied.

"Okay, let's get her on her feet," Joe announced.

He and one of the men moved to each side of Katie, and with a hand under each arm, lifted her gently to her feet.

Katie groaned, as, on standing, dizziness threatened to send her crashing back to the ground again. Her legs went weak and Joe and the second man had to throw their arms around her and support her. Leaning more against Joe, Katie closed her eyes, willing the pain in her head and the dizziness to abate.

They stood in frozen sculpture for long minutes until Katie straightened and opened her eyes. "Okay," she murmured, "let's go."

"You sure?" Joe asked.

"Yes," Katie answered, "otherwise we'll be here forever."

Slowly, concentrating on keeping her head as still as possible, so it did not increase the pain, Katie and her two escorts moved toward the marines guarding the perimeter of the area. Joe was issuing orders into his radio, and by the time the three of them had reached the other marines, all members of the patrol had formed themselves into a protective cordon with Katie and her two escorts and Joe at its center.

Joe turned to Katie. "I'll leave you with these two guys. I have to keep my eye on things," he said.

"Okay," she said, glancing at his face.

Joe winked at her then moved off, talking into his radio as he went.

The second marine took the place of Joe and put his arm around Katie's back, linking his arm with the second marine on her other side.

"All right, ma'am?" he asked.

"Thank you, I'm fine," Katie answered.

In a few minutes, it appeared that the patrol was ready to move out. Katie glanced back over her shoulder at the burning helicopter, muttered a silent apology for her colleagues who were still inside, then turned to her front once more. Through the flickering darkness, she could see Joe at the front of the patrol, and she watched as he raised his hand and gestured forward. She also noticed that all the marines surrounding her had their weapons raised and facing outward.

"Are we in danger?" she asked.

"You can call me Bonio, ma'am, and my buddy on your other side is Slither," the marine on her left said. "There's a sitrep of some bad guys heading in our direction but the old man should get us out of here so there's nothing for you to worry about."

"Where's my bergen and weapon?" Katie asked.

Bonio attempted to reassure her again but Katie was adamant.

"I'd like my weapon, please. Can somebody get it for me?" She raised her chin in a stubborn tilt.

Bonio thumbed the button on his PRR and spoke quietly into it. Minutes later Sergeant Eastman approached them with Katie's medical bergen and weapon in his hands.

He nodded at Katie. "All right, Corporal Walker?" And handed over her weapon and bergen.

"Fine, thank you, Sergeant," she replied and offered him a small smile, shrugging painfully into her bergen and slinging the strap of her rifle over a shoulder. "Thank you for hanging on to my equipment."

Sergeant Eastman inclined his head and went back to his position in the patrol.

The patrol and Katie with her two escorts began to move forward, making their way slowly and carefully away from the crash site and into the pitch-blackness of the desert. The pace was slow and careful in keeping with Katie's own movements, marines on either side of her guiding her around obstacles that appeared out of the dark suddenly and without warning. Katie could see that their eyes moved constantly, even though they were in the center of the patrol, and their arms were strong about Katie's back as they supported her.

The desert maintained its usual silence with the exception of the sound of distant gunfire. The firefight did not appear to be getting any closer, nevertheless there was an air of urgency amongst the squad at getting Katie to the coordinates where the medevac would be meeting them.

Katie felt embarrassment at this squad having to protect her. She wanted Joe with her but knew that he was unreachable at the moment. He had a responsibility to his men to get them to safety. She stumbled suddenly and almost cried out with the pain in her head. Bonio prevented her from falling.

"Oopsy-daisy, ma'am," he said.

Katie suddenly felt cold, although sweat was dampening her face and running down her back. She began to tremble, then, without any warning, she leaned forward and vomited.

"Ma'am?" Bonio queried, concerned, his arm preventing her from tumbling forward. "Are you okay?"

Katie's response was to retch dryly, her stomach completely empty. Her head was pounding, her vision was becoming blurry, and she couldn't prevent a small moan from escaping her dry lips.

"We need the medic over here," Slither suddenly called in a voice just loud enough that the rest of the squad heard and came to a stop. The marines automatically went down on one knee and raised their weapons.

Katie staggered slightly and Slither said, "Okay, ma'am, I think you need to sit down for a bit. The medic will be here in a few to check you over."

They led Katie to a low rock. Someone brought out a pad from his bergen and laid it on the ground then the two marines who had been assisting her helped her to sit down. Katie closed her eyes and leaned back against the rock. A few minutes later, the medic who had treated her at the crash site came to her side. He spoke briefly to Bonio and Slither then crouched down beside her. The remaining members of the squad immediately established a perimeter around them, facing out into the dark desert.

"Feeling rough, ma'am?" the medic asked. He reached out and took her wrist, feeling for her pulse.

Katie opened her eyes, feeling her body shivering and a cold clamminess on her forehead. "My head hurts," she explained quietly.

"Yeah, I bet it does," the medic replied. "We need to get you warm—"

At that moment, Joe appeared out of the dark and crouched down at her other side.

"What's wrong, Corporal?" he asked the medic, gazing at Katie's ashen face and closed eyes with consternation.

The medic rose to his feet and gestured to Joe to join him a few meters away from Katie. "She's started to suffer from shock, Staff Sergeant," he explained. "Her pulse is a bit rapid and her body temperature is dropping, probably due to a lowering blood pressure. She's in a lot of pain. She's not in any danger, but the longer she's on her feet, the worse the symptoms will get. We need to keep her warm and get her onto a medevac ASAP."

Joe listened carefully, his face expressionless, emotions under control as happened when he was under pressure or in a difficult situation.

"Very well, Corporal," he eventually replied. "Let's get her an extra jacket first."

He thumbed his PRR and spoke on the open squad band so everyone would receive his transmission. "All on this net, we need a spare jacket if everyone can search their equipment bergen and report to me by the casualty—on the double."

Within minutes, a marine jogged up to them with a spare combat jacket and handed it to Joe then jogged back to his position in the perimeter.

Joe turned to the medic and two marines. "Give us a few minutes, guys," he ordered. The three men obeyed the order without a word and all moved away a few meters and turned their backs.

Clutching the jacket, Joe crouched down beside Katie, who hadn't moved. "Katie," he called gently and rested a hand on her leg. "Hey, sweetheart."

Katie murmured and stirred. She struggled to open her eyes, resentful that someone had disturbed her. She saw Joe beside her and offered him a small painful smile. "Hi," she whispered weakly. "I'm so sorry."

Joe managed a grin at her, although he had never felt less like smiling in his life. "Sorry doesn't exist in my vocabulary. Honey, I need to put this jacket on you. The medic has said you need to keep warm. Can you help me get it on you?"

Katie nodded, wincing, and leaned forward slightly. Joe managed to get one of her arms inside the sleeve of the spare combat jacket, slung it around her back, and got her other arm into the second sleeve, straining to close it across her body armor. Eventually he was able to fasten the Velcro that held the jacket together. Exhausted, Katie slumped back against the rock and closed her eyes again.

"Katie I need to talk to you—explain what we're going to try to do. Come on, Katie. Stay with me." Joe gently shook her hand and Katie groaned and opened her eyes again.

"Let me sleep," she said irritably.

"Uh-huh, nope," Joe replied. "You listen to me, lady. We have to get you on your feet and keep going. We have about two clicks to go then the medevac will be there to take you back to base. You can rest up in the CTH. Do you understand me?"

"I hear you. I'm not deaf," Katie snapped grumpily. "If I have to, I have to."

"That's my girl," Joe grinned, knowing that it was the head injury that was making her irritable. He rose to his feet and called the medic and two marines over. "Let's move out," he ordered.

The two marines managed to get Katie to her feet, the patrol formed up as before, and they moved off again.

At the site of her extraction, Katie promptly slumped to the ground, body trembling from the quickly spiraling shock taking control of her limbs, and closed her eyes. Joe saw how extremely difficult the last two clicks of the march had been for her and that it was only by sheer force of will she had managed to remain on her feet and keep going.

Joe immediately got on the radio and sent a transmission advising that they had reached the agreed coordinates and the causality was ready for the extraction. Relief filled him as he was advised that the CTF was fifteen minutes out from their location and Katie would be in safe hands in a short time.

While the marines kept watch from their security perimeter, Joe went to Katie's side. "The medevac will be here in fifteen," he explained.

Katie opened her eyes and managed a small smile for him. "Sorry to disrupt your patrol," she said, trying to infuse some strength into her voice.

Joe said soothingly, "Hey, it's okay. The crash was hardly your fault. Just remember, we'll be together tomorrow night. Just do as you're told and get well, otherwise you'll be kept in the CTH."

"That'll happen," Katie retorted with a little of her old spirit.

Glancing casually over his shoulder and noting that his squad was minding their own business, turned away from him, he took one of Katie's hands and stroked it. "I love you, sweetheart," he said softly. "You'll be fine."

In her weakened state, Katie felt tears fill her eyes, "I love you too, Joe," she replied, her voice trembling.

At that moment, Joe became aware of the sound of a helicopter approaching at low level from the south, and when he straightened up and glanced up at the night sky, he saw the flashing red lights of the CTF helicopter descending toward them. A member of the squad struck a red flare and threw it some distance from where the marines were positioned. Its smoke rose in a red cloud, marking the landing zone for the helicopter.

"Come on, Corporal, on your feet," Joe ordered, and bending down, he put one of Katie's arms across his shoulders and an arm around her waist and lifted her.

The Chinook touched down gently, and a member of the CTT team jumped out from the side door, ducking to avoid the huge, slowly spinning rotor blades, and jogged toward them. He took Katie's other arm and slung it around his shoulder and together the two men helped her toward the helicopter. The CTT member hoisted himself aboard then bent down, putting his hands under Katie's armpits and gently lifting her into the helicopter. As he did, Katie glanced anxiously at Joe.

"Joe," she began, but he shook his head slightly and offered her a reassuring smile. He then backed away from the Chinook while Katie was helped inside the cabin.

Joe kept his eyes on the helicopter, waiting for it to take off, wanting Katie to be all right. He had a feeling that showing his feelings so blatantly for a non-com, while on active duty out in the field, might not show too well on his career record. If his CO heard about it, he supposed he would be in for a lecture or two and it wouldn't be of the fatherly kind. As far as he was concerned, he didn't care. This was a very strong admission for him but the main priority for him now was Katie. All he wanted was this woman who was being treated aboard the medevac helicopter. He realized finally how much she meant to him, how much he loved her.

He watched as the rotor blades of the Chinook sped up, and as the engines reached full power, the nose tilted up and it rose gracefully into the air. It banked to the left and took off at speed.

Tense and stressed, Joe stood with his hands on his hips, gazing after the helicopter, hearing the noise of its engines fading into the distance. He eventually became aware that Sergeant Eastman had come to stand beside him and was talking to him. He turned abstractedly away to face his sergeant.

"Take it easy, Joe," Louis Eastman advised quietly. "She's safe now. Loosen up."

"Yeah," Joe replied, still staring in the direction of where the helicopter had disappeared.

"Joe, you need to get a grip. We have a patrol to finish and the men are getting antsy. We all know you're seeing the young lady but you need to focus," Louis continued.

"Roger that," Joe responded. He turned on his heel. "Let's get to it."

Chapter Twenty-Four

Once inside the helicopter, one of the CTT took Katie's bergen, helmet and weapon from her, and led her to a stretcher and helped her lie down. She immediately sighed and closed her eyes. She could feel someone taking off her jackets and placing a blood pressure cuff around her upper arm before pumping it up. During this time, the engines powered up and the helicopter took off with barely a jolt.

A woman's voice spoke to her asking, "Katie, can you hear me?"

Katie didn't want to open her eyes but the voice persisted in calling her name. Eventually she focused on the female Corporal CTM leaning over her, vaguely recognizing her as Angie Wilson. Corporal Wilson smiled. "Hi there," she said soothingly. "Can you tell me your name?"

Katie smiled slightly. "I know the drill," she murmured. "My name is Katie Walker, rank Corporal, serial number WA8061, and date of birth five July, blood group B positive. I have had loss of consciousness, symptoms of shock, dizziness, vomiting, bangs and bruises, no broken bones and a terrible headache."

The CTM smiled in appreciation. "Well, you're pretty oriented all right. Can we look at that bump on your head?"

Katie went to nod, thought better of it and agreed. "Yes."

After lifting removing the gauze dressing—some of the surgical tape was sticking to Katie's hair, causing her to wince—the CTT surgeon studied it carefully. "Nasty," he said, "but no major damage, although it'll hurt like hell for a few days." He shone a penlight into each eye. "Okay, Corporal, as you probably already know what's wrong with you, I'll just give you a brief rundown. You have a concussion from that bang on the head. You're also a bit dehydrated through the vomiting, your blood pressure is a little low, and you're suffering from a bit of shock. We'll get you assessed at the CTH and they'll probably admit you for twenty-four hours, just to keep an eye on you, get you rehydrated, and your blood pressure up a bit. As for now, we'll start a drip. It'll make you feel better. Is that okay?"

"Yes, sir," Katie answered.

She was left alone for a few minutes then somebody rubbed the back of her hand with a cold solution, and as per the standard medical statement, someone said to her, "This might sting a bit," which was an understatement, as patients generally found out. There was a sharp scratch then a stinging pressure as the cannula slid into the thin skin and muscle of the back of her hand. She felt the cannula taped to the back of her hand then she was covered in a tin foil blanket with an Army blanket on top. For the first time that night, she felt warm and relaxed. The headache had diminished slightly and she found herself drifting off. The last thought in her mind was whether she would be released from the CTH in time to meet Joe the next night.

Katie next became aware of a slight jar as the helicopter landed then the ramp at the rear lowered. Two ambulance medics came up to lift her stretcher and take it down the ramp.

"I don't need all this," Katie protested in a murmur.

The female CTM laughed. "Come on," she teased. "We all know that doctors and nurses and medics make the worst patients. Be a good girl."

After being loaded into the back of an ambulance, it drove off to the CTH. On arrival, a trauma team was waiting out front and they placed Katie on a gurney and wheeled it through the doors. Once in a trauma room, they lifted her from the gurney onto an examination table.

"Hello, Katie, how are you feeling?" a trauma nurse asked, leaning over her and smiling.

"Need a new head," Katie replied and smiled weakly.

As she had done many times before on patients of her own, members of the trauma team gave Katie a full body assessment, took her vital signs, changed her IV bag, stripped her of her combats, and dressed her in a hospital gown before giving her a painkilling injection.

"This will make you a bit sleepy, Katie," a corporal CTM explained, "but you need to rest. The captain says you have a nasty bang on the head and concussion. We're going to send you for an MRI, see if there are any fractures, but we're not expecting to find any. Then we'll put you to bed and you can sleep."

Katie nodded. They wheeled her into the MRI room, and for the next twenty minutes, her skull and brain were battered with noises from the MRI scanner. She had to wait until a technician checked the scans before he gave her the all-clear and she was wheeled to a ward where she was transferred to a bed.

Finally left alone in the ward, which was comfortably dim and empty of casualties, she experienced peace and quiet for the first time that day. She didn't have time to think any thoughts about Joe before she fell into a deep, exhausted sleep.

Chapter Twenty-Five

Heavy bergen on his back and combat helmet held loosely in one gloved hand, Joe walked up to the CTH and pushed open the doors. Exhaustion evident on his face, his eyes red from the desert dust and chin covered in stubble, he was tired, dusty, and dirty, but his concerns for Katie far outweighed his physical feelings or looks. He had arrived back from patrol, gone straight to debriefing, then without even showering—let alone sleeping—made his way to see her.

Now he entered the cool, clean interior of the medical facility, briefly marveling at how spotless the floors and walls were. After being out in the desert for twenty-four hours, he was embarrassed about his dusty, sweaty attire, but he wasn't about to leave until he had seen for himself that she was okay. He could then maybe find some peace and get some sleep.

Placing his weapon in the weapons room, he hovered just inside the doors, unable to see anyone around, although he could hear voices from the far end of the corridor. He decided to visit there first, perhaps discover where Katie was.

He started walking toward the sound of the voices, his combat boots squeaking on the floor, but had gone only a short distance when a man stepped into the corridor and began to walk toward him. As the man approached, Joe saw that he was a Sergeant.

"Can I help you, Staff Sergeant?" the sergeant asked, stopping in front of Joe.

"Yeah, Sergeant. I'm looking for a Corporal Walker. She was brought in by medevac early this morning. She was in the CTF helo that went down last night. My patrol went to the crash site to rescue survivors. I came to see how she was."

The sergeant was studying Joe with an intense, fathomless gaze, assessing him. Joe held the sergeant's stare without flinching.

"Is she okay?" Joe asked slowly and firmly. "I'd like to see her if I can."

"Katie is fine," Sergeant Webster began. "She's asleep at the moment. She has a concussion, is a little dehydrated, and is suffering from shock, but there's no major damage."

Joe straightened slightly, his face expressionless. He had heard a slight tone of over-protectiveness with regard to Katie in the sergeant's voice. "I'd like to see her, Sergeant," Joe reiterated, his voice a little firmer, not quite bordering on authoritative.

"Excuse me for saying so, Staff Sergeant, but Katie is a good girl and she's well liked here and around the camp."

Joe nodded, feeling a little annoyed but accepting the hidden warning. "I'm well aware that Katie is a good girl, Sergeant, and she's going to stay that way. Now, if you'll show me where she is, I'll pay my respects and leave."

Sergeant Webster hesitated for a moment longer but then, clearly unable to think of a suitable reason to prevent this man from visiting his CTM, he turned abruptly and said, "Follow me."

The two men walked silently along the corridor and Sergeant Webster led Joe into a ward and pointed to a bed halfway along the large room.

Joe thanked him and walked slowly to where Katie was lying, asleep. Sergeant Webster turned and left.

Joe quietly shrugged out of his bergen, putting it down on the floor and balancing his helmet on top. He gently lifted a chair from beside the bed, turned it round, and sat astride it, resting his arms on the back. He sat there silently, gazing at Katie's face. There was a large dressing on her temple and extending below it down her left cheek an angry graze and livid bruising on her cheekbone. Her skin was pale, her copper-colored hair a bright flaming halo. Glancing at her slim arms, he saw more grazes and bruises and a drip inserted into the vein of her right hand.

He continued to watch her, wishing she would wake up, but knowing that she needed her rest. He was glad that she was all right physically, but who was to say that the whole incident had not upset her mentally. He suddenly yawned, unable to stop himself, and decided to leave. If and when she was discharged, he would see her tonight. Quietly, he went to get up when suddenly Katie moved, and Joe froze.

She moaned softly, eyelids fluttering, then her eyes opened and she gazed directly at him. They were so green against her white skin that Joe thought they resembled emerald ice. She stared at him as though not recognizing him, and then smiled. "Hi," she whispered.

"Hey, honey," he whispered back.

She reached out her left hand to him. He got up from the chair, came to her bedside, and sat down on its edge beside her. He took the offered hand and leaning forward, kissed her gently on the mouth.

"Thirsty," she murmured.

"Wait one," Joe said, and standing up again, he went to the bedside cabinet and poured some water from a jug into a plastic cup. He went back to the bed and gently lifted her head and let her sip the cool water.

Katie sighed blissfully, and after a few more sips, rested her head back on the pillow. Joe put the cup on the bedside locker and sat back down. He took her hand again and squeezed it. "How are you?" he asked.

"Okay," Katie answered. "Bit of a sore head, but I'll live. You look so tired."

"Yeah, it was a tough night," Joe answered lightly. "I'll get some shut-eye later."

"Thank you for getting me out of there," Katie began. "I don't know what I would have done if you hadn't found me." She swallowed, partly from a dry throat and partly from the threat of grief building up inside her chest.

Joe was shaking his head. "No thanks are necessary," Joe answered, "but you scared the crap out of me."

"I was terrified," Katie murmured. Her eyes became a little distant as she thought back to the crash. A safety mechanism in her brain, designed to protect her mentally, dismissed the images of the burning helicopter and the dead sergeant. She jerked back to reality and noticed that Joe was studying her intently.

"Would you rather give tonight a miss?" he asked. "We can always arrange another night."

"No!" Katie exclaimed. "I'm going to be all right. Don't cancel, Joe. I need to be with you alone, even if it's not for…what we'd planned."

Joe grinned slightly and squeezed her hand again. "Okay. I'll come and collect you from your tent at about 2000 hours if you are discharged. Now, I'd better leave you before that protective sergeant of yours comes and chucks me out." He stood up from the bed and bent over her. "Get some sleep, sweetheart, and I'll see you later." He gently kissed her, and noticed with amusement that Katie's eyes were almost closing.

"Love you," he heard her whisper.

"Love you too," he replied softly.

Joe collected his bergen and helmet and, taking a last look at her, loving her so much, he backed away from the bed and left the ward. There was no one around so he walked as quickly as he could to the entrance and left the building, making his way to his tent in Camp Roosevelt.

* * * *

Katie slept for another few hours and woke up feeling sore and bruised but with a much clearer mind and a diminished headache. She remembered Joe visiting and her heart soared when she remembered his face. She propped herself up in bed and glanced at her watch, which had been placed on the locker beside her. It was 1400 hours, and she realized that she felt a little hungry, which was surely a good sign that she was recovering.

At that moment, there was the sound of boots squeaking on the flooring, and Lance Corporal Barrow entered the ward.

"Harry," Katie greeted.

"Hey, Katie, how are you feeling?" The CTM approached the bed, took her chart from its position where it hung at its foot, and began to take her blood pressure, pulse and other vital signs, making notes on the chart as he went.

"I'm feeling better," Katie replied. "What's the verdict?"

"Everything stable," Harry answered. "Blood pressure is back to normal and pulse normal. How's the head?"

Katie pulled a face. "I'll survive," she replied. "When can I get out of here?"

"Ahhhh, the million dollar question," Harry laughed. "You know the procedure, Katie, twenty-four hour observations, followed by a doctor's assessment at 1700 hours. I'm going to get you something to eat. You're due some more painkillers then I'm afraid you'll have to be patient until the doc's rounds. I think you'll be okay for discharge later. Just behave yourself and be a model patient."

Katie pulled a face and smiled wryly. "Patience is not one of my virtues," she commented, "but I promise I'll be good."

"I'll order you up some lunch. See if you can eat something," the lance corporal said, placing the chart back on the foot of the bed and leaving the ward.

A few minutes later, Sergeant Webster came in. "Good to see you awake, Katie," he greeted.

"Yes, Sergeant, thank you," Katie replied.

"Met a staff sergeant coming here to visit you," Sergeant Webster announced casually. "Hope you know what you're doing, Corporal." He held Katie's eyes with a knowing, concerned look in them.

Katie held his gaze. "I do, Sergeant. Everything is fine."

Sergeant Webster nodded, turned, and left the ward.

Katie spent the rest of the afternoon dozing and reading magazines. As time passed, she began to think of the night to come. She was excited and impatient. She couldn't wait to be with Joe in a private place, alone, away from prying eyes. She wanted to be in his arms, reassured and safe. At the moment, the thoughts of the crash were pushed to the back of her mind, sealed away to be brought out when she felt able to deal with it, but there was a hard ball of grief in the pit of her stomach that was firmly held in check. If she relaxed her control, she would break down and cry, and she wasn't about to allow that to happen.

As the afternoon passed, she grew more and more restless, wanting to be out of the CTH. Once back in her tent, she could rest until she was due to meet Joe, but prior to that and more importantly, she needed to pass the doctor's assessment before that could happen.

At 1700 hours, she finally heard the sound of voices and a group of medical personnel came into the ward.

"How are you, Corporal Walker?" Captain Williams asked as he approached the bed.

"I'm fine, Sir," Katie answered, determined to convince the surgeon that she was well enough to be discharged.

"Any headache?" he asked.

"Touch of one, sir, but nothing major."

"Okay. Well, we'll check you over and decide whether we can release you or not."

"Thank you, sir."

The captain did a thorough examination, checking the pupil reaction of her eyes, blood pressure, and pulse. He also had one of the CTMs with him extract the cannula from the back of her hand. Once he was satisfied that everything was as it should be, he smiled at Katie and said, "You appear to be on the mend, Corporal. But there will be conditions for your discharge. You'll need to rest for forty-eight hours, keep your fluid intake up, no rushing around, wild dancing, anything like that. I'm going to prescribe you some painkillers because no doubt you still have a headache, no matter what you tell me." He raised an eyebrow knowingly. "If you start to get any double vision or vomiting—or if the wound starts to get infected—you're to get right back here. Is that understood?"

"Yes, sir," Katie replied meekly, but inside she was tingling with excitement and happiness. She would be able to meet Joe that night.

"Okay, Corporal, you are discharged. Sergeant Webster will bring you your pills and I believe there is someone waiting for you out in the corridor."

He smiled as Katie said, "Thank you, sir," then he and his team left. Katie was briefly left alone until Wanda suddenly put her head around the door. "Hey, babe," she greeted in her usual cheerful manner.

"Wanda!" Katie exclaimed, pleased to see her friend. "What are you doing here? How did you know?"

"A little bird told me," Wanda replied, coming in to the ward carrying a holdall. "No, actually a Sergeant Webster contacted me and said that you might need some uniform brought in and some help getting back to the tent."

Katie thrust the covers back and swung her legs around to sit on the edge of the bed. For a brief moment, she felt lightheaded and a little sick. Wanda saw the expression on her friend's face and hurried to her side.

"Are you sure you should be getting out?" she asked.

"You're damn right I should be," Katie retorted. "Can you help me stand up, please?"

Wanda placed the holdall on the floor and, grasping Katie's arm, waited until Katie placed tentative feet on the floor then assisted her to stand upright. Katie swayed for a minute and put a hand to her head.

"I need a shower," she stated.

"Okay," Wanda said, "but I've been told to keep an eye on you, so where are the showers. I'll take you to 'em."

"God, you don't have to do that," Katie stated a little irritably. "I'm perfectly capable of taking a shower on my own."

"Nope, orders are orders, mate," Wanda replied firmly. "Now, let's go. Otherwise we'll never get you out of here."

"Well, you'll have to walk behind me," Katie advised. "These hospital gowns don't exactly cover someone's modesty and I'm not about to let the whole of the CTH see my bare backside."

With Wanda holding the back of the hospital gown together with one hand and the holdall with the other, the two women walked slowly out of the ward and in the direction of the shower rooms. They were halfway down the corridor when an alarm went off. Wanda jumped and glanced around. "What's that?" she asked.

"Incoming casualties," Katie replied. "I should be working."

"No, you're supposed to be resting," Wanda answered firmly. "No arguments."

The CTH came alive as medical personnel left the R&R room and hurried down the corridor toward the two women. Nobody seemed perturbed or surprised to see Katie walking down the corridor in a hospital gown. She heard comments, offered with friendly smiles, such as 'Good to see you're doing okay, Katie' or 'Glad to see you up and about', however, nobody wasted time stopping for a conversation. They had a responsibility to the incoming injured.

Katie and Wanda made it the shower rooms and Katie grabbed her towel and toiletries and went into one of the showers while Wanda sat down on the bench in the adjacent locker room.

"If you need me, just shout," Wanda urged.

"I will," Katie agreed.

While in the shower, having taken off the hospital gown, Katie took a moment to glance down at her body. She was a little horrified to discover that she had large, livid bruising over most of it, including enormous purple bruises on her left hip and elbow and raw abrasions and angry-looking grazes on her stomach and chest that were painful when she touched them. It was no wonder she felt stiff and sore.

"Jesus," she murmured. "I look like a human punch bag." Joe was going to take one look at her tonight and think that she looked horrible.

Feeling a little depressed, Katie turned on the shower and stood under the hot spray. It eased some of the soreness in her muscles, and after a little while, she was able to bathe herself and wash her hair. Once she had finished, she dried herself then called to Wanda.

"Can you bring my uniform to me, please?"

"Yep," Wanda answered and there was the sound of booted footfalls on the tiles of the shower room, the sound of a bag unzipping, then various parts of her uniform appeared over the top of the door.

"I've got your boots as well," Wanda said, "but there's blood on them."

"That's okay," Katie replied. "I'll have to wear them. They're the only pair I have."

Spraying herself liberally with deodorant, Katie managed to dress herself without irritating the bruises and grazes. She towel-dried her hair and fluffed it up then let herself out of the shower. Walking to the long mirror on the wall, Wanda watching, she glanced at herself in it and couldn't stop herself from gasping.

"Oh crap, I look a fright," she exclaimed, and her voice sounded a little tearful. Her face was still pale and drawn and there were faint, dark circles under her eyes. The bump just above her temple was still evident with a livid gash across it. A graze and a multicolored bruise ran down the left side of her face almost to her jaw line.

Wanda placed a soothing hand on Katie's shoulder. "You look fine," she reassured gently. "Anyway, you're alive."

Katie paused and turned to glance at her friend.

"Want to talk about it?" Wanda asked.

Katie shook her head. "No, Wanda. Not yet."

"Okay, whenever you're ready. Now, shall we get out of here before they change their minds and keep us both here?"

Katie laughed slightly and nodded, "Yeah, let's go."

The two women left the showers and went back out into the corridor. The CTH was busy and they hurried to the doors and let themselves out into the evening air. Katie could hear the sound of an ambulance and almost wanted to go back inside and join the teams, but there was something more important she had to do that night—be with Joe.

The two women walked slowly away from the CTH, making their way toward the tents.

"Do you want something to eat?" Wanda asked as they approached the Mess.

"No, I'm not hungry," Katie answered. She hesitated then, glancing at the other woman said, "Wanda, I'll be staying out tonight."

Wanda's step never faltered at Katie's sudden announcement, but she did raise an eyebrow and issue a whistle. "Are you sure you should?" she asked slowly.

"I'm sure," Katie answered.

"Is it with your staff sergeant?"

"Yes, with my staff sergeant. He has keys to a friend's room and we're going to stay there. He's coming for me at the tent at 2000 hours. I had to tell you so you would know where I was."

"Okay," Wanda replied slowly then continued, "I hope you know what you're doing, sweetie."

"No lectures please, Wanda. I just want to be alone with him — not for sex — but since we've met, our time together has always ended abruptly and we're both sick of it. An opportunity has presented itself, and we've decided to take it."

"Good for you, Katie," Wanda replied.

The two women remained silent as they continued on with the walk back to the tent. Once inside, Katie was welcomed back as though she had been absent for longer than twenty-four hours. Nobody asked her what had happened. Everyone on the base was well aware that a CTF had gone down and personnel killed. The British camp's Union Flag was at half-mast and the whole of the base's communications were restricted to emergencies only until families back in the UK had been informed.

"I'm going to lie down for a bit," Katie advised her friend, once the noise in the tent had subsided. "I'll take some pills first. Can you wake me at 1930 hours if I fall asleep, please?"

"Will do," Wanda answered. "I got you some bottles of water and they're in your bergen."

Katie looked at her friend gratefully, took out the pills the doctor had prescribed and swallowed them with some bottled water. She lay down on her bed and closed her eyes. Her head was thumping and aching and her muscles were protesting. She sighed. In a few short hours she would be with Joe and she could immerse herself in him, even if she did look as though she had gone ten rounds with a Samurai warrior.

As the strong painkillers did their work, Katie closed her eyes and, feeling relaxed for the first time in two days, she drifted off to sleep.

It seemed only minutes later that someone was shaking her arm. Groggy and feeling hungover from the painkillers, Katie opened her eyes.

Wanda was bending over her. "Wake up, sleepyhead," she urged gently.

Katie groaned and sat up. "Oh my God," she moaned. "I feel like death warmed up." She rubbed her face and swung her legs over the side of her bed.

At that moment, somebody came into the tent, stopped just inside and said, "There's a rather attractive staff sergeant waiting outside for some lucky lady. Who does he belong to?" And she looked pointedly at Katie.

Katie laughed, all grogginess and tiredness vanishing instantly. "He's mine," she replied and stood up.

"Katie, you dark horse," one of the women called across the tent.

"Yes, and I'm going to stay that way. Now, I need to go." Grabbing her combat jacket, she slowly put it on. "I'll say goodnight, ladies, and don't wait up," Katie announced, and the there was laughter and ribald comments.

Katie waved to them all and left the tent. It had grown dark but lights shone out of the openings in the tents and there was the usual music playing and the sound of laughter.

Joe was standing on the beaten-down path, and when she appeared, he immediately straightened and came toward her. Katie met him halfway and went hastily into his arms. She winced as Joe's arms squeezed her bruises and the sore parts of her body, but she sighed as she snuggled her body against his and peace overcame her. "Joe," she murmured and felt the icy lump in the pit of her stomach begin to dissolve slightly.

"Hey," she heard him whisper gently, "how you doing?"

Katie glanced up at him. "I'm okay now you're here," she replied softly.

"Let's go," he said. He took her hand and led her away from the tents. On reaching the road leading to Camp Roosevelt, they crossed it and continued walking until Joe turned right onto a well-worn path. At the end was a two-story prefabricated building. Night was coming on quickly and there were one or two lights on in the building, but otherwise the rest of the rooms were in darkness.

As they paused at the end of the path, Joe turned to Katie. "Are you sure —?" he began.

Katie didn't let him finish. She placed a gentle finger on his lips to prevent any further talk. "I'm sure," she answered. "I've never been surer about anything in my life."

Joe smiled and heaved a sigh, "Okay, let's get inside the room quick. Follow me as quietly as you can."

He led her toward the building and stopped at the back of the first room. Keys were already in his hand and he swiftly unlocked the door, pushed it open and urged Katie through into the room beyond. He followed after her and quietly closed the door, locking it behind them.

Chapter Twenty-Six

Nervously, Katie stepped a few paces inside the room and glanced around. Compared to her tent it appeared large and luxurious. There were two windows, making it appear light and airy, one facing out onto the grounds at the front of the building the other to the left, facing the footpath. It was furnished with a sink, chair, bedside locker with lamp, and a camp bed covered with a sleeping bag. It was quiet and vastly different from being in her tent. How was she ever going to get used to a room, let alone a house again, if this was her reaction to one small, prefabricated room?

Joe dropped his bergen to the rubber floor then quietly went to each of the windows to pull down blinds, shielding them from anyone walking past the building. He then placed a lit torch on the locker beside the bed. The room now dimly lit, he turned and stood watching her, waiting patiently.

Katie turned to him slowly, becoming aware that he was watching and waiting for her reaction at them finally being alone. For brief seconds they stood regarding each other, observing each other's expressions, searching for any doubt, and then Katie hurried toward him almost throwing herself into his arms, desperate to be close to him, to feel his arms around her and to feel his body against her own. Joe uttered a small moan then he was kissing her passionately and she was kissing him back, their bodies pressed against each other, realizing that they were now alone with nobody to disturb them and nothing to separate them for the whole night.

Without any hesitation, Katie fumbled with the front of Joe's jacket, ripping apart the Velcro fastenings, trying to push the sleeves down over his arms before the jacket was fully off his shoulders. Realizing that she was struggling, Joe laughed gently and shrugged out of the jacket, letting it drop to the floor. Katie gently traced the rippling muscles up his arms with her fingertips, causing him to shiver slightly. Reaching his shoulders, she put her arms around his neck, running her fingers through his short hair, pulling his head down so that his hot mouth was crushed against hers. Joe tugged her T-shirt out from the waistband of her combat trousers and thrust his hands up inside it, resting the warm palms of his hands against her skin, the muscles in her stomach quivering and contracting at his touch. She winced as his fingers came into contact with some of the bruises and grazes but was not about to let him know. She had been waiting for this moment for what seemed like forever and was not about to call a stop to it now.

Dropping her arms from around his neck, she shrugged off her jacket, allowing it to fall at her feet then, pulling Joe's T-shirt free, put her own hands up inside it, drawing her palms against smooth, warm skin, feeling firm stomach muscles and a well-muscled back. Their breathing was loud in the quiet room but it didn't matter to Katie. It meant that she and Joe were somewhere private and could remain oblivious to everything other than both their arousal.

Joe took his mouth away from Katie's soft moist lips and began to trail warm kisses along her neck and down to her shoulder. Blood sizzled in her veins and she arched her neck so he could gain easier access while grasping the waistband of his trousers and tugging him closer. She could feel how hard he was and she gently moved her hips in small circles, rubbing her own pelvis against his. He moaned softly and one of his hands traveled up her stomach and came to rest on one of her breasts. There he paused, as though he thought that he may have gone too far, but Katie pressed her hand on top of his, a signal that urged him to continue.

Joe quickly grasped the bottom of Katie's T-shirt and tugged it upward over her head. It joined the increasing pile of clothes on the floor. He paused, breathing raggedly, and stared at her, her white lace bra dazzling white against her tanned skin. "My God, you are so beautiful," he exclaimed huskily.

"Take off your T-shirt," Katie ordered breathlessly, and without hesitation, Joe obeyed. Katie immediately saw the black elaborate tattoo of an eagle on the left side of his chest. Its lower body covered half his ribcage, the upper body and head the upper part of his chest with the wings flowing up to his shoulder and down the upper part of his left arm. The bird flexed and rippled as though alive when Joe moved.

Katie placed the palms of her hands on Joe's chest, marveling at the ripple of muscles. Sensuously she ran her hands down his sides and curved in along his stomach, eliciting a strong contraction of his stomach muscles. He went to reach for her again but she looked at him, smiled slowly, and shook her head. "Wait," she whispered. Tenderly, sensuously, she trailed her fingers down to the waistband of his combats and slowly, taking her time, she undid the fastening then grasped the zip. Joe caught her hands in his and shook his head quickly.

"Wait," he said, smiling slightly, teasingly, then he lifted her in his arms and was walking hurriedly toward the bed. He laid her down on top of the sleeping bag then slid over her to lie down beside her. Immediately she went into his arms. Joe brought his hand to her breast again, but struggled to get his fingers inside the cup of her bra. Eventually he said sheepishly and with frustration, "How do you get this damned thing off?"

Giggling softly, Katie reached her arms up behind her, and in a moment, the bra was falling away from her breasts.

Joe felt the air leave his lungs as though he had been holding it in, then he was pulling her toward him so that their skin was touching and his mouth was on hers again, hot and eager. His hand clasped one of her breasts and his thumb gently circled her erect nipple, causing Katie to gasp and press against him, but he pushed her gently onto her back, and leaning over her, he licked at her nipple, leaving a glistening trail. Katie arched her back, her hands thrusting into his hair. Joe's tongue circled her nipple then he took it into his mouth, his tongue teasing the hard bud. He moved away from the firm mound, leaving gentle kisses on the way, licking a swirling trail down her stomach.

Exquisite sensations coursed through her body at his touch. Wanting him so much, Katie writhed and arched her back. Reaching down, she grabbed the waistband of his combats and urged him with small tugs to move over on top of her.

She heard Joe laugh softly. "In a hurry?" he asked against her mouth.

"Yes," Katie answered without any hint of shyness, her voice husky with arousal. "I want you, Joe."

Joe groaned and quickly moved over to lie between her legs. They both lay still for a moment then he began to move against her, the friction of their combat trousers making the sensations more intense. He rubbed himself against her for some time, until Katie was moaning softly, trying to muffle the sounds against Joe's bare shoulder.

Joe suddenly didn't wait any longer. Raising himself on his elbows and lifting his pelvis slightly, he reached down and began to undo her combat trousers. Katie suddenly put a hand on his, arresting his movement.

"What?" Joe asked distractedly.

Katie giggled softly. "My boots," she whispered.

Joe regarded her as though she was talking a foreign language, "Boots? What do you mean, boots?" Then realization dawned and he grinned. "Crap," he exclaimed. Getting to his knees, he shuffled backward to the end of the cot and began to undo the laces of her boots. His hands were shaking slightly but eventually he managed to undo them and tug them from her feet, tossing them haphazardly onto the floor. Then he reached back up, finished undoing her trousers, and slowly pulled them down her legs, throwing them over his shoulder. He then moved back up to lie between her legs.

Katie put both of her hands between them, causing him to raise his hips slightly, supporting himself on his elbows. All the time he was watching her.

Katie carefully pulled the zip down of his combat trousers and ran her finger down inside, moving it teasingly back and forth, her fingertip caressing the tip of his penis. Joe flinched and moaned then, foregoing any further foreplay, she grasped the waistband of his trousers and pushed them down, followed by his underwear, releasing him from confinement. She grasped the full hot length of him, gently and tenderly.

Joe groaned, "Wait, Katie. Be careful."

Katie released him and pulled his hips downward so he was pressed against her. Joe fumbled with her panties, trying to pull them down until there was a sudden ripping sound and the delicate material came away in his hands. He tossed them aside and Katie opened her legs to allow him entry. He was suddenly and smoothly inside her hot, moist warmth, thrusting into her, moving slowly at first, almost teasingly, and Katie arched her back, almost unable to bear the exquisite sensations that were beginning to explode inside her. She could feel his hard erection, gently thrusting in and out, his mouth against hers, hot and burning. Katie matched his movements then raised her legs to place them around his hips, pulling him in deeper. Their movements became faster and more frantic. Joe grasped both of Katie's wrists and held them above her head. He slowed his movements, gritting his teeth, slowly pushing in and out, teasing her, trying to control the feeling that was growing in intensity.

"Tell me you want me," he whispered, his voice husky and thick with arousal.

Katie moaned and raised her hips, wanting him to go back to thrusting harder.

Instead, he almost fully withdrew himself from her and stopped. "Tell me you want me, Katie."

"I want you," she gasped. "I want you, Joe, for God's sake." Pulling her wrists from his grasp, she clutched his back, her fingernails digging into his skin, and she flexed her internal muscles until they were clenching around him in little sensual movements.

Joe groaned again and this time he thrust into her roughly. A few seconds later, Katie felt the onrush of her orgasm. She bucked her hips, tossing her head from side to side, uttering small whimpers.

Katie suddenly gasped and uttered a long, drawn-out moan, and that sound of release sent Joe soaring on his way to his own climax. He thrust in and out rhythmically, harder, faster, and deeper until—for what seemed like an eternity—both hung at the peak of ultimate pleasure, then both began to sink back to reality. Joe rested on top of her, supporting himself on his elbows, the fingers of his hands playing with her damp hair, taking deep slow breaths in an attempt to slow his rapid breathing. Katie lay with her eyes closed, feeling his heart pounding against her chest, her own heart hammering, and feeling a sense of pure satisfaction and contentment that she had never felt before in her life. Happiness filled her and wrapped her in its warm embrace. When she finally opened her eyes, she felt a tear trickle down from the outer corner of one eye.

"Hey," Joe said softly, gently wiping it away. "Why the tears?"

"Oh, just happy," Katie whispered, giving him a tremulous smile.

"I'll never understand women," Joe rejoined, offering a grin, "but I love you so very much." He leaned forward and kissed her tenderly on the mouth.

Katie gazed at Joe's face, taking in every detail. "I love you, Joe," she responded. "I don't ever want to leave you."

"You won't have to," Joe replied. "We finish our tours in a little over three weeks and then we'll be together. I promise."

Katie nodded, and then to her embarrassment, she suddenly yawned. "Sorry," she murmured.

"Boring you, am I?" Joe asked a chuckle in his voice.

"Never," Katie answered. "Being with you makes me feel safe and protected. I don't want to be anywhere else."

Joe slid off her onto his side and took her into his arms, pulling up the rumpled sleeping bag to cover them both.

"Go to sleep, sweetheart," he said gently and kissed her on her forehead. "Go to sleep."

Placing a hand on the warm, firm muscles of his chest, Katie snuggled against him and allowed her eyes to close. "Love you so much," she murmured and slipped into sleep.

Joe lay gazing down at her, feeling tired himself but not wanting to close his eyes in case he missed a change in her expression or she woke up again. He wanted to remember everything about tonight. He watched Katie sleep until exhaustion eventually overcame him and his head slumped back on the pillow and he too slept.

The alarm on Joe's wristwatch went off at 0500 hours and he instantly awoke and switched it off, glancing quickly at Katie to see if the noise had wakened her. At some point in the night, she had moved slightly away from him. She now slept with one fist tucked under her chin. He wanted to touch her, to feel her smooth skin, to wake her up and make love to her again, but she needed to sleep. Sleep was healing and she had been through so much over the last few days. Instead, he rested his head on the palm of a hand and watched her.

This woman lying beside him had irrevocably changed his life forever. He had never loved anyone as he loved her. He couldn't begin to put into words how he felt, how deep his emotions went. Their lovemaking had just been a small part of it because what he felt for her went much deeper than that. He wanted to protect her, keep her safe, and love her always.

He watched as she pursed her lips in her sleep then lowered his eyes to her breasts, which were bare. He remembered caressing them, and her reaction last night, and he began to grow hard again. He squirmed slightly and contemplated waking her gently. As though she had read his thoughts, Katie's eyes opened and a slow smile of delight spread across her face.

"Hi," she greeted softly. "I thought it was all a dream."

"No dream," he said, smiling lovingly at her.

Katie raised herself slightly, moved closer, and kissed his chest with little pouting kisses. Reaching his nipple, she licked it slowly then bit into his skin, not enough to hurt, but it caused tingling sensations to shoot down into his groin. When he moved to put his arms around her, she stopped the kisses and glanced up at him.

"No," she murmured. "No touching. It's my turn. Lie on your back." Katie moved slightly to accommodate him on the bed.

Watching her, Joe obliged, and Katie ran her eyes down his body, her breathing slightly rapid. Bending forward, she kissed the tattoo on his shoulder and chest, working her way down his ribcage, returning to his nipples again and licking them, nipping slightly in one place then another. With her left hand, she ran her fingertips down the center of his chest then his stomach, trailing them lower and slower until she reached his groin. He was fully erect and hard and she gently traced her fingers up and down the length of him and circled the crown. She raised herself up slightly on her knees and proceeded to kiss and lick down the center of his stomach, nipping gently with her teeth.

Joe began to moan softly as her mouth trailed wet kisses toward where her hand was tenderly playing with his cock. Reaching it, she licked along the underside, causing him to jerk involuntarily.

Joe suddenly grabbed her hair firmly. "Katie," he warned.

Katie glanced up at him with a sensuous look on her face. He moved to pull her up toward him, to roll her onto her back, but she held him at bay.

"It's my turn," she repeated huskily, and gracefully straddled him, pressing her down and rubbing her against him, creating an exquisite friction.

Joe watched her face as she threw her head back, her hips grinding against him, her mouth slightly open and her eyes closed. Joe reached up and clasped her breasts, massaging her erect nipples, causing Katie to moan. As though she couldn't wait any longer, she raised her hips and, opening her eyes and staring deeply into Joe's, she grasped him gently and guided him into her then sat down with a single smooth movement until he was deep inside her, as deep as he could go, until it almost hurt. Joe felt her heat and the small squeeze of muscles as she clenched around him and he wanted to explode right at that moment. He gritted his teeth and continued to watch her. She sat frozen for a moment, enjoying the sensations of having him inside her, then she began to move, rocking backward and forward, sometimes rising up until he was almost out of her then sitting down with that same smooth motion until it nearly drove him mad.

As their passion rose, their movements became faster and harder and Katie began to utter the little moans that told him that she was nearing her climax. He was well on his way to his own and both peaked virtually at the same time. Katie slumped on top of him, murmuring little endearments, and nuzzling his lightly sweating chest. He put his arms around her and rubbed his face against her head. They both stayed in that position for a long time, until Joe eventually stirred. He managed a surreptitious glance at his watch and sighed. "I'm sorry, sweetheart, but we have to go."

Katie made a little choked sound of reluctance. "Don't let me go, Joe, please."

Joe raised her chin with his finger. "I don't want to," he answered. "Believe me. But we'll both be in big trouble if we stay here."

"I know," Katie said, and her voice sounded so sad that he wanted to give in and stay in the room with her in his arms. But she climbed off him and sat on the edge of the bed. Joe climbed off the camp bed beside her and stood up.

Katie admired his body as she ran her eyes up and down him, a small smile playing about her mouth.

"Don't look at me like that, lady," he said. "I might change my mind." He started to put on his underwear and combats and Katie reluctantly began to put on her own uniform. Once they were both dressed, Joe suddenly took her hand and led her back to the camp bed.

"Sit down," he said. "I have to talk to you."

Katie obliged, wondering what he was going to say.

Joe put his hand in the pocket of his jacket and pulled something out. "I want you to have this," he said, and handed her a gold ring.

Katie looked at it and saw that it was a large gold and onyx ring with the letters JA entwined in raised gold on the black stone. "Joe," she gasped. "It's beautiful."

"It's my class ring," he said. "I've given it to you in lieu of an engagement ring."

Katie gaped at him, open-mouthed. "Are you asking me to marry you?" she asked breathlessly.

"Yes I am, if you'll have me," Joe replied solemnly. "I know people will gasp in horror. Everyone will—with good intentions—say that it's too soon. We don't know each other—the usual advice—but I know what I feel about you, honey. I want you with me for always."

Katie looked down at the ring then back at Joe, nodding frantically. "Yes," she answered delightedly. "Yes, I will." She threw her arms around his neck, kissing him excitedly all over his face.

Laughing, he held her tightly, kissed her deeply on the mouth, and then held her back. "I also have to tell you something else. I don't mean to rain on our parade but I'm going out on patrol tonight and won't be back for five days. It's a big mission. We're being flown behind enemy lines. That's all I can say about it, but when I get back, we'll come here again."

Joe watched as worry and anxiety appeared in Katie's eyes. "God, Joe!" she exclaimed.

"I'll be fine, Katie. I'll be back. You won't lose me now." He took her in his arms again and she snuggled against him. Her joy at his marriage proposal was dampened by the news that he was going out on patrol again, and this time a more hazardous one than usual. An intense surge of fear suddenly took over her body and she clenched her jaw and closed her eyes, determined not to let her terror overcome her but unable to free her of the sense that being so happy would bring about something bad.

"Now," he began, "we really have to go."

They spent the next few minutes tidying up the room and remaking the bed, checking that they had left nothing behind. Almost reluctantly, Joe unlocked the door, and going outside into the early morning, they fled along the path to the road.

Joe took her back to her tent and they stopped outside. Taking her in his arms, he kissed her hard and at length. "Remember," he said. "I love you and I will be back."

Katie's eyes filled with tears, "Joe," she whispered, her heart in almost physical pain as she gazed into his face. The terrible feeling that something was going to happen to destroy their love, that a nightmare was now in motion by them spending the night together, one that would change them forever, still remained like a physical weight in her stomach.

Joe released her and stepped back. As though he couldn't take his eyes from her, he walked backward until he reached the end of the path, then he raised a hand briefly, turned and walked away.

Katie felt the tears on her face as she watched him disappear into the misty, early morning light, missing him so much already, loving him beyond words and dying a bit inside as he eventually disappeared without looking back.

Chapter Twenty-Seven

Katie woke suddenly, her eyes flashing wide in an instant. She had been in a deep sleep and dreaming. She couldn't remember what the dream had been about and the sleep had done nothing to refresh her. She was exhausted and worried beyond comprehension. Her tent was full of murmured conversation from the other women with the faint sound of the radio and a film on somebody's laptop sounding in the background. The light was dim and shadows of movement played on the tent walls like shadowy ghosts. Katie closed her eyes again. There was something wrong. She could sense it throughout her body. Joe had been out on patrol now for three days, nothing worrisome in that. He had said on the night they had spent together that he was going to be gone for five days, dropped behind enemy lines. He hadn't been able to say anything more but from experience, Katie knew that it was more than likely to be a dangerous mission. He was due back in two days and was to meet her here at her tent and they would spend the night together again in the room belonging to Joe's friend. She should feel excited about being together again, but instead she was frightened. A strong feeling of foreboding sat like a lump of lead in her stomach and she was tired and edgy.

Sitting up on her bed, Katie swung her legs over the side. She glanced around the tent and saw a couple of the women looking in her direction. She noticed immediately that their expressions held sympathy and concern. She felt ice form in her veins. The women saw that she had noticed them staring and hastily turned away in silence.

"Hey," Wanda said, coming to sit beside her friend. "How are you?" Wanda's tone was soft and gentle, totally unlike her usual strident tones, and Katie glanced at her curiously.

"I'm okay," she answered, paused, and then asked, "What's going on?"

To Katie's consternation, Wanda's face took on the same expression of concern as the two women who Katie had caught staring at her.

"Nothing's wrong," Wanda answered. "You just don't look well."

"I feel like you all know something I don't," Katie went on. She looked down at her hands. "I feel… I feel like something's wrong—with Joe." She glanced at her friend again. "I'm so scared, Wanda. Something's happened to him. I know it."

"Hey." Wanda put a soothing hand on Katie's shoulder. "You're imagining things."

"No." Katie shook her head. "No, I don't think so."

At that moment, the tent flaps moved aside and a female lance corporal entered. She looked directly at Katie and announced quietly, "Katie, there's someone waiting outside to speak to you."

Katie froze where she was seated, excitement suddenly welling up inside her. *Joe! It has to be Joe. Who else can it be?* But he wasn't due back from patrol yet. Jumping up, she hurried to exit the tent to see who it was.

The early evening air was slightly chilly in extreme contrast to the soaring temperatures of the day and she shivered. She glanced to where Joe usually waited for her but there was nobody there. Frowning, she glanced in the opposite direction, and saw somebody standing in the shadows. Turning, for a second she thought that it was Joe, but the dark figure moved out into the dim light and Katie recognized him. It was Sergeant Louis Eastman. Katie knew instantly that her feelings of fear were about to be confirmed.

The sergeant walked toward her, limping slightly. "Corporal Walker? Katie?" he asked hesitantly.

Katie remained where she was, rigid with a powerful fear. As he drew nearer, she saw that his arm was in a sling.

Sergeant Eastman stood before her and the look on his face was one of grief and shock. She started to shake her head, her green eyes wide and staring, mouth trembling. She lifted a shaking hand to ward off what she suspected she was about to hear.

Sergeant Eastman cleared his throat and when he spoke, his voice trembled. "Katie, he's missing."

Silence seemed to envelope Katie like a shroud, and the words he had just spoken didn't make sense in her suddenly chaotic mind. "Missing?" she echoed in a small, husky voice.

Sergeant Eastman nodded, looked down at the ground, and then raised his head, pain at the loss of his friend etched into his drawn face. "We were out on patrol, search, and rescue. We had gone to a compound where Intel reported that there were some hostages. The Intel was false. They were waiting for us—full-on

Taliban attack, heavy weapons, the lot. Some of our guys were killed. Joe and a couple of others went back to rescue some of them and they never came back. When backup arrived, they searched but there was no sign of them. His helmet and weapon were found, but nothing else."

"He's not dead then?" Katie asked, her voice trembling, on the verge of screaming a denial.

Sergeant Eastman sighed heavily. "We couldn't find him," he replied simply.

Katie gazed around her, seeing the black night sky, the bright stars, feeling a chill wind against the heat of her face. She turned her gaze back on the sergeant.

"Thank you for coming to tell me, Sergeant Eastman. It was good of you." Her voice was emotionless, as though all feeling had gone from her, and she registered dully that Sergeant Eastman felt bad for her.

"Wait," he said. "Before we went out on patrol, Joe asked me to give you something." He reached into his combat jacket pocket and withdrew two envelopes. He handed them to her and, Katie clutching them, felt something inside her die a little as each second passed.

"I'm so sorry, Katie," Sergeant Eastman reiterated. "He was a good buddy to have. I'd better go. If you need anything..." With that last statement, he gave her a half salute, turned, and disappeared into the darkness.

Katie stood where he had left her, gazing down at the letters, the pain in her heart so severe that she wanted to crumple to the ground then and there and scream out her heartache. She barely acknowledged Sergeant Eastman's goodbye, and when she finally looked up, he had gone.

She gazed around her, at the tents, the dim lights, confused and shocked. She didn't want to read the letter addressed to her. To do that would make the last ten minutes a reality and just confirm that Joe was missing. She walked slowly toward her tent and went inside. She stopped just inside the entrance, glancing around, not seeing anyone, or hearing the exclamations of concern as the women saw the expression on her face. She went abstractedly to her bed and sat down.

Wanda, glancing up as her friend came in, winced at the look on her face.

Katie looked down at the two envelopes again. One was addressed to her in Joe's handwriting, the other addressed to a Mr. and Mrs. Anderson with a Virginia, USA, postal address. With shaking hands, she ripped open the envelope with her name on it. She extracted the single sheet of paper, unfolded it, and began to read. Halfway through, the tears began to fall, blurring the handwriting, and a howl of wounded pain began to build up inside her. She must have made a small sound because Wanda was instantly by her side, putting an arm around her friend's shoulders.

With tears streaming down her face, Katie turned to Wanda. "He's gone," she choked, the sobs becoming harder to control. "He's missing Wanda. He's missing." Then she broke down, the sobs heart wrenching and full of pain.

Wanda's own eyes filled with tears and she pulled Katie into her arms and hugged her tightly, stroking the other woman's hair as you would a child. "I know, Katie, sweetheart. We already know," she said, her usually strong voice cracking with sympathy and compassion. "Let it out, Katie. Let it out."

Katie cried as though her heart was breaking, the sobs making her whole body shudder. At one point, attempting to break free from her friend's enfolding arms, she saw that one or two women in the tent had glanced in her direction but turned away as she had raised her head, as though to go and comfort her would cause the same thing to happen to them. She watched a few other women, concern, and heartfelt sympathy etched on their faces, approach her bed space, sink down on the floor before her, and encircle her and Wanda. Mirrored in their own faces were Katie's grief and pain.

The circle of women stayed surrounding Katie for a long time, until her sobs began to taper off and, exhausted, she sat slumped, head bowed. Then they rose to their feet and wandered back to their own tasks and thoughts. Wanda remained beside Katie, comforting her, sitting in silence, waiting for Katie to speak.

At last, Katie straightened and wiped her wet face. "Thanks," she said, sobs still causing her voice to hiccup. She turned to face Wanda. "You said you already knew?"

Wanda nodded. "Yes. My section informed me that some members of a patrol had gone missing. All the flags are at half-mast, then your Sergeant Webster contacted me and told me that the staff sergeant—your man—was one of the ones missing. I told the rest of the girls here. We couldn't say anything. We were ordered not to, not until you had been told yourself."

Katie nodded, feeling nothing. She was completely numb now, which she was grateful for, and hoped that she would continue to remain so.

"Do you want to talk about it?" Wanda asked.

Katie shook her head. "No, thank you," she replied. "I can't, not yet. I want to go to bed, forget about it for now." She stood up, still clutching the letters.

Wanda gazed up at her friend worriedly. "Okay, girl, but if you need me, just shout."

Katie nodded, turning away before the tears could start again. Wanda rose from her seat beside her friend and went back to her own bed space. Without undressing, Katie lay down on her bed and dragged her sleeping bag over her. She put the envelope addressed to Joe's parents under her pillow and held Joe's now-crumpled letter under her cheek. Although her mind was in turmoil, she wanted to close her eyes, and if Joe was not going to be with her, never wake up. Katie's exhaustion was borne of emotional chaos and she instantly fell asleep, her sleep deep and dark with black images flitting about in her mind all night long.

* * * *

For the next forty-eight hours, Katie functioned on automatic. She did her job with her usual competence and skill but was numb to all emotions. Her Joe had gone and that was all that mattered. Her work colleagues did not ask any questions of her but they showed their sympathy in the gentle friendly touches on her arm and shoulder, the small smiles of concern when they passed her in the corridor and rooms of the CTH. Sergeant Webster, at one point, called her into his office and awkwardly let her know that he was there if she needed him, as was everyone else. Not able to speak, in case she broke down, Katie had nodded her understanding and abruptly left his office.

The night that she and Joe had been due to meet after he returned from his patrol, Katie went outside her tent at 2000 hours in the unreasonable belief that he would be waiting for her. Inside her was a fleeting hope that it was all a bad dream and that she would get to see his wide grin and the love he had for her reflected in his dark blue eyes. She waited until 2130 hours, pacing the worn down path in front of the tent but there was no sign of him. Finally, the pain of realization unbearable, she went back inside the tent, knowing at last that Joe was not coming back, hope that he might still be alive blotted out by the shadowy blackness that was taking over her heart.

At 1100 hours the next day, Katie was summoned to Sergeant Webster's office. As she entered, she was startled to see Sergeant Eastman seated there. Katie looked lethargically at them both.

"Katie," Sergeant Webster began, his voice unusually gentle. "They're having a small memorial service on Camp Roosevelt for the casualties from Sergeant Eastman's patrol. He came here to ask if you would like to attend. If you do, he will escort you there and back. It's up to you."

Katie froze, her first thought to offer a hysterical refusal, but she thought of the members of Echo squad whom she knew and who might be dead or missing, those who had helped her on the night of the helicopter crash and she changed her mind.

"Thank you," she said in a small voice. "I'll get my kit."

In the locker room, she slowly and tiredly put on her military cap and sunglasses. Sergeant Eastman was waiting for her outside and together they walked in silence down the long corridor and outside into the heat of the day. Neither of them spoke as they walked the long distance to Camp Roosevelt. As they approached the USMC building, Katie could see a large crowd of marines and Army personnel standing in a half circle. They were silent, heads bowed, helmets and caps in hand. She slowed almost to a stop, panic striking at her, reluctant to go any further, not wanting to see the grief displayed so openly from Joe's men and colleagues.

Sergeant Eastman turned and must have seen the pain and fear in her eyes, and he touched her arm.

"You okay?" he asked. "You don't have to do this."

Katie swallowed. "Yes, yes I do," she replied. "I have to do this for Joe."

The sergeant and Katie continued to walk in the direction of the crowd. As they reached it, Sergeant Eastman led Katie to the front of the half circle of soldiers. She saw that there were perhaps half a dozen marines separate from the crowd, kneeling down on one knee, arms across each other's shoulders, heads bowed. In a line in front was a row of combat helmets placed on upright rifles with boots neatly paired together in front of each helmet and rifle. Scattered in front of the boots were dog tags and various personal effects. Some of the kneeling soldiers had their hands resting on helmets or boots.

The meaning behind this display was not lost on Katie. It was a serious memorial for those lost in battle, first begun back in the mists of time—the Battlefield Cross. Katie knew that a rifle with bayonet placed downward into the ground or in the boots signified a soldier killed in action. It also signaled a time for prayer, a break in the action to pay tribute to a friend and hero. Dog tags identified the soldier's name so that he or she would never be forgotten. The helmet also symbolized the great sacrifice and combat boots represented the final march of the soldier in his or her last battle.

Feeling as though she were intruding, Katie followed the sergeant to the half circle of kneeling marines. Nobody looked at her, they were all deep in their own grief.

Katie gazed through blurred vision at the poignant row of helmets and boots of those who had died or were lost. *Was one of the helmets Joe's? A pair of boots or his dog tags all that was left of him?* She moved slowly along the line of men toward the last helmet, knowing beyond doubt that it belonged to Joe. She stopped by the single helmet and rifle and saw the dog tags lying where the boots would have been, if there had been any.

She didn't want to look, didn't want to verify that they did indeed belong to him, but she couldn't resist, needed to know once, Then maybe she could begin the long journey of moving on.

Bending forward, she looked at the dog tags, trying to see the name. They were lying so that she couldn't read what was on them. Aware that this was probably not the right thing to do, she gently touched one dog tag and turned it so that the name was facing upward. She flinched as though it had burned her fingers.

The name Joe Anderson seemed to leap out at her and she recoiled backward. She forced herself not to cry out. It was too quiet here, so many people suffering their own grief and loss. She put her hand across her mouth and closed her eyes, her shoulders shuddering silently. She wanted to be away from this lonely place, lonely because of the tangible atmosphere of loss and suppressed emotions. But something made her reach out for the helmet, balanced on top of the butt of the weapon. As she touched it, it rocked slightly, unbalanced, from side to side. She placed the palm of her hand on the top. Warmed by the sun she could feel the roughness of the camouflage material of the cover and tears began to build up, threatening to overwhelm her. She bit her lip hard, tasting the coppery essence of her own blood. She grasped the rim of the helmet, and without conscious thought, lifted it from its precarious perch on top of the rifle. Turning it upside down, she looked through tear-blurred eyes at the name written in felt tip along the inside—Anderson.

Katie suddenly clasped the helmet against her stomach and uttered a small moan of desolation. She pressed the helmet against her and slowly sank down on one knee, bending forward until she was hugging the precious helmet as though it were a lifeline. She tried to suppress the harsh sobs that were coming fast and furiously. In a small part of her, she felt that she was almost certainly making an exhibition of herself but could not control her grief. It was almost too much to bear.

She became aware that someone had knelt down beside her, a shoulder brushed against hers, and an arm placed around her shoulders. Someone else knelt down on her other side and another arm went around her shoulders. Looking up, Katie saw that the marines, who had been kneeling in front of the line of helmets and boots, had surrounded her. She recognized Corporal Carver on her right, and as he glanced at her, he nodded, his own eyes wet with emotion, and squeezed her shoulder, letting her know that she wasn't alone and letting her know that she had a right to be there.

Chapter Twenty-Eight

The next two weeks were a living hell for Katie. She completed her duties in a dazed numbness, grateful that she felt nothing. On the final day of her tour, another worry had arisen. For a few days, Katie had been feeling sick, and on two occasions had vomited while at work. She felt tired and her breasts hurt. She knew what these symptoms meant but could not believe that the single night she had spent with Joe could have resulted in her becoming pregnant. She hoped with all her heart that it was true, but she was going to wait until her return to the UK before she confirmed it.

Now here she was boarding the C-130 Hercules for home. The first leg of her flight was to Base Chora, where she would catch a commercial flight to the UK. She was leaving Afghanistan but more importantly, she was leaving Joe behind. There had been no further news. Everyone had moved on with their lives, their duties, their commitments, except for herself. She felt like she was stuck in limbo with the pain of loss always with her.

Taking her seat on the aircraft, she locked the seat belt around her waist and turned her gaze to the window. Outside, the sky was an uncaring blue. A heat haze caused the airfield buildings to ripple and shimmer. Conversation inside the aircraft surrounded her, the voices excited and enthusiastic as most of the passengers were going home either having completed their tours of duty or going on leave. She felt isolated and alone. She didn't want to leave. She was leaving Joe, and it felt as though she were giving up on him.

The engines of the aircraft grew louder and it began to taxi toward the runway. Katie moved closer to the window, her nose pressed against the cold glass, head turned sideways so that she could see the buildings of Base Independence. She felt as though the life was being wrenched out of her. The aircraft reached the end of the taxiway and turned onto the runway, its engines rumbling, waiting for clearance before taxing. Katie wanted to scream out, telling the aircraft not to take off, begging to be allowed off the aircraft. *What am I thinking? Joe could still be alive and I'm deserting him.*

The engines rose in pitch before the aircraft hurtled down the runway, Katie watching as Base Independence raced past. She pressed the palms of both hands to either side of the window and the tears ran down her face. Joe's name coursed through her brain, as she called to him silently, over and over again.

Then they were lifting off the ground, the landing gear retracting with a thump and Base Independence disappearing into the heat haze. Katie sobbed silently until she became vaguely aware that someone had sat down beside her. Startled, she turned, and the female sergeant aircrew handed her some tissues with sympathy showing on her face, as though she had done this a hundred times before. "Leaving someone behind?" she asked quietly.

Katie choked, couldn't find the words for a minute then said, "He's missing," and completely broke down.

The sergeant quickly put her arms around Katie, pulled her close, and held her.

Chapter Twenty-Nine

A hundred kilometers away from Base Independence, at the foot of the northern mountains of Afghanistan, hidden among rocky hills and a tree line of native trees and thorny scrub bushes, lay a Taliban compound, its sand and mud walls blending into the surrounding desert and rocky terrain. A few days earlier, the compound had been alive with boisterously loud Taliban insurgents, celebrating their latest success against the 'white dog Americans'. Now, advised of an approaching US contingent of troops, they had moved on, dragging along with them the innocent villagers to be used as hostages.

Outside the walls of the compound knelt a man, a US marine, alone without food or water, hands tied behind his back and a two-inch thick rusty chain wound around his neck then staked to the ground. Tethered in this position for over two weeks, he was extremely dehydrated and sick. His dark blond hair was wet with sweat, his face sunburned, bloodied, and swollen from the beatings he had sustained. There was a deep, infected cut that ran from his right eyebrow to the corner of his mouth. Blood had leaked from the wound and crusted on his neck and body armor, and day and night flies buzzed around it, landing and taking off like aircraft from an aircraft carrier. He had lost roughly twenty pounds in body weight and his lips were dry and cracked, his tongue swollen from lack of water. Flies landed continuously on his face, drinking his blood and sweat, and where he had frantically tried to tear the bonds around his wrists, deeps cuts festered and wept with infection. He was sure that he had a couple of broken ribs where they had kicked him and hit him with their rifle buttstocks. His combat trousers were soaked with urine where he had had to relieve himself where he was kneeling, and he was covered in dust and sand. He stank.

Joe Anderson knelt with his head lowered and eyes closed, dozing under the hot sun. He was grateful for the warmth. The nights out in the open were torture, the temperatures almost at freezing with the area being so close to the mountainous region as it was, the season edging toward autumn. He felt that one night he would end up falling asleep and die of hypothermia.

None of the Taliban had been near him for two days now, and he couldn't hear any noise drifting from the compound. He suspected that they had left him to die. He was so thirsty he could kill for one cool mouthful of water. As it was, he couldn't see any coming any time soon. He struggled with his bonds again, frustration and fury giving him added strength, but he was becoming weak, dehydration, and hunger taking its toll with the pain in his wrists increasing. He needed medical treatment, as he sometimes shook with fever and suspected that an infection in his cuts was beginning to spread throughout his body.

The only image that distracted him, that kept him going, kept him sane, chained up as he was like some kind of dog, was that of Katie. His memories of her were like a brilliant flaming torch in the darkness of his mind. He could picture her face with crystal clarity, her startling green eyes — how she looked at him, how her smile lit up her whole face, her stubbornness. He remembered how she felt in his arms, and sometimes he allowed the memories of their lovemaking during the night they had spent together to intrude into his thoughts, but the memories were more than he could tolerate. He remembered that she was due to fly back to the UK today. She was leaving without knowing that he was alive. He was going to lose her, and the pain in his gut was like a live thing. He had lost most of his men and now his woman. Frantically and viciously, Joe wrenched at his bonds, but they only dug deeper into the flesh of his wrists and fresh blood started to flow freely, dripping onto the sand and dusty earth. He suddenly raised his face to the sky and uttered a howl of pure pain, like an animal that had lost its young and mourned them.

Joe suddenly overbalanced and crashed to the ground onto his right side, the resultant pain in his ribs blotting out all reason. He groaned, closed his eyes, and curled into a ball. "Katie," he murmured hoarsely. "Katie, I love you." Then he passed out.

* * * *

Awakened by gentle hands on his body, Joe felt himself turned onto his back. On opening his eyes, he discovered that it was night and cold with a strong, icy wind blowing down from the mountains. He was burning up but shivering violently. He could hear the murmur of voices speaking in Pashto, the native language of Afghanistan, and hands were unwinding the chain from around his neck. Some of the links were embedded in his flesh and he hissed with pain. Another pair of hands checked his wrists then he felt the repetitive movements of a sharp object sawing through his bonds. As his wrists fell apart—no longer bound—his arms fell down by his sides and he almost cried out with relief. He could barely move them because they had been in the same position for so long. Someone helped him to sit up and a heavy blanket, smelling strongly of goat, was flung around his shoulders. Someone crouched down beside him and handed him a goatskin bladder that sloshed with water.

Joe looked up into the face of an old Afghan peasant, bearded and grizzled but with kindness directed at him out of wrinkle-surrounded, deep-set eyes.

He took the water, nodded his thanks, and upended the water bladder so that the water trickled into his mouth. It was the sweetest taste he had ever sampled. He drank the water slowly, knowing that if he gulped it, he would probably throw it back up. He became aware that a rickety old truck, in great need of a paint job, was backing toward them, and a vague hope surfaced that he might now be safe. This was confirmed when the old man beckoned for him to stand up. Joe tried but he was too weak, however another equally old man joined the first and together both of them helped him to stand, offering silent support as he strove to remain standing on legs that had not supported his weight for some weeks. Once he was steady, they led him to the back of the truck. With their continued assistance, he climbed awkwardly onboard, where he sank down onto the metal floor and closed his eyes. He had no idea they were to take him now, but wherever it was, he was sure that he could make it back to a friendly unit.

"Katie," he murmured, "I'm coming home."

Chapter Thirty

Joe took Katie in his arms, a warm look of love and longing etched on his face. His arms were tight about her and there was a smile of tenderness on his mouth. "Hey," he whispered gently, "I love you and miss you so much."

Katie smiled through her tears. "Is it really you, Joe?" she asked, raising a hand to stroke his face. "Where have you been? I've missed you so much."

"Away," Joe answered evasively, "and I can't get back. Not yet. But remember that I love you very much and always will."

"But you're here..." Katie began, panic beginning to rise inside her, "and I have something to tell you."

"I have to go," Joe said, his voice fading slightly. "Don't forget me, Katie. Keep on loving me and keep believing in me."

His face became insubstantial as though disappearing into misty darkness. Katie tried to hold on to his arms but within a few minutes, he was gone and she was clutching at air. She screamed his name and awoke with the scream on her lips.

With dry, painful sobs, Katie sat bolt upright in bed, heart hammering, unable to catch her breath. It had been another nightmare, nothing but a heart-wrenching dream, and Joe was still gone. He had never been there at all, although the warmth of him and the sound of his voice had seemed so real. Katie hugged herself, feeling as though her heart was breaking all over again. She wanted to moan like a wounded animal, crawl back beneath the covers, curl up into a ball, and never move again. She closed her eyes, willing the numbness to return and block out the painful thoughts and feelings. "Oh, my God," she murmured in a choked trembling voice. "Joe, where are you?"

Burning tears threatened to spill over onto her cheeks and she felt as though she was going to choke with the upwelling of desolation and loneliness inside her. Struggling to compose herself, she violently wiped away her tears and swung her legs from beneath the covers to sit on the edge of the bed. The electric clock on her bedside table said 0630 hours and it reminded her that she had something to do this morning, something that would almost certainly change her whole life. But she still didn't move from her position on the bed. She gazed at the heavy curtains hung at the window and at the small crack of gray daylight, but didn't register it in her mind. She was exhausted with emotional pain and worry. Joe was on her mind ceaselessly and it was draining her resolves and resources, leaving her apathetic, without energy, as if her life had stopped moving forward, leaving her trapped in a nightmare with no way out.

Katie abruptly stood up. She needed to get this thing done, find out once and for all, and then she could begin to plan her future. On getting to her feet, she felt instantly lightheaded, and a wave of nausea enveloped her. Putting a hand to her mouth, she murmured, "Oh, here we go again." She hurried quickly to the en suite bathroom, heading straight for the toilet, where she spent the next few minutes bent over the bowl, retching dryly, perspiration beading her forehead, her wretchedness adding to her mental anguish. Once her stomach had settled, she wiped her mouth with a swatch of toilet paper, pressed the button to flush the toilet, and went to the sink. She glanced emotionlessly in the mirror, seeing pale skin with freckles standing out distinctly and brilliant green eyes that seemed dim and dull without their usual sparkle. Her soft mouth trembled with suppressed grief. Katie hastily looked away from her reflection, took her toothbrush and toothpaste from its ceramic holder on the shelf above the sink, and began to brush her teeth. Afterward, she washed her mouth out with mouthwash, grimacing as the mint taste threatened to upset her stomach all over again. She stood motionless again, as though she had forgotten what she should be doing, then glanced toward the toilet cistern and the box lying on it jogged her memory. Sighing, she moved back toward the toilet. "Okay, here goes."

Picking up the pregnancy test, she glanced briefly at the front of it, reading the name, and then opened it, shaking out the small thermometer-like object inside. She shook the box again and the instructions slipped out to join it. For a few minutes, she read the instructions thoroughly then spent another two minutes carrying them out. Once she had flushed the toilet again with a shaking hand, she set the test on the cistern. The instructions said one minute for the results. Sixty long seconds to wait before she would know. Filled with trepidation and excitement, she knew that whatever the result she would have to sit down and think about her life without Joe in it.

The next sixty seconds were the longest of her life. She paced the bathroom floor, glancing every few seconds at her watch, her breathing rapid and uneven. As the seconds ticked by, she became increasingly shaky, eventually loudly telling herself to calm down. Finally, a minute passed and slowly she walked to where the test was resting. Her hand trembled violently as she reached out to pick it up. As she looked at the result, at first she couldn't see it as her vision was blurred with tears, and one fell as she eventually saw that there were two horizontal pink lines across the small window, and beneath it read four weeks.

Sobs threatened to overwhelm her and the tears came faster, running down her cheeks and dripping from her chin. She had known all along what the result of the test would be, had even known before she had left Afghanistan. The nausea, the early changes in her body, and intuition had already told her that the one night she had spent with Joe had culminated in her expecting his child. Now, the ski slope of life-changing decisions would begin, once she had visited an Army doctor to confirm the test.

Katie threw the test into a wastebasket and left the bathroom, making her way downstairs to the kitchen. She put the kettle on to make coffee. She couldn't face drinking tea anymore — it made her feel sick — then she sat down at the kitchen table. She gazed around the large kitchen, feeling some small comfort at her familiar surroundings. The house had belonged to her parents, and when they died, it had passed to her. The décor was a little shabby and worn but she loved it and hadn't wanted to decorate or change any of the furniture. She felt at peace here, as though her mother and father were watching out for her. Now, she had plans to make. One decision she had already made was that she was going to keep Joe's baby. There was absolutely no argument with that. The Army would help her, her job, as a CTM would be safe. She would take as much maternity leave as she could to bring up her child the best way she knew how, and during that time, perhaps Joe would come home. She was convinced that he was alive, somewhere. A search and recon mission did not find his body, only his helmet, dog tags, and weapon. That gave Katie cause to feel a faint hope that he was a prisoner somewhere with every chance of escaping. She needed to keep that desperate belief alive. It was a small spark of hope among the heartbreak, but it was better than nothing.

However, she first had to see a doctor to confirm her pregnancy, then the doctor would notify the WRAC personnel officer and there would be interviews, particularly as she was single. This wasn't going to look good on her record, but she couldn't care less. Her first priority now was her baby. A vague plan had sprung into her mind during the many nights when she had lain awake, the pain of loss and love banishing sleep. She was unsure whether it was legal, or even if it could be done. She would have to get the Army's help to bring it about, but for now, she had to ring the medical center at the base and make an appointment. Thereafter, she would consult with the relevant people and go from there. At the moment, she was still on two weeks disembarkation leave, given to service personnel so that they could reorient themselves back into military life after a deployment. For the first time since Joe's disappearance, a small sense of excitement rejuvenated her and some of her energy returned. Forgetting the boiling kettle, she went into the lounge and lifted the receiver to begin dialing the medical center's number.

* * * *

A week later, Katie sat in front of the WRAC personnel officer, Captain Lee. The office was silent as the female officer read Katie's personnel file, placed on the desk in front of her. Eventually, she looked up, closing the paper folder. She sat back in her chair and folded her arms, regarding Katie with a look of sympathy and a little concern on her ageless face. "I'm sorry for your loss, Corporal Walker," Captain Lee began warmly.

Katie cleared her throat, swallowing the lump of emotion that had suddenly developed there. She wanted to scream, 'Not dead, not dead', but instead forced herself to nod in acknowledgement. "Thank you, ma'am."

The captain continued to regard Katie silently then continued, "I have been informed that you are pregnant?"

Katie nodded again, "Yes, ma'am."

"And you want to keep the child, which is due in...April?" At Katie's nod, Captain Lee also nodded. "I see. And the father of the child is Staff Sergeant Anderson, who is missing in action?"

As she nodded again, Katie felt like she was one of those old-fashioned dogs with the head that wobbled backward and forward on the back shelves of cars, "Yes, ma'am."

"So, Corporal Walker, please tell me what you would like to do."

Katie hesitated, gathering her courage. "As I've already said, ma'am, I want to keep my baby. I would like to take the usual maternity leave if possible. I have enough funds from the death of my parents to look after my baby and bring it up."

Captain Lee nodded. "I think that can be arranged," she agreed. "So you will want to remain in the Army?"

"Yes, ma'am. There is one other thing I would like to run past you. My... Staff Sergeant Anderson's parents live in the States. Before... Before he went missing, he asked a friend of his to give me a letter to send to them if anything was to happen to him. I am going to do that but I am also going to inform them about the baby. It will be their grandchild after all, and with Joe—Staff Sergeant Anderson—missing, I think they deserve to know. I also think that they deserve to be a part of its life. It might help to ease their grief over their missing son, so I was wondering if I could transfer from the British Army to the US Army. I love my career as a CTM and I am sure that even though I will have a child, I can still be of some use to either Army." Having finished the heartfelt plea, Katie's mouth snapped shut.

Captain Lee's expression was unfathomable. "Your request is highly irregular. You do understand that, Corporal Walker?"

Unbidden, Katie's eyes filled with tears. "I'm well aware of that, ma'am. I appreciate what you are saying but..." To her mortification, her voice choked on a sob.

Captain Lee sat forward in her chair and opened up Katie's file again.

"You have had an outstanding career, Corporal Walker. Your assessments, both as a soldier and a CTM have been excellent. It would be a loss to the Army if something couldn't be done in regards to doing some research into your request to see whether it is feasible. I cannot promise you anything. The chances are that it cannot be done. It could take months, but in the meantime, we will have you put on maternity leave as of today's date. I know that it's very early but the doctor has recommended that you rest and look after yourself.

You'll receive full pay for six months and then maternity pay for the following six months if you decide to extend your maternity leave. Go home now and you will be contacted for a further interview when we have some news."

Katie rose to her feet, saluted the officer, and said in a trembling voice, "Thank you, ma'am." Executing an about-turn, she marched out of the office, insides quivering with nerves and praying that her plan would come to fruition.

* * * *

A month later found Katie sitting on her bed holding the letter from Joe that Sergeant Louis Eastman had given to her. The paper of Joe's letter was well worn from being handled and in some places, the writing was blurred with tearstains. Katie had read and reread the letter many times and knew it by heart. That and his class ring, which he had given to her the night that they had spent together, were the only personal items she had of his.

She read the letter again with tears in her eyes.

My Darling Katie,

If you are reading this then you know something has happened to me and I am sorry with all my heart that you are going through this. Since I met you, you have been my world, always in my thoughts. I am not one for words but I hope you believe me when I say that I love you with all my heart and have loved you since the first moment I saw you. I wanted us to spend the rest of our lives together but, my love, that is not to be now. I need to believe that you will go on. Live your life in the Army. Do what you do best and carry on being the best CTM that you are.

My buddy Sergeant Eastman will give you another letter. Please send it to my Mom and Dad. They know about you already, know how much I love you, and they will be waiting to hear from you.

I have to sign off now. They're calling me to go out on patrol, the nasty one I told you about. Take care, my love, and remember always how much I love you.

Joe

Once again, the tears fell onto the letter as Katie sobbed quietly. Every time she read Joe's words, it renewed her sense of loss. She reached into the envelope and withdrew the ornate gold and onyx ring with the letters JA entwined in raised gold on the stone. She gazed at it, feeling the cold metal against the palm of her hand, knowing that Joe had once worn it. She brought it to her lips and gently kissed it, closing her eyes, and then she rubbed the initials softly across her cheek. She lay back on the bed and curled into a ball, the ring still pressed to her cheek and gentle, sad tears ran down her face, soaking the quilt cover beneath her. Before very long, her eyes closed and she fell asleep.

Katie awoke a bit later, lay for a while staring at the ceiling, then got up off the bed. Still clutching the ring, she folded Joe's letter and put it back in its envelope. She needed to write to Joe's parents, tell them about the baby, what her plans were and also, she wanted to send them Joe's ring. Getting up from the bed, she collected a pen and writing pad and went to the dining room table. It took an hour before she was satisfied with the results. She hadn't wanted Joe's parents to think that she was after some monetary compensation for carrying Joe's child. All she wanted was to let them know that they were to be grandparents and to advise them that if they wanted to be part of its life then she would welcome that. She kissed Joe's ring one final time and enclosed it with the letter to them then made a small package of it in a padded envelope. It might be some weeks before she received a response, if any, and in the meantime, she could receive news from the Army about a possible transfer.

* * * *

And that was how it worked out. Katie received a telephone call from the WRAC personnel officer to attend an interview some two weeks later. By then Katie was nearly three months pregnant. She had had her first scan and carried the resultant picture around in her bag. She attended the interview with Captain Lee, her nerves frayed with expectation at what the outcome might be. Inside the captain's office, Katie seated herself in the same chair as before. Captain Lee smiled. "And how are you, Corporal Walker? You look well. How is your baby?"

Katie offered a small smile. "We're fine, thank you, ma'am," she replied.

"Good. You're looking much better than the last time we met. Now, I'll not keep you waiting for an answer to your request for a transfer to the US Army. It would appear that even though you and Staff Sergeant Anderson were not married, you are expecting his child and in the rules we unearthed, your child will have dual citizenship—British as well as American. This means that you, as the child's mother, would be able to travel to and live in the US. However, there is a rule that you would need somebody to act as sponsor for you, vouch for you, and so forth. We took the liberty of contacting Staff Sergeant Anderson's parents and they have agreed, wholeheartedly I might add, to act as your sponsors. I assumed that you had already written to them and I did not think it was out of order. Now, the answer to your request is yes, your request for a transfer to the United States Army is approved. All your transfer papers and all the relevant forms have been prepared, including your new orders, ready for you to sign. After your maternity leave, you will report to MSB Quantico where you will join your new platoon as a CTM working with the Marines. You have a flight booked on 30 September, two weeks from now. Now, there is a lot of paperwork to sign. Once that is done you are free to go."

Katie was stunned, and, for the first time in a long time, exhilarated. She couldn't believe in two weeks' time, she and her unborn child would be flying out to the States to start a new life. She would be meeting Joe's parents and become a part of their lives, and hopefully she and Joe's child would ease some of their loss.

For the next hour, Katie signed form after form in the captain's office. Finally, she was done. Her new orders, transfer papers, and travel documents were safely in her bag and she was ready to leave the British base for the last time.

"I wish you all the best, Corporal Walker," Captain Lee said warmly as Katie stood ready to leave.

Katie saluted smartly and said, "Thank you, ma'am, and thank you so much for everything you've done." She immediately about-turned and left the office.

With imaginary wings on her feet, Katie hurried home and let herself into the house. She instantly saw the letter on the floor, and her heart flew into her mouth. Picking it up from the floor mat, she went into the kitchen, placed her bag on the table, and immediately slit open the envelope and extracted the thin blue sheets inside.

What was written in the letter caused Katie to dissolve into heart-rending sobs.

Our Dear Katie,

Jack and I were delighted to hear from you and thank you from the bottom of our hearts for our son's ring. He had already written about you and he told us how much you meant to him. He loved you very much. We are overwhelmed about your news that you are pregnant. It has filled our hearts with joy that there will be something remaining of Joe. We are looking forward to seeing you and, of course, you will be living with us – that is, if you want to. It is entirely up to you. A Captain Lee has contacted us to verify that we will be your sponsors. We cannot wait to meet you. We have your flight details and we will be at the airport to meet you. Katie, you have given Jack and I everything to live for, something to hope for. We understand completely your reference in your letter that you are asking for nothing, however, anything you ever need, you only have to ask.

With much love
Maggie and Jack

* * * *

Two weeks later, Katie was at the airport. The period of time leading up to this day had gone by so fast that it felt as though her feet hadn't touched the ground. The decision to sell her house was made with much regret. It had fetched a far higher price than she expected and had sold so quickly that she'd had to stay in a hotel for some days before her flight. Some of her furniture had also gone, the rest put in storage. All that was left of her previous existence were two suitcases, now probably loaded into the cargo hold of the aircraft she was about to board, and all her personal papers and jewelry.

Boarding the aircraft, Katie felt a moment of sadness at leaving her country behind. She had lived in the UK all her life and it was a wrench, but she would be starting a new life and she would be sharing it with her Joe's child.

Eight hours later, Katie's aircraft descended into Dulles International Airport. Feeling very tired, she disembarked and followed the signs to Customs and Security, going through after she had produced all her military papers to collect her luggage. Using a trolley, she waited at the baggage claim until her flight's cargo came through and she collected her suitcases. Wheeling the trolley awkwardly, she followed the directions for arrivals and found herself in a huge arrivals lounge where crowds of people were waiting. She stopped dead, feeling a little lost and exhausted, looking at the sea of faces and wondering in panic how she was supposed to recognize Joe's parents. Her eyes scanned the many faces, swept past one older couple who were staring at her, and froze. Her eyes darted back to them, to the man specifically, and her heart began to pound frantically. It was Joe. The same tall powerful body, the dark blond hair, and the same facial features. In a split second, she realized that it wasn't Joe but a carbon copy. The couple still stared at her and Katie smiled tentatively, her eyes filling with tears. The man pointed at her then he and the woman began hurrying toward her, beaming smiles on their faces. As they stopped by her, the tall, plump woman asked, "Katie?"

Katie nodded. "Mr. and Mrs. Anderson?"

Katie began to cry with the almost overwhelming pain over the loss of Joe, with sympathy for Maggie and Jack Anderson and with the beginning of hope in the form of Joe's child. She felt that at last she had come home.

Epilogue

The older couple stood together in front of French windows, open to let in the fragrances of a mild spring day. The tall, soldierly erect, blond-haired man had his arm around the woman's shoulders, who was equally as tall as her husband but plump in a motherly way with a mass of softly waving gray hair. Silently they stared out through the windows into the garden, watching the young woman with her baby. A gentle breeze stirred the older woman's hair and she raised a hand that shook slightly to brush back an errant strand.

The room they were in was large and elegantly decorated in dove gray and dusky pink. It obviously belonged in a house of wealth, but was homely and lived-in, with vases of fresh flowers positioned on small side tables and on the hearth of the spacious marble fireplace. Numerous gilt-framed photographs of children and family members stood in groups on shelves and on a vast antique dresser. The furniture was comfortable with oversized plush pillows and scatter cushions piled haphazardly on sofas and armchairs. The air smelled of cinnamon, lemon-scented furniture polish and the fresh scent of flowers. A large, framed picture of a US marine in dress uniform hung above the fireplace, below it on the mantelpiece sat an ornate candle together with a single red rose in a slim, long-stemmed vase.

The woman turned her face up to her husband's and regarded him with misty dark blue eyes. Her lips trembled and there was grief etched on her face. "Jack," she began in a soft American voice, "I'm worried about Katie. She looks so lost and sad. You would think that over these last few months with baby Josie to distract her, her grief would have eased, but it hasn't."

Jack Anderson turned his attention to his wife, looked down at her, and squeezed her shoulders gently. "Maggie, has your pain diminished a little as the months have gone by?"

Maggie Anderson's eyes filled with tears and she shook her head. "The pain of losing my son will never go away," she replied in a trembling voice.

"Hey," Jack said, stroking his wife's arm, his voice quavering slightly. "We don't know that Joe is dead. He's just missing in action. They never found his body. Until they do, we have hope, just like Katie has hope."

"Does she, though, Jack? Does she really? Does she honestly think that Joe is going to come walking through the door? It's been nearly a year and there's been no word," Maggie continued, the grief she was feeling a massive burden on her shoulders.

"Honey," Jack soothed again, trying to raise his wife's spirits. "You can't talk like that. To lose hope is to betray our Joe and all that he stood for. You have to think positive. Katie is here and so is our granddaughter. We have to love Katie like Joe said in his letter. We have to love them both, look after them, and believe that he will come home one day."

A tear trickled down Maggie Anderson's lightly powdered, smooth cheek, "I would love to believe that," she said, and a soft sob escaped her.

"Well, I believe," Jack responded firmly, "he will come home." He turned to look back out of the French windows again at the slim figure standing some distance down the broad expanse of garden.

Katie looked down at her tiny daughter asleep in her arms and wondered how she could love this little girl so much. From the time the baby had come screaming from her womb, looking so much like her father, with Joe's deep blue eyes and her own copper-colored hair, Katie had been consumed with a love so strong that she wondered how it could be real. The presence of this little life that she had nurtured and adored, even before she was born, had slightly eased the devastating pain and loss of Joe's disappearance. Her child had given her something to live for, something to cling to while she tried to cope with the loss of the man who she had loved so much.

Now she tenderly kissed her baby's forehead and carried her slowly and carefully to the pram. Bending down, she laid the child in its cool, shadowed interior, the little girl barely stirring, and made sure the baby's body was shielded from the sun by the protective shade from the old-fashioned canopy. She smiled slightly, tenderly cupped the little girl's delicate head, and then went to sit down in the garden chair that had been placed close to the pram.

The spring breeze, fragrant with the smell of flowers, pine trees and green grass, tossed Katie's curly hair with teasing fingers. She could hear the rustling of the branches of the tall pines and firs that formed a dense forest at the bottom of the garden, and birds called and sang abundantly.

Ordinarily, those sounds would have been peaceful and soothing, but Katie barely noticed them or the beauty of her surroundings. She felt numb and empty of all emotion, the loss of Joe leaving behind nothing but a dark shadow inside her. She had lost the one thing in her life that had meant something to her. She had loved him more than she had thought possible, and for those last few weeks in Afghanistan, he had been everything to her. Having lost her parents tragically some four years before, she knew what loss and grief were all about, but Joe's disappearance had torn her very world apart. If it hadn't been for the birth of her baby, she suspected that she would have been hard-pressed to go on without him. She sat with bowed head, hands clasped limply, staring at her lap, wondering where the detachment of self that had served her so well in Afghanistan had disappeared to. She needed it desperately, now more than ever. Katie closed her eyes as they filled with burning tears, something that happened very frequently nowadays and that she tried so hard to control, but she failed dismally. One silvery drop eventually trickled down her cheek.

"Joe," she murmured brokenly, "where are you, Joe? Please come home to me." Her shoulders suddenly jerked with grief and a small wrenching sob escaped her.

Back inside the house, Maggie Anderson straightened her shoulders and turned away from her view of the forlorn-looking figure seated in the garden chair. "I'm going to put the kettle on," she said. As she spoke, there came a single heavy knock at the front door.

The man and woman glanced at each other with expressions of fear mirrored in their eyes. Jack's lips thinned with concern. Over the past months, a knock on the door or the ringing of the telephone had filled them both with pessimistic terror, in case it signaled bad news.

"You get the kettle and I'll get the door," Jack announced firmly.

Maggie nodded silently and the couple left the lounge, Maggie going into the large kitchen and Jack continuing on across the large, spacious hallway to the front door.

Maggie filled the kettle with water and put it on to boil then went to the kitchen window and stood motionless, staring out into the garden, not seeing the expanse of smooth green grass or the sunlight playing on the colorful flowers in the cottage-style flower beds. She was thinking only of her missing son and feeling the terrible sense of loss deep within her heart. Sighing deeply, she began to set a tray with a complement of sugar bowl, milk jug and cups and saucers. She remained absent-minded and preoccupied with her thoughts until an odd noise coming from the hallway caused her to turn her head in that direction and stiffen, her hand freezing in the act of setting teaspoons on the tray.

The noise had sounded as though someone had choked just once. Holding her breath, Maggie tried to hear if the sound repeated. All remained silent in the house except for the rapidly boiling water in the kettle. She shrugged and continued to prepare the tea tray. Her head jerked up again when she heard another sound, only this time it was a soft moan. Heart leaping into her throat, Maggie called out, "Jack?" There was no response, and feeling a little unnerved, she moved toward the door of the kitchen that led out into the spacious hallway. "Jack?" she called out again and went into the hallway, turning in the direction of the front door.

Maggie stopped dead in her tracks, staring in shock and disbelief at the scene before her. Jack and a tall soldier clad in camouflage combats stood in a still-life tableau just inside the front door, the soldier with his hand on Jack's shoulder. Maggie's hand, shaking as though with palsy, fluttered to her throat and her heart began to pound heavily in her chest. She couldn't speak and her legs suddenly threatened to collapse beneath her. Reaching out a trembling hand to support her against the wall, she continued to stare with dazed eyes at her ashen-faced husband and what she thought must be a ghost standing next to him.

The soldier turned from the gasping man and surveyed the elderly woman across the hall. "Mom?" Joe Anderson queried.

Maggie heard the familiar voice of her son and her shocked immobility was broken. She almost ran across the hall, calling Joe's name repeatedly, as though not to say his name would cause him to disappear and therefore be a figment of her imagination.

Keeping one hand on his father's shoulder, as though to keep him upright, Joe held out his other hand to his mother and upon Maggie reaching his side, he clasped her to him in a bear hug. Maggie began to cry as though her heart would break and clung onto her son, feeling his uniform and the warmth of his body through it and finally realizing with pitiful joy that he was real and blessedly alive. For a long time, there was emotional confusion until Maggie, wiping away her tears, looked up at Joe and was horrified at what she saw.

Joe's face was thin and haggard, almost to the point of gauntness, his eyes sunk deep in their sockets, where they gleamed a deep blue. However, it was the expression in them that caused Maggie to wonder in anguish about what her son had been through. There was an extraordinary pain, anger, and grief that had dulled the usual brightness in her son's eyes, but she believed that those emotions went far deeper than expressed in his gaze. A livid scar ran from his right eyebrow to the corner of his mouth, but the worse thing of all was the angry red web of scar tissue encircling his neck. He looked exhausted, and had lost far too much weight, his uniform looking far too big for his body and hanging from his frame.

"Joe, my God," Maggie exclaimed. "What…?"

"Mom." Joe raised a trembling hand in a warding off gesture. "Don't ask me any questions yet. I can't—and don't—want to talk about it."

Maggie was horrified as she saw tears fill her son's eyes. She had never seen him cry and it nearly broke her heart.

"Come on, son." Having regained his composure, Jack put his arm around Joe's shoulders. "Your mom was just about to put the kettle on. Let's get you into the lounge. Leave your bag where it is. We'll collect it later."

Joe nodded silently and the three of them, clinging onto each other, moved awkwardly across the hall toward the lounge. Maggie was again horrified to see that Joe now walked with a bad limp, and she realized then that he must have gone through something terrifying out in Afghanistan. She bit her lip, refraining from asking any further questions. Joe would talk when he was ready. It was enough for now that he was home, safe.

Jack and Maggie stopped at the doorway of the lounge and watched as Joe walked slowly into the room, paused, and glanced around him, surveying the furnishings as though he had never seen them before. He appeared restless and uneasy, as though he was unsure of where he was or what to do next. Turning, he walked to where there was a row of framed photographs set on a table. Bending slightly he looked at each of them in turn but remained silent. He straightened without comment, turned and began to walk to the opposite end of the room. Jack and Maggie tensed and looked at each other with alarm on their faces. If he looked out into the garden, he would see Katie and the baby. They needed to tell him first, warn him that she was there — to lessen the shock — but then it was too late.

Walking past the open French windows, Joe glanced out into the garden. At first, what his eyes perceived out there did not register and he continued on for two more paces before he stopped abruptly, as though he had crashed into a wall. His whole body went rigid with tension as he continued to stare at the woman in the long white dress bending over a stroller. He would have recognized that short, gleaming copper hair anywhere.

The room was deathly quiet as — still keeping his eyes focused on the scene in the garden — he turned slowly. Finally taking his gaze from what he had seen, he turned to face his parents.

"Who's that?" Joe asked. His voice was devoid of emotion, completely at odds with the expression on his face — his body and his mind under an iron-hard control.

Maggie walked toward her son and placed a hand on his arm. He instantly recoiled and she knew that there was something deeply wrong with him. "Joe," she began gently. "That's Katie. She's been living with us here for eleven months now."

Joe turned to stare out into the garden again. He cleared his throat. "What's that in the stroller?"

The tears began to trickle down Maggie's cheeks. "That's your daughter, Joe. Katie was pregnant before she left Afghanistan but didn't find out for sure until she returned to the UK. She was pregnant when you went missing. Josie was born about two months ago. Katie sent us the letter you asked her to send to us and one of her own, telling us that she was pregnant and asking us if we would want to be a part of the baby's life. She also managed to transfer from the British to the US Army. Your father and I jumped at the chance and we invited her over to live with us. She refused at first. She's a stubborn woman."

At that statement, a small smile twitched about Joe's mouth, "Yeah, that's Katie."

"Anyway, she came over and gave birth to Josie here. Joe, Katie never gave up hope, never gave up the belief that you would come home. She said that you were still alive. She believed in you. She kept us going."

Joe still hesitated. "I've changed," he said sadly. "I'm not the man she once loved."

"Son," Jack began in a choked voice, "you'll always be the man she loves, and you'll always be our son, no matter what. War changes everyone. There's no shame in that."

Joe glanced at his father, doubt in his eyes, about to say something in contradiction to his father's statement, but then he took a hesitant step toward the French windows, followed by another.

Katie, on hearing a small whimper from the pram and shaking herself out of her self-pity, had risen from the chair and gone to her child. The baby was still sleeping, and placing a gentle hand against the rose petal soft cheek, she checked to see that the child wasn't too hot. Straightening up, she looked around the large garden and decided apathetically that she would take her daughter for a brief walk around the boundary. It would give her some exercise and might help her to relax. She was just about to release the brake on the pram when she froze.

The hairs on the back of Katie's neck were rising and it felt as though someone was watching her. Nervously, she glanced around the garden, in particular toward the forest, but all appeared normal. The feeling, however, was becoming stronger and more uncomfortable, so she turned around abruptly in the direction of the house. Completely stunned and disbelieving, she swayed, as the world spun around her and all noise seemed to fade away to nothing as she saw the tall soldier standing on the steps leading from the patio down into the garden. The combat-clothed figure was completely still as if watching her. Katie would have recognized the man anywhere.

They both remained motionless, gazes locked on each other until Joe moved laboriously down one step. Katie saw that he limped badly and watched breathlessly as he descended another step. Even over the expanse of grass, she could see the difference in him — how thin he was and how his once-upright stance was now stooped, as though with mental as well as physical exhaustion. She watched as Joe finally reached the foot of the steps and stopped. The dark shadow inside her, representing months of loss and sadness, suddenly dissolved, and a white-hot blaze of immense joy and happiness soared inside her. It *was* Joe. He was home. Katie began to move toward him, slowly at first, and then she was running, flying across the grass as though she had wings on her feet, laughing and crying, calling out his name over and over again. Joe held out his arms and as Katie reached him, she threw her arms around his neck and Joe swung her off her feet in a circle. He quickly lowered her to the ground then he was kissing her, tenderly at first then hungrily, his arms crushing her to him as though he would never let her go again.

Sobbing with overwhelming emotion, Katie clung to him, kissing him back with all the longing and intense love that she felt. She couldn't believe he was here. She could feel his arms, his kisses, smell his skin, but part of her mind was insistent that she had fallen asleep in the hot sun and this was a nightmare, because when she woke up, he would be gone again.

Joe stopped kissing her and drew back to study her face.

Katie watched in horror as his eyes suddenly filled with tears, then he was crying, great heart-rending sobs that shook his whole body. Katie's heart tore at his grief and she put her arms around him, holding him as she would have held a child. She felt the bony gauntness of his body, felt him trembling, and held him tighter, but such was Joe's exhaustion and grief that his legs began to buckle and he fell to the ground on his knees, dragging Katie down to the ground with him.

Kneeling on the ground in front of him and holding his head against her shoulder, she hugged him as hard as she could, trying to instill her strength into his exhausted body. "Sssshhh, Joe, I'm here. You're home. You're safe," she murmured to him soothingly, but he was unable to stop crying. His sobs were pitiful and came from some deep well of grief and pain inside him, some place where even Katie couldn't reach and comfort him. She had always remembered him as being strong and tough, and she had never seen him in this much pain. He held her in a crushing grip, and even though it hurt, she ignored the pain and held him. After a long time, his crying began to abate and he lifted his face away from her shoulder and ran a hand across his face. "What a dumb fuck," he said in a choked voice, embarrassment evident in his tone.

Katie gently stroked his hair then put a hand against his face, feeling the wetness there. "No," she said softly, "just tired and hurt." She saw the empty look in his dull blue eyes, saw his scars and the haggard, exhausted look on his face, and was well aware of what the storm of emotions was about.

"I have someone you should meet," she said. "Can you get up?"

Joe nodded, but his injured leg wouldn't support him and Katie had to help him to his feet. Waiting until he was steady, she took his hand and led him slowly across the expanse of grass toward the pram. A few feet away, she dropped his hand and said smiling, "Wait here."

She went the rest of the way to the pram and peered inside. Josie was awake, waving her small fists in the air and kicking her small legs. Katie said, "Hello, little girl. Your daddy is here to meet you." Using the words sent a thrill of delight through her and she gently lifted the tiny baby from her pram and, turning, walked back to Joe.

Joe was standing where she had left him, an intense look on his face as he stared at the child.

"Joe, meet your daughter, Josie Rebecca Anderson." She held out the child, offering her to her father.

Joe hesitated, looking from Katie to the baby, and then he tentatively took the small child from her mother. He studied the little girl in wonder, seeing the wide open blue eyes as they looked up at him, almost as though she knew who he was, and the fine copper-colored hair. There was a gentle expression on his face. "She's beautiful, like her mom," he said softly.

Katie put one hand on Joe's arm and the other on her child's head and glanced up into Joe's face, all the happiness that she could ever feel there in her heart. "She has her daddy's eyes. That's what makes her beautiful."

Inside the house, Jack and Maggie, observing the scene, clasped each other with happiness.

"And now we help him to pick up the pieces," Jack said.

"Yes," Maggie said. "Now the healing begins."

About the Author

Sharon spent eight and a half years in the Women's Royal Air Force. Originally based in London, after she met her husband, Sharon relocated to Scotland to settle in Edinburgh. Already loving the country after having been stationed there during her time in the military, Sharon has never looked back. She lives with her husband and rescue West Highland Terrier, Snowie, (who thinks that she is a Rottweiler in disguise).

In 2014, Sharon started to have visions of writing a contemporary military romance. The ideas started to pile up and there was nothing for it but to get them down on her laptop, regardless of time and place.

Sharon Kimbra Walsh loves to hear from readers. You can find her contact information, website and author biography at http://www.totallybound.com.

Lightning Source UK Ltd.
Milton Keynes UK
UKOW02f1543180116

266612UK00001B/87/P